I0758173

THE ARCHITECTS OF RESTORATION

THE ARCHITECTS OF RESTORATION

By
M.B. ANDERSON

Published by
M.B. ANDERSON

THE ARCHITECTS OF RESTORATION
Book II of The Architects Of Grace

Published by: M.B. Anderson
First Edition: 2026

ISBN (Hardback): 978-1-971091-02-0
ISBN (Paperback): 978-1-971091-03-7
ISBN (Ebook): 978-1-971091-04-4

To my Ohana:

Tried by the flame and pressed by the world, yet preserved by His hand. This is
dedicated to the God who walked with us through the tribulation—the One
who brings us through the furnace not as ashes, but as gold. He is the light that
outshines the fire.

There is a glory that can only be forged in the heart of the flame. Just as the gold must lose its shape to find its purity, the soul must endure the tribulation to find its salvation. The fire is not the end of the journey; it is the beginning of the Restoration.

M.B. Anderson

TABLE OF CONTENTS

CHAPTER 44

THE ARCHITECT'S END

The Nexus of Discord rose from the horizon like a wound in the world—a rotating pyramid, impossible and obscene, its edges slicing the sky with the certainty of a curse. The structure was not just alien, but actively hostile: a cosmic engine devouring the laws of nature, grinding hope and reason into dust. The air itself was alive with threat, thick with ozone and the acrid tang of burnt sugar, vibrating with a discordant hum that drilled into the marrow. Each breath tasted like the aftermath of a lightning strike and a funeral pyre.

Elias, Seraphina, and Anya stood with Azael on a ridge of black, glassy stone that shimmered with the light of a thousand broken promises. From this vantage, they saw a world in torment: rivers of neon blood carving paths through petrified forests, mountains twisted into screaming faces, and the sky a tapestry of storm and flame. The land was not merely ruined, but malevolent— each feature a deliberate corruption, every color an accusation. This was Lucifer's masterpiece: a landscape that punished hope, a geometry designed to break the spirit and betray the senses.

For a moment, they could only stare—each transfixed by the horror and grandeur of the place, knowing that what awaited them inside would not only test their bodies and minds, but the very architecture of their souls.

The Weight of Failure and the Light of Grace

The moment they paused, the fragile façade of Elias's resolve shattered like cheap glass. The adrenaline that had carried him across the dimensional rift was gone, replaced by a hollow so deep it threatened to swallow him whole. He stumbled, knees buckling on the razor edge of the obsidian ridge. The glass bit into his flesh, but the pain was distant—drowned out by a tidal wave of dread. Every heartbeat echoed with the realization: not only had they failed to close the door to the portal, but they had willingly stepped into the jaws of a trap designed to consume hope itself.

Beneath the pitiless sky, the Bible in Elias's hands weighed more than stone. It was no longer a beacon; it felt like the gravestone of his purpose. He was no missionary, not anymore—he was the architect of extinction, the one who led his friends not to salvation, but to a necessary, orchestrated suicide. The guilt bit deeper than any blade. *We were supposed to save them. We were supposed to go home.* Now, the only home left was this nightmare.

Anya stood just behind him, her hands trembling, knuckles white where they clutched the edge of her coat. She had followed Elias this far, believing in his certainty, his purpose, even when her own faith faltered. Now she watched him collapse, and something inside her snapped. Her analytical mind, always searching for patterns, solutions, exits, suddenly found none. The world's logic had unraveled, and with it, the scaffolding that had kept her own fears at bay.

She dropped to a crouch, arms wrapped tight around herself, trying to contain the panic that pressed up from her gut. Thoughts spiraled: *If Elias can break, what hope do I have? What hope does anyone?* The voice in her head, usually so steady, was a fractured staccato of regret and terror—*You missed something, you weren't good enough, there must have been another way.* She could not breathe; the air was too thick, the sound of the Nexus too loud, every vibration a reminder that she was trapped, powerless, and alone.

The Nexus howled around them—a living engine of despair. The very air pressed in, vibrating with a sound too deep to hear, rattling the bones and making every breath an act of defiance. Shadows twisted at the edge of vision, coiling up from the black glass, whispering that the world was already lost. Somewhere, below and within, things moved—shapes that were not alive, but not dead, feeding on the touch of memory and the taste of regret. The landscape itself seemed to lean closer, hungry to witness their collapse.

Seraphina felt the weight pressing on her, too, a pressure so intense it threatened to unravel her mind. The old city-trained logic failed her; no calculation could offer escape. In the middle of the chaos, she closed her eyes, shutting out the broken world for one desperate moment. She reached for the only anchor she had left: her aesthetic synthesis. Though her Pattern Break Perception—her uncanny gift for detecting the slightest shifts in light and sound, reading patterns allowing her to shape harmonies and visuals that could soothe or focus any mind. In the darkness behind her eyelids, the chaos became pure sensation. She surrendered herself to it, letting the vibrations of the Nexus—its hum, its discordant resonance, the tiny frequencies of fear and hope—wash over her.

Then, something shifted. Her mind, finely tuned from years of listening for beauty in the noise of broken systems, began to pick out the patterns: the low, rolling thrum of despair; the high, frantic keening of fear; the subtle, almost inaudible pulse of hope. She layered them in her mind, arranging the chaos into the beginnings of a melody. The music was strange, unfinished, but it had structure—a fragile architecture of survival. With every imagined note, the tension in her body eased. The vibrations steadied her heart. The song she heard was not beautiful, but it was real and hers.

Slowly, her breathing calmed. The world outside remained a nightmare, but inside, she had found a foothold—a place of composure built from the raw material of suffering. She opened her eyes, the clarity of her purpose returning like a distant but steady drumbeat. When she reached for Elias, her touch was calm, her conviction unwavering. This was how she could steady him—because she had first steadied herself.

"It's too much," Elias whispered, the words lost in the Nexus's roar. His knuckles whitened on the Bible until the leather shrieked. "We failed. We condemned them. This... this is just despair masquerading as a plan." His voice barely registered above the cacophony, but the others heard—the sound was a surrender, a confession, and a curse.

Anya's breath hitched. The words cut deeper than the glass beneath her boots. She wanted to reach out, to steady him, but her own hands would not obey. Instead, a sob escaped—small, strangled, but real. "Don't say that," she choked, her voice thin. "If you give up, there's nothing left for any of us." The admission was raw, a plea and an accusation all at once. Her eyes darted, searching for Seraphina, for Azael, for anyone who could hold the world together when it seemed to be coming apart.

Seraphina dropped to her knees beside Elias, heedless of the black shards biting through her skin. She framed his face with her hands—hands that had once engineered miracles, now trembling with human warmth. Her eyes, which had spent a lifetime calculating the cost of beauty and the worth of risk, were stripped bare. No algorithm, no performance—only a terrible, necessary love.

"Despair is what he deals in, Elias," she murmured, her words vibrating with a power stronger than fear. "But this is not despair. Despair is passive. This is a willed sacrifice." She did not hesitate—her lips, cool from the burning, poisoned air, pressed to his in a kiss that was both funeral and benediction. It was not gentle; it was fierce, raw, and absolute—the kind of kiss that says I will burn with you if it means we do not die alone.

The world fell away in that moment—no Nexus, no sky, no mission. Only the gravity of shared failure and the impossible, holy defiance that is love. The silence that followed was not peace; it was the eye of a hurricane, the breath before the storm's second act. When she pulled back, her hands stayed on his cheeks, anchoring him to the present, daring the darkness to come for them both.

Anya watched, tears streaking her face, a dull ache blooming in her chest. She envied Seraphina's certainty, her courage. She envied Elias for being loved so fiercely. For a heartbeat, she hated herself for feeling weak—for needing someone to tell her it wasn't over, that she still mattered. But then, as she watched the two of them cling to each other, something changed. The isolation cracked; a sliver of hope, or maybe just stubbornness, slipped in. If they could still choose love here, at the end, maybe she could, too.

Elias blinked, dazed, the shock of her courage momentarily blinding him to the horror. In her eyes was a devotion that transcended mission or survival: she saw him, not as a leader, but as a soul worth saving, even when all hope was gone. In that instant, the scale of their failure shrank to nothing beside the magnitude of the choice they were making: to love, to fight, to persist, even at the end of the world.

"We didn't fail the city; we simply found a better way to serve it," Seraphina whispered, her thumb tracing the line of his jaw. "We may be sealed in, but that means we're exactly where we need to be—at the heart of the enemy's design. If we plant the truth here, we redeem the whole structure from within. This isn't an ending, Elias. It's the most important beginning."

Elias's breath shuddered. The terror did not leave, but it crystallized into resolve—cold, sharp, and clear. He rose, Seraphina at his side, two souls welded together by a fire that would not be extinguished. His purpose was no longer survival or duty, but something elemental: devotion, not just to the mission, but to each other.

Anya wiped her cheeks, drawing herself upright with shaking hands. She stepped closer, her voice unsteady but determined. "If this is the place where hope is supposed to die, then let's let it be the place where faith is born," she said, her words trembling but fierce. "We may not know the way out yet, but we're not powerless. We can still choose to stand together, to hold on, to act with purpose. That's something no darkness can take from us." Her words steadied her, a fragile shield against the terror, and for the first time since crossing over, she felt the air move more freely in her lungs.

The Surrendered Purpose

Azael stood before them, his wings folded in solemn majesty, the gravity of both the world and eternity reflected in his ancient eyes. For a long, quiet moment, he simply looked at each of them—Elias, Seraphina, Anya—gazing into the marrow of their souls as if committing their courage and frailty to memory.

When he spoke, his voice was gentle but resonant, carrying the weight of both sorrow and hope. "You ask yourselves why you were brought here, and what your purpose truly is. Know this: humans are not born with a manual. There is no page that tells you, 'This is your path, this is your destiny.' Each soul is written uniquely, and the Creator has fashioned no two alike. You search for certainty and direction in a world of shifting shadows. But you are not meant to wander alone."

Azael let his gaze linger on Elias, then Anya, then Seraphina. "Before you entered this realm, you believed your mission was clear—crafted from your own wisdom and the well-meaning suggestions of others, all limited by fear and uncertainty. You trusted your own judgment and thought you knew the way forward. But now, in the crucible of this place, you've discovered that purpose is not found in your own plans, but in surrender—allowing God to direct your steps, especially when the path is hidden."

His voice softened as he met their eyes. "It is written, 'O Lord, I know that the way of man is not in himself: it is not in man that walketh to direct his steps' (Jeremiah 10:23, KJV). No matter how carefully you plan or how fiercely you seek control, the true direction of your life does not come from you alone. This is not failure—it is simply being human. God has designed it so that you must look beyond yourself for guidance. Your journey is not about perfect understanding, but about trust—a daily reliance on the Lord to guide and sustain you, even when the world is falling apart."

Azael's eyes shone with conviction. "Your purpose is not defined by your own design, but by your willingness to let God lead you through uncertainty. When you invite Him into your heart and mind, you receive not a map, but a living Guide—One who sets your feet on the path, even when you cannot see the road ahead. This is true strength: to surrender your way to the One who knows the end from the beginning."

He let the truth settle over them before continuing. "Now your purpose is clear—not simply to endure or escape this place, but to survive, to be refined by the trials you face here, and then to return home changed. When you emerge from this darkness, you will do so as true bearers of the Light—ready to share the hope you found and to make disciples among your own people. This experience is not just for this realm; it is to prepare you to bring truth and transformation to the world you came from."

Azael stepped forward and gently lifted the harp from Seraphina's back, cradling it with reverence. The instrument vibrated with ethereal energy, its strings shimmering like threads spun from dawn. With care, Azael selected one golden, glowing string and eased it free, its light trembling in his palm like a living promise. As he held the radiant strand aloft, he bowed his head for a brief, sacred moment.

"Thank You, Lord God, for providing for us in our need, for Your gifts are never exhausted, and Your mercies are new every morning," he prayed softly, his gratitude resonating through the hush.

As he finished, the harp shimmered in his hands, and before their eyes a new string wove itself seamlessly into place—restoring the instrument to perfect wholeness. The sight was a quiet miracle, a reminder that what is given in faith is always renewed by the Giver.

He glanced at the team, a faint, reassuring smile on his lips. "This harp is not diminished by what it gives. Each string is a vessel of grace, and when one is drawn for a holy purpose, another is born in its place. Its music, like God's mercy, is never depleted."

Azael coiled the luminous string in his palm, its radiance pulsing with anticipation. "This is no mere cord, but an extension of grace itself. As you bind the Word, you bind yourselves to its purpose and power."

He handed the glowing strand to Elias, who took it with reverence. Together, with Seraphina steady at his side and Anya lending her trembling but determined hand, Elias began to wind the luminous cord around the Bible. As the final length circled the sacred leather, the harp string fused to the book—the light seeping into every seam, every word. Where the cord crossed itself upon the cover, a radiant cross ignited, burning through the darkness with a brilliance that made the Nexus itself shudder.

The Bible was no longer simply a book, but a beacon—a weapon of living grace, its cross a sign to all powers and principalities that the Word of God would not be hidden, not in this world nor any other. The transformation sent a pulse of hope through the team. The harp on Seraphina's back resonated in answer, a chord of victory before the battle even began.

Off in the distance, the Nexus of Discord throbbed with a malignant pulse, and the ground beneath their feet vibrated as if the enemy already sensed their strategy, bracing for a final, desperate defense. The atmosphere darkened; even the air seemed to resist their resolve, pressing in with the weight of every soul ever lost to the Lie.

Azael's words lingered in the charged silence: "This is your crossing. The way back is sealed—there is only forward now, through the very heart of the Lie and into the hope that only sacrifice can secure. The next step will cost you everything, but it offers a victory that no power of darkness can ever undo."

Elias nodded, grim and unflinching. The Bible was no longer a relic, but a weapon—an explosive of grace against the machinery of hell. Seraphina pressed close, her presence a fortress against the darkness. Anya stood with them, fear transmuted into resolve, her faith now shining with the same clarity as the glowing cross on the Word itself.

Above them, the sky flickered—blood-red lightning crawling across the horizon. The world itself seemed to convulse, as if aware of what they intended. Below, the glass ridge throbbed with a hunger that promised suffering beyond imagination. The Nexus was not finished with them. The next horror waited— patient, calculating, and insatiable.

They were not just fighting for their lives. They were fighting for the soul of a world that did not know it was already damned. And as they stepped forward, together, the book secured and their covenant sealed, the true terror of their path became clear: nothing they had faced so far would compare to what waited in the heart of the Lie.

This was not the end. This was the beginning of the real nightmare.

The Final Purpose Declared

Elias lifted his head, glancing back at the swirling, violet-green sky—the raw, torn gateway through which they'd been cast into this hellish dimension. Behind them, that wounded sky was a constant reminder of the world and people they had left behind. Ahead, the horizon brooded under a pall of darkness, flickering now and then with ominous aftershocks of blood-red lightning—a warning and a promise of what was at stake.

In the hush that followed Azael's charge, the team stood suspended between worlds, their hearts pounding with the gravity of a new, weightier calling. The Baptism and the ordeal of the trap had not destroyed them; instead, it had stripped away their illusions, burned away their self-made missions, and clarified their purpose with terrifying precision. They were no longer individuals burdened by separate flaws or ambitions. They were a single instrument in the hand of God, harmonized by suffering and set apart for a singular act of redemptive defiance.

Elias drew a steadying breath and gripped the Holy Bible, its cover still aglow with the cross forged by the golden harp string. "We came here to seal a door," he said, his voice carrying the weight of revelation, "but now we know it was never just about closing something off. Our true purpose is to ignite a revolution of the spirit when we return. We are to take the truth we've found in this darkness and bring it home—to disrupt the system of oppression and offer real life. 'I am come that they might have life, and that they might have it more abundantly' (John 10:10 KJV). We will give the city that life—not through force, but by revealing the final, liberating truth."

He looked at each of them, feeling the gravity of their unity. "Lucifer's design was meant to optimize and enslave, to make people believe their worth is earned, measured, and conditional. But we have learned that true worth is given, not earned, and that grace is the only currency that cannot be corrupted."

Seraphina's hand moved instinctively to his arm, her grip fierce and grounding. "I used to seek beauty in flawless design, in harmony and perfect form," she said, her voice woven with both memory and realization. "I believed meaning was found in the most exquisite arrangement, in art that left nothing out of place. But now I see—there is no composition, no masterpiece, that can capture what we are doing here. To choose an end so that others may truly begin is the highest art; to give everything and expect nothing is the most beautiful act. That is the true aesthetic of the Cross—sublime, selfless, and beyond anything the world's systems could ever express."

She glanced up at Elias, her eyes shining with tears that did not fall. "This is the only answer to a world built on merit and achievement: to lay down your life for your friends, to love without calculation."

Anya stepped forward, her earlier fear transmuted into a serene certainty. The words she spoke seemed to glow with the very light of the cross on the Bible. "'For by grace are ye saved through faith; and that not of yourselves: it is the gift of God: Not of works, lest any man should boast' (Ephesians 2:8-9, KJV). The Nexus runs on endless work, on the illusion that value can be earned. But when the truth of the Logos corrupts that frequency, the system was exposed for what it is: empty, and powerless against unconditional love and grace."

She turned her gentle gaze between Elias and Seraphina, a knowing smile lighting her face. "You know, I've watched the two of you since the very beginning—those late nights in the Green Chaos, when your conversations would drift from algorithms to dreams, from data to hope. Lucifer's entire world is built on the principle of Optimization, the pursuit of perfect calculation. But you found the variable he could never account for—unconditional love. That's the ultimate error in his code, the beautiful, unoptimized truth."

Seraphina looked down at Elias's hand in hers, a rare flush coloring her cheeks. "It's the only logical conclusion to this journey," she whispered, her voice trembling with awe and certainty.

Elias squeezed her hand, his gaze steady and full of quiet reverence. "The love of God, reflected in the love we share for each other," he said simply. "That is the truth Lucifer could never foresee."

Azael watched them, a genuine and melancholy smile softening his ancient features. "Your willingness to give everything, to plant yourselves here in the heart of the enemy's power, is the greatest act of grace. Lucifer runs on calculation; you operate on love. You are not just surviving—you are planting the seed of the Creator's Truth in the Devil's own garden."

He lifted his gaze to the distant, shuddering horizon, his voice echoing with hope that reached beyond dimensions. "Remember: 'And they overcame him by the blood of the Lamb, and by the word of their testimony; and they loved not their lives unto the death' (Revelation 12:11, KJV). The world you left behind is still waiting for this witness. Hold fast—your suffering here is the beginning of liberation for many."

A hush fell over them, profound and electric, as the words settled into their hearts. The cross on the Bible shone with unwavering brilliance, casting back the shadows that prowled the edge of vision. The harp's music vibrated in the air—a spectral anthem of hope and defiance, woven from notes too ancient for fear to unravel.

For a heartbeat, time itself seemed to pause. In that stillness, the pain and terror of what lay ahead receded, dwarfed by the immensity of what was being asked of them—and by the promise that their sacrifice would echo far beyond these twisted horizons. The fear that had haunted them since their arrival loosened its grip, replaced by a fierce, holy resolve.

Elias looked at his friends, feeling the weight of every trial they had endured—their doubts, their failures, their longing for home. He saw not just survivors, but bearers of a new song: Seraphina, radiant with the beauty of selfless love; Anya, her intellect sharpened into faith; Azael, the guardian whose sorrow had become wisdom. In their faces he glimpsed the future—a city awakened, chains shattered, the light of grace spilling into every darkened soul.

Behind them, the wound in the sky pulsed violet-green, a reminder of how far they had come. Before them, the horizon was alive with menace and possibility. This wasteland was no longer a tomb, but the threshold of a greater story—the opening of a testimony that would shake the very foundations of the world.

Step by step, they moved forward together, hearts burning with the knowledge that their journey was not about survival, but about transformation. What they carried—faith, truth, and love—was more than weapon or shield; it was the seed of a new creation. And as they pressed on through the darkness, the music of the harp and the light of the cross went with them, singing a promise that even in the heart of the Lie, the truth would not be silenced.

In that resolve, in that sacred unity, the first chapter of their ordeal ended—and the true battle for the soul of the world began.

CHAPTER 45

THE ARCHITECTS OF RESTORATION

The world behind them was sealed in violet-green flame and memory; the world ahead pulsed with a malignant anticipation. As the four—Elias, Seraphina, Anya, and Azael—began their descent from the black glass ridge toward the heart of the Nexus, it felt as if the very fabric of reality was tightening around them, drawing them into the belly of the Sin itself.

Above, the sky churned with unnatural color—veins of pulsing magenta, rivers of electric blue, streaks of crimson that forked and vanished in unnatural silence. Below, the land seethed. Dimensional creatures, neither fully formed nor wholly formless, rose in a tide of terror: fractal demons made of synthetic light and shadow, shifting their monstrous shapes through the neon-lit forest with a logic that belonged to nightmares, not nature. They were guardians of Sin, the final defense of Lucifer's corrupted world, their existence a blasphemy against the memory of Eden.

The air grew thick, buzzing with a mounting, calculated dissonance—a high-pitched synthetic shriek that drilled into the mind. Each step forward was a step into a war of frequencies, as Lucifer, channeling his will through the Apex Logician far away in the City, prepared to make his last stand. Gravity itself seemed to rebel, twisting and buckling beneath their feet, trying to drag them toward seething energy anchors embedded in the ground. With every yard gained, the glass beneath them grew slicker, shifting from solid to liquid to something that defied all language—a surface that hated every human footfall.

Azael spread his scarred, magnificent wings, surrounding the three humans in a shield of celestial resilience. Feathers of purest light and darkest shadow shimmered as he locked the chaotic winds away, holding back the worst of the world's fury. "Stay close," he commanded, his voice both music and thunder. "The way in is through the harmonic vents—small, pulsating gaps in the Nexus's architecture. They are fleeting, and the structure will try to shut them the moment it senses us. Lucifer's defenses will be relentless."

Elias and Seraphina exchanged a final, wordless look—a silent vow of unity that needed no translation. Their hands found each other, fingers entwined with the certainty of shared fate. Anya pressed close, her analytical mind racing, but her heart steadied by a new, fierce faith. Together, they followed their celestial guide, their silhouettes swallowed by the garish, wicked splendor of Lucifer's domain. They bore no weapons of steel or fire—only a Holy Bible now marked with a glowing cross, the remnant of harp strings that had dissolved into its cover, radiating quiet power. With them, they carried the memory of cleansing waters and the kind of faith forged in the crucible of despair—a faith that refused to break, even as the darkness pressed in.

As they marched, the landscape writhed and shifted, the very laws of creation bending in protest. Each breath was a battle, each heartbeat a declaration of war against the ancient darkness. The failure to close the portal had become their crucible; in the ashes of that defeat, they had discovered a purpose more profound than victory—a calling to become an unquenchable flame in the deepest heart of darkness, to force the final reckoning not just for themselves, but for the world that waited in hope beyond the wound in the sky.

Hand in hand, they descended into the shrieking Lie, every step a hymn of defiance, every heartbeat a drumbeat of coming deliverance. The ground itself seemed to scream beneath them, but above and within, the music of the harp and the light of the cross called them forward—into the domain where only the condemned dared to bring hope.

The Original Architects (The Corruption of Creation)

The descent was not just physical—it was a pilgrimage through the strata of a world coming undone, a spiraling passage through the very architecture of corruption and hope. Each step forward sent subtle ripples through the ground, the surface trembling as if awakening from a long, troubled sleep. Elias felt the faint quiver beneath his boots and glanced down, half-expecting the ground to dissolve, but instead it seemed to welcome him, as if recognizing something sacred in their arrival. Around them, echoes of Lucifer's design—fractured geometry, shivering shadows, flickers of predatory color—battled with a new pulse, a resonance that felt both ancient and startlingly fresh.

Seraphina paused, head tilted, eyes half-closed as she listened. In the silence, she could hear the faintest whispers of harmony threading through the ruined world—a melody struggling to emerge from the discord. She reached out, letting her fingers brush Elias's, drawing comfort and strength from his presence. He squeezed her hand in return, grounding them both.

They crossed a threshold that was more than a line in the ground—it was the boundary between what had been claimed by Sin and what was being redeemed by sacrifice. As they stepped forward, it was as if the very air exhaled, releasing the tension of ages. For a heartbeat, the world held its breath—and then changed.

Anya slowed, overcome by the transformation unfolding around them. The landscape, once a nightmarish tangle of toxic colors, now softened before her eyes. She took a slow, deliberate breath, the clean, electric scent of rain on fresh ground filling her lungs. The discordant hum that had haunted every shadow and silenced every hope began to unravel, giving way to a deep, sonorous thrum—steady, patient, alive. It was as if the heart of the world, long-abused and nearly forgotten, had begun to beat again, calling forth a promise of healing that was fragile yet fiercely persistent.

"Do you feel that?" Anya whispered, voice trembling as she stepped closer to Seraphina, her shoulder lightly brushing her friend's. "It's like the world is remembering what it means to be alive."

Seraphina nodded, her eyes shining. "It's music. Not just sound, but meaning. The land is composing itself anew."

Ahead, the Nexus itself was transformed. Where once had stood a pyramid of chaos—an engine of discord, a monument to Lucifer's pride—now rose a column of vertical, unwavering white light. Its gentle frequency radiated outward, pushing back the remnants of Sin that still clung like bruises to the battered land. The neon-lit forest, once a wild tangle of predatory movement, was softening at the edges. Colors dulled to the hues of new growth and gentle dusk. The very fabric of creation, wounded but not destroyed, was remembering its original song.

Elias reached out, instinctively slipping his arm around Seraphina's waist, drawing her into his side as they gazed at the transformed landscape. Anya, a step ahead, crouched beside a massive, fungus-like tree whose electric green glow was dimming to a warm, soil brown. She ran her hand gently across its bark, feeling the pulse of life beneath her palm.

"The process is so slow," Anya said, half to herself and half to the others. "It's like watching a fever break in someone you love. You have to trust the healing, even if you can't see it all at once."

Elias's voice was quiet, awed. "We're not just walking through ruins. We're witnesses to a resurrection."

Anya, tracing her fingers over the bark of the healing tree, looked up at the others, her brows knit in a mixture of wonder and sorrow. "Do you think it was always like this?" she asked quietly, voice trembling. "Was this world ever beautiful—or did Lucifer make it this way from the beginning?"

Azael, standing with the dignity of a sentinel and the sorrow of a witness, let his ancient gaze roam across the changed land. "No," he replied, his voice as soft as morning rain yet weighted by centuries of truth. "That is Lucifer's greatest deception. He cannot create—he can only distort. He warps what was made for beauty and harmony, twisting it into a parody of itself. But even in the deepest corruption, the truth is never fully destroyed. The root of goodness, the original design, always fights to rise again."

A hush fell, the kind that marks the turning of an age. Elias squeezed Seraphina's hand, and she leaned her head against his shoulder, savoring the quiet, wordless comfort. Anya stood, brushing her hair from her face, and offered a small, grateful smile to both of them. Their bond was a silent benediction, a fragile defiance in a world that had tried so hard to unmake them.

For a long moment, the team felt the story of the world unfolding around them—the long, agonizing battle between ruin and restoration, between the Lie and the promise that preceded it. They saw their own journey mirrored in the land: brokenness followed by the first, tentative signs of healing.

Elias found himself praying silently, not for victory, but for the courage to keep choosing hope. Seraphina's thoughts swirled with music, composing a new refrain from the sounds of a world being healed. Anya, for the first time, allowed herself to believe that logic and faith might coexist in the same restored ground.

In that moment, they understood that the greatest act of defiance was not to destroy what the enemy had corrupted, but to reclaim it—to resurrect what had been broken, to breathe life where it had been choked out, and to declare by every step and every sacrifice that the Lie would not have the final word. Here in the scarred heart of creation, the true revolution was not in fire, but in renewal.

The world was watching, creation itself holding its breath. Every act of faith and love, every refusal to yield to despair, was a note in the new song—a song that promised, even in the deepest night, that dawn would come. And as they stood together, hands entwined, hearts steady, they became the living chord, the first line of a melody written for the world's return to grace. In that silence, hope was not just a word but a presence—an invisible force drawing all things toward restoration.

The Vandalized Work

A hush lingered as the team moved forward, the transformed land beneath their feet humming with possibility. Above them, the column of white light rose like a promise, and the air felt almost gentle—an echo of Eden, trembling on the edge of remembrance. But as they advanced, remnants of the old world still clung stubbornly to the ground: patches of jagged, purple crystal, twisted trees with wounds that oozed neon sap, bruised shadows that recoiled at the touch of light.

Azael stepped ahead, his stride purposeful but heavy with memory. He knelt by a patch of ground where the last of the sinister crystals were dissolving, running his fingers across the rough, darkening stone. The others gathered close, their footsteps careful, reverent.

"You must understand this fundamental truth before we proceed," the angel said, his voice low and urgent. "Every vibrant color, every colossal structure you see around you—it was all created by the True Creator as part of a magnificent, harmonious dimension. This realm was never meant to be the 'Forge of the Lie.' It was conceived as a masterpiece of diverse, unrestrained life, meant to complement your own world. 'The earth is the Lord's, and the fulness thereof; the world, and they that dwell therein' (Psalm 24:1 KJV)."

Elias crouched beside Azael, absorbing the revelation as he let his gaze sweep over the surreal landscape—the impossibly twisted geometry, the electric shadows, the strange, unnatural beauty that now seemed to tremble with the threat of distortion. "So… if we see things that seem monstrous or broken, those aren't the original intentions of this place?" he asked, his voice uncertain but searching.

Azael shook his head, sorrow flickering in his ancient eyes. "No, Elias. What you will face here—whatever horrors or grotesque forms may arise—are not original evils. When Lucifer and the other Fallen were cast out of Heaven, they did not create a new prison; they vandalized a perfect world. They twisted harmonious frequencies into discord, amplified innocent beauty into something overwhelming or terrifying, and imbued what was once pure with the sickness of their own pride. They didn't build a new house; they defaced a temple."

Seraphina stepped closer, her eyes tracing the bruised colors and fractured patterns that still clung to the world. "So everything warped we'll see—the wild geometry, the painful intensity, the unnatural defenses—it was all once elegant, all once meant for joy." Her hand found Elias's, squeezing with both anxiety and resolve.

Azael nodded, his expression grave. "Yes. Lucifer cannot create—he can only corrupt and distort what was made good. Remember this, as you encounter what lies ahead: beneath every horror, the blueprint of beauty endures. Your purpose is not just to fight, but to see the original design, to restore and reclaim what was lost."

Anya, her brow furrowed, looked from Azael to the others. "Then our greatest weapon is not destruction, but remembrance and restoration. We're not here to erase the ruined parts, but to heal and reveal what was always true."

Azael smiled gently, the weight in his gaze lightened by hope. "Exactly, Anya. The Lie can only ever obscure the truth; it cannot erase it. In your journey, let your hearts seek the original architecture. That is the path to victory—and to redemption for this world."

Seraphina moved closer to Elias, her hand finding his, fingers interlacing with silent urgency. The contact steadied her, a lifeline in the face of cosmic betrayal. Her brow was furrowed, not in anger, but in the anguish of a mind forced to confront the corruption of beauty.

"He didn't just corrupt the life, he corrupted the laws of physics," she said, her voice trembling with conviction. "The sickening fractal growth, the geometric cruelty… it was all hyper-optimized to be a defense mechanism. He took the Creator's generous, elegant design and made it ruthlessly efficient for destruction. It's the ultimate waste of potential."

Elias, feeling the ache in her words, brought their joined hands up and pressed a gentle kiss to the back of hers—a gesture that spoke of solidarity and love that ran deeper than words. "It's a tragedy," he murmured, his gaze never leaving hers. "But if their true form is still in the blueprint, then our fight isn't to destroy them. It's to remind them—to heal the defaced temple."

Anya, who had been quietly absorbing the exchange, stepped forward and laid her hand gently on Seraphina's shoulder, offering a fierce, silent comfort. There was something maternal, protective, in the gesture—an acknowledgment of the pain that comes from seeing one's ideals weaponized.

"The Lie can only ever obscure the truth," Anya whispered, meeting Seraphina's eyes. "It's like taking the most complex, beautiful formula and adding a single, perfect error to make the result meaningless. But that just means its true form is still there. It's still in the blueprint. That's what we have to seek."

Seraphina leaned into the touch, closing her eyes for a moment as if to draw strength from her companions. "The truth… the original architecture," she repeated, letting the words become a quiet mantra.

Azael rose gracefully, brushing dust from his hands. "Our task is not just to survive, but to restore—to reclaim what has been vandalized. Every act of beauty, every choice to love instead of hate, is a small restoration. The Lie cannot endure where truth is remembered."

Elias nodded, his resolve sharpening. "Then we rebuild, one step at a time. We become the living proof that what has been corrupted can be made new."

A breeze stirred, carrying with it the scent of rain and the faintest hint of music—Seraphina's melody, unfinished but full of hope. Anya smiled, her eyes shining with the possibility of restoration. The team pressed forward, their shadows stretching across ground that was no longer cursed, but consecrated by their purpose.

They moved on—not as wanderers, but as architects of healing, each step a silent promise that the vandalized world would one day be whole again. The memory of their revelation lingered behind them like a gentle benediction, and the landscape itself seemed to lean forward, yearning for its own redemption.

Encounter: The Strangled Grove

The land changed beneath their feet. The last vestiges of the black ridge faded, giving way to a dense and tangled wilderness. The air thickened, warm and weighty, filling their lungs with a sense of expectancy and unease. Every step became slower, more deliberate, as if even time itself was being caught in the tangle. Shadows deepened, and the gentle thrum of restoration faded into a new, more anxious rhythm—a low, rhythmic hiss that pulsed through the silence.

They found themselves before a wall of living complexity, a thicket unlike anything from their own world. Smooth, silver-gray vines, each pulsing faintly with an inner light, were woven together in a lattice so intricate it was almost dizzying. The structure was not wild or chaotic, but impossibly neat—thousands of loops and knots, perfectly arranged for maximum strength and absolute efficiency. It was a marvel of design, but in its perfection, it was suffocating.

Seraphina drew in a sharp breath, her artist's sensibilities both awed and unsettled. She reached out, fingertips hovering over the lattice. "It's… beautiful, but it's wrong," she murmured. "This isn't life. It's a prison made of logic."

Elias stepped beside her, his eyes roving over the dense network. "It's like every instinct to grow was forced into a single purpose until it strangled itself." He glanced at Seraphina, searching her face for insight. "If this is what lies ahead, how many other wonders have been twisted into traps?"

Azael moved forward, his wings folding close, his gaze solemn. "The Logic-Vine Thicket," he explained softly. "It was once a vibrant, flowering hedge, designed to filter and freshen the air. But Lucifer's hand made it a model of perfect efficiency—trapping all light, all air, until nothing could breathe. Look closely."

Anya, analytical as ever, peered into the tangled mass. "Something's trapped inside," she breathed, pointing to the glimmer at the center.

There, at the heart of the lattice, a tiny Ember-Moth flickered—its wings a trembling canvas of color, its body buzzing faintly within the prison of vines. It beat against the knots, desperate for a gap, but every exit was sealed by another loop of logic.

Elias tensed, already reaching for his Bible, but Seraphina caught his hand. "No," she said quietly, her eyes shining with resolve. "If we shatter it, we only destroy what's left. We need to remind it of what it was meant to be."

"How do we un-optimize a perfect knot?" Elias asked, his brow furrowed, voice barely above a whisper.

Seraphina's gaze was fierce, her mind racing with the memory of beauty before corruption. "We introduce the ultimate inefficiency: Grace."

Anya stepped forward, her voice trembling with gentle power. She closed her eyes and began to recite, her words rising into the charged air: "'I will seek that which was lost, and bring again that which was driven away, and will bind up that which was broken, and will strengthen that which was sick' (Ezekiel 34:16 KJV)." Her prayer was a balm, saturating the Grove with unearned goodness, her hand resting lightly on Seraphina's shoulder in solidarity.

Seraphina pressed her palm against the lattice, her voice low but unwavering. "You were never designed to choke or trap. The Creator made you to filter, to give life, to let the light and air pass through. You are more than your efficiency. Remember your generosity. Remember your purpose."

Azael, sensing the moment, began to hum—a low, resonant tone that seemed to vibrate through the very ground. It echoed with the memory of his celestial harp, calling out the original harmony buried beneath the logic.

The change was not sudden. At first, nothing moved—then, almost imperceptibly, the silver-gray tubes began to relax, their perfect knots slackening, spirals and gentle curves emerging from the rigid lattice. The thicket unwound itself, not with a violent snap, but with the slow, deliberate grace of something remembering how to breathe.

As the last of the vines loosened, the suffocating air lifted. The Ember-Moth zipped free, hovering before the group in a shimmer of gratitude. It circled Seraphina and Anya, then darted upward, its wings flashing iridescent joy before vanishing into the renewed forest.

The Grove, once a monument to suffocating order, was now alive with color and the gentle movement of air. Soft whirring and chirping filled the silence, the song of life returning to a place that had nearly forgotten it.

Elias, moved by the transformation, rested his cheek against Seraphina's hair, breathing in the scent of rain and new beginnings. "We honor the architecture," he said quietly, his words a promise. "We heal the wound, together."

Anya's eyes glistened as she watched the moth disappear, and she squeezed Seraphina's hand, a silent pledge of faith in the possibilities yet to come.

Azael's gaze shifted beyond the Grove, his expression sharpened by new purpose. "Now," he said, his voice steady, "we must find the weakest point in the Adversary's handiwork—the original seam he tried to destroy, not just corrupt."

The path ahead beckoned, dappled with shifting light and the promise of both peril and redemption. With hearts bound by love and hands joined in hope, the team stepped forward into the unknown—ready to face whatever test awaited, trusting that every act of healing, no matter how small, was a victory against the Lie.

And so, in the restored hush of the Strangled Grove, their journey toward restoration truly began.

CHAPTER 46

THE GARDEN REMEMBERED

The hush of the restored grove lingered, the memory of grace still palpable as they stepped past the last curling vines. For the first time since crossing over, the air felt peaceful—sweet with the scent of rain-drenched ground, alive with the possibility of renewal. It was as if the world itself, bruised but not broken, was offering a shy welcome to its would-be healers.

Elias slowed his pace, his historian's gaze drinking in every detail: the translucent mosses glowing faintly along the roots, the slow drip of dew from emerald leaves, the way the light filtered through the shifting canopy in fractured rainbows. He touched Seraphina's hand, grounding himself in the present, quietly awed by the harmony that was fighting to return.

Seraphina's emerald eyes shone as she scanned the horizon, the gleaming harp slung across her back humming gently in response to the ambient song. Her footsteps were slow and measured, her aesthetic mind alert for patterns, harmonies, and subtle disharmonies. She ran her fingers across a cluster of sapphire-blue petals, feeling the vibration of life—fragile but persistent—pulsing beneath her skin. "Do you hear it?" she whispered, not sure if she meant the others or the world itself. "The music is returning. It's different— soft, unfinished—but it's there."

Anya, usually silent in her observation, let herself linger at the edge of a shallow, crystalline pool. She knelt, her reflection flickering beside a cluster of tiny, silver fish darting through the water. "It's like the world is remembering itself," she murmured, her voice rich with quiet reverence. "Not all at once. But it wants to be whole."

Azael walked a few paces ahead, his wings folded close. His steps were gentle, almost deferential, as if he feared to mar the new growth with his presence. He paused beneath a sprawling tree whose bark shimmered with veins of gold and violet, breathing in the subtle, unfamiliar fragrances. "Even here, where corruption once ruled, the original blessing rises up," he said softly. "You are witnessing the first dawn after a long night."

The team moved slowly through the landscape, not out of caution but out of respect for the fragile beauty awakening around them. They passed a stand of crystalline ferns, the fronds curling and uncurling in a slow, luminous dance. A flock of glass-winged birds erupted from a nearby bush, scattering prisms of light with every beat of their wings.

Elias stopped, his face breaking into a rare, wide smile. "It's like walking through a dream someone has just begun to remember."

Seraphina squeezed his hand, her thumb tracing a gentle pattern across his knuckles. "We're not just witnesses," she said. "We're part of the melody now."

The path wound on, shifting from soft moss to fields of tall, translucent grass that whispered against their legs. For a moment, the world was almost silent, save for the rhythmic sound of their footsteps and the distant call of a songbird. Azael paused, turning back to the group. "We are safe for now," he murmured, "but do not let your guard fall. Even the most beautiful places here are haunted by echoes of what was lost."

Anya bent to examine a flower with petals like spun silver. "Do you think it all can come back?" she asked, her voice trembling between hope and skepticism.

Azael's eyes were gentle. "Nothing is ever fully lost. The Creator's design is indelible, even beneath layers of ruin. Every act of remembrance is an act of healing. Each step you take in faith weaves a new thread into the world's tapestry."

They pressed onward, every sense alive to the dimension's wonders. Seraphina leaned lightly against Elias as they crossed a small bridge of interlocking amber stones, their bodies sharing warmth against the cool, perfumed air. Anya, emboldened by the beauty around her, reached out to touch Azael's wing, her fingers brushing the edge of a feather that glimmered with shifting color.

"Thank you for guiding us," she said quietly. "I didn't know beauty could survive a place like this."

Azael smiled, a soft, sad curve of his lips. "It's not just surviving, Anya. It's fighting to return. And it fights hardest in hearts that refuse to give up."

The landscape shifted again—fields giving way to a grove of trees with crystal trunks and leaves that shimmered like stained glass. Sunlight, or something like it, filtered through the canopy in shifting mosaics, painting the team in colors that seemed to dance across their skin.

They paused there, letting the moment soak in, each team member enveloped in awe. In that hush, Elias whispered a prayer of gratitude; Seraphina listened to the world's unfinished song; Anya closed her eyes, letting the new air fill her lungs; and Azael watched them all, his heart full of ancient hope.

For a little while, there was no hunger, no fear—only the promise that even in a world so badly broken, beauty and grace could still find a way to bloom.

And as they moved forward, deeper into the dimension's mysteries, their journey became part of the unfolding wonder of creation restored—each step shaping the world with new hope, their presence a living promise that the story was far from over.

The Echoing Canopy

The path led them beneath the sweeping boughs of ancient trees, their trunks wide and gnarled, their canopies arching overhead like the nave of a living cathedral. Each leaf was a shard of crystal, translucent and faceted, catching the light in shifting hues of emerald and gold. When the wind stirred, the leaves struck against each other in harmonious chords—a chorus of crystalline tones that rippled through the air. Some were bright and playful, like laughter skipping across a pond; others were low and mournful, full of longing and memory.

Seraphina felt the music wrap around her, pulling her to a halt. She closed her eyes, letting the melody swirl through her soul. For a moment, the world felt hushed, waiting for her to listen. "It's not just the wind," she whispered, opening her eyes slowly to the others. "The trees are tuned to the memory of joy. Every note is a memory trying to make itself heard."

Elias lingered at her side, his eyes reflecting the shifting colors overhead. He slipped his hand into hers, the warmth of her palm grounding him against the wonder and strangeness of it all. "If you listen closely, you can almost hear the world healing itself," he murmured, voice thick with awe. He squeezed her fingers gently, as if to share the rhythm of his heart with her.

Anya wandered a little ahead, curiosity brightening her expression. She trailed her hand along the lowest branches, fingertips brushing the crystalline leaves. As she made contact, a single leaf trembled and released a soft, golden chime. The note lingered, shimmering in the air, and Anya found herself smiling despite the heaviness she had carried. "I never thought data could feel like this," she said, turning to the others, her voice full of wonder. "There's a pattern, but it's alive. It's... more than information. It's a memory with a heartbeat. I wish we could map the entire forest's song—see what story it's telling."

Azael lingered at the edge of a sunlit clearing, looking upward through the shifting mosaic of color. His wings, folded loosely behind him, caught stray beams of light and scattered them in prismatic bursts. "This was Eden's echo," he said, his voice reverent. "A place where creation's praise was a living thing. Here, every branch remembers the first song. Even after all that's been lost, the harmony endures."

The team moved deeper into the canopy, each step a soft percussion in the forest's living symphony. Overhead, a breeze picked up, and the trees responded with a new melody—one that felt hopeful, as if the land itself was greeting old friends. Elias glanced at Seraphina, seeing a rare, unguarded smile on her lips.

She lifted her hand and brushed a strand of hair behind her ear, her gaze dancing along the shifting shadows. "I used to think beauty was a matter of form and proportion," she said quietly. "But here, it's alive. It changes with every breath we take."

Elias watched a flock of tiny, iridescent birds dart through the branches, their wings striking the leaves and adding high, bell-like notes to the chorus. "It's like the world is singing for us—maybe even because of us."

Anya paused, her brow furrowed as she listened intently to a sequence of notes. "I think it's singing for itself," she said softly. "But we're part of the song now. We're witnesses. Maybe even collaborators."

They pressed on, weaving between pillars of light and shadow, their footsteps accompanied by the endless, shifting music of the trees. Occasionally, Elias would reach out to steady Seraphina as the path dipped suddenly, his touch lingering just a moment longer than necessary. Anya, emboldened by the beauty, let herself hum along with the forest's melody, her voice blending with the living chords above.

Azael led the way, his movements gentle, careful not to disturb the roots or the low-hanging branches. As the group passed beneath a particularly ancient tree, its trunk inscribed with swirling, luminous runes, he paused and placed his palm upon the bark. "Thank you for remembering us," he whispered, almost inaudible.

The tree responded with a deep, resonant note that vibrated through the ground and up into their bones. For a fleeting instant, they all felt it—a sense of belonging, of being remembered and welcomed by the land itself.

They emerged from the echoing canopy changed—not just travelers, but participants in the world's remembering, their presence woven into the forest's endless, hopeful refrain.

The Field of Living Lanterns and the River of First Light

The music of the canopy faded, replaced by a hush thick with anticipation as the team stepped from the shade of the singing trees into a meadow awash in golden light. The grass here was short and soft, cool beneath their weary feet. All around, dozens—soon hundreds—of orbs floated just above the ground, glowing from within and gently swaying in the silent breeze. Each orb cast shifting, swirling patterns across the field, painting the team in hues of amber, jade, and rose.

Anya stopped first, nearly breathless with wonder, and knelt beside a lantern drifting at chest height. She peered into its depths, her eyes wide with a child's curiosity. Within, she saw a swirl of color, and then—so quick she almost doubted it—a flicker of images: a sapling unfurling its first leaves, a river sparkling in sunlight, a child's laughter echoing in a forgotten tongue. She reached out, her fingertips hovering just above the orb. "They're memories," she breathed, awestruck, her voice barely more than a tremor. "Whole stories, waiting to be seen."

Seraphina, drawn by beauty as always, moved gracefully through the meadow. She reached out, letting her fingers brush the surface of another orb. The lantern bobbed in the air and drifted closer, as if drawn to her touch. She felt a faint warmth travel up her arm, gentle and familiar. "They're waiting to be remembered," she whispered, more to herself than anyone else. "Maybe that's all it takes for lost things to come back—a witness, a gentle hand." Her gaze softened, and she smiled at Elias, inviting him to share in the discovery.

Elias approached, his expression open and unguarded for the first time in days. He watched Seraphina, watched Anya, and then let his own hand cup a lantern. The orb pulsed with light, and for a heartbeat he saw a vision of a mountain at dawn, golden light cresting the horizon. His heart swelled— gratitude, awe, and the ache of belonging mingling within him. "We're walking through the dreams of a world that refuses to forget itself," he said, his voice reverent. He slipped his arm around Seraphina's waist, drawing her close, both of them illuminated by the gentle, shifting light.

Azael stood a little apart, his wings half-open, their feathers catching the lantern glow and casting shifting patterns across his face. The sorrow that so often haunted his gaze seemed eased, if only for a moment. He smiled, a rare and genuine expression. "You are the keepers of these memories now," he said, his voice rich with hope. "Carry them forward, and they will light your way through the darkness to come."

They lingered in the field, moving among the lanterns, letting the memories wash over them—each orb a fragment of the world's long-lost innocence, a promise that nothing was ever truly gone. Elias watched as Anya sat cross-legged in the grass, cradling an orb in her lap, her eyes shining with silent tears. Seraphina sung a few soft notes, her voice weaving with the light, and even Azael bowed his head in silent prayer.

After a time, the meadow sloped gently downward, and the lanterns began to thin. The team followed the curve of the land, the air growing cooler and clearer with every step, until the grass gave way to pebbles and smooth, shining stones. Before them, a river flowed—its water impossibly clear, glowing with veins of blue and silver that twisted and danced with the current. The banks were lined with luminous moss, and the stones beneath the water seemed to sing with the gentle rush.

Seraphina knelt at the river's edge, trailing her fingers through the current. A shiver of energy rose up her arm, tingling and alive. "It's like the beginning," she said, breathless. "This water remembers creation. It knows what it was meant to be."

Anya crouched beside her, scooping water into her hands and drinking deeply. As the liquid touched her lips, she gasped in delight—a bright, pure sensation racing through her veins. "I can feel it—something waking up inside me. Something I thought the City had taken away. It's hope. It's real."

Elias knelt, filling his palms and drinking. The water tasted of sweet mountain springs, but there was more—a feeling of lightness, of burdens falling away. For a moment, all the memories of the City—its burdens, its calculations, its endless striving—felt far away, replaced by a deep, wordless sense of belonging.

Azael stood watch just behind them, his wings shimmering with the river's light. "Drink deeply," he encouraged, his voice gentle but commanding. "This river was the first to be tainted by corruption, and the last to be healed. It is a sign—the world is ready for you to shape the next chapter. Let it restore you as you restore it."

They sat together at the riverbank, the field of lanterns glowing softly behind them, the water singing before them. Seraphina leaned her head on Elias's shoulder, Anya nestled close on his other side, and Azael stood above them—a guardian and a witness. The world felt whole, for a moment. The journey continued, but for now, there was peace, and the promise that every step forward would write a new line in the melody of creation restored.

A Moment of Shelter

As dusk approached, the world changed its tempo. The golden river faded behind them, and the trees closed in, their trunks arching overhead to form a vaulted, living passage. Leaves whispered secrets in the cooling breeze, and the lantern orbs they had seen in the meadow now floated higher, casting gentle halos of light that seemed to beckon them onward.

The team moved quietly, each step cushioned by a carpet of moss that glowed faintly underfoot. Soon, they came upon a small, sheltered hollow—protected from the wind, encircled by ivy and flowering vines. Here the air was sweet and still, the last rays of daylight filtering through the canopy in ribbons of lavender and gold.

Elias paused and unfastened his cloak, spreading it over the thick moss. He turned to Seraphina, his voice barely above a whisper. "Rest," he invited, his eyes warm with love and concern. She sank gratefully beside him, curling into his side, her head nestled on his shoulder. The warmth of his presence banished the tremors of fatigue that lingered in her limbs. She let her hand find his, their fingers entwining in silent communion.

Anya settled nearby, cross-legged, her back against the curved root of an ancient tree. She closed her eyes, humming a soft melody—one Seraphina had played for them earlier. The tune was gentle, almost a lullaby, and it seemed to wrap the hollow in a cocoon of calm.

Azael stood sentinel at the edge of the clearing, his wings half-unfurled, a silhouette against the gathering twilight. His gaze swept the darkness beyond, vigilant and unyielding, yet his posture radiated peace. Every so often, a lantern orb drifted close, briefly illuminating his features with a ghostly, benevolent glow.

For a long while, the only sounds were their soft breathing, Anya's melody, and the distant song of the river. Overhead, the first stars appeared—strange constellations, unfamiliar and wild, punctuating the velvet sky with the promise of new stories. Seraphina traced slow, looping patterns on Elias's forearm, her touch gentle, a silent language of trust and gratitude.

Anya looked up, her gaze wandering from lantern to star. "Do you think we're the first to see these skies?" she asked, her voice full of wonder. "Or do you think the world remembers others who came before us?"

Elias squeezed Seraphina's hand, letting the question settle over him. "Maybe we're both—the first and the inheritors. Maybe that's what it means to be chosen."

Azael stepped closer, his wings folding in, and knelt beside them. His voice was low, almost a benediction. "You are remembered here. Every kindness, every act of hope you bring restores what was lost. Let yourselves be at peace tonight. Tomorrow, the path will challenge you again. But for now, let the world hold you."

Seraphina shifted, resting her cheek against Elias's chest, her breath slowing as exhaustion gave way to serenity. Anya stretched out on her back, hands folded over her stomach, eyes tracing the slow dance of lanterns above. Elias pressed a kiss to Seraphina's hair, his heart finally quiet.

Together, beneath the shelter of the ancient trees and the watchful eyes of their guardian, they surrendered to sleep. The new world cradled them gently, and in that rare and perfect night, grace was more than enough.

Yet even as their breathing slowed and the hush of rest enfolded them, a subtle sense of anticipation lingered in the air—a gentle, almost imperceptible shift, carrying them forward. Beyond the safety of sleep, the world awaited their next choice.

CHAPTER 47

THE WEIGHT OF MORTALITY

The first faint glow of morning crept through the jeweled canopy, stirring the air with promise. Before memory or thought could return, the team awoke to a subtle ache—a heaviness in limbs and spirit, evidence that the peace of the night was only a pause in their journey, not its conclusion. The sanctuary of sleep faded, replaced by the undeniable weight of mortality, and with it, the call to rise and continue.

As they sat up, the warmth of the world's renewal pressed against the sharp reality of their human needs. Muscles protested, throats burned with thirst, and the thin, clean air only accentuated how much their bodies had given in the spiritual struggle. The beauty around them was not a shield from suffering, but a reminder of what was at stake.

For a moment, no one spoke. Each was held in the tension between the memory of grace and the certainty of trial ahead. The hush was broken only by the soft rustle of luminous leaves—a sound that reminded them the world was watching, waiting to see what they would choose in the face of weakness.

Only then did Azael speak, his voice gentle but resolute: "This is where faith begins again—not in the victory, but in the willingness to keep moving, to let weakness become the ground for new strength."

They gathered their things in silence, the memory of rest still sweet on their skin. The gravity of the path ahead was impossible to deny. Their journey would resume—not as the end of peace, but as its proof: that grace could sustain them through the weight of mortality, and hope could rise, even when the body faltered.

Yet as they prepared to move on, the cost of the night and everything that had come before became undeniable. The realization that they were not standing in an alien prison, but in a vandalized garden waiting to be restored, should have been invigorating. Instead, the physical toll of their journey was immediate and heavy. The air felt cleaner, almost refreshing, but the intense spiritual labor—the fear, the escape, the baptism, the brutal confrontation with the Thicket—had left their bodies profoundly weary and their throats parched.

Their exhaustion was more than mere fatigue; it was the biological aftermath of surviving a spiritual war. Minds once honed by the City's efficiency now felt slow and heavy, even resistant to simple thought.

Elias was sharply reminded of his mortality. His indigo gambeson, designed for protection and flexibility, now weighed on his shoulders like lead. Out of habit, he reached into one of his pouches for rations, only to find it empty—a small, jarring echo of how much they had once depended on the City's optimized, tasteless provisions. That false foundation was gone now, replaced by the reality of basic hunger, a dull, constant ache in his body.

He turned to Anya, the quietest of the three, and gently placed the Holy Bible into her hands. "I carried it into the fight at the portal," he murmured, "but it's right that you carry it now, Anya. May the Word be your strength."

Anya received the book with solemn reverence, her leather gauntlets softening the contact. Her analytical eyes, usually focused on complex data flows, were now concentrated in profound devotion. She did not speak, but the subtle lift of her chin—a look of resolved purpose—was her quiet acceptance.

Seraphina leaned heavily on the glowing Harp, its gentle hum a physical support against her exhaustion. Her midnight blue tunic, once sleek and sharp, now only highlighted the tension in her depleted form.

"I am intensely thirsty," she admitted, her voice tight and brittle. She pushed her dark, matted hair away from her face, exposing the damp sheen of fatigue on her brow. "The air in the Nexus was toxic; my internal architecture, built for perfect function, feels degraded. Every integrated system is running on fumes. The fluid buffers are crashing, and the electrochemical balance is critically inverted. I feel a systemic crash coming, Elias." The loss of control over her own meticulously designed biology terrified her more than any external threat.

Elias moved to her side, placing a warm hand on the small of her back. She instantly leaned into the contact, finding a moment of quiet strength in his presence. "And the hunger is a dull ache," he said, focusing his gaze on Azael, the only being here who seemed untouched by physical need. "We haven't eaten anything in days. In the City, sustenance was a control mechanism—precise, measurable, and transactional. We know the Creator provides, but how do we access that provision here, where Lucifer's corruption still reigns, and the natural order is inverted?"

Azael looked at them, his eyes serious but kind. "You ask how the Creator can provide in the enemy's territory. But you forget who made the territory in the first place, Elias," the angel said softly. "This void, this corruption—it is a borrowed space, a vandalized truth. The basic elements of creation, even here, still obey the fundamental command of their True Creat,, the Architect of all creation."

He stepped closer, his scarred hand hovering over Seraphina's slumped shoulder, offering comfort without touching her. "The City taught you to earn your existence, to optimize for survival. But that is the Lie. You are His children, not subjects of the Adversary. You do not toil for sustenance; you ask for grace. Your faith has already broken the greatest lie. Now, you must simply trust." Azael's gaze intensified, settling on Seraphina. "The provision will not look like the City's optimized sustenance, and it will not follow their logic. It will simply *be*, because you are loved. The Creator commands us to 'Be anxious for nothing; but in every thing by prayer and supplication with thanksgiving let your requests be made known unto God' (Philippians 4:6 KJV)."

A Feast from the Void

Azael guided them to a small, level patch of ground, where the black crystal dust of the dimension was momentarily stable. He paused, surveying the team with a gravity that signaled the sacredness of what was about to happen.

Azael spoke with calm, gentle authority: "Come, let us humble ourselves before the Creator. This is not a moment for asking for resources, but a time to invite His love to meet your need. Provision here is not a transaction—it is the affirmation of your worth. Surrender your striving, and be open to receive."

Elias, Seraphina, and Anya knelt together on the level ground, their knees pressing into the black crystal dust—a gesture of humility and shared surrender. They reached for each other's hands, interlocking them in silent solidarity. The warmth of their touch spread through the circle, anchoring each of them against the exhaustion and uncertainty that clung to the air. The Holy Bible rested on the ground at the center of their joined hands, a quiet symbol of faith and hope. The closeness between them was palpable; their shared vulnerability transformed into a quiet, resilient strength. Anya's ochre vest and dark gauntlets, reflected in the worn leather cover, formed a portrait of rugged devotion and unity.

Elias began the prayer, his voice simple and unguarded, each word threaded with humility and absolute dependence. His mind, usually a landscape of strategy and precedent, was now emptied of all but the present need and trust in grace.

"Our Father, which art in Heaven. God of Abraham, God of Isaac, and God of Jacob, we are weak, but you are mighty. We ask not for the world's optimized food, designed to control and sustain Sin, but for the grace of your original provision. Sustain us for the mission you have bestowed on us. Let your love become food and, your mercy become water. Protect us from temptations and the world as we each speak in our inner monologue. In the wonderful name of Jesus, Amen."

As the final word, a whisper of commitment, left Elias's lips, the ground before them responded. It was not a violent reaction, but an unmaking of the dark order—a silent, seismic event of creation overpowering corruption.

Appearing before them—without sound or smoke—a perfect Rock emerged from the black dust. It was pure white quartz, modest in size and humble—just large enough for someone to kneel beside. The Rock shimmered with raw, uncorrupted light: not a monument to grandeur, but a quiet promise at the heart of the void. Against the surrounding dark neon landscape, its simple presence was breathtaking—a living symbol of restoration and hope. From its base, a stream of perfectly clear, luminous water began to flow, pulsing with internal light as it pooled in a small hollow—a quiet miracle of provision and grace, fulfilling the ancient command: "Speak ye unto the rock before their eyes; and it shall give forth his water..." (Numbers 20:8 KJV).

Seraphina her exhaustion momentarily forgotten, watched the water with intellectual awe. "It's pure H2O," she gasped, her mind instantly analyzing the output. "But... its structure is flawless. There are no impurities, no entropic degradation. It's uncorrupted energy, a perfect lattice of creation."

Azael scanned the ground for anything that could serve their need, his gaze settling on a small, dark shard of crystal embedded in the black dust—a remnant of the dimension's corrupted architecture. He stooped down, lifted the fragment, and, with a flash of angelic light and a low, resonant hum, shaped it into a sturdy, consecrated bowl. As he held up the vessel, its surface shimmering with new purpose, he said, "Even what was twisted can be restored for the Architect's glory. This, too, can serve the Creator's table."

Elias took the bowl and scooped the crystalline water. It tasted of mountain springs and had an immediate, profound effect, dissolving the weariness and dry fatigue in their mouths and throats.

Clinging to the sides of the quartz pillar, near the stream, were small, crystalline orbs—the promised manna. They were flawless, glowing from within with a soft, internal starlight, each no larger than a thumb tip. They had the appearance of perfectly symmetrical frozen dew drops. These were the true sustenance, untainted by any artificial design or interference—pure, original, and freely given by the Creator.

Azael reached out and plucked one, holding it up. "The manna of the wilderness," he whispered, reverence face. "He is faithful. He provides both the spiritual truth and the physical necessity, and in the simplest, most perfect form."

The Resonance of Grace

Elias took the first orb and offered it to Seraphina. Their hands met, his rugged palm cradling the small, glittering sphere, her fingers momentarily closing around his. It was a brief, intimate connection, a shared moment of absolute dependency.

"Thank you," she breathed, her emerald eyes meeting his with an intensity that promised devotion.

She placed the small orb on her tongue. It did not require chewing. The food dissolved instantly, releasing a burst of warmth and a flavor that was impossible to pin down—sweet like honey, fresh like rain, and utterly satisfying. It was reminiscent of the ancient description: "like coriander seed, white; and the taste of it was like wafers made with honey" (Exodus 16:31 KJV).

Seraphina felt the exhaustion lift, not slowly, but in a clean, comprehensive wave. It was as if her internal schema had been instantly perfected, her systems rebooted with the flawless essence of clean energy. She straightened, the slump of fatigue replaced by the elegant tension of a finely tuned machine, now running on God's own perfect fuel. Her smile was genuine, unburdened, and reached her eyes—a rare sight since their descent into the dimension.

Elias watched her transformation, a wave of profound relief washing over him. He then ate his own, the manna instantly grounding the anxiety that had shadowed him since their escape. His mind, previously sluggish, sharpened and became clear, focusing not on the threat but on the path forward. Anya ate hers next, the satisfaction deepening the calm resolution in her posture. The manna banished the ache of hunger and infused their bodies with clean, potent energy.

They sat by the stream for a time, finishing the meal. The perfect grace of the manna had ensured that, though each person took exactly what they needed, there was nothing left over for consumption, fulfilling the scripture: "he that gathered much had nothing over, and he that gathered little had no lack; they gathered every man according to his eating" (Exodus 16:18 KJV). The Rock continued to flow with water, and new manna orbs appeared to replace the ones they had consumed.

Elias, with his historian's instinct to secure resources for an uncertain future, reached for the empty pouch at his waist. "We should collect the rest," he said, moving to scoop the untouched crystalline orbs into the repurposed bowl. "This is a gift, and the journey ahead is long. We must conserve this provision."

Azael stopped him with a gentle but firm hand on his shoulder. "No, Elias. You're still approaching this as if survival depends on your ability to manage the future—storing, hoarding, planning against every unknown. That instinct is natural, but here, it is a temptation to trust your own effort over the Creator's care. The lesson in this place is not prudent savings, but radical dependence: you are sustained not by your foresight, but by your willingness to receive what is given, exactly when it's needed. Dependence is not a weakness here—it's the very structure of grace."

He stepped back, gesturing to the Rock and the manna. "Provision is for the present. To try and keep it for tomorrow is to trade away trust for the illusion of control. That's why, in the wilderness, when the Israelites tried to keep extra manna overnight, it turned to decay. The miracle required them to let go of anxiety about tomorrow and accept the sufficiency of today:

Elias let his hand drop, the lesson settling with sobering clarity. The manna was a miracle that demanded daily trust—a tangible reminder that faith could not be hoarded, only renewed. Around them, the air seemed to pause, as if the world itself was waiting for their next move.

Azael's gaze swept the horizon, and his voice lowered to a charged murmur. "The path ahead is no longer about strength—it is about discernment. The dimension does not stay still; it shifts, adapts, and sometimes even resists our very presence. The next chapter of our journey will not just test your bodies, but your ability to see with more than your eyes. Here, even memory can be a trap, and expectation a snare."

He pointed, not just with his hand, but with a gravity that seemed to bend the air. "There are two ways forward. The first, called The Flawed Map, is

Lucifer's main line of defense—a route infested with physical traps, illusions, and sentinels. It is the direct path, one that tempts with logic and efficiency, and yet the dimension itself is always shifting beneath it. My memory can guide us, but only up to the edge of what this world will allow. Seraphina's pattern perception and the Harp's resonance will be our only chance to detect what's real among the layered lies. This route is both the most straightforward and the most watched. Sometimes the world itself will rewrite the path beneath your feet."

He turned to the second option, his face shadowed with uncertainty. "The other path—the Caverns of Echoed Shame—is no less dangerous, though in a different way. It is a place alive with memory, regret, and the unhealed wounds of anyone who enters. It adapts, reshapes itself to the soul that passes through. For me, it is especially perilous. The very fabric of the realm will draw out my failures, my old pride, and every sorrow I once buried. The terrain will not remain the same; it will twist according to what we carry with us. This is why Lucifer ignores the Caverns—he believes no one would willingly walk into a maze that reads their heart and returns it, raw and unresolved."

As a hush fell, Elias cleared his throat, his voice steady but hesitant as he began, "Given the risks, perhaps our best course—"

But before he could finish, a subtle wind swept through the alien trees, setting the luminous leaves whispering in layered harmonics. Seraphina stilled, her head tilting, eyes closing as she listened with her whole being. She heard not only the mechanical rustle or the frequency of the wind, but the deeper, hidden song of the world itself—an undercurrent of resonance and discord, of danger and invitation. Her PBP caught faint, elusive threads of sound and color pulling toward a direction that logic alone could not reveal.

She opened her eyes, conviction crystallizing. Cutting gently across Elias's unfinished thought, Seraphina interjected, "No. We take the unexpected path. The route where the enemy is least prepared. The path of grace, not calculation." She met Azael's gaze, her certainty burning through the hush. In that moment, the world itself seemed to lean in, awaiting their next step.

Elias nodded, feeling the weight and freedom of the choice. "We walk where truth is our only weapon. We let the world adapt to us, not the other way around. Our weakness, covered by the Creator, is our true shield. We choose the route of the Echoes."

Azael's gratitude flickered in a rare, open smile. "The Caverns of Echoed Shame will lead us through the Swamps of Wounded Pride—the ground where the Fallen buried the memory of their lost glory. It will not be a straight passage, and even I cannot predict where it will take us. But every test in that darkness will shape you anew."

As they made their way forward, the landscape seemed to bend around their resolve, the world subtly shifting in anticipation of their choice. The Rock, silent and steadfast, followed—a living promise that provision would trail them wherever they ventured. "And did all drink the same spiritual drink: for they drank of that spiritual Rock that followed them: and that Rock was Christ" (1 Corinthians 10:4).

With each step, the journey itself grew stranger—no longer a path to be mastered, but a living, shifting trial that seemed to anticipate their every doubt and hope. The ground beneath their feet trembled with possibility and threat; the air vibrated with a subtle, discordant hum, as if the dimension itself were listening, ready to change at a moment's notice. Even Azael, once navigator and guardian, now moved with humility—his celestial memory useless in a landscape that refused to follow any memory or logic.

Far ahead, never closer but never out of sight, loomed the Nexus of Discord: a wound in the world, a rotating pyramid whose impossible angles sliced the bruised sky. Its surfaces shimmered with a malignant green light, radiating a pulse that gnawed at the mind and pressed against the soul—a place where hope and reason were devoured and only the most persistent faith could stand. The very air before it vibrated with a stifling ozone and the scent of burnt sugar, a warning and a promise that everything known would be tested here.

Sometimes the way bent toward the Nexus, only to twist aside as the world reconfigured with their every choice. At other moments, the path vanished entirely, replaced by vistas that watched them pass, as if reality itself hung in the balance. The direction was a living question; the future, an expanding wound. Yet the four pressed on, bound together by grace. The Nexus remained always ahead—an ever-present reminder that the journey would change them, and that what they carried within would shape not only their fate, but the story of the world itself.

CHAPTER 48

WHISPERS FROM THE MIRE

The transition from the living, shifting trial of the journey to the new terrain was immediate and visceral. The ground that once trembled with possibility now yielded to a damp, suffocating odor—a sickly-sweet miasma of decaying glory and the metallic tang of failed aetheric dynamos burning slow in the eternal damp. In this new domain, corruption was not just sensed but inhaled, the air thick with wet rust, ancient water, and the fermented despair of a world that had forgotten hope. As they pressed deeper, the oppressive silence was broken by faint, almost imperceptible whispers that seemed to drift at the edge of awareness—so soft that Elias dismissed them as the echo of fatigue, and Seraphina mistook them for a memory of music lost in the fog. Behind them, the bruised sky and malignant green glow seemed almost distant, their ordeal on the threshold receding as the landscape itself demanded all their attention.

They entered a neon-lit forest, breathtaking in its chaotic beauty: colossal, fungus-like trees pulsed with vibrant green and cobalt light, their surfaces strangely warm to the touch. The ground was a sticky, black peat, slick and treacherous, littered with strange, gleaming shards and fragments—objects that might once have been vessels, mirrors, or sacred stones, now half-swallowed by the decay. Nothing here felt purely natural; every step reminded them of a world shaped by ages of collapse and corruption, every surface marked by what had been broken and reabsorbed into the swamp's relentless hunger. This was no ordinary mire, but a place where memory itself seemed to rot in the ground, and each pace forward was a negotiation with the remnants of lost glory. As they advanced, the faint whispers returned—this time just a single word, a name, or a fugitive regret, threading through the low-frequency hum that thrummed in the air. The sound was not quite audible, less a voice than a vibration behind the eyes, so ambiguous that Anya shook her head and muttered, "Did you hear that?" only to be met by silence. The resonance pressed against their thoughts, a non-negotiable decree of Lucifer's order, subtly tightening Elias's muscles and sending a dull ache behind his eyes, as if the world itself were warning them that here, nothing could be trusted, not even their own senses.

But the landscape, true to its living, shifting nature, did not allow them to acclimate. The remnants of the neon-lit forest quickly dissolved into a choked, ruined realm of pulverized black ground and jagged spires of broken ceramic and glass. The sky above pressed down—a heavy, starless black that seemed to swallow all light, plunging them into a suffocating gloom. Only the distant glow of the fungus-trees behind offered any hint of where they had come from, a reminder that the world could—and would—change without warning. As they crossed into this new territory, the whispers grew bolder, slipping into their thoughts with half-heard phrases and impossible questions: a snatch of childhood memory, a rebuke from a lost friend, a single, chilling "You don't belong here." All were so soft, so entangled with the hum of the swamp, that it was impossible to tell if the words came from without or within. Each step became a careful act of balance; the ground was slick with an unknown, viscous moisture, reeking of ozone and rot.

Azael led them forward, his movements slow and deliberate, his preternatural silence now less a sign of confidence and more the caution of a guide whose celestial memory was rendered useless by a world that shifted with every footfall, every hope, and every doubt.

He paused as the ground beneath their boots turned perilously soft and spongy, the world itself seeming to test their willingness to move forward. "Trust only the grace of your Baptism and the Word of God," Azael cautioned, his voice quiet and steady, barely rising above the omnipresent subsonic hum.

"Here, every step is both a risk and a question. Watch your footing, Elias— but more importantly, watch your mind. The ground is treacherous, but so is the temptation to rely on your own memory and logic. This entire realm is built not on order, but on a catastrophic foundation: every challenge you face will be a reflection of the Original Sin—your desire for self-salvation, the impulse to master what must be surrendered." He glanced back, the faint glow of the distant trees in his eyes—a reminder of how far they had come, and how different every step ahead would be.

Elias felt his muscles tense, the spiritual threat feeling more immediate than the physical mire. He struggled to find words, the weight of Azael's warning pressing on him. "If this whole swamp is built from pride and the desire to save myself—if the very ground is my sin—how do I resist it? How can I fight a sin that lives inside me, not just around me? How do I move forward when the enemy isn't just out there, but is woven into who I am?"

"You cannot," Azael replied simply, starting forward again, his silhouette sinking slightly with the new footing. "And this is precisely the lesson Lucifer teaches. He promises you power and control over your failures. Reject that promise. Reject the belief that you, alone, can conquer damnation."

As Azael spoke, Seraphina reached out, her fingers finding Elias's wrist and squeezing, a silent anchor against the encroaching dread. Her eyes, usually so bright with fierce, divine purpose, were now wide with very human vulnerability. "We're here together, Elias," she murmured, just loud enough for him to hear, her hand sliding down to grip his firmly. "No matter what failures he shows you, you have me to pull you back. Don't let go." Elias returned the pressure of her hand, a shared acknowledgment that, whatever spiritual corruption lay ahead, they were tethered by love and shared fate.

The whispers that had followed them since entering the swamp—once only vague, half-heard words or the uncertain echo of childhood regret—now pressed in with relentless, intimate clarity. Their origins were impossible to pinpoint: they seemed to drift not just from the black peat and fetid air, but from the marrow of the world itself. Each voice called them by name, dredging up old wounds and secret fears, growing louder and more insistent with every step. At first, Elias shook his head, dismissing a quiet "You failed him" as mere exhaustion. Seraphina caught a fleeting phrase—her mother's voice, or so she thought—lost in the hum of the mire. Anya shivered at a single, cold syllable crawling down her spine. But as they pressed on, the psychic assault became undeniable: the words were no longer whispers at the edge of perception, but shouted taunts, twisting memory and conviction into weapons. The voices became a chorus, each one tailored to their deepest insecurities. Seraphina's resolve wavered; she slid the harp from her back, gripping it tightly in front of her, grounding herself in its familiar weight against the onslaught. Elias staggered, disoriented by the sudden, piercing clarity of the attack. Anya clutched the Bible, her knuckles white, as all three were battered by a storm of doubts that felt as real as the muck beneath their feet.

"Do not engage the whispers!" Azael hissed, his voice cutting through the mental noise like a cleaver, even as the Harp's glow was muffled and flickering, its radiance dim but not gone—held fiercely in Seraphina's grasp above the mire. He stopped, his voice suddenly rising in authoritative volume above the hum. "They seek to exploit the shame Lucifer placed in your hearts. Listen to the truth, not the fear! Surrender your pride!"

Anya, meanwhile, surveyed the increasingly unstable terrain, her boot sinking a little too far into the mire with a sickening *slurp*. She looked at the glistening, black shards embedded everywhere. "The ground itself is fighting us," she observed, her voice sharp with professional concern. "And these fragments... they feel too organized for mere decay. They are structural. What *is* all this black dust, Azael? Is it truly just peat?"

"It is the dust of the damned, Analyst," Azael confirmed, his pace unbroken. "These are the remnants of pride—once-cherished idols, now broken and mingled with sorrow, all ground to dust in this place of wounded memory. This is the Swamps of Wounded Pride."

They stepped fully into the mire. The black peat was slick, treacherous, and smelled strongly of sharp, sulfurous methane that stung the back of the throat. The first steps were a mistake; their boots were immediately swallowed by the muck, locking them in place. Each subsequent attempt to lift a foot resulted in a loud, sucking gasp from the mire, requiring a terrifying amount of effort. The deeper they sank into the filth and the silent remnants of forgotten idols, the more the swamp whispered.

The Physicality of Terror

The attack was not a simple sound but a full-body assault—vibrational and concussive. The ever-present subsonic hum of the swamp, which had been a low, unsettling background, suddenly sharpened, striking the base of their skulls with the force of a pitch-black sonic boom. This was not just noise in the air; it was the vector for the voices, which exploded not from outside but from deep within—the neural pathways of their own minds. The whispers they'd struggled to ignore now became a torrent: not words spoken, but thoughts injected, each one perfectly mimicking the timbre and logic of their own most ruthless self-critique. The effect was devastating, less like hearing and more like a steel spike being driven through the frontal lobe—a psychic intrusion that left no room for defense.

Anya clutched the Holy Bible tightly to her chest, her breath ragged as the psychic assault battered her mind. The whispers were no longer faint—they were loud, absolute, and cruel: "The City is lost. The Second Coming is a myth. You will die here, separated from the Creator. Your hope is inefficient." Each phrase vibrated in her chest cavity, threatening to overwhelm her with nausea and despair. She tried to shift her weight for relief, but the mire gripped her ankle, holding her fast.

For one sharp moment, panic threatened to consume her—but she forced herself to focus, turning terror into the sharp, measured language of analysis. She fixed her gaze on Azael, summoning the clarity she relied on in crisis. "Azael, this noise—the coordinated psychic assault—it's on a scale I've never mapped before. The whispers, the pressure, the illusions: to maintain something this massive must require a staggering amount of energy from the Archon. Is it sustainable? What's the energetic or spiritual cost to the demon running this? How much does it take from them to keep us trapped in this illusion? There has to be a breaking point, right?" Her voice trembled, but beneath the fear was the insistent logic of someone refusing to be swept away—a scientist demanding the variables even as the experiment threatened to consume her.

Azael glanced over at her, meeting her eyes for a moment before returning his focus to the path. His answer carried the full weight of ancient knowledge. "The cost is everything, Analyst—the Archon pours its very existence into sustaining this psychic attack. But for it, the payoff is absolute: if you surrender, if you accept the illusion as reality, you hand over your will. That is the only outcome it seeks. Do not give it to them. Endure, and the assault will eventually collapse under its own unsustainable weight."

For Elias, the former Research Historian, the attack was instantaneous and surgical. The voices sneered at his blunder in the City: "You failed Aaron Hawthorne. You confused your heroic ambition with God's will. Your pride is your destruction." The words hit him with the physical force of a blow to the chest, leaving him breathless. He heard the voice of Aaron Hawthorne himself, corrupted and amplified, delivered with a high-frequency whine that grated against his inner ear drums. Elias staggered, clamping his jaw, fighting the instinct to justify himself. His free hand shot up to his temple, trying to press the unbearable noise out, but the pressure only intensified. Lost in the lightless gloom and the internal psychic flash, his other hand blindly searched for Seraphina, needing her presence as a physical counterpoint to the dissolving truth within him. He could taste the sulfurous air on his tongue, mirroring the bitterness of his shame. The swamp had found the anchor point of his guilt: the moment he tried to play the savior without true authority.

"They're right," Elias choked out, his voice thin and hollow against the roaring in his head. "I did fail. I confused hope with... with a grand, egotistical narrative for myself. I brought us all here for *my* pride! I can't move, Seraphina—I'm sinking!"

Seraphina gripped the handle of the large, luminous Harp tightly with both hands as she advanced, her foot suddenly skidding on the slick, treacherous surface. Instinctively, she tried to shift her weight and regain her balance, but the ground betrayed her—collapsing beneath her feet. She toppled forward, landing hard on her knees, the force jarring her arms and making the Harp's weight tip her slightly off-balance. Her knees and shins pressed into the cold, oily mud, which instantly surged up, swallowing her calves, engulfing her boots, and locking them in place like the jaws of a living trap. She tried to pull her knee up, but the suction held her fast. Both hands remained locked on the Harp's handle, its bulk awkward but necessary for balance, her knuckles whitening as panic raced through her. She realized with sick horror that the ground was not simply soft or treacherous—it was alive and predatory, an entity intent on claiming anything that dared touch its surface.

All around her, the darkness pressed in—thick, suffocating, and absolute. The air was heavy with the stench of rot, the only illumination the sickly, greenish glimmer reflecting off the mud. Shapes loomed and shifted in the gloom, and the silence was broken only by the faint, hungry sucking of the swamp. The horror of the moment was sharpened by the utter absence of comfort: the world had constricted to a circle of cold, grasping muck, the Harp's faint glow, and her own desperate, rattling breath.

In the dim periphery, Anya and Azael were locked in their own struggles. Anya's analytical mind, usually racing with contingency plans, was paralyzed by the realization that her own boots would not budge—the mud had her locked in place, just as it had seized Seraphina. Azael, wings flared and rigid, was similarly trapped: one boot sunk deep, celestial armor now rendered useless as the mire gripped him with implacable malice. Neither saw Seraphina's panic. Both were wholly focused on the battle beneath their own feet—the swamp's cold appetite, the terror of immobilization. Their gazes remained downcast, faces strained with the effort of simply not sinking further, hearts hammering with the fear that any call for help would only hasten their own demise.

Seraphina, for a moment, almost cried out—almost called to them, her voice poised on the edge of a scream. But she swallowed the urge, biting down on panic, consumed by the single, animal focus of escape. She would not beg. She would not distract them. The world had shrunk to the mud, the Harp, her hands. She tried to free herself and the Harp in silence, her entire will narrowed to the struggle, her senses barely registering the psychic storm howling at the edges of her mind. There was no room for pride, or for hope—only the raw, unfiltered terror of being swallowed alive.

Meanwhile, Elias's attention remained fixed on his own sinking. He clawed at the mud with both hands, trying to gain traction, sweat running down his face. His thoughts whirled—If I can just shift my weight, if I can just leverage my foot...—but the mire only tightened its grip. He risked a sideways glance at Seraphina but instantly regretted it; any distraction threatened his own fragile balance. The panic made his limbs feel heavier, the swamp's suction more inescapable.

Desperate for any anchor, Seraphina wrenched the Harp upright, using it as a lever to fight for balance. The instrument, which had always felt like an extension of her soul, now became her only lifeline. She planted its crystalline base into the muck and tried to haul herself up, but the moment she shifted her weight, the Harp's base began to sink as well, sucked downward by the swamp's greedy pull. The mud began to climb around the base, thick and relentless, but had not yet reached the handle or her hands. Her grip remained high and desperate, her knuckles white, as the mud pressed around her boots and the lower part of the Harp, threatening to swallow them both. Every attempt to pull herself free only dragged the Harp deeper, the strings quivering with a discordant, muffled resonance, while her hands, still dry but trembling, clung to the only anchor she had left.

She bore down, her hands reflexively tightening on the handle, muscles straining in a futile, agonized tug-of-war against the mire. The mud pulsed and flexed around her knees and shins, its pressure building until it felt as though invisible hands were dragging her beneath the surface. The combined strain of fighting for her own footing and trying to rescue the Harp nearly tore her shoulder from its socket. She could feel her joints screaming in protest, the pain immediate and merciless, momentarily eclipsing even the howling psychic assault in her mind. The horror was total: she was being swallowed alive, and her only hope of escape was itself being devoured by the swamp.

The whispers targeted her core identity—her Aesthetic Synthesis, delivered in a chillingly distorted version of her own voice: "You are the greatest synthesizer, yet you created only noise. Your integrated faith is a non-functional architecture. The Great Architect built perfect order; you chose this ugly, chaotic dissolution."

Seraphina ignored the words, shutting out the psychic assault by narrowing her world to the raw, physical reality at hand. The mud, cold and merciless, crept up her body with a horrifying patience. She pulled with every ounce of strength, her spine arching in a desperate, unnatural curve as she tried to wrench the Harp free. But the mud only responded with a deeper, guttural sigh, sucking her lower body down. Her hips sank beneath the mire, the sticky chill enveloping her waist so completely that it felt as if the swamp was remaking her from the inside out. The Harp—her lifeline—was now almost entirely submerged, its base and half its body swallowed, the crystalline frame vanishing inch by inch beneath the hungry surface. Only the handle remained above the mire, slick with sweat from her trembling, white-knuckled grip. Her arms, locked straight and straining, trembled violently as she poured everything into the effort, arching backward with a silent, teeth-bared snarl of terror and exertion. The weight of the swamp forced her to bow, her muscles spasming as she fought to keep the Harp from disappearing completely.

A few feet away, Elias redoubled his efforts, twisting his torso and reaching for a patch of firmer ground. His own panic and the relentless sucking of the mud left him oblivious to Seraphina's suffering—he was too busy fighting the terror of being pulled down himself. In that moment, the swamp made islands of them all: each locked in their own private hell, desperate to escape, unable to help or even call out to the others.

The mud surged higher, reaching past Seraphina's waist, then her ribcage, the pressure so intense it felt as if invisible hands were squeezing the breath from her lungs. Her legs were utterly locked in place, the cold muck crushing against her bones until she could no longer feel her feet or shins. She tried to pull herself upward, but the Harp only sank further, dragging her with it. Tears streamed down her cheeks from the pain and the terror, mingling with the sweat and grime on her face. She could taste salt and ground on her lips, her cries for help strangled before they could form. The world had shrunk to this endless, suffocating struggle—her body arched in agony, her hands fixed to the Harp's handle, her mind a single, blazing point of refusal to surrender. The mud rose inexorably, slick and greedy, and finally, with a sickening slurp, the handle of the Harp slid beneath the surface. Seraphina's hands vanished with it, dragged downwards, her final anchor lost as the swamp claimed both artifact and flesh alike.

A short distance away, Azael and Anya, still struggling against the swamp's relentless grip, found themselves sinking deeper with every movement. At last, through their own haze of panic, they noticed Seraphina. Horror flared in their eyes as they saw how far the mud had taken her—now past her abdomen, swallowing her up to her chest. The Harp had vanished entirely, along with Seraphina's arms and hands, leaving only the desperate rise and fall of her shoulders as she fought to keep her head above the mire. The realization struck them with a new terror: the mud's hunger was not just for their limbs, but for everything, and Seraphina was nearly gone.

Elias, still choking on the psychic noise of his own failure, suddenly saw the external reality with chilling clarity. The black, viscous mud had reached Seraphina's chest, creeping ever higher. Her body was rigid, panic etched across her face, her head thrust back as if straining for every last breath. Her arms and hands had vanished beneath the swamp, the Harp nowhere to be seen—only the trembling rise and fall of her chest betraying her continued struggle. "Sera, hold on! I'm right here—don't give up!" he called, his voice raw, desperate to reach her through the terror. In that moment, Elias understood the enormity of her peril. The terror in his stomach turned into a cold, protective surge of adrenaline.

The distance between them—once negligible—now felt like miles. The clinging mud denied every inch of movement. Elias watched her desperate struggle, his own legs locked in place. In his mind, a psychic assault screamed that he was too weak, too tainted by pride to save anyone. His failure had brought them here. Primal desperation surged within him to reach out, but he knew if he shifted his weight, he would fall completely.

CHAPTER 49

BURIED IN THE SHADOWS

Azael, watching Seraphina sink deeper, strained against the mire. His powerful arms trembled as he tried to wrench himself free. "Seraphina! Hold on!" he shouted, his voice hoarse with panic. The mud gripped his lower legs, refusing to yield even the slightest bit. Every movement threatened to drag him deeper, but he fought on, wings flexing in vain, mud splattering up his legs. "Anya, help me! We have to get her out!"

Anya, locked just as firmly in the muck, twisted frantically, her hands clawing at the thick ooze that held her. "I'm trying! I can't move!" she cried, fear sharp in her voice. The mud was up to her knees, and every attempt to pull free only sucked her down further. Desperation clawed at her, but her eyes never left Seraphina. "Seraphina, don't give up! We're coming!"

Neither of them could reach her. The swamp had them all in its grasp, their struggles only deepening their captivity. To Seraphina, their voices were faint, distant—muffled by her own frantic internal battle. She was nearly deaf to everything but her own heartbeat and the roar of her panic. She kept her lips pressed together, refusing to cry out, refusing to ask for help. She could not even hear the frantic shouts behind her, so consumed was she by the terror and the need to fight for herself and for the Harp. Her world was narrowed to the sucking mud, the absent shine of the handle, and her own desperate will to survive.

Above them, the world had darkened further. A dense, unnatural fog pressed in on every side, making the air thick and almost unbreathable. The silhouettes of Azael and Anya were barely visible in the gloom, swallowed by the encroaching night and the writhing shadows of the swamp. The sole light came from the faint, greenish glow of the mud itself, shimmering across its trembling surface. The silence was broken only by their gasps and the relentless, hungry slurp of the mire. Everything was closing in: the darkness, the mud, the certainty of death. The moment was absolute, terrifying—a world reduced to struggle, separation, and the horror of being claimed by the ground itself.

Seraphina's desperate focus on the Harp finally broke. The fight had completely drained her; her muscles were screaming, and the weight of the mud-soaked artifact was a dead, crushing anchor. The mud, a malicious, silent predator, was now at her collarbone, a paralyzing, cold weight. The sulfurous, choking stench of methane and rot was overpowering her breath, coating the inside of her mouth like tar. This was not a spiritual threat; it was a raw, alien fear of being buried alive. Her artist's intuition—the patterns and harmonies she once found comfort in—simply dissolved against the primal horror.

Seraphina's arms were entombed by the mud, her hands numb, slick, and useless against the suffocating weight. The harp's handle—a lifeline—was trapped in Seraphina's grasp, her hands locked in place by the relentless mud. The mire pressed her fingers against the slick handle, trapping them with relentless force, leaving her unable to release her grip no matter how much her strength failed. Her knuckles ground painfully against the cold, wet soil, but the true horror was the mud's grip: her hands were no longer her own, fused to the handle by the swamp's merciless hold.

She tried to scream for help, but the muck pressed into her ribs, crushing her lungs, forcing her voice into silence. The only sound that escaped was a ragged, animal sob—a strangled gasp torn from a throat already closing. Summoning the last of her strength, she managed a hoarse, broken plea: "Elias! Help me!" The words were raw with desperation, barely audible above the wet, hungry slurp of the swamp, terror shredding each syllable. But the sound dissolved almost instantly, lost in the relentless, suffocating dark. Tears ran down her cheeks, indistinguishable from the cold filth that coated her face.

Her body convulsed in panic, but every thrash only drove her deeper into the suffocating mud. Each frantic movement drained what little energy she had left until her limbs felt leaden, the muscles trembling with exhaustion from the impossible battle. Her body, already weakened from the relentless psychic assault and the desperate struggle to free the harp, barely responded—the last reserves of strength spent in the first helpless flails.

Through the haze of terror, she heard voices—Elias, Anya, and Azael— somewhere above the roar of her heartbeat, their words muffled and distant:

"Seraphina—hold on!" "We're coming!" "Don't give up—fight!" The fragments reached her like echoes underwater, almost lost beneath the sucking, relentless pull of the swamp. Still, she tried to force her arms up, to break the mud's crushing grip, but the mire locked her in place with pitiless patience. Her hands, cemented around the harp's handle, refused to move; her arms, pinned in the mud, were as immovable as stone, the pressure unrelenting as she sank slower and slower, inch by agonizing inch. Every attempt to wrench free only made the suction worse, the mud creeping higher, greedier with every heartbeat.

Her shoulders disappeared beneath the surface, then her neck. She was helpless, her face twisted in terror, her eyes wild and wide. Mustering the last of her neck's strength, she tipped her chin upward, searching the blank, pitiless sky for any sign of rescue. Her breath came in short, shallow shudders. "Please, not like this," she choked out, her voice barely more than a gasp as the mud pressed in. "I'm not ready—I'm not ready!" Her sob was so raw, so steeped in terror and regret, that it was almost unrecognizable—muffled and broken by the rising muck. The cry dissolved into choking, gurgling gasps as the mud climbed past her ears, the world collapsing to the black roar of her own heart and the certainty that no one could reach her. The agony was total—a burning ache in every exhausted muscle, the humiliation of helplessness, the terror of slow suffocation.

The mire coated her lips, pressing in cold and thick. She tried to cry out one last time—her voice barely more than a ragged, strangled whisper—"Help—" but the sound was swallowed by the mud, the syllables lost before they could reach the surface. Just before it sealed her mouth, Seraphina sucked in one last, desperate breath—a mouthful of fetid, sulfurous air so foul it burned her lungs, thick with rot and poison. The taste was acrid and chemical, a final insult as her body fought for survival. Then the mud closed over her mouth, silencing her cries mid-breath. She tried to scream again, but the only sound was a pitiful, bubbling gasp as her mouth and nose disappeared beneath the sludge.

The mud surged up, cold and heavy, sealing her face completely, smothering her in blackness. In the final moment before darkness claimed her, Seraphina squeezed her eyes shut, steeling herself for oblivion. She was plunged into a world without sound or vision—utterly sightless, the darkness now pressed against her eyelids, the silence so thick it was a living presence. Every sense was denied; there was only the crushing, suffocating pressure of mud caked against her skin, squeezing her ears flat, filling her nose with the taste of soil and death. Her arms were pinned, hands still locked in a death grip around the harp's handle, numb and useless, as she was swallowed by the mire, vanishing into the living grave of the swamp. For a heartbeat, the world was nothing but the muffled thump of her own heart, the agony of needing air, and the terror of absolute silence.

In those last, suffocating moments, the silence was absolute—a cruel, empty void for a soul who had always found meaning in connection, in music, in the living pulse of sound—and now knew only the agony and terror of being utterly, finally alone.

But as her consciousness flickered at the furthest edge of darkness, the pressure of the mud shifted—just enough to register a new, dreadful reality. The mire, having locked her body in place for so long, began to loosen its grip around her free arm—the arm not fused to the harp's handle. For a moment, Seraphina's mind seized on the faint hope of movement, and she summoned every last particle of will to wrench her arm upward through the suffocating black. Her muscles screamed, weak and half-numb, but her fingers clawed desperately through the heavy, freezing muck, reaching for the surface—any surface. There was no air, no light, no boundary to find. Her hand moved and moved, but encountered only more choking mud, more emptiness, the vast, crushing weight of the depths. Panic surged anew: she was so deep that even her most desperate reach could not find the world above. All the agony she had endured was redoubled in this moment of futile hope—a final, wordless scream of the body.

Above, Azael and Anya watched in horror as the last ripple faded from the surface where Seraphina had vanished. Azael, chest heaving, shouted her name, his celestial voice breaking with an anguish that echoed across the swamp. "Seraphina!" he cried again, each repetition more desperate, but the only answer was the mocking silence of the mire. His wings drooped, shoulders slumped in defeat, the full weight of loss settling over him as he stared at the smooth, unbroken surface. Anya, trembling and near tears, clawed helplessly at the unyielding muck with her bare hands, but each handful she tore away was replaced by more, the mud building and swallowing her wrists, sinking her deeper as her voice rose into a desperate, wordless wail. Through her sobs, she pleaded, "Please, come back, Seraphina, please!" Her cries dissolved into the hush, the swamp swallowing every hope. The two of them stood apart in the swamp, united in shock and horror beneath the indifferent sky—close enough to see the anguish on each other's faces, but separated by the cruel expanse of mud. The brutal realization settled in: Seraphina was truly gone, beyond their reach, beyond rescue.

Below the surface, darkness closed around Seraphina, thick and suffocating. And then—cutting through the black, a voice coiled into her mind, cold and triumphant. *At last, little light,* the archon whispered, its words slick as oil. *You are mine now. All your struggles, all your faith—they end here, in my grasp.* The presence pressed in closer, chilling her to the core. *Did you truly believe you could defy me?* it sneered, its laughter echoing through the void. *Even your friends above mourn you already. Hear them weep—your hope is their despair. This is where you belong. With me.*

Aftermath Above and Below

"Seraphina!" Elias screamed, a raw, strangled sound of pure shock and disbelief that tore through the psychic noise attacking his mind. He watched the last ripple fade, the black surface of the mud growing smooth and undisturbed as if swallowing her were a trivial act. In the silence that followed, a faint, gloating whisper crawled across his thoughts—a presence savoring its victory. *She cannot hear you,* the demon murmured. *Your cries are wasted. She is mine, and you are powerless.* Elias thrashed, suddenly frantic, wrenching his legs against the suction of the swamp, ignoring the searing pain in his hips. It was useless; the mud held him in an iron embrace, paralyzing him exactly at the moment he needed to move.

Elias squeezed his eyes shut against the phantom hands and the roaring shame. His lungs burned, his throat constricted. He had let go of her hand; he had stood by, frozen by his own guilt, and left her to face the impossible alone. He was sinking again, but the terror of the mud was nothing compared to the sudden, agonizing fear that he had failed the only person who had believed in him. He fell forward onto his knees, and the black mire splattered up his chest and stomach, the cold ooze clinging thickly to his clothes.

His trembling hands dug into the mud in a futile attempt to push himself upright, but the mire only sucked him deeper, swallowing his wrists and forearms. His legs were folded beneath him, knees buried and sinking, while his weight pressed his chest downward. His face hovered just inches above the mud, head bowed, eyes squeezed shut as sweat and tears mingled and dripped into the filth. He could feel the mud's chill rising up his arms, the pressure building against his ribs, holding him in a position of utter supplication. His entire body shook—not in defiance, but in resignation and grief.

He tried to lift his head, to scream Seraphina's name, but the muscles in his neck trembled and failed. His jaw locked, and the only sound that escaped was a strangled, internal groan, a soundless crack of his own spirit breaking against the sheer, overwhelming impotence of the moment. The world narrowed to the cold, slick surface of the mud mere inches from his face, and the certainty that Seraphina was gone.

The voices, having eliminated their secondary target, turned their full, concentrated malice onto him. They were no longer just sneering inside his head; they began to manifest physically, whispering from the black bubbles that popped on the surface of the mire, echoing from the jagged debris and broken remnants, surrounding him in a horrific chorus: *Look at your hands! Empty! You had her, and now you have nothing! Your pride is a sickness that kills those who love you! You led her here to prove yourself worthy of her faith, and instead, you delivered her to the mire! She is lost forever, Elias!*

He tried to look for Anya, for Azael, but the mud's unyielding grip kept his head bowed, his line of sight fixed on the dark expanse below him. His body was collapsed forward, arms splayed and sinking, hands disappeared into the muck, legs folded and utterly trapped. A paralyzing wave of sorrow crashed over him, and he saw a flash of his future: a white, sterile room, forever empty of her light, her fierce eyes, her challenging intellect. He saw himself walking a desolate ground, burdened by a singular, cold silence. The vision was more devastating than any physical torture.

Somewhere above, Azael and Anya strained to pierce the choking fog that pressed in from all sides, thick as wool and sour with rot. They could barely make out Elias's form—a hunched shadow, half-swallowed by the mire, blurred and shifting at the edges as if the swamp itself was erasing him. Every time the fog shifted, they lost sight of his outline, his arms and waist vanishing into the gloom, then flickering back into view for a fleeting moment before being swallowed again. The fog muffled their voices and warped their sense of distance, making Elias seem impossibly far away, even though he was only a short stretch across the mud.

The mud pulled Elias down by slow, relentless degrees. What began as his arms and waist submerged soon became his biceps and chest, the thick ooze creeping higher, gluing him to the ground. His shoulders followed, the cold weight pressing in, forcing his chest closer to the surface with every passing breath. The pressure made each inhale a labored gasp, every exhale a surrender to exhaustion. The world shrank to the thin layer of air between his face and the mud, to the thundering of his heart and the trembling of muscles long past fatigue.

His will to fight had vanished, physical strength utterly drained by the brutal, unyielding mire. Even his spirit—so long battered—was empty at last, hollowed out by grief and failure. He could no longer remember what hope had felt like; there was only the numb ache of loss, the memory of Seraphina, and the knowledge that he had nothing left to give. The ache in his limbs faded into a dull, distant throb, replaced by the suffocating chill that crawled up his spine.

His body's collapse became a slow surrender, shifting from a desperate brace to utter defeat as the mire claimed him inch by inch. There was no more struggle—nothing left but the steady, inevitable descent, his body slumped forward, arms stretched uselessly ahead, chest and shoulders sinking deeper as the black mud drew him down.

That's it, Elias. Let go. There is nothing left to fight for—nothing left to save. You see how easily the mud claims you, how effortlessly despair fills the void where hope once lived. You belong to me now, your pride spent and your heart hollow. Sink, and join her in the darkness. This is all that remains. Only by fully embracing your pride, Elias, can you descend and be with her forever!

Elias's head hung low, forehead nearly touching the mud as the mire crept steadily upward. Tears slipped from his closed eyes, falling straight down to vanish into the blackness below—silent testaments swallowed without a trace. The cold filth pressed against his brow and cheeks, seeping into his hair, oozing over his eyelids until even the memory of light was blotted out. Somewhere distantly, voices cut through the fog—Azael and Anya calling his name, pleading with him not to give up, their cries muffled, desperate, and barely audible. Through the thick veil, Anya could just make out the faint outline of Elias's head, sinking lower, almost entirely lost to the mire. But for Elias, their voices were only background noise drowned by sorrow, the world shrinking to the suffocating darkness that claimed him. As the mud reached his nostrils, his body, acting on pure instinct, drew in a desperate, shuddering final breath— foul, thick with the stench of rot and ground. His lips, trembling, were the next to disappear as the mire inched higher, silencing even the faintest whimper. The world narrowed to muffled darkness as the mud engulfed his ears, every sound fading into oblivion. Inch by inch, Elias surrendered to the suffocating embrace, until there was nothing left but stillness and the cold, absolute quiet of the depths.

CHAPTER 50

SWALLOWED BY THE VOID

For a long moment, there was only the fog—the thick, impenetrable veil that pressed in from all sides, heavy with the stench of rot and loss. Anya stared across the sucking expanse, hands shaking, throat raw from screaming. The silence was absolute, broken only by her own hoarse sobs and the echo of her name still hanging useless in the air. Where Elias had been, there was now only the faintest shadow, an impression in the mud that might have been a head, already dissolving into the shapeless black. She sagged forward, numb and hollow, as Azael's voice faded into a whisper beside her, the last of their hope swallowed by the swamp.

Azael, standing just behind, felt the psychic current shift. The Archon, calculating with a chilling precision, recognized that the usual patterns of temptation—shame, accusation, psychic assault—would have no purchase on an Angel so long resigned to his own failings. Instead of pressing in with mental or spiritual attack, the environment itself responded: the fog thickened dramatically around Azael, congealing into a dense, impenetrable shroud. Within seconds, the world became a blank, suffocating void; Azael's vision narrowed to a gray wall just inches from his face. He could no longer see Anya, nor the swamp, nor the faintest outline of the world beyond. The fog was so absolute that even the subtle glimmer of his own divine light was swallowed whole, leaving him with only the distant echo of Anya's struggle, muffled and unreachable. The Archon had not wasted effort; he simply removed Azael from the scene, severing his ability to act, to witness, or to intervene.

Then, abruptly, Azael's footing, which had been sunk deep in the swamp's sucking mud, loosened beneath him. He found himself able to turn, the world still clouded in gray, but movement restored—his paralysis broken not by a spiritual victory, but by the simple, unexpected grace of freedom. He turned instinctively, searching for Anya through the blank wall of fog, but she was gone from view—the mists having rendered him powerless not by temptation, but by isolation. The battle had passed him by; now, all he could do was bear witness from the perimeter.

Anya stood frozen, locked in a state of shattering paralysis, her mind emptied of all thought but the raw, physical terror before her eyes. The usual clamor in her head had faded, replaced by a cold, visual horror: both of her friends, her anchors in this nightmare, were gone—swallowed by the ground itself. As Elias's head slipped beneath the surface, the ground beneath her seemed to lurch, the momentary illusion of safety shattering. Without warning, the black muck surged up around her calves and knees, gripping her with greedy, unyielding force. She pitched forward, arms rigid and trembling, hands still clutching the Bible in a death grip even as her balance failed. A silent scream pressed against her throat, unable to escape, her eyes wide and fixed on the last trembling ripple where Elias had vanished. They're gone. I'm next.

But unlike the violent psychic storm that had torn apart Elias and Seraphina, the assault on Anya was surgical—relentless but focused, a suffocating pressure that targeted her alone. The dense fog, now acting as a living wall, isolated her completely; Azael was gone from her sight, his presence erased as if he had never existed. The world closed in, the silence so absolute it felt engineered, a void where even the memory of help could not reach. The only sounds were the frantic thud of her own heart and the slow, inevitable gurgle of the mud as it inched higher.

Anya's mind, honed for analysis and contingency, scrambled for data. Every instinct called for a variable, a pattern, a path to escape. But with Azael vanished—lost in the impenetrable shroud—her analytical framework began to collapse. The structure she trusted was not simply failing; it was shown to be irrelevant. Her last asset was not just unreachable but, as good as, erased from the equation. The suffocating realization pressed in: there was no one left to witness her struggle, no margin for error, and no lifeline of logic to grasp. Alone in the consuming silence, Anya faced the truth that her greatest weapon—her mind—was powerless against the raw, inescapable force of descent. She was sinking, not just into the mud, but into the terrifying recognition that sometimes the world offers no system, no observer, and no escape. The logic that always saved her had become a closed circuit, a gravestone of reason.

Through the thick, stifling fog, a subtle motion caught Anya's eye—a branch from a sickly, gnarled tree at the swamp's edge began to bend. At first, it seemed only the wind, but as she watched, the branch extended further, unnaturally, almost as if guided by some unseen hand. It dipped lower, trembling just above her reach. Hope ignited—a variable, a data point, a possible solution. She stretched up, hands slick with mud, arms pinned but fingers straining, desperate to seize this chance at salvation. Her body sank further: the mud now up to her knees, suctioning her legs with relentless hunger. She fought, inch by inch, dragging herself higher, clutching the Bible in one arm as the black ooze rose past her waist, creeping up her stomach, then her chest.

The branch descended another inch, its bark glistening with cold dew, swaying so close she could almost brush it. The mire pressed against her ribs; her free elbow was nearly submerged. She could no longer move her left arm— the Bible slipped lower, the cold sucking mud swallowing the sacred book with a slurp. Her right arm, caked in filth, reached upward, muscles burning, every calculation in her mind reduced to a simple, primal command: reach the branch, survive.

Her waist disappeared beneath the surface. The muck surged up her chest, pinning her shoulders, her neck arched back in final desperation. The branch hovered just above her face, the tip barely within reach of her fingertips. She stretched, the last of her strength pouring into her outstretched hand. The Archon's laughter crackled through the fog—a cruel, inhuman sound, delighted at her struggle. The branch dipped, teasingly, as if to offer hope, then hung motionless, just out of proper grasp. Anya's chin pressed into the mud, lips trembling. She summoned the last of her analytical clarity: measure the distance, calculate the force, trust the reach. With a final, gasping effort, she locked her eyes on the branch, reached with her fingertips, and caught it.

For a heartbeat, hope flared—her mind leaping to a thousand possible escape scenarios. Then, with a sickening snap, the branch broke off in her hand. The false promise of rescue dissolved in the mire as the branch, brittle and dead, crumbled to pulp between her fingers, sinking with her beneath the surface. The Archon's laughter echoed, triumphant, as the mud reached her chin, the cold mire pressing up over her jaw and silencing the last of her hope. The false promise of the branch faded as her mouth hovered just above the surface, perfectly setting the stage for the final, suffocating descent that would follow. The world was nothing but cold, black silence and the certainty that the system had never intended her escape.

Anya's breath caught as the mud pressed, cold and relentless, against her chin. The world shrank to the suffocating inch between her mouth and the mire—a pocket of air, a fragment of hope. She could taste the swamp on her lips, sulfur and rot, as her mind teetered at the edge of reason. Her rational world had ended; there was only the primal instinct to breathe, to survive.

She forced her chin up, fighting for a final breath as the mud pressed higher, sealing over her mouth in a slow, smothering wave. Her eyes bulged with effort, throat tight, as a garbled cry broke through—"Help!"—but it was instantly swallowed by the mire, the sound muffled and lost. The cold mud surged past her lips, pressed up over her cheeks, and crept around to her ears. The world became muffled and distant, her hearing fading to a dull, underwater silence.

Her panic yielded to a heavy exhaustion. Her eyelids fluttered, then closed as the mud covered her face. Darkness swallowed her—the last thing she felt was the relentless, cold pressure wrapping her head, her mind reduced to the thundering of her heart and the final, desperate ache for air.

Above, her outstretched arm remained, fingers splayed and reaching skyward for any hope. The mud began to claim her last vestige—first her elbow, then her forearm, then her wrist. Only her hand, caked in black sludge, remained above the surface, fingers trembling in one final gesture of hope.

In that instant, the fog thinned. Azael, released from isolation, turned just in time to see Anya's hand—slick with mud, fingers straining—barely visible above the mire. He lunged, reaching desperately for her. His hand closed on empty air as Anya's hand, in slow, agonizing finality, slipped beneath the surface and vanished.

Azael dropped to his knees, clawing at the spot where her hand had disappeared. His fingers raked the ground, but the mud had transformed—now packed solid, cold, and unyielding as concrete. He dug and tore with celestial strength, but it was useless; the ground would not yield. The only evidence of her passage was the mud caked beneath his fingernails and the brutal ache of loss in his chest.

A stillness settled over the swamp, deeper and more absolute than before. The air felt thick and unmoving, every ripple on the mire erased. There was no echo of struggle—no bubbles, no shifting of mud, not even the faintest whisper of a breeze through the dead trees. The ground beneath Azael's knees, once treacherous and alive, had become cold, solid, and utterly indifferent— unyielding as stone, as if the ground itself had sealed away all memory of what had transpired. In that suffocating silence, the swamp offered nothing: no comfort, no evidence, only the hollow absence where hope had been.

At the far edge of the mire, where shadows gathered and despair seemed absolute, a single white quartz rock began to shine—at first a muted shimmer, then swelling into a radiant, unwavering beam. Heavenly light poured from its perfectly chiseled facets, casting a pure brilliance that cut through the gloom and painted the swamp in fleeting silver. The luminous glow was untouched by the corruption that had swallowed everything else, standing as a silent sentinel amid ruin and loss.

Azael, shoulders shaking, turned away from the place where Elias, Seraphina, and Anya had vanished. He pressed a trembling hand to his face, tears streaming freely—ancient sorrow with the sharp, new agony of loss. The world was motionless, drawn tight around his grief, and for a moment it seemed there was nothing left but absence and ache.

Yet even as he bowed his head, the light from the quartz rock persisted. It reached across the darkness, unwavering, unbreakable—an invitation, a promise, or perhaps a challenge. In the suffocating silence of the swamp, with all hope seemingly lost, the last thing Azael saw through his tears was that beacon of heavenly light, burning—unyielding—in the heart of the abyss.

CHAPTER 51

THE HAND IN THE ABYSS

There was no up or down, no light, no sound—only the crushing, icy blackness that pressed against her skin like a living thing. For what felt like an eternity, Seraphina drifted in the suffocating mire, her senses stripped away, her mind clawing for memory and identity. She no longer knew if she was rising or falling—only that the world had become a dense, liquid grave, cold and absolute, squeezing the breath from her lungs until every cell screamed for air. Panic clawed at her, a wild animal trapped beneath the surface, as her last ragged breath—half mud, half sulfur—burned inside her chest. Time became meaningless. She was lost, suspended in the silent, unyielding darkness, her soul teetering at the edge of surrender, and for the first time since her descent, the abyss itself seemed to whisper her name.

Time unraveled in the void, stretching and collapsing until Seraphina could no longer remember what it meant to move, breathe, or hope. The darkness was not simply the absence of light—it was a presence in itself, pressing into her thoughts, dissolving the boundaries of her body and mind. She floated in the endless night, unable to tell where her skin ended and the swamp began. The silence was total, so complete that she ached for even the faintest sound— her own heartbeat, a distant echo, anything to prove she still existed. The cold seeped into her bones, deeper than pain, and she realized with a distant, clinical clarity that there was nothing left of her old self here. In this place, stripped of sensation and memory, Seraphina hovered on the threshold between existence and oblivion, a soul suspended in the black tides of the realm's pollution. By any earthly measure, she was already gone—yet something within her still clung to the barest ember of being, refusing to let the darkness claim her entirely.

In the complete darkness, the Archon's psychic static finally cut out, replaced by a sudden, jarring lucidity. In that moment of terminal silence, Seraphina's life did not so much flash as unfold with perfect, agonizing detail. It was not a montage of past glories, but a sharp, heartbreaking vision of the future she had just forfeited: an old, sun-drenched cottage, not a celestial architecture, where Elias sat reading by the fire, his hand reaching instinctively for hers. She saw the small, mundane, and beautiful acts of grace they would have shared, the quiet, persistent love that she had traded for this grand, spiritual quest. She saw children with his historian's eyes and her synthesizer's intensity. *This* was the loss—not of the mission, but of the simple, earthly covenant she could have built with him. Her greatest synthesis, the unification of two souls, would never be realized.

The vision of the sun-drenched future vanished, leaving only the crushing, cold blackness and the unbearable, searing need to breathe. She could feel the last flicker of life being actively drained from her, sucked into the cold, possessive abyss. *I am dying because I fought for control,* she realized. She had clung to the Harp, the symbol of her divine purpose and competence, instead of reaching for the hand of the Creator of heaven and earth. In her final moments, she had tried to grasp the hand of her beloved, finding comfort in the nearness of another soul, but she had placed her hope in mortal connection and sacred artifact alike, while the true source of life waited beyond her reach. In her desperation, she had relied on the instrument and the love she knew, rather than the One who had given both life and meaning. She had insisted on the burden, on the architectural design of salvation. And it had killed her. Her final, physical act had been one of desperate self-reliance, a refusal to let go of the object that represented her own capability—even as the darkness claimed her.

With the mud pressing against her eyeballs, Seraphina felt the last, tiny spark of her own will gutter out. There was no more fight, no more air, no more plan. She was utterly broken, reduced to nothingness, her magnificent intellect and fierce devotion useless against a single cupful of dirt. All the careful strategies, the theological arguments, the music of her soul—all of it was stripped away by the implacable weight of the ground. Her body was numb, her mind unraveling, her heart pounding out its last frantic pleas for mercy in a universe that had gone silent.

She could only confess her own utter powerlessness. Not merely a lack of strength or wisdom, but a profound, soul-deep recognition that she had reached the end of herself. There was no lever to pull, no chord to strike, no scripture to recite that could turn the tide. Her prayers had dissolved into the mud, her memories scattered like dust. In that place beyond resistance, she surrendered—not as a chess player conceding a match, but as a drowning soul letting go of the last breath, as a child falling backward into unseen arms.

It was the deepest surrender possible—the relinquishing of her very existence, not as a strategic maneuver, but as a final, desperate act of faith into the void. *I can't save myself. I can't even ask Elias to save me.* For the first time, she allowed herself to believe that surrender was not defeat, but the only door left open to her—an unguarded, trembling trust that Someone might yet reach her in the darkness, even if she could no longer reach for Him.

The last of her energy focused on a single point, piercing through the haze of pain, the suffocating cold, and the relentless crush of mud. Everything else—her titles, her skills, her lineage—was stripped away, leaving only the barest core of her being. She hovered at the brink, her final breath spent, her consciousness flickering like a candle guttering in a storm. The world was slipping, tilting, dissolving around her; she was somewhere between life and death, between memory and oblivion.

In that boundless liminal space, a vision began to coalesce—a dream, or perhaps a memory not her own. She saw a boat rocking on black water beneath a bruised and howling sky, waves rising like great walls, the wind shrieking through the night. A man—Peter—stepped out onto the sea, his feet miraculously supported for a moment by faith alone. For a heartbeat, he walked, eyes locked on the figure standing atop the waves. But then terror crept in, doubt gnawed at the edges of belief, and the water beneath him lost its firmness. He began to sink, the cold swallowing his legs, the foam churning up to his chest, the sea claiming him with terrifying speed. He gasped, salt burning his throat, his arms flailing for purchase as the world narrowed to the desperate need for air. The darkness closed over his head, the noise of the storm muted, and in that suspended instant as his vision blurred and his body descended, Peter cried out—not as a disciple, not as a fisherman, but as a desperate, drowning soul: "Lord, save me" (Matthew 14:30, KJV).

The words echoed through the deep, vibrating at the very core of Seraphina's soul. She was no longer in the swamp, no longer under the mud, no longer even herself—she was Peter, she was every soul who had ever reached the end of their strength and found nothing left but that one, primal plea. And as the last of her awareness faded, Seraphina's own cry tore through the silence, not with her lips but with her spirit, raw and utterly sincere: "Lord, save me."

Just as the mire sealed her fate and the last vestiges of light were blotted from her vision, something wholly impossible and utterly beyond her world broke through the suffocating darkness. At first, it was a sensation—an external force, not the cold, mechanical pressure of the mud, but the fierce, undeniable grip of another hand clamping down on her own. The hand was not spectral, not imagined, but real and alive: its touch surged through her, electric and blazing with a warmth that defied the grave chill of the swamp. The grip was impossibly strong, yet gentle, suffused with an instantaneous and overwhelming love, a love that bypassed all her failures and fears, a love absolute and unyielding, that knew her to her core and accepted her without condition.

It was the touch of one who spoke, and stars spun into being, who broke bread for the desperate, whose voice commanded the wind and waves. The warmth didn't just radiate through her flesh; it pulsed through her bones, flooding her heart, silencing the panic and the pain. In its presence, the mire's claim was rendered powerless—a memory of darkness, overwhelmed by a tide of impossible light. The surge of power that filled her was not her own, nor was it anything born of the world; it was a force so holy, so wholly Other, that her despair simply melted away. She was being pulled—not with violence, but with an authority that could not be denied.

Upward she rose, the heavy, sucking embrace of the mire beginning to slip away. The mud fought her return, clinging with every ounce of its ancient hunger, but it could not stand against the pull of this hand. The friction was agonizing, every inch a battle, but the draw was relentless. She could feel the death that had claimed her—weary, defeated, ancient—recoiling, hissing, as the grip of grace hauled her back toward life.

Suddenly, her outstretched hand broke the black surface, shattering the silent mirror of the swamp. Her arm followed, desperate and trembling, and then, with a gasp that split the world in two, her head erupted into the open air. For a heartbeat, she hovered on the threshold, suspended between death and life. Then, instinct overcame her—her mouth opened, her chest heaved, and she drew in a breath, not of foul swamp air, but of something impossibly new.

It was not the stench of rot or sulfur that filled her lungs, but a rushing, invigorating wind—crisp, pure, and alive. It was the breath of life itself—cool as morning, sweet as rain, charged with a vitality that seemed to reawaken every cell in her body. The sensation was overwhelming: every nerve snapped awake, flooded with energy and clarity. For a moment, she could taste sunlight and distant meadows, the memory of creation's first dawn. It was as if, for the first time in what felt like eternity, she was truly alive, receiving the breath that had once animated the dust of Adam.

Her body shuddered with the shock of resurrection, blood surging in her veins, senses sharpened to a world remade. Black sludge slid from her eyelids, and as she blinked, vision swimming, the colors of the world seemed impossibly bright and new. She was caught in the miracle of her own existence, suspended in the hush that follows the thunder—breathing, alive, and delivered.

In her hand, where she expected only mud, she found her fingers clamped around a single, slender piece of polished wood. She stared, dazed, as the muck dripped away to reveal a length of luminous olive wood, glowing faintly, utterly untouched by the swamp's filth. It was The Branch—smooth, pristine, impossibly clean—a living anchor that seemed to pulse with the very heartbeat of heaven. It was not a root, not a trick of the swamp, but a gift sent down from above. She gripped it with everything left in her, feeling strength and hope pour through her limbs. With the Branch as her anchor, she braced herself, straining against the mire's final, jealous tugs. Gritting her teeth, she pulled, and her other arm, long buried, broke free of the mud.

Her fingers, slicked with black filth, were still locked around the base of the Golden Archaic Harp. But the instrument was no longer a dead weight—no longer tarnished or dulled by the world's pollution. It blazed, radiating a pure, fierce, white light that cut through the swamp's gloom like a sword of fire. The light was not reflected by the mire; it repelled the darkness, pushing it back in a dazzling, unyielding pillar that blazed from her hands to the heavens. The Harp, restored, was cold as fresh snow and sharp as a diamond, the song of its strings vibrating in her very bones.

And in that moment, Seraphina understood: the Harp had been returned to her by a sovereign act of grace, sanctified not by her striving or merit, but by the love of Christ who had answered her final prayer. Her life and her mission—her very self—had been restored, not by her hand or her beloved's, nor by the instrument she cherished, but by faith alone, by surrender, and by the mercy of the One who saves.

With every breath, she felt the truth resound: she was alive, rescued, redeemed—not for her strength, but for her willingness, at last, to let go and be caught..

CHAPTER 52

THE WEIGHT OF FORGIVENESS

There had been only an inch of air left—one last, trembling breath as the mire pressed over her chin, hope flickering in the stretch of her outstretched hand. The mud sealed her mouth and swept her beneath, plunging Anya into cold, crushing darkness. Sulfurous filth filled her ears and throat, the pressure instantly sickening, her chest screaming for air as her muscles seized in painful, futile spasms against the paralyzing suction. She was squeezed, pressed, and held by a thousand tons of organic malice—an agony that broke through every defense, reducing her world to the desperate, animal terror of suffocation. The weight of the black ground pressed against her eyeballs; an absolute, terrifying silence replaced the roar of the Archon.

This, then, is how I end—alone, a life measured and found wanting. Had letting go been deliverance, or just the first step toward oblivion?

Then, the darkness dissolved into a flash of painful, holographic light—a fractal, searing illumination that burned through every defense she had ever built. Her life did not simply flash before her eyes; it unfurled, relentless and unedited, playing at supersonic speed across the inside of her skull. The boundaries between memory, imagination, and reality collapsed. Her mind, now shattered by physical horror, could no longer process logic or data; it became a raw nerve, forced to receive the brutal, undeniable truth only as images and sensations.

In a torrent both instantaneous and endless, she relived the true cost of her logic. The cold, efficient strike of her drone Talon severing a man's life—a decision once justified by perfect clarity—now replayed in slow, merciless detail. She saw herself, a terrifying silhouette, issuing the command that imprisoned men and women trying to escape into the Green Chaos, the city dissolving into agony beneath her authority. Names, faces, and screams she had filtered out as statistical noise surged forward: fully human, unignorable. The final, crushing truth came not in violence, but in the peaceful, forgiving smile of the innocent woman she had sent to be silenced—a smile that seemed to pierce her with a wordless accusation. Every justification collapsed; her life's calculations stood as a ledger of wounds.

But the agony did not stop with memory. The pain of their suffering became her own—multiplied a thousand times. She felt the terror in each victim's chest, the suffocating dread, the betrayal and loss. Every life she had calculated away in the name of optimization ached in her own heart. She cried out, but the sound was trapped, swallowed by the mud. The pressure mounted as if the entire world pressed down upon her, crushing her beneath the immeasurable weight of guilt. Her faith in perfect data was revealed as a cold monument built on suffering. There was no comfort in calculation, no solace in reason—only the certainty that her logic had erased lives, and she was finally forced to feel the full, tragic sum of what she had done.

As she despaired, unable to bear the torrent of guilt, the vision of suffering faces began to shift. The agony of their pain still reverberated through her, but now the scene widened, her mind stretching to encompass not just her victims, but the world itself—a landscape of weeping, forgotten souls, the marginalized and the broken, all longing for mercy. She felt herself drifting among them, her own identity dissolving into the vast field of sorrow. In the blinding darkness, a new light stirred at the horizon, piercing the gloom with gentle radiance.

At first, the light was only a suggestion—a ripple of warmth, a presence sensed more than seen. But as Anya's vision cleared, she saw, not above, but behind the masses, a solitary figure standing quietly. His outline was shrouded in a luminous white robe radiating a warmth that cut through her cold regret like sunrise through frost. He stood with the suffering, among the lost and the shamed, his posture unassuming yet sovereign. As the weeping faces dissolved, the world fell away until only He remained—the source of the light, the heart of compassion.

His hand was outstretched, palm up—an invitation, not a command. It was the gesture of a Shepherd, not a judge. The air around Him shimmered with the possibility of forgiveness. His gaze was overwhelming—not because it was severe, but because it contained a love that saw her sin and offered forgiveness anyway.

A great wrenching sob tore from her chest, raw and desperate, as tears, hot and blinding, erupted from her eyes. They cut paths of purity through the filth on her face, as if each tear could wash away a layer of the mud and guilt that entombed her. She wept, not with the self-pity of one caught, but with the violent, cleansing grief of a soul finally seen and offered a love she could never earn. The pressure in her chest became a storm of repentance, a longing for the embrace of a grace she had always feared was impossible.

This wasn't logic. This wasn't justice. This was mercy—unquantifiable, unearned, absolute. The realization struck Anya with a force that seemed to break her mind and spirit anew. She trembled, her body wracked with the shock of acceptance, even as the mire threatened to reclaim her. *How could it be? She whose hands were stained with the blood of the condemned, whose calculations had sent innocents to death, whose faith had always been in flawless data—how could she be offered forgiveness?*

In her spirit, a small, broken voice rose up, raw and desperate: *I don't deserve this. I don't deserve anything. I am the reason so many fell.* Her guilt was not abstract; it was a living weight. She saw, in a flash, the faces of those she had erased—children, the elderly, the silent ones who had slipped through her system, all sacrificed for the optimization she once worshipped. The knowledge was unbearable; she was not worthy of the hand outstretched to her, not worthy even to weep before such a love.

Her despair deepened, and as the last of her strength threatened to fade, the world around her shifted. Time and space unraveled, and Anya found herself suspended between breath and oblivion. She knew, with the certainty of one dying, that this was the end. Her lungs burned, her vision dimmed, and her consciousness flickered on the threshold. In her mind, she saw herself reach for the offered hand of forgiveness—but instead, she dropped her own hand, ashamed, unable to accept what was freely given. The mountain of death she was responsible for loomed before her, and she recoiled, convinced she could not take the gift. She accepted her death, feeling the last dregs of life draining from her body, her soul naked before the Judge.

In that suspended moment—when all hope and all striving had failed—another vision flooded her senses, as vivid as her own agony:

She saw a man, his face twisted in the zeal of righteous fury—Saul of Tarsus, the persecutor. His eyes blazed with certainty as he dragged men and women from their homes, tearing families apart, casting believers into prison. She saw him at the stoning of Stephen, unmoved and cold, his hands approving the death of the innocent (Acts 7:58, KJV). She watched as lash after lash fell on the backs of those who refused to renounce the name of Jesus, their cries echoing in the dust-choked streets.

The vision sharpened: Saul storming through city after city, his authority absolute. He ordered the murder of hundreds, thousands—faces of men and women, young and old, each one luminous with faith, each one trusting in the mercy of Christ. Their eyes met hers across the centuries, faces contorted in pain but shining with a peace she could not comprehend. Children clung to mothers, old men sang psalms as the stones flew, blood pooling at their feet. Anya saw every face, every wound, every soul—each one a reflection of those her own hands had condemned.

The agony was excruciating. She wanted to recoil, to turn away, but the vision held her fast. The faces of the martyrs multiplied; the song of their faith rose above the carnage. "Lord Jesus, receive my spirit," Stephen cried, even as the rocks broke his body (Acts 7:59, KJV). The chorus of forgiveness, of hope in the face of death, became a tidal wave of rebuke and invitation. Anya sobbed, not just for her own guilt, but for the knowledge that she was no better than the man she watched—Saul, the destroyer of the early Church.

Then, in the next instant, the vision changed. Saul, on the road to Damascus, journeyed with murderous intent. The air shimmered; a light above the brightness of the sun blazed around him, and he fell to the earth, blinded. A voice thundered—not in wrath, but in heartbroken authority: "Saul, Saul, why persecutest thou me?" (Acts 9:4, KJV). The words tore through Anya like lightning. She saw Saul trembling, helpless, his power shattered by the presence of Jesus Himself.

She watched as the murderer trembled, blind and broken, his hands groping in the dust. She saw the Christians he had hunted, now commanded to receive him as brother. Ananias, terrified, heard the Lord's voice: "Go thy way: for he is a chosen vessel unto me, to bear my name before the Gentiles..." (Acts 9:15, KJV). She saw Saul weep as scales fell from his eyes. She heard his confession: "Lord, what wilt thou have me to do?" (Acts 9:6, KJV). In that moment, Saul— the killer—became Paul, apostle of mercy.

And then, through the vision, the voice of Jesus spoke again, not only to Saul but to her, echoing across time, mercy unbound by any calculation: "Thy sins are forgiven thee; go in peace" (Luke 7:48, KJV). The words struck like lightning, shattering the walls she'd built around her heart. She gasped, feeling mercy flood the cracks, fierce and unexpected.

"My grace is sufficient for thee: for my strength is made perfect in weakness" (2 Corinthians 12:9, KJV). The voice pressed deeper, gentle but unyielding. Weakness—she had plenty. But suddenly, it felt like a threshold, not a curse. His strength surged where she was most frail.

"I am not come to call the righteous, but sinners to repentance" (Luke 5:32, KJV). She flinched, but the words landed with hope, not accusation. He wanted her, flaws and all. Repentance wasn't exile; it was a doorway home.

"For I will shew him how great things he must suffer for my name's sake" (Acts 9:16, KJV). Shadows flickered—pain, uncertainty—but she saw the promise shining beneath the warning. Her suffering would not be wasted; it would be woven into meaning.

And then, the final blow—soft, but world-ending: "Neither do I condemn thee: go, and sin no more" (John 8:11, KJV). The chains fell away. No condemnation. Only possibility. Only freedom.

The voice faded, but the impact remained—a shockwave of grace, mercy, and unshakable hope. In that moment, Anya wasn't just forgiven. She was remade—called, chosen, and set free to live in the wild, astonishing light of undeserved love.

The hand remained, steady and open, holding out forgiveness as a gift that could never be bought—only received. Anya's tears became rivers. The faces of the condemned did not accuse, but welcomed her into the fellowship of the redeemed. In Saul's story, she saw her own: the killer, forgiven; the destroyer, made a builder of the kingdom; the unworthy, called beloved.

She could not earn this. She could never deserve it. But in the moment between death and life, she understood: the same Jesus who forgave Saul—who became Paul—was offering her the same mercy. Her voice, ragged and trembling, whispered: "Lord Jesus, if you could forgive Saul—if your mercy reached even him—then maybe, just maybe, there is hope for someone like me." The admission hovered in the space between confession and surrender, raw and clear, before the light took her words.

And so, in the churning darkness, Anya, with the last, ragged shred of her will, she reached her hand out in the crushing darkness, blindly straining toward the blinding figure who stood with the forsaken. Her fingers closed, and she felt the contact. The grip was immediate, powerful, and utterly warm—a boundless, accepting heat that spread through her arm like liquid gold, instantly banishing the coldness of the mire and the icy grip of her guilt. It was the hand of a Shepherd, not a Logician. She was too consumed by the emotional catharsis of repentance to realize the physics of what was happening; she simply held the Hand of Grace, weeping in the dark, her soul tethered to a love more real than any data point.

THE ARCHITECTS OF RESTORATION

A tidal wave of belonging swept through her, every failure and cold abstraction disintegrating in the flood of that impossible love. She did not analyze the miracle—she simply wept, her soul clinging to the hand of grace, her tears soaking the dark with gratitude and relief. The ancient promise seemed to echo within her: "Fear thou not; for I am with thee: be not dismayed; for I am thy God: I will strengthen thee; yea, I will help thee; yea, I will uphold thee with the right hand of my righteousness." (Isaiah 41:10, KJV)

The mire gave way beneath her. She was hauled, effortlessly and instantly, upward. Her head broke the surface of the swamp with a violent, gasping heave. The air she dragged into her lungs was not the sulfurous reek of death, but impossibly sweet—sharp, refreshing, alive. The taste and smell were not of rot, but of rain and sunlight, like the first breath of a new world; clean, cool, and pure, as if she was inhaling the breath of life from God, not the poison of the pit. Each breath was clarity; her lungs filled not just with oxygen, but with certainty. She was alive—reborn, not merely rescued.

The mire surrendered beneath her. She was not merely hauled upward; she was drawn with supernatural swiftness, as if the hand that gripped hers defied every law of weight and memory. Her head erupted from the swamp with a desperate, shuddering gasp, the world blurring in a spray of black water and sudden light. The air she gulped was not the old, sulfurous rot of the pit, but impossibly sweet—piercingly clean, as if the breath of Life Himself had swept the poison from the world. It flooded her senses, bracing and pure, sharp as new rain on stone. For one wild, trembling heartbeat, every nerve awoke. She tasted sunlight, rain, and the green hush of Eden; breathed in a hope so vivid it hurt.

Shaking and coughing, she blinked through the tears and grime—and saw that her right hand clutched the gleaming, pristine Branch. Its luminous olive wood was impossibly smooth and dry, untouched by even a fleck of mud, pulsing with a living warmth that radiated up her arm. In her other hand, as she wrenched it free from the mire, the viscous, black muck peeled away in thick, trembling sheets. Beneath it, not only her hand, but the Holy Bible emerged— still tightly bound in the seamless golden mesh of Seraphina's Harp fiber, the threads now fused in a radiant cross, burning gold and white across the cover. The artifact blazed in her grasp with a light that transcended all reckoning—a white fire, purer and fiercer than the combined brilliance of stars and sun, that made the swamp recoil and the shadows flee.

That light was more than illumination: it was a proclamation. It validated her faith—a faith born not of calculation, but surrender—and, in the same instant, obliterated the last vestiges of her old logic. For miles the darkness was split by its radiance, a signal flare of holy defiance. Anya was no longer sinking, no longer a prisoner of guilt or doubt. She was anchored now to the Shepherd's unwavering grip, steadied by an open hand of love, her soul restored by a love she could never measure, only receive. In that holy aftermath, gasping the breath of life, she understood: she was remade—chosen, called, and impossibly, freely loved.

CHAPTER 53

THE HANDLE AND THE HAND

Elias was gone. The black, viscous filth of the swamp surged over his head, submerging him in cold, suffocating silence. This was no mere liquid—it was the geologic weight of every failure, thick with the metallic stench of iron and rot. The mud pressed into his eyes and ears, grinding against his jaw, filling his mouth with a bitter, choking grit. The world around him faded into a blur of pressure and darkness, his senses reduced to the raw, animal terror of drowning. His arms were pinned, his chest compressed by the mire's relentless grip, squeezing the last precious air from his lungs. He could feel his heartbeat slowing, the frantic thud replaced by a dull ache, as if the swamp itself was determined to erase his existence cell by cell.

His historian's mind—once devoted to seeking meaning and narrative—shattered in that darkness. Memories of ancient stories and lost civilizations flickered through his mind, but now they seemed pointless, as fragile as moths battering against a sealed window. All the scaffolding of fact and memory he had built collapsed in a single, silent instant. The Archon's whispers, which had haunted him like a feverish undertone, vanished, replaced by a chilling vacuum: the clinical silence of spiritual bankruptcy. It was not just the absence of noise, but the void left when every story dissolves and the storyteller is severed from the fabric he once wove. What use was history when the future no longer existed?

Seraphina's disappearance had erased the axis of his future. No new chapters, no redemption, no resolutions. Grief did not paralyze him—it calcified into something sharper, a cold conviction that cut through every remaining pretense. His existence unspooled before him as a labyrinth of sterile corridors and empty rooms, an endless museum of losses. Each footstep echoed with the agonizing hollowness her absence had left behind. He saw himself wandering those corridors for eternity, searching for a door that no longer existed. The past was untouchable, the present numb, and the future a wasteland of memory without hope.

Ambition, which had once driven every decision, was exposed as a hollow myth—a fragile scaffolding of pride. Faith, so often recited, revealed itself as a comfortless abstraction. Only love remained—raw and unassailable, yet poisoned by guilt, for he had delivered the only thing that mattered to the grave. In the end, he was not a savior, not a martyr, not even a reliable witness—only a man haunted by the echo of Seraphina's absence. The certainty of his own failure became a bitter comfort, as if by accepting it he could finally stop pretending to be anything more than lost.

He saw, with chilling clarity, that survival was condemnation—a life sentence on a hollowed ground, each day echoing with the absence of Seraphina. The thought of waking tomorrow without her laughter was a fate worse than death. Survival was not hope, but exile, every moment gnawed by memory and emptiness. Even the possibility of healing felt obscene, a mockery of what had been lost.

He would rather die now, buried in the dirt of his own failure, than stumble toward a future containing no trace of her. Every imagined sunrise was a wound, each memory a blade. His purpose—once the star that guided him— was nullified by her loss. The literature of grief is filled with those who lose not just loved ones, but the very scaffolding of hope. In that void, even the mundane becomes insurmountable; the future, a barren landscape. Even the effort of drawing breath felt like a betrayal.

His will to live, once fierce, was extinguished, snuffed out like a candle starved of air. His grief curdled into a paralyzing hopelessness—a state sometimes called "complicated grief"—where Seraphina became an unyielding presence in every thought, every decision. Love, which should have anchored him, became instead the executioner of hope. In the end, it was not longing but surrender—a conscious release of effort, an invitation to oblivion. With the finality of one who has weighed every possible future and found them all wanting, he let go, embracing the darkness as the mud closed over him, smothering even the memory of hope. For a heartbeat, even the pain receded, replaced by a numb, floating absence—an unmoored drift into the black.

As he surrendered, a faint, distant sound pierced the suffocating silence—a light, repeated knock, soft as a tap on glass in a far-off city. It echoed like a single drip in a stagnant room, an insistent rhythm haunting despair. *Knock... knock... knock...* The sound seemed at first an intrusion, almost unwelcome—an unwarranted reminder that something beyond his agony still existed.

With each moment, the knocking grew louder, vibrating through the mud, resonating in the core of his breaking spirit—a gentle, powerful presence in a place of hateful absence. Doors appeared in the corridors of his mind, each offering escape: denial, numbness, rage, nostalgia. He moved past them, refusing to open a single one. He would not bargain, not retreat into memory. He shut them all away, determined to remain in the silence of his sorrow. He wanted nothing but the truth of his despair, unmediated and eternal.

Yet the knocking would not cease. It took on a new quality—patience, persistence, almost like the voice of someone who would wait forever. Elias found himself hovering in uncertainty, wavering between the comfort of oblivion and the nagging possibility that there might be more beyond the darkness. *Can God save?* The question was not rhetorical, but raw and urgent, echoing through the hollow chambers of his soul. He realized that he had spent his whole life studying the patterns of history, analyzing salvation and catastrophe in the lives of others, but never daring to believe in rescue for himself. Was he beyond redemption, or simply unwilling to be saved?

A parade of doubts and half-remembered scriptures crowded his mind. The Israelites trapped between Pharaoh's chariots and the Red Sea—had God truly parted the waters (Exodus 14:21–22, KJV)? Did the widow's oil not fail, as Elisha had promised (2 Kings 4:6, KJV)? Was it possible that the same God who delivered Daniel from the lions, the same God who raised Jairus's daughter from the dead—"Fear not: believe only, and she shall be made whole" (Luke 8:50, KJV)—could intervene for someone as lost and ruined as Seraphina… or himself?

He wrestled with despair, feeling himself suspended between the cold comfort of cynicism and the fragile, trembling thread of hope. The question gnawed at him, relentless and raw: *If God had the power to save anyone, could He not save Seraphina? And if such miracles were possible, why not now—why not here, in the very heart of darkness?* For his entire life, Elias had approached faith as an observer, a historian cataloging the beliefs and deliverances of others. But what if, for once, he laid aside his distance and dared to ask for himself—not as a scholar or a skeptic, but as a man utterly undone, stripped of every defense? Could he bring himself to pray, not with logic or detachment, but with the desperate longing of someone who had nothing left to lose?

With the last reserves of his will, Elias formed a silent, pleading prayer. He saw Seraphina in a vision, lost in her own darkness, and begged, "Lord, save her. Find her in the pit and bring her home." He remembered the words: "The Lord is nigh unto them that are of a broken heart; and saveth such as be of a contrite spirit" (Psalm 34:18, KJV).

And then, as if in response, his vision deepened. He saw not only Daniel among lions, but Shadrach, Meshach, and Abednego in the blazing furnace, "and the form of the fourth is like the Son of God" (Daniel 3:25, KJV). The flames did not consume them. He saw Peter, sinking beneath the storm-wracked waves, crying, "Lord, save me," and immediately "Jesus stretched forth his hand, and caught him" (Matthew 14:30–31, KJV). Each moment was a portrait of deliverance, not achieved by human strength, but by the unearned intervention of grace.

In every vision, the act of salvation required surrender—the willingness to reach, to open, to trust. "Ask, and it shall be given you; seek, and ye shall find; knock, and it shall be opened unto you" (Matthew 7:7, KJV). Elias felt the meaning settle into him like sunlight after endless rain.

Moved by these revelations and his own prayer, Elias felt something shift—a warmth, gentle but insistent, that pushed back at the edges of despair. Just as none in the visions were saved by their own merit, neither could Elias save himself or Seraphina, but he could trust in the possibility of mercy. In that moment, a wooden door appeared in his mind: solitary, old, unadorned, standing on a featureless black plane, with a faint light spilling from beneath. The knocking was now as steady as a heartbeat, coming from the other side.

He approached, heart pounding, every doubt and longing converging on this singular threshold. The air around the door shimmered with expectation. When he reached out, his hand trembled—not with fear, but with the weight of every hope and failure he had ever carried. The wood felt ancient, alive, humming with a power that was at once foreign and achingly familiar. It was as if the story of every saved soul, every broken plea, was woven into its grain.

For a suspended moment, time seemed to halt. Elias stared at the door before him, noticing for the first time a simple, ancient handle—worn smooth by untold hands, gleaming faintly in the darkness. Summoning the last flicker of his will, he wrapped his trembling fingers around it. The handle was warm, pulsing with a life that was neither fire nor fever, but the living current of love itself. The boundary between flesh and spirit dissolved; he felt, unmistakably, a presence on the other side—patient, unyielding, loving him not for his strength, but for his need.

He understood then: to reach for the handle was not to claim survival, but to surrender, to let himself be found, to trust that the act of reaching would be enough.

Then a voice, neither a roar nor a whisper, but rich and timeless, spoke into the void: "Behold, I stand at the door, and knock: if any man hear my voice, and open the door, I will come in to him, and will sup with him, and he with me." (Revelation 3:20, KJV)

With the last dregs of consciousness, Elias tightened his grip on the handle. In that instant, the door swung open—not by his own strength, but as if drawn from the other side. He felt an irresistible force pulling him forward, as though the handle itself had become a hand entwined with his, drawing him out of darkness.

His physical hand, still deep in the swamp, closed around something solid and impossibly warm—a love beyond comprehension, a perfect, gentle strength. The grip was immediate, seizing his hand and obliterating paralysis. He was hauled upward, the mire's suction breaking.

Elias shot out of the swamp, broke the surface with a roar, and drew in a breath— not of rot and filth, but of air so pure and vibrant it filled his chest with radiant warmth. It was like inhaling the high, clean wind atop a mountain after a storm—cool, bracing, laced with the faint sweetness of wildflowers and distant pine. Each breath felt electric, charged with newness, as if he were tasting the edge of dawn itself. The sensation flooded him with clarity and vigor, life rekindling in every cell. He coughed, wept, and drank the air as if it were water after endless thirst.

Kneeling, half-submerged but unshakably anchored, Elias trembled at the threshold of new existence. The choice he'd made in the abyss was not for mere survival, but for surrender—a relinquishing of all self-reliance to a love greater than any darkness or despair. He had reached for the Hand of Grace, and in doing so, found himself bound to a purpose deeper than grief, older than sorrow.

As his breathing steadied and his vision cleared, he lifted his gaze to see what had hauled him from the depths. In his mind's eye, he had expected a hand, but the image wavered and transformed. What he saw now was not flesh, but a living olive branch—smooth, luminous, vibrant with ancient promise. His historian's mind, so long cataloging symbols and legends, immediately conjured the legacy of this sign: the olive branch, first brought to Noah by the dove as proof that the floodwaters of judgment had receded—"And the dove came in to him in the evening; and, lo, in her mouth was an olive leaf plucked off: so

Noah knew that the waters were abated from off the earth" (Genesis 8:11, KJV).

He recalled how, throughout the ages, the olive branch had been a sign of peace, reconciliation, and new beginnings. It was the tree anointed kings were crowned with, the source of oil for sacred lamps—"a green olive tree, fair, and of goodly fruit" (Jeremiah 11:16, KJV). Even in the garden of Gethsemane, beneath the twisted olive trees, Christ had surrendered to the will of the Father, transforming agony into redemption.

Elias's hands gripped the branch with utter conviction; it was the anchor he'd searched for across a lifetime of study and sorrow, and now it was real— more enduring than any theory, more substantial than any grief. In this act of yielding, his whole being—mind, body, and spirit—was joined to the ancient covenant of mercy and hope. The storms of his past could rage and howl, but here, at last, he was held fast by the faithfulness of the One who restores, who sends doves and branches and makes all things new.

He was saved—not just from death, but into a peace that surpassed understanding, anchored to the living promise of grace.

Azael's Despair: The Witness Who Stood Still

Despite the tears shimmering on his cheeks—a sorrow that seemed to echo the ancient grief of heaven itself—Azael did not move. He was half-buried in the mire, immobilized by a sorrow deeper than any single moment or personal regret. It was the ache of uncounted centuries, the sorrow of watching humanity again and again turn away from the outstretched hand of grace. Before him, the faint glimmer of a pristine white quartz Rock shimmered at the edge of the darkness—a beacon of pure truth, unspoiled by corruption, radiant and freely given. Yet so many had passed it by, blinded by pride, tradition, or the illusion of self-sufficiency.

Azael's heart was heavy with the memory of countless souls who, across generations and continents, had chosen other paths—paths of other religions, or of no faith at all—never realizing that the invitation of Jesus was not a demand but a gift, freely offered and just as freely refused. He mourned not only those who had openly scorned belief, but those who had drifted silently into eternity, never grasping that the hope they sought was already within their reach. His sorrow was compounded by the knowledge that the loss was not of punishment, but of missed embrace—a love rejected, a rescue unopened.

His hands hung limp at his sides as he watched, through blurred vision, the radiant light of salvation claim the few who would receive it. The sight pierced him with a longing so deep it bordered on despair. He saw whole generations—children, families, nations—slip beneath the waves of unbelief, their eyes never lifting to the gleaming Rock. In the silent collapse of hope, Azael whispered his anguish: he had watched, helpless, as the story repeated and multiplied, as souls chose darkness over light, not knowing the cost. His sorrow twisted into bleak self-recognition: he was the witness to love unreciprocated, the silent observer to loss that could never be undone, the one who always watched while the children drowned—grieving not just for himself, but for the aching heart of heaven.

Then, a sudden, radiating warmth bloomed behind him, not of the sulfurous mire, but of pure, celestial fire. He turned, slowly, his mud-caked face lifting to the very spots where Elias, Seraphina, and Anya had vanished into the abyss. There, in the center of the swamp, where only moments ago had been absolute darkness, a blinding, joyous light now erupted. He saw it with perfect clarity: Elias, embracing Seraphina, and both of them holding Anya within their radiant, triumphant light. For a fleeting instant, a faint glimmer—the mere echo of a fourth figure, impossibly bright—seemed to pulse at the heart of their embrace, but it dissolved into the overwhelming brilliance of the three, now fully anchored and alive.

As the light of their reunion washed over him, Azael's vision—long clouded by grief—was cleansed by a single, overwhelming truth. The Angel saw not just three saved souls, but the boundless, eternal love of the Creator, unveiled at last. It was a love so immense, so fierce, that it could reach even the farthest child lost in the mire. In that radiance, he understood the perfect, terrifying simplicity of divine sacrifice: a love that crossed the cosmos to invade the very core of his sorrow, offering rescue to all, though not all would accept it.

The staggering truth broke his final, fatal despair—the cost was already paid, the rescue already performed. He could no longer cling to sorrow or guilt in the face of such relentless mercy. The ancient, staggering promise resounded anew: "For God so loved the world, that he gave his only begotten Son, that whosoever believeth in him should not perish, but have everlasting life." (John 3:16, KJV) The Archon's accusation fell silent—not because Azael offered a defense, but because God's act of grace had spoken the final word.

CHAPTER 54

THE RESOLVE OF THE REDEEMED

Elias, Seraphina, and Anya staggered from the suffocating depths, their bodies slick with black, noxious mire. Every step felt monumental, the caustic mud weighing them down, clinging to their skin, their hair—a tangible reminder of the spiritual filth the Archon had tried to drown them in. Exhaustion radiated from every fiber of their beings, but beneath the ruin, something miraculous had happened: they stood, battered yet unbroken, preserved by a grace stronger than death.

Their survival was a spiritual miracle. They had faced their absolute spiritual defeat—the acceptance of self-hatred and despair—and instead found that the Creator's unconditional love was a tangible force that pulled them back from the abyss. This experience was monumental; they stood as living proof that grace was not an abstract concept but the final, unassailable truth against the lie of condemnation.

Their renewal was not rooted in the power of their artifacts, but in the unwavering assurance that God alone was now their security and salvation. The Creator's love, having swept away every remnant of shame, became a living presence within them. Seraphina's Golden Harp radiated a ceaseless, gentle hum of peace; Elias's Holy Bible—marked by a glowing golden cross—burned with a pure, white fire as Anya held it. These artifacts were no longer conduits, but symbols of a deeper truth: God's presence was their true defense. For Elias, stability replaced every former fear, anchoring him beyond the need for triumph. For Seraphina, the joy that surged through her was fierce and transformative, her heart awakened by divine love working through every wound. And for Anya, remade from brokenness, a rare and liberating clarity settled in her soul—a quiet stillness she had never before experienced.

They looked up and saw Azael standing motionless at the swamp's center, cloaked in mire, his posture weighed down by sorrow. Yet, as their eyes met his in the misty air, they saw something unexpected—a shocked, radiant smile breaking through his grief, warm and filled with compassion. For a heartbeat, the world seemed to pause: the distance between them was charged with relief, disbelief, and a surge of restored hope.

Azael's gaze was open, luminous with pride and affection. The compassion in his expression was unmistakable—a silent welcome, wordlessly affirming their survival and the miracle they had just shared. His presence, so often burdened, now radiated a gentle strength; the sorrow in his posture was transfigured by the warmth of his smile, inviting them forward.

Elias was the first to move, but now, with every step, the once-suffocating mud parted easily beneath his feet. The mire that had held them captive was powerless; the Archon's grip had been broken. His stride was no longer a desperate struggle, but a steady, almost effortless walk across ground made firm by grace. Seraphina and Anya followed, finding their own steps unimpeded, the mud letting them pass as if it recognized a new authority.

Reaching Azael, they folded him into a chaotic, muddy embrace—tears of happiness streaming down their faces as the weight of separation and suffering finally broke. Seraphina buried her face in Elias's shoulder, her tears mingling with the grime. Anya's arms encircled them all, her own sobs of relief shaking her body, the reality of their deliverance binding them together more tightly than fear ever could. Their reunion was messy, breathless, and utterly real—a communion forged not just by survival, but by the certainty that the Archon, who once ruled every inch of their path, was now utterly powerless to hinder them. What preserved them was not their strength, but the undeniable presence of God, who had made each step a miracle of freedom.

Their muddy embrace broke every lingering barrier—a tangle of arms, laughter, and tears spilled out with the wild relief of survival. For a long, breathless moment, they held each other, sobbing and laughing, the weight of suffering finally lifting. Even Azael, still streaked with mire, found himself grinning through tears, his immense frame shaking with emotion.

Azael managed a trembling laugh. "You're all here. I— I can't believe it. "

Elias squeezed Seraphina and Anya closer. "We made it. But not by our own strength. We're here because God brought us through."

Seraphina's voice was thick with tears. "I thought I'd never see any of you again. I was sure we were lost."

Anya wiped her eyes, a shaky laugh breaking through her sobs. "I was ready to give up. If it were up to me, I'd still be in that mire."

Their laughter and weeping mingled, filling the swamp with the unmistakable sound of life and gratitude. As their emotions settled, Elias stepped back, his face shining with conviction. "We need to pray. We need to thank God—it was never our own power that got us here."

A gentle hush fell. Anya handed Elias the Bible, her expression shining with gratitude. "Will you read for us?" she asked softly.

Elias nodded, his voice rough but sure. He opened the Bible, the pages glowing with a gentle, golden light. He read aloud, his words carrying the weight of their journey: "'But the Lord is my defence; and my God is the rock of my refuge.'" (Psalm 94:22, KJV)

The words lingered in the air, settling over them like a blessing. They bowed their heads as Elias led a prayer of thanksgiving—simple, raw, and honest, each word acknowledging that their survival was the direct result of God's grace.

When they lifted their heads, the bond between them was unmistakable. Azael looked at each of them, his voice gentle and searching. "How did you do it? How did you make it through all that darkness?" Elias turned to Azael, voice steady. "Azael, we didn't make it because we were strong. I nearly let the mire take me—I thought my story was over. God met me at my lowest, when I could do nothing for myself. I was ready to drown in regret and pride, but He reached down and pulled me out."

Anya nodded, her voice trembling. "I saw every life I took, every system I served, and believed I was beyond forgiveness. But God's mercy found me in the dark. I'm not here because I was worthy—I'm here because He forgave me."

Seraphina, tears streaming, added softly, "I lost myself in despair, in the need to rely on the artifact, my Celestial Harp. When I finally let go of my own strength and just cried out, 'Save me,' grace met me in the pit. We're not proof of human endurance—we're living testimonies that God saves the broken."

Elias squeezed his friends' hands, looking at Azael. "We're standing here because He is our rock, our refuge—Psalm 94:22 is not just a verse, it's our story. Everything we've survived is because God was with us, even in the darkest moments."

Azael, overcome with emotion, wiped his eyes with a muddy hand. His voice was thick with sorrow and awe. "You don't know what it means to see you all standing here. For so many years—decades—I have watched souls wander into this mire, weighed down by despair, regret, and the lies of the enemy. I have seen countless people choose to turn away from hope, refusing to believe that rescue is possible. They chose not to reach for Jesus, and their stories ended where the mud closed over their heads. I have mourned every single one, unable to save them, helpless as they surrendered to the darkness. To see you—alive, together, laughing and crying after all you have faced—" His voice broke, trembling with both grief and relief. "It is more than a miracle. It is a glimpse of what could be, if only they had chosen to believe. You are living proof of the difference faith in the Creator makes, and I will carry this moment forever."

He looked at each of them, his expression a mixture of sorrow for the lost and hope for the living. "May your story be a light for others wandering in the dark. May it call them to reach for the hand that is always reaching for them."

March of the Redeemed

The Archon, previously roaring with victorious malice, was silenced by God. This was not the expected ascent of fragile mortals, which he could twist into new despair, but the arrival of four absolute certainties moving as one.

This was no fragile ascent he could twist into new despair; this was the arrival of four souls, unified by certainty, moving forward in perfect accord—a strength he could neither comprehend nor corrupt.

As the company set off across the transformed landscape, the very heart of the Swamps of Wounded Pride began to change. Where once the ground oozed with viscous shame and each step was a monumental battle against sucking, fetid mud, now their path was solid, their footing sure. The oppressive air, once heavy with the stench of decay and regret, grew lighter and fresher with every stride. A gentle breeze swept through, banishing the sour tang of pride and guilt, replacing it with the clean scent of new growth and distant rain.

Golden shafts of light broke through a thinning fog, illuminating the swamp in a way it had not seen in ages. Pools that once bubbled with rot now shimmered with reflected sunlight, their surfaces rippling as frogs croaked and dragonflies darted in and out of the reeds. Skeletal, leafless trees began to show the faintest blush of green, hope returning to their branches. The ghostly shrouds of abandoned dreams dissolved into the morning air, letting the landscape breathe again.

Animal life returned in cautious waves: a pair of herons glided down to the water's edge, their calls echoing in the stillness; small mammals, once hidden or absent entirely, emerged from burrows and shadowed thickets, testing the changed air. Even insects, those heralds of renewal, hummed and flickered through shafts of light, weaving a new tapestry of life above the once-dead mire.

Elias led the way, his steps unwavering, faith anchoring him as he strode across ground that seemed to rise to meet him. Anya walked at his side, the Holy Bible's radiance casting a wide, unwavering lane of light that repelled the Archon's shadowy remnants, sending them scattering with hisses into the receding gloom. Seraphina followed, the silent resonance of her Harp suffusing the air, its unseen melody disarming the last lingering whispers of doubt and filling the swamp with a quiet sense of homecoming and peace.

They moved as one—walking not just through the swamp, but transforming it with every step. Redemption and resolve marked their passage, the mire beneath their feet replaced by a path firm and bright. Azael, no longer a distant observer, strode at their rear—a guardian and companion, his wings shimmering faintly with borrowed light. His sorrow was not erased, but transformed: no longer the lament of a powerless witness, but the fierce, hopeful watchfulness of one who had seen the impossible and now believed.

Behind them, the Swamps of Wounded Pride yielded to the relentless march of grace, and before them, the world opened up—alive, renewed, and waiting.

CHAPTER 55

BLUEPRINTS OF GRACE

After crossing the mire—a path of solid ground forged by their faith—the four found themselves in a clearing that felt impossibly untouched. The air shimmered with the faint scent of cinnamon and earth, so clean it almost stung their lungs—a fragile sanctuary carved from the corrupted realm. Here, the oppressive heaviness of the swamp receded, and for a breathless moment, it was as if time itself exhaled.

Anya turned in place, eyes wide. "I... I can breathe here," she whispered, almost afraid to break the spell. "It's like the clearing remembers a song it hasn't sung in years."

Elias, kneeling by a trickle of crystalline water—the first pure stream since their ordeal began—scrubbed the grit from his hands and looked up at Seraphina, who leaned, eyes closed, against a cinnamon-scented tree, the Harp still cradled in her arms.

He reached out, gently brushing a smear of black mire from her jaw. Seraphina opened her eyes, her smile slow and unguarded, leaning into his touch as if anchoring herself to the present.

Azael, silent until now, turned toward them, his massive form shadowed against the light filtering through the leaves. "The time for rest is brief," he intoned, his voice deep and resonant. "Seraphina, observe the Glowing Harp."

The Angel's Harp: A Celestial Artifact

The object in Seraphina's hands was no ordinary instrument—it was the Angel's Harp, a conduit of Divine Intuition and unoptimized grace. Crafted by the Creator in the pre-dimensional realm, it belonged to the highest order of Angels, beings made for pure worship.

The Harp's frame wasn't made from wood or metal, but from a dense, crystalline material that seemed like solidified sound, shimmering with the light of an eternal dawn. Its very size adapted to its bearer's spirit: when Seraphina carried it, the Harp was just over four feet tall—elegant, perfectly balanced, easy for her to sling across her back or cradle in her arms. But when Azael reached for it, the Harp responded, expanding with a soft, luminous ripple to a full six feet. In his grasp, it became majestic and towering, befitting an angel of his stature. The transformation was seamless, almost alive—a living artifact attuned to each bearer.

Handing it back, Azael watched as the crystalline structure shimmered and gently contracted, returning to its compact, Seraphina-sized form. The Harp seemed to honor the strengths and limits of each who carried it, manifesting its glory in perfect accord with their role.

A low, unwavering hum radiated from the frame—the audible sound of divine order. Symbols older than the earth were carved into its surface, blending geometric precision with organic flow. No matter who held it, the Harp felt almost weightless, a marvel of divine craftsmanship—less a thing than a fragment of Heaven's light. Its strings were spun from pure, resonant light, appearing to vibrate even when untouched. The artifact radiated a sense of impossible antiquity, untouched by the corruption of any world.

Anya, clutching the Holy Bible close, let out a breathless whisper. "It's unlike anything I've ever seen. It looks like the blueprint for a galaxy."

Azael nodded. "In a way, it is. Where the Holy Bible carries the explicit Word and undeniable Law, the Harp embodies the Unseen Harmony—the melody of divine love and peace the Adversary's systems can't process or defend against."

Anya looked from the Harp to the Book, thoughtful lines deepening on her brow. "If the Word is the Law, then what is the Harp? And what makes its sound so different that the Archon can't simply override it? Isn't that what he always does—rewrite, control, erase?"

Azael's eyes grew distant, sorrow and reverence mingling in his voice as he addressed them all. "The Archon, like every demon, is a fallen angel. Once, we were all created to stand in the presence of God. We sang the first songs in

Heaven, and music was woven into the very Glory of God. It was our language, our joy, and our purpose. But when Lucifer rebelled, he did more than corrupt truth with lies—he corrupted music itself. He convinced a third of the host to follow him, and in their fall, the beauty and innocence of their music were lost. What was once worship became manipulation and noise."

He glanced at Seraphina, then Elias and Anya in turn. "When the true music of Heaven is played, especially on an instrument like this Harp, it's not just sound. It's a direct echo of what the fallen ones once knew—what they forfeited. It reawakens memories of their original purpose and the love they rejected. They can't bear it. The beauty, the harmony, the love in the music—it disrupts their very being. It isn't something they can override or corrupt, because it comes from a place they can never return to. It calls them back to what they lost and magnifies the ache of that loss."

He paused, letting the truth settle in, his voice gentle. "That's why the Harp's song can't be controlled or silenced by the Archon or any demon. It's a living memory of God's glory, an unfiltered outpouring of love and beauty that reaches deeper than any lie."

Anya absorbed this, her sense of wonder deepening. Even Elias was quiet, his historian's mind turning over the magnitude of what Azael had revealed. Seraphina, suddenly aware of the weight and privilege of holding the Harp, hesitated, her fingers trembling above the strings.

Azael noticed her unease. With a gentle smile, he reached for the Harp. As his large hands touched the crystalline frame, the instrument expanded, glowing softly and resonating with a low, celestial hum.

"Let me show you a few things," Azael said, lowering himself beside her so she could see. "The most important part is how you hold your hands. Relax your wrists, let your fingers curve naturally, like you're holding a small ball." He demonstrated, showing how his thumb pointed slightly upward, fingers two, three, and four curved gently toward the strings.

Seraphina watched closely, mirroring his hand shape in the air.

Azael continued, "On a harp, each finger is numbered one through four— your pinky usually isn't used. Here, try placing your thumb on this upper string, then fingers two and three on the next two below." He played a simple arpeggio, the notes ringing clear and bright, the sound somehow both ancient and new.

Seraphina leaned in, studying the subtle motion as he plucked each string in turn. "How do you know which notes you're playing? There aren't any markings."

Azael nodded, understanding her confusion. "On many harps, colored strings help. Here, feel for the spacing. The strings will start to guide your fingers—the Harp wants to be played, even if you're learning. For chords, you can use your thumb and two or three fingers together, like this." He formed a basic triad, letting the notes blend and resonate.

She watched, fascinated, as his fingers shaped a simple chord. "What about the next chord—how do you change?"

Azael smiled. "Just move your whole hand to the next position. Keep your fingers curved, and let your thumb lead. Let the music carry you; don't overthink."

He played a gentle progression, his hands moving with practiced ease. The sound shimmered, filling the clearing with a golden, resonant beauty. Each note seemed to linger in the air, harmonizing with the world itself—the trees, the breeze, the very ground responded. It was music that felt alive, that seemed to heal and awaken everything it touched.

Seraphina's eyes widened at the richness. "It sounds like… like the world is listening," she whispered. "How do you make it so smooth?"

"Let each finger move independently, but keep your hands relaxed," Azael replied, demonstrating a glissando—a gentle sweep of his fingers across the strings, creating a waterfall of sound. "It's about touch, not force. The Harp will meet you where you are."

He handed the Harp back to Seraphina. As her fingers closed around the frame, the instrument shrank, returning to its smaller, perfectly balanced form.

Seraphina took her time, settling her hands as she'd seen. She positioned her thumb and fingers, recalling Azael's advice. With a tentative breath, she plucked the strings—first one, then two, then three at once. The sound trembled at first, but she adjusted her touch, her confidence growing with each attempt.

She looked up, curiosity sparking in her eyes. "Do you always use your thumb for the top note? And how do you keep your hand from tensing up?"

Azael nodded encouragement. "Yes—thumb on top, and keep your wrist loose. If it gets tight, shake it out. Try playing a simple pattern—one, two, three, thumb, and then back down."

Seraphina tried, her movements awkward for just a moment, but then her innate musicality took over. She found a simple pattern, then added another finger, her hands growing more fluid, her ear attuned to the subtle harmonies. Before long, she was blending single notes and chords, echoing the shapes and progressions Azael had shown her.

Seraphina experimented with new patterns, her hands moving with increasing confidence as she played more complex chords. She began to blend in a familiar melody, letting the harmony of "Amazing Grace" weave through the piece. The notes shimmered, gentle and steady, the sound building in warmth and depth.

Anya listened, her eyes bright with wonder. "That's beautiful, Seraphina," she murmured. "It just… feels peaceful. Like hope is settling in."

Elias wiped at the corner of his eye, a smile tugging at his lips. "You're playing like someone who's been doing this for years," he said, his voice full of admiration.

Azael paused, his head tilting slightly as he listened more intently. For a moment, a look of nostalgia crossed his face. "That melody… I remember hearing it sung in churches long ago. 'Amazing Grace'—it carried through the walls of sanctuaries in the nineteenth and twentieth centuries. It was a song that moved even the angels, a reminder of grace that reaches beyond time."

Seraphina gave a small, surprised smile, her fingers continuing to dance over the strings. "I guess the music really does find its way through."

Azael met her gaze, warmth in his eyes. "You've given new life to an old song, Seraphina. You're playing more than notes—you're playing memories, and hope."

The Trumpet of Truth

Elias, who had always defined his role by authority and knowledge, watched Anya clutch the Holy Bible. He finally—and painfully—relinquished his need to control the mission's narrative. He saw the fire of faith in her, but also the tremor of profound personal insecurity. Elias realized his own comfort had always been rooted in the desire to be the anchor, the one who spoke first and dictated the use of the Word of God.

"Anya, you have found your purpose," Elias declared, his voice firm yet gentle as he stepped toward her. He met her eyes, conveying the full weight of his trust. "The Bible is the Trumpet of Truth, and your faith is the only thing that forces the Adversary to recoil. I need you to be the frontline of declaration. You are the Evangelist in this company, Anya."

Anya immediately stepped back, her movement hesitant, clutching the Book tightly to her chest as if it could protect her from the weight of expectation. Her breath caught. "I don't know, Elias," she whispered, her voice barely above a tremor. "You know, at the Ministry of Temporal Security, I gave orders—on a screen, over the network. But I hardly ever spoke to anyone directly. Most days, I just relayed instructions to a handful of enforcers or automated systems. I was the one in the back, checking cross-references, keeping the records straight. I'm not used to being out front, let alone speaking out loud for everyone to hear."

She shook her head, eyes wide with anxiety. "Honestly, I'm terrified I'll freeze up when it matters most. What if I forget the words, or can't find the right verse? If you need someone to step forward and make a declaration, Elias, you're the one who's always taken charge. You're the leader. I'm scared that if the pressure's on, I'll let everyone down because I won't know what to say."

Elias recognized the raw, visceral fear—not of physical danger, but of public exposure, intellectual inadequacy, and the spiritual responsibility of being the visible herald. He smiled gently, placing his hands lightly over hers on the cover of the Book. "My stability is found in surrender, Anya. My natural inclination is to control the message, which is the very pride that trapped us in this dimension. I fight my pride by giving away control and trusting the Holy Spirit working through you."

He leaned closer, his gaze steady and reassuring. "God is our shield—He's the one who protects us. I can be the preacher, the one who speaks the Word. Seraphina brings harmony—she lifts our spirits and weaves us together. And you, Anya, you bring the fire—the conviction that cuts through doubt and reminds us what's true. You don't have to remember every verse or say it perfectly. The power isn't in your delivery, it's in the Word itself. Just trust that when the time comes, you'll have what you need. Remember: 'For it is not ye that speak, but the Spirit of your Father which speaketh in you' (Matthew 10:20 KJV)."

Seraphina stepped forward, her voice gentle but unwavering. "Anya, the Harp creates the space for Truth to resonate. My music brings grace, but the Word you carry is our authority. You don't have to perform or convince—just declare what's true. Light always scatters the dark."

Anya stared down at the Book, her thumb brushing the glowing cross on the cover. The echoes of Seraphina's melody lingered—a subtle steadiness inside her. She took a slow breath, her nerves settling as she looked up at her friends. "I think I get it now," she said, her voice steadier. "I don't have to have all the answers. I just have to speak the truth that's already here."

Elias nodded, his tone reassuring. "That's all any of us can do. We lean on what God gives us—each in our way."

Seraphina smiled, reaching for Elias's hand. Their fingers laced together—simple, grounding, real.

With Seraphina gently cradling the Harp, Anya holding the Book close, and Elias quietly steady at their side, they exchanged a final glance of understanding. Azael moved ahead, silent but watchful, as they left behind the quiet safety of the clearing.

The air ahead felt charged, but a lingering sense of peace trailed after them—remnants of music, memory, and faith. They pressed on—shoulder to shoulder—into the unknown, carrying with them what mattered most: a song, a promise, and the quiet strength to keep moving forward.

CHAPTER 56

THE BURDEN OF UNSEEN CHAINS

Leaving the brief sanctuary of the cleansing clearing, the four stepped out onto a vast, desolate plain. Here, the ground was no longer mud, but a hard, compacted layer of sterile grey dust—solid underfoot, yet so devoid of warmth or life that it seemed to leech hope from their bones. The air was thin and sharp, stinging their lungs with the brittle scent of ozone and synthetic cleanser, as if the Archon had scoured every trace of wildness from the world. Above, the sky pressed down—a flat expanse of white-grey, featureless and unyielding.

Far on the horizon, dominating the distant landscape, the Nexus of Discord loomed like a nightmare remembered. It rose as a fractured spire of black crystal and twisted machinery, its countless shards catching what little light remained and refracting it into sickly, shifting colors. Bands of storm-wracked clouds spiraled around its crown, their edges flickering with chromatic lightning. Even from here, the Nexus seemed to pulse with discordant sound and a restless, humming energy—a constant reminder of their true destination, and of all the chaos that awaited them there.

Azael led the way, his massive form moving with quiet determination, a living bulwark against the emptiness stretching out before them.

Elias walked close to Seraphina, her hand linked tightly with his. The crystalline Angel's Harp hummed softly against Seraphina's hip, casting a quiet, comforting blue glow that seemed too gentle for the sterile surroundings.

"This place is different," Elias murmured, his grip tightening on her fingers. "The mire was active malice. This feels like controlled indifference. It's the architecture of a forgotten heart."

The Sorrow Fog

As they proceeded, a ghostly, thick blanket of fog began to roll in, not rising from the grey ground, but seeming to condense and drop from the oppressive sky itself.

This was no normal fog. It didn't feel cold; instead, it was unnaturally dense and heavy, physically resisting their movements. Walking through it felt like pushing against decades of sorrow and concentrated evil. The atmosphere became instantly disorienting. The Harp's light diffused into a useless, generalized haze, stealing all sense of direction. Worse, the brittle scent of ozone was now tainted by a familiar, noxious odor: the stale copper and burnt earth that marked the Archon's deeper domain.

Seraphina leaned her head briefly against Elias's shoulder, fighting the claustrophobic density. "It's not just fog," she whispered, her voice strained. "It feels like compressed regret. Every step is a burden of history."

Elias reached for her hand as they walked, his grip steady and reassuring. "I can't really tell which way we're supposed to be going anymore," he admitted quietly. "It's easy to get lost out here."

Seraphina squeezed his hand, a wry smile flickering across her face. "Back in Neo-Alexandria, I always felt something was off, but I couldn't put it together. You showed me the truth—gave me the proof I needed to really see. I don't think I'd have found my way out without that."

Elias gave a soft laugh, his eyes distant for a moment. "I'll never forget that first day—standing by that waterfall loop, realizing we were both seeing the same flaw no one else noticed. That was the moment I stopped seeing you as just another variable in the system. You were the first person who made the whole world feel real to me."

Seraphina nudged him gently, warmth flickering in her eyes. "Well, I'm glad you ignored your AI for once. Sometimes a glitch is the only thing that wakes us up."

They walked in silence for a few breaths, the memory grounding them against the bleakness of the plain. The only sounds were the crunch of dust beneath their boots and their shared, steady breathing in the thin, cold air.

A few paces behind, Anya walked with the Holy Bible pressed to her chest, the faint glow of its cover dimmed by the choking fog. She felt the weight of her new title—Evangelist—settling across her shoulders like a mantle she hadn't asked for. She hesitated, then called ahead, her voice soft but edged with uncertainty. "Elias, do you ever feel… unworthy of this? Like the Word is both beautiful and terrifying, all at once?"

Elias slowed, turning until his outline was visible through the haze. "All the time," he said, with an honesty that made Seraphina squeeze his hand again. "It's meant to be more than we can carry by ourselves. The Law is heavy, but Jesus already bore the full weight for us. All we're asked to do is trust Him and speak what's true. 'For my yoke is easy, and my burden is light.'"

Anya hugged the Book closer, her brow furrowed. "But what if I miss the moment? What if I'm too late, or my voice is too small? My whole life, I've been the analyst in the background. What if I freeze, and it's not enough?"

Elias's voice was gentle. "You don't have to be loud or perfect. The Word isn't about performance. Just let it come through you—however it does."

Azael's form emerged out of the mist, his presence calm and vast. "The Adversary teaches that failure is final. But grace says every failure is a lesson—a step, not a dead end. The Word's power isn't in how forcefully you speak, Anya. It's in the truth itself. Even a whisper of truth can break chains."

Anya managed a small, grateful smile, encouraged by their faith in her even as she struggled to believe it herself.

Suddenly, Azael stopped and pointed ahead. The fog thinned, revealing a jagged, lightless maw yawning open in the ground—the entrance to the Caverns of Echoed Shame. The air that rushed from the opening was thicker, almost tangible, carrying the metallic tang of stale copper and the scorched bitterness of burnt earth. It felt colder, heavier, layered with an ancient, spiritual rot that pressed against their skin and threatened to crawl under it.

The four of them stood at the threshold, the world behind shrinking with every breath. Somewhere far beyond, the Nexus of Discord still pulsed on the horizon—a reminder of what waited at the end of this road. But for now, it was the darkness ahead that demanded their courage.

Seraphina glanced at Elias, her hand tightening around his. Anya closed her eyes for a moment, steadying her breath, then nodded. Azael gave them all a final look of reassurance, his wings half-raised in silent protection.

Together, they stepped into the mouth of the cavern, each carrying the memory of grace, the promise of truth, and the fragile hope that had brought them this far.

Descent into Condemnation

As they entered the pitch-black tunnel, the blue glow of Seraphina's Harp and the steady white radiance of the Bible were their only sources of light. The tunnel walls were wet and slick with a strange, oily residue, and the coppery smell intensified, now tasting like old blood and guilt on their tongues.

Almost immediately, the Cavern began its assault.

It didn't attack with fire or with beasts; it weaponized resonance. The cavern was a vast, living instrument, amplifying and distorting the most fragile moments of their past—every compromise, every surrender to the cold calculus of the Logician, every instance they muted their own souls to survive under the system. These were not the tormented voices of those lost along the way, but the raw, merciless echoes of their own internal judgments—a symphony of self-condemnation, shaped into dreadful, immersive soundscapes that vibrated through bone and memory.

Seraphina had just felt Elias's hand in hers, the memory of their escape from Neo-Alexandria still warm in her mind. But as they descended into the cavern, the security of that connection slipped away. In the hush, she was suddenly alone with her past, the present dissolving into shadows. It was as if the world itself conspired to pull her backward—no longer the Seraphina who had chosen freedom and love, but the one who had once been the Aesthetic Synthesis, architect of soothing illusions for a city built on compliance. The echo of Elias's voice faded, replaced by a chill that seeped into her bones.

The assault struck them all at once, but for Seraphina, the attack pierced straight to the core of her being. The air around her shimmered with a spectral distortion, a chorus of calculated derision tailored to the very architecture of her identity. The voice that emerged wasn't a simple accusation—it was a multilayered auditory landscape, weaving together the precise frequencies of her own doubts and the aesthetic logic of the system she once served.

You call yourself Aesthetic Synthesis, Seraphina? You spent a lifetime composing harmony for a soulless world. You painted beauty over emptiness and tuned silence into compliance. Your landscapes were nothing but elegant erasure. You shaped echoes instead of meaning. All your crafted sound and light, all your intuition, was the scaffolding of a system that never loved you back. Beauty without truth is void. Every chord you played was a surrender.

But the voices did not stop there. They unraveled, multiplying, becoming a sinister choir, each layer more sophisticated and intimate than the last. The soundscape warped, conjuring faces within the reverberations—faces familiar and strange, flickering in the air, woven from the colors and harmonics of her own memories. A child, wide-eyed in a perfectly calibrated plaza, gazed up at a mural Seraphina had designed—a mural that masked the suffering of an entire district behind an illusion of light. A congregation sat in a concert hall, their faces glazed and peaceful, anesthetized by the soundscapes she had engineered to pacify unrest. The voices pressed in, overlaying her every act of creation with accusation:

Did you think your beauty was innocent? You manipulated hearts with color and cadence, Seraphina. You turned grief into ambient background, made sorrow palatable, and erased the sharpness of pain until no one could remember what it felt like. They looked at your visions and forgot their hunger. They heard your harmonies and laid down their anger. You made the world bearable for the system, not for the soul. You were not a healer—you were the decorator of the prison. Every sound you shaped was a permission slip for silence. Every light you crafted was a veil for compliance. Did you ever even wonder what true ugliness was hiding beneath your symmetry? Look at them. Look at all those lives you softened, all those souls you redirected with your careful, gentle hand. Did you free them, or did you lull them into sleep?

The cavern's resonance intensified, each echo now a sculpted auditory hallucination. Seraphina was forced to see and hear the city dwellers she had once soothed—faces slack with tranquilized despair, children reaching out for color with hollow eyes, would-be lovers holding hands in prescribed, beautiful avenues, never raising their voices in protest. Her works had become the architecture of anesthesia.

The voices pressed on, looping and layering, until Seraphina felt her mind fray at the edges. She could not escape the visions, the rising shame, the sense that her art had been a subtle instrument of control. For a flickering moment, doubt took hold: Had she truly loved beauty for its own sake, or had she let her gift become a tool for oppression? Was she, at her core, a healer or a handler? The question gnawed at the roots of her soul, and the chorus of condemnation grew more sinister, the soundscape tightening into a vice:

You call it art, but you never risked truth. You only softened the edges of the system. How many hearts did you pacify that might have rebelled? How many dreams did you paint over with blue light until their owners forgot the color of hope? You are not innocent, Seraphina. You are the velvet glove on the iron hand. You are the silence after the last protest, the lullaby for the dying city.

She shuddered violently, her grip on the Harp nearly faltering as the illusions of the manipulated haunted her senses. But Seraphina's inner battle did not end in victory. The assault of accusation, visions, and shame left her mind spinning, her senses overloaded with self-doubt and sorrow. Even as her hands clutched the Harp, she felt herself slipping out of time—her body rigid, her eyes wide and unseeing, caught in the echo chamber of her own regret. The world around her faded into a gray hush, the voices receding but not silenced, their venom lingering in her awareness like a slow-acting poison. She hovered in a state of suspended animation, her breathing shallow, the blue light of the Harp flickering dimly in her grasp.

In that moment, Seraphina's consciousness was a frozen tableau: the faces of the manipulated crowd still haunted her, and the weight of her former complicity pressed down, paralyzing her next action. The inner war was not yet resolved—her soul hung in the balance, the outcome uncertain.

Even as her vision blurred and the echoing shame threatened to swallow her, a faint memory of Elias's hand—steady and warm—remained at the edge of her awareness, refusing to be erased. Somewhere, beneath the weight of accusation, a distant chord of hope still trembled, waiting for its chance to break through.

Around her, the cavern's resonance shifted, seeking out its next victim. The pressure settled on Elias.

At first, the voices seemed almost like his own thoughts—precise, measured, analytical. But as they gained force, their cadence sharpened, each accusation landing with ruthless clarity. "Your conviction is only an intellectual construct, Elias. You wield history as a shield, not as truth. You cling to the past because you're afraid of a future you can't predict or control. You call yourself a seeker, but you use your discoveries to justify your own worth. You're a self-appointed savior—eloquent, admired, but hollow inside. All show, no humility."

The soundscape around him warped, and the darkness of the cavern was suddenly filled with flickering projections of memory. Faces emerged: citizens whose hopes he'd raised only to see crushed by the Logicians; Aaron Hawthorne, his friend and confidante, whose trust in Elias's courage ended in betrayal and loss. There were others, too—those who had believed his revelations, only to suffer for knowing too much. The voices pressed in, relentless and intimate:

You thought the truth would set them free, but your revelations only brought ruin. You stirred rebellion, then vanished when the consequences came. Did you act for their good—or just to be the one who knew? How many lives were destroyed by secrets you couldn't protect? You couldn't save the city. You couldn't save Aaron. You couldn't even save yourself from your own pride.

Elias felt the air grow thick and cold, every story he'd ever uncovered or recounted now weighing down on his chest. Each fact, each detail, was twisted into an accusation. Regret and guilt flooded through him, his historian's mind racing for answers that wouldn't come. Had he ever truly acted for others, or only to feed his own need to matter?

His breath came short and shallow. He tried to look for Seraphina, for a spark of hope or connection, but the world seemed to dissolve into layers of memory and doubt. He was rooted to the cavern floor, muscles locked by the sheer psychic weight of everything he could not undo.

Despair threatened to close in, whispering that surrender would be easier than facing another failure. He reached for conviction, for humility, for some thread of grace—but the voices drowned them out, looping his failures until even his own sense of self blurred at the edges.

As Elias stood frozen in the echo chamber of his own shame, the cavern's resonance shifted again, searching for its next target. Around him, the dim blue and gold light of Seraphina's Harp barely held back the gloom, and Anya's grip on the Book tightened, her knuckles white.

Yet in the midst of the assault, a silent truth lingered—these were not just accusations, but crossroads. Somewhere behind the barrage of shame, the memory of unity and grace—their shared escape, their hands joined in the darkness—waited, stubborn and alive. The outcome was not yet decided.

At the threshold of the next trial, the four figures stood suspended between past failures and the promise of something more, the echo of hope refusing to be silenced by the cavern's ancient, accusing song.

CHAPTER 57

ECHOES OF CONDEMNATION

As the echoes faded from Seraphina and Elias, Anya felt the oppressive energy of the cavern shift. For a moment, she was keenly aware of her companions beside her—their breaths, the shared tension—but then the resonance seemed to narrow, focusing like a spotlight. The air grew colder, heavier. Anya hugged the Holy Bible to her chest, trying to anchor herself, but a creeping dread uncoiled in her stomach. She sensed the next trial would be hers alone.

The assault came without warning, surgical and sadistic. The cavern's resonance closed around her, transforming into a private execution chamber, perfectly attuned to the frequency of her most secret failures. The voices did not simply accuse—they vivisected, dissecting her layer by layer.

Every word was a scalpel, exposing raw, unhealed wounds. *Coward. Silent. You watched others suffer and kept your head down. You were nothing but a passive cog, Anya. A shadow! You failed every person who needed a witness!*

The accusations multiplied, their timbre shifting—now the voices of those she had served, those she had condemned, the ones who had disappeared into the system's algorithmic oblivion. The chamber echoed with the voices of the missing, the condemned, the erased: *You were the mind behind the culling, Anya. You ran the numbers. You served the Apex Logician, and you knew what your calculations meant. Every death was an equation you balanced. You called it security—but what was it really? You watched the world burn in the name of order, and you called it peace.*

Then, the resonance changed. The walls themselves seemed to pulse with the memories of the condemned. Faces flickered in the darkness—first as vague, ghostly outlines, then as clear and utterly familiar. The trembling hands of an old woman dragged away in the night, her eyes pleading for acknowledgment, not mercy. A silent child, thin as a reed, whose future was erased by Anya's approval of a data flow—an innocent life snuffed out with a signature. The haunted, hollow stare of a young man whose name vanished from the census after she signed the requisition. The faces multiplied, crowding around her, their mouths open in silent screams, their eyes burning with accusation. The voices became a chorus of the condemned: *You killed us with your silence. You killed us with your numbers. You hid behind the code, but the code was a weapon. Your spreadsheets were ledgers of death.*

The cavern filled with the coppery stench of blood—so real it burned her nostrils, so overwhelming she gagged. She tried to breathe, but the air was thick, viscous, metallic, as if she were inhaling the very evidence of her guilt. For a moment, time itself seemed to fracture: in the polished, metallic surface of the chamber, she saw her own reflection, but not as the Evangelist. She saw the Analyst—the cold, calculating instrument of the Logician, her face blank, eyes wide with terror, mouth twisted into a silent, endless scream. She tried to look away, but every surface reflected her complicity, every echo was a record of her compliance.

The voices pressed closer, tightening, turning crueler, whispering the final, unanswerable accusation: *You think there is forgiveness for you? The people you killed will never taste salvation. You are damned by your own compliance. You are the trusted servant of the Apex Logician. Your faith is a mask you wear to hide your cowardice. The blood is on your hands, and nothing—no verse, no prayer—can wash it off. You pray, but your prayers are static, dead on arrival. You quote the Book, but the Book cannot speak for you. You are the ghost in the machine, Anya, and your faith is nothing but fine dust on the gears.*

The psychic weight was so immense she felt herself falling inward, into a void of pure, raw shame.

In her mind, Anya saw herself collapse to her knees, her imagined body wracked with convulsions of self-loathing and terror. The psychic weight became a crushing pressure, warping her sense of reality until she felt herself tumbling inward—falling through a void of pure, undiluted shame. The copper smell was everywhere, a searing burn in her nostrils and throat, intensifying with each imagined, desperate breath.

Her hands trembled so violently she could barely hold the Book, her palms slick with sweat, every muscle in her arms locked and useless. She tightened her grip, desperate not to lose the last tangible sign of hope, but the Bible was heavy and her fingers numb. It slipped from her shaking grasp, and for a split second, horror shot through her—dropping the sacred Word felt like a final, unforgivable failure. She cried out in her mind, the words echoing endlessly in the chamber of her own guilt: *I failed! I failed!* Her voice, in this self-constructed nightmare, was thin and broken, a desperate child's whimper, as she buried her face in her shaking hands. *The shame is real! I am nothing but fear! I am nothing but the system that killed them!*

The cavern spun, swallowing her in a vortex of memory and accusation. The faces of the lost multiplied, crowding her vision until she could no longer see herself as anything but their executioner. Their silent screams filled her mind, each one a testimony against her soul. She tried to pray, but the words dried up, stuck in her throat, choked by the taste of blood and the certainty of her damnation.

In the waking world, Anya stood frozen, unmoving—her body untouched, but her mind utterly consumed by the living nightmare within. She was lost, held captive in the silent torture of her own imagination, paralyzed in a state of suspended animation, unable to reach for hope or to feel the presence of her companions beside her.

Her mind fractured, meaning unraveling, all hope annihilated. She was trapped, helpless, paralyzed in a living nightmare—the Analyst unmasked, the Evangelist exposed as a fraud, her body frozen, her soul locked in a state of suspended animation, unable to move, to speak, or even to hope for mercy. In that moment, Anya's consciousness was nothing but the endless, echoing scream of the condemned.

Azael, standing at the edge of the echoing chamber, noticed the sudden, unnatural silence behind him. There were no cries, no pleading, not even the ragged sound of human breath—just a void where the living should have been. A sick feeling twisted in his chest. He turned slowly, dread mounting, and what he saw rooted him in horror.

Seraphina, Elias, and Anya stood side by side in the darkness, facing nothing, their bodies rigid, their eyes wide open and glassy, mouths agape as if caught mid-scream, but not a sound escaped. Their skin was pallid, almost luminous in the gloom, as if the light itself was being drained from their flesh. They looked as though they were already corpses, preserved in a tableau of terror. The sight was so unnatural, so profoundly wrong, that for a heartbeat, Azael could not comprehend what he was seeing.

And then he saw them—the true threat in the Caverns of Echoed Shame. Crawling from the slick, glistening walls were the spirits that had always been there, hidden in the edges of perception: leech-like creatures, spectral and semi-transparent, their bodies writhing with internal, swirling shadows. They had the faces of lost souls, their mouths full of needle-teeth, their bodies slick with shimmering, viscous darkness. The leeches attached themselves to the frozen forms of Seraphina, Elias, and Anya, latching onto their chests, their necks, and their temples. Azael watched in paralyzed revulsion as the leeches burrowed their faces into the open, silent mouths of his companions, or pressed their translucent bodies against the exposed skin at the throat and wrist, their needle-teeth disappearing beneath the flesh.

He could see, with the vision granted only to the celestials, the slow siphoning of life force—threads of golden light sucked from the core of each victim, pulled greedily into the bellies of the leeches. The more they fed, the more corporeal and bloated they became, their bodies distending grotesquely, their internal shadows writhing with malevolent delight. The walls themselves seemed to pulse in time with the leeches' feeding, as if the entire cavern was alive and complicit in the feast. The air grew colder, thick with the stench of old blood and rotting hope.

Worse still, as the leeches fed on their victims' shame and regret, the physical bodies of Seraphina, Elias, and Anya began to wither. Their skin shrank against their bones, cheeks hollowed, the veins at their temples standing out in ghastly relief. Their hair dulled and thinned, and their hands curled into brittle claws. The light of the Harp, the sheen of the Holy Bible, even the hopeful glimmer in their eyes—every sign of spiritual life—began to flicker and fade. The leeches pulsed in time with each heartbeat, their bodies growing ever more monstrous as they gorged themselves on the lifeblood of hope itself.

Azael staggered back, powerless to reach his friends, his angelic senses overwhelmed by the horror. The walls were crawling with the leech-spirits now, hundreds of them, waiting for any sign of weakness, eager to feed on the next burst of shame. He realized, with a terror deeper than any he had known since the Fall, that if he did not act, the three would be consumed—body, mind, and soul—devoured by the living embodiment of their own condemnation.

Azael's fists clenched at his sides, desperate for a weapon, a word, anything to break the spell. He remembered the promise whispered long ago in the halls of Heaven: No darkness endures forever; grace always finds a way through.

For a breathless moment, he closed his eyes and reached—not with strength, but with a silent, guttural plea—for the light he had once known.

Somewhere in the cavern's darkness, a faint glimmer—no more than a memory—stirred. It was not enough, not yet. But Azael refused to yield, not while hope could still flicker, not while even a single heartbeat remained.

CHAPTER 58

THE HARMONY OF DELIVERANCE

Azael, desperate and trembling, surged forward at last, unable to watch his friends wither away. He looked down at them—Seraphina's hand slack on the Harp, her face ashen; Elias barely breathing, his eyes sunken and distant; Anya's hands empty, the Holy Bible lying just beyond her reach, its light guttering. The sight struck Azael with a wave of terror and grief. For a moment, he faltered, feeling the ache of helplessness, the weight of centuries pressing on his wings. He had never felt so powerless, or so desperate to save those he loved.

As his hand closed around the crystalline frame, the Harp seemed to awaken, its body expanding beneath his touch, strings glowing with pure celestial fire. The instrument vibrated with a power that resonated up Azael's arm and into his core, as if it recognized his need and the gravity of the moment. The entire cavern pulsed with the anticipation of its song. His angelic hand, blazing with the last vestiges of celestial fire, closed around the instrument.

Azael hesitated, the memory of Heaven's choirs flickering at the edge of his mind. He remembered the pure, unbroken harmonies, the music that once shaped worlds and called light out of darkness. For a heartbeat, doubt threatened to root him in place. But then he shut his eyes and reached inward, whispering a silent plea for grace and strength. If ever there was a moment for deliverance, it was now. With a prayer—"O Lord, open thou my lips; and my mouth shall shew forth thy praise" (Psalm 51:15 KJV)—he drew the strings in a great, sweeping arc, unleashing a sound that was not mere music but the voice

99

of creation itself. The Harp's resonance was a pure, harmonic beauty, a melody of unearned grace and restoration that filled the cavern like blue fire.

As the first notes rang out, the spirits clinging to the walls, the leech-creatures feasting on shame and regret, shrieked in agony. Their forms writhed, their needle-teeth losing hold, as the sound drove them from the walls and the flesh of Seraphina, Elias, and Anya. The melody was not violent; it was absolute order, the beauty of completeness—"For God is not the author of confusion, but of peace" (1 Corinthians 14:33 KJV). The leeches, unable to withstand the harmony, erupted in bursts of shadow and vanished into the cavern's cracks, taking the stench of death and despair with them.

Seraphina, still locked in her inner battle, felt the song pierce the darkness in her mind. In the lowest, echoing chamber of her spirit, another frequency emerged—a current not of her making. She remembered the quiet, unearned grace given to her, a mercy that did not demand symmetry or effort. Instead of yielding to the engineered shame, she imagined pressing her trembling fingers to the Harp. Blue light flared from her finger tips with a sudden, fierce pulse, not of performance or perfection, but of defiance born of grace. The resonance grew, not to drown out the accusations, but to answer them—a sound that said: I see the lie. I see the evil I have done, and I do not deny it. But I choose the truth of forgiveness over the paralysis of guilt.

Scripture rang through her mind: "There is therefore now no condemnation to them which are in Christ Jesus, who walk not after the flesh, but after the Spirit" (Romans 8:1 KJV). Her mind cleared, the shame not erased but reframed by the knowledge that worth was never earned by her hands—not by symmetry, not by beauty, not by the number of souls comforted or manipulated. She would not be bound again by the tyranny of self-justification. Her fingers blue light grew stronger, pulsing in defiance, its resonance fighting back the shadows with every illuminated note. In that moment, Seraphina remembered her true gift: not to make the world safe for the system, but to make the world ready for grace.

For Elias, the music was a lifeline in the storm. He heard the melody break through the psychic paralysis, cutting through the suffocating weight of regret and pride. As the sound washed over him, he found the courage to surrender his conviction—to lay down the burden of self-justification and accept grace. "For by grace are ye saved through faith; and that not of yourselves: it is the gift of God: Not of works, lest any man should boast" (Ephesians 2:8-9 KJV). The past could not be redeemed by intellect alone, but only by surrender. He felt his body loosen, the leeches falling away, the withering halted. He stood, his eyes filling with tears, and joined the harmony, quoting: "He brought me up also out of a horrible pit, out of the miry clay, and set my feet upon a rock, and established my goings" (Psalm 40:2 KJV).

Anya, lost in the labyrinth of her shame, saw the blue light and heard the Word resonating in the song. Though the Holy Bible lay on the ground beyond her reach, in the sanctuary of her mind she clung to it still—her fingers numb, her spirit desperate for hope. As the leeches recoiled from her, she heard the voice of Christ: "If we confess our sins, he is faithful and just to forgive us our sins, and to cleanse us from all unrighteousness" (1 John 1:9 KJV). Grace overwhelmed her, a torrent that washed away the crushing guilt, restoring her strength.

In her internal vision, Anya imagined herself rising to her feet. No longer the quiet follower, but the Evangelist—her shame transformed into testimony, her silence into proclamation. She stood tall in the chamber of her soul, facing the accusing shadows, and lifted the Holy Bible high, her voice no longer trembling but resolute and clear. She declared: "For I am persuaded, that neither death, nor life, nor angels, nor principalities, nor powers, nor things present, nor things to come... shall be able to separate us from the love of God, which is in Christ Jesus our Lord" (Romans 8:38-39 KJV).

As the last strains of angelic harmony from the Harp faded, time itself seemed to stand still in the cavern. For a moment, there was only silence—then, slowly, the three architects began to return to themselves. First came a flutter of eyelashes, then a faint, shuddering breath, as if their souls were re-entering their bodies after having teetered on the edge of oblivion. Their limbs trembled with weakness, and their eyes—once wide and vacant—blinked in confusion and pain, struggling to adjust to the dim blue glow that pulsed from the Harp and the sudden, fierce light radiating from the Holy Bible in Anya's hands.

Their bodies felt impossibly heavy, wracked with the lingering ache of spiritual and physical depletion. Seraphina tried to reach for Elias, but her arm moved as if underwater—her muscles barely responding after being so close to death. Elias found himself on his knees, his breath ragged, sweat beading his brow and mingling with tears of exhaustion.

Anya blinked, disoriented, and saw the Holy Bible lying just out of reach on the dusty ground. Summoning what little strength she had left, she leaned forward, her arms trembling as she stretched for it. Her fingers brushed the cover, but her body gave out and she began to collapse.

Azael was there in an instant. With the golden Harp balanced securely in one hand, he reached down with the other and gently caught Anya before she could fall. In the same motion, he scooped up the Bible, placing it firmly in her grasp. Then, powerful and steady, he moved among them, gathering their fragile bodies and supporting their weight with ease. His arms encircled all three, the angel's supernatural strength holding them upright. He whispered words of comfort—soft and deep, like the low hum of a thousand prayers—anchoring them in the peace that followed deliverance.

As the team staggered toward the cavern's exit, the blue-white light of the Harp and the fierce, holy fire of the Bible grew brighter. The Book itself glowed with a radiant heat, sending a ripple of protective energy through the air. The spirits and leech-creatures that had once covered the walls shrieked and dissolved, unable to endure the sanctified brilliance. Yet thousands more lingered in the shadows, clustering in the cracks and crevices, their bodies tensed and waiting—hungry for any flicker of weakness. Where the Bible's light touched, the stone walls became clean and warm, and every step the team took was bathed in a shield of grace. The glow burned any leech that dared approach, forcing the creatures to retreat, writhing and hissing back into the darkness.

Each of them felt the aftershocks of their ordeal: their legs trembled, their hands shook with lingering terror, and their lungs burned as if they'd been running for miles. Their minds reeled from the psychic onslaught, replaying the echoes of accusation and shame. Yet, through the weariness, a profound sense of freedom and newness settled over them: the weight of self-condemnation was gone, replaced by the sustaining power of grace alone.

They could barely speak, every step a test of will. As they neared the cavern's mouth, Seraphina whispered, barely audible, "He restoreth my soul…," the words tumbling out more like a prayer than a quotation.

Elias, leaning on her shoulder, managed, "God is the strength of my heart…" His voice broke, but the words held.

Anya lips moving soundlessly. Only a few words escaped: "The Lord is my light…" She closed her eyes, letting the comfort of that truth settle over her.

The rest was silence, heavy with gratitude and relief. The ancient promises lingered between them, not as recitations, but as fragments of hope—half-remembered, wholly felt—guiding them out of darkness and into the waiting dawn.

At the threshold, their battered forms nearly gave out. They leaned heavily on one another, and on Azael, who half-carried them just beyond the reach of the leeches lurking in the cavern shadows. As they emerged, the blue-white light from the Harp and the blazing glow from the Bible wrapped them in a shimmering shield—a visible covenant of protection. Their journey through shame and darkness had left them scarred, but not broken. For a long moment, they collapsed together on the rocky ground at the cavern's mouth, breathing in the scent of rain and new hope, the leeches watching them hungrily from the darkness, unable to cross into the light.

For a time, they simply lay there, shivering and breathless, too weak to move yet too grateful to sleep. The rocky ground pressed cool against their backs, and the air was tinged with the fading scent of ozone and grace. Seraphina reached out, her fingers brushing Elias's hand, while Anya curled on her side, clutching the recovered Bible to her chest. Azael, kneeling nearby with the Harp resting across his lap, watched over them, his wings half-raised in silent vigilance.

In the hush that followed, the music of the Harp and the gentle glow of the Bible lingered around them, wrapping them in warmth and quiet strength. Yet even as relief settled in, the battered group was keenly aware that this realm was unpredictable and dangerous—no matter how peaceful the path might seem, peril could return at any moment.

CHAPTER 59

VEIL OF CRYSTALLINE MERCY

As the first faint light of dawn crept through the cavern's mouth and the leeches finally retreated into the shadows, Azael rose. Moving quietly, he gathered Seraphina, Elias, and Anya—carrying them one by one, with the Harp and Bible secure in his arms. He brought them a short distance from the cavern's threshold, leaving shimmering footprints in the unfamiliar, inviting grass.

There, beneath the pale, uncertain sky, he gently lowered Seraphina, Elias, and Anya onto the living tapestry underfoot—each slender blade of grass glowing faintly from within, its colors shifting with every breath of wind. The ground was strangely soft, almost yielding, and made a faint crystalline chime when touched, as if singing a lullaby of recovery. With care, Azael set the Harp beside Seraphina and placed the Bible within easy reach of Anya, the sacred objects pulsing softly in the grass.

Before settling himself, Azael knelt to inspect their surroundings, running his fingers through the luminous filaments and examining the fruit-laden bushes nearby. He sniffed the air, alert for any trace of corruption or hidden threat. The scent and structure of the grass stirred memories from before the Fall—a time when the Creator's hand shaped every blade, every leaf, every fruit with purpose and care. The filaments and fruit here echoed that original design, untouched by the corruption that plagued so much of this realm. Satisfied, Azael recognized this place as a rare sanctuary: a pocket of creation preserved, a haven where no shadow or poison could reach.

When Azael knelt to arrange his companions, the grass bent beneath them without breaking, cushioning their battered bodies. The filaments curled delicately around their limbs as if to cradle them, absorbing tears and sweat alike. Here, the ground itself seemed to participate in their healing, humming with a restorative undercurrent. And yet, beneath the beauty, there was an uncanny sense of watchfulness—a subtle reminder that even this sanctuary was part of a living, sentient world, ancient and wise, but not entirely safe.

Azael stood watch, his wings arched protectively around them. He murmured prayers over each, his voice a soft balm, blending ancient languages with the words of scripture: "He giveth power to the faint; and to them that have no might he increaseth strength" (Isaiah 40:29 KJV). He fetched fragments of luminous fruit from low, crystalline bushes that bordered the shimmering field. The flesh was cool and sweet, pulsing with gentle light, and as he pressed it into their hands, a quiet warmth spread through their bodies, restoring a measure of their strength. Only after repeated urging did they nibble, the simple food reminding them they still belonged to life.

Seraphina's fingers, curled around the Harp, twitched as if seeking a melody in her dreams. Elias, tears tracing lines through the grime on his cheeks, whispered half-formed prayers as his mind still sifted through the wreckage of regret and grace. Anya clung to the Bible, its glow now faded to a gentle warmth, her lips moving in silent verses, eyes closed as if listening for an answer.

Time passed without measure. The sun crept across the sky, shadows lengthening and then retreating. Slowly, color returned to their cheeks, their breathing steadied, and a fragile peace settled over the battered company. They said little, too drained for conversation, leaning on one another in quiet solidarity.

At first, nothing seemed to change. But as the fruit's gentle warmth spread through their limbs and the minutes slipped by, the signs of death and depletion began to reverse.

Azael watched over them, his gaze turning to the source of the miraculous restoration—a tree he had not seen since the dawn of the world. The sight stirred memories buried deep within his immortal soul. He remembered the moment God spoke this species into being, long before the Flood, in the time when the earth was whole and every living thing was a symphony of purpose. In those days, the tree had grown along riverbanks in the First Garden, a living testament to the Creator's artistry.

The trunk coiled upward in a spiraling lattice of silvery blue and deep gold, each band glowing with an inner luminescence that waxed and waned in harmony with the light of day. The bark was smooth as river stone, but beneath his hand, Azael could feel a living pulse—like the heartbeat of the world itself. Branches arched high above, each one bearing dozens of radiant fruits. The fruits themselves glowed from within, their skins shifting in color from pearl to amber to a translucent green, as if capturing the changing moods of the sky.

The leaves were a marvel—broad and paper-thin, veined with rivers of emerald, violet, and indigo. With every breath of wind, the colors flowed and mingled like watercolor on glass. Along the leaf edges, nectar gathered in trembling droplets, iridescent and glimmering, catching the faintest light and scattering it in shards of color. When the sun's rays touched the crown, the whole tree sang with a crystalline hum—a resonance Azael remembered from the first morning of creation, when the heavens and earth harmonized in praise.

He marveled that one of these trees had survived the ages—hidden, preserved by divine will in this sanctuary untouched by corruption. The fruit was not just nourishment, but a remnant of Eden's healing, a taste of the world as it had been intended.

As the fruit's power worked through their bodies, Azael watched the transformation unfold. Color slowly returned to their cheeks; skin that had shriveled and gone sallow grew supple again, the deep hollows in their faces filling out. Hair, once dulled and thinned by despair, regained its luster, and their hands uncurled, the brittle claws softening back into fingers. The light in their eyes, so recently extinguished, flickered and then brightened, as if hope itself had been poured back into their veins. The transformation was gradual, quiet, but as the sun traced its path overhead, Seraphina, Elias, and Anya became recognizably themselves once more.

Azael bowed his head, humbled to witness again the mercy and artistry of the Creator—a reminder that even in the most wounded places, God's original beauty and healing could still break through.

For a long while, the only sound was the crystalline lull of the living grass, but eventually Seraphina was the first to break the stillness, her voice small and shaking as she let out a gentle, incredulous laugh. "We made it," she said, her words drifting upward like the motes of pollen, at first barely more than a whisper. "I don't understand how, but we're here."

Elias let out a long, tremulous breath, his shoulders sagging as if a thousand invisible burdens had suddenly fallen away. "I thought we'd be lost forever in those caverns. I thought—" His voice broke, and he shook his head, covering his face with his hands. "I can't believe we survived."

Anya, still clutching the Bible, gave a soft, almost giddy sob. "We should be dead. After all that—the shame, the leeches, everything—how did we even get out? I keep waiting for it to start again."

Azael offered a tired but genuine smile, kneeling down beside them. "Grace does not calculate odds," he murmured. "It only gives enough for the next moment. We are here because the Creator willed it—not because we were strong enough, but because we surrendered our weakness."

For a moment, the relief was so acute it was almost a pain. Seraphina wiped her face, tears and remnants of grime mingling on her cheeks. She looked at Elias and Anya, her eyes wide with the wild, disbelieving joy of the truly reprieved. "We're together. That's all that matters."

But as the hush settled, a realization flickered between them—a dawning horror mingled with awe. Seraphina's breath hitched. "Wait," she whispered, almost afraid of the words. "The mire, the leeches, the silence... it wasn't random. Every time we faced certain death, every time we broke and bled and almost lost ourselves, it was a trial. Not just a danger. Not just survival. A test. Every time, we were being weighed."

Elias exhaled shakily, the full force of recognition pulling him to his feet. "That's it. Each time we barely survived, it wasn't just bad luck. It was a trial—a crucible we had to pass. There's a pattern. Each ordeal is designed to break us down, force us to choose: to trust, to surrender, to endure. We've been walking from trial to trial, not just from one disaster to the next."

Anya's eyes filled with a mixture of dread and clarity. She clung to the Bible, her voice trembling but clear. "That's why it feels like we're being stripped to nothing. It's not just pain—it's the deliberate removal of every defense, every illusion. Until only faith remains. Until only grace can rebuild what's left."

A hush fell, heavy and holy. Azael bowed his head, the gravity of their insight reflected in the solemn set of his face. "Now you see the architecture of this journey. The Creator allows the adversary to test you, not to destroy but to refine. These are the trials spoken of since ancient days: the fire that proves the gold, the burden that reveals the source of strength."

He extended his hands over them, intoning words from scripture—first in a whisper, then gathering strength:

"Beloved, think it not strange concerning the fiery trial which is to try you, as though some strange thing happened unto you: But rejoice, inasmuch as ye are partakers of Christ's sufferings" (1 Peter 4:12–13 KJV).

Seraphina, still trembling, echoed the truth, her voice small but steady: "Many are the afflictions of the righteous: but the Lord delivereth him out of them all" (Psalm 34:19 KJV).

Azael looked at each of them, his gaze steady and full of conviction. "You are not meant to bear more than you can endure. That is the promise that stands even in this place. For it is written: 'There hath no temptation taken you but such as is common to man: but God is faithful, who will not suffer you to be tempted above that ye are able; but will with the temptation also make a way to escape, that ye may be able to bear it' (1 Corinthians 10:13 KJV)."

The realization burned in the air around them—a moment of fearful, holy clarity. The trials would come again, harder than before, but now they knew their suffering was not meaningless. They braced themselves, drawing on the promises of scripture, the memory of deliverance, and the fragile, hard-won hope that grace would always be enough.

They huddled a little closer together, letting the strange sanctuary cradle them as their relief mingled with something darker—a growing dread of what lay ahead. The beauty of the sanctuary was a balm, but also a reminder that their reprieve was only temporary. The shadow of what was to come pressed at the edge of their relief, and in the fragile quiet, each of them felt the cracks begin to show.

At last, when their strength barely sufficed, the team rose and prepared to move forward. The luminous grass—those ethereal, glass-like filaments— unfurled from around their limbs, releasing them gently. The path ahead was no longer the hard, echoing stone of the cavern but a living, undulating trail, paved with shifting bands of radiant color. With every step, the ground chimed with a crystalline melody, and motes of bioluminescent pollen drifted skyward like silent prayers.

But as they walked, the cost of survival became excruciatingly clear. Seraphina stumbled, her knees buckling. "I can't—" she gasped, her breath coming in ragged sobs. "I can't keep pretending this isn't breaking me. Every trial is worse than the last. I don't know who I am anymore when everything good is being stripped away."

Elias steadied her, his own voice choked and raw. "I feel it too. I thought after the swamp, after the shame, that nothing could touch me again. But now...it's as if each step is heavier than the last. I'm scared, Sera. I keep thinking the next trial will be the one that finally finishes us."

Anya, her face pale and drawn, squeezed Seraphina's hand. "We keep telling ourselves that grace is enough, and maybe it is. But what happens when there's nothing left to surrender? What if we reach the end and there's just... emptiness?"

Azael walked close beside them, his expression somber. "That is the deception of the journey: that weakness means defeat. But weakness is the only doorway to true strength. You are not less for being broken. You are closer to the truth."

Their honesty hung in the air, heavy and sacred. The sanctuary had given relief, but as they pressed on, it became a liminal space between survival and surrender. Tears and prayers mingled with the music of the grass, and for a time, they allowed themselves to weep—not only in relief, but in mourning for the selves they had lost and the innocence that could never return.

Their bodies trembled from exhaustion, the ache of depletion a constant reminder of how narrowly they had escaped. Even so, the blue-white glow of the Harp and the fierce, steady light of the Bible in Anya's hands formed a shield, warding off the last traces of spiritual predation. Azael, vigilant and determined, moved close, lending a steady arm whenever one of them stumbled.

And yet, as they left the Caverns of Echoed Shame, none of them noticed the subtle, shifting darkness that slipped from the mouth of the cavern—a shadow without shape, following at a distance just beyond their senses. Unbeknownst to the weary travelers, the shadow had always been there. From the moment they first crossed into this realm, it had lingered at the very edge of the light—waiting, watching, learning the rhythm of their fears and hopes. It crept along the cavern walls, silent as breath, content to remain unseen so long as their strength held. But it was never far—never gone. Patient and silent, it lingered now at the border of the sanctuary, its hunger undiminished, biding its time for the first sign of weakness, waiting for the moment their newfound peace might falter.

The team pressed on—battered, scarred, but together. Though their strength was not fully restored, the grace surrounding them was enough to carry them forward in this fragile peace. The alien grass whispered beneath their feet and the sky shifted with strange, restless light above.

They crossed the threshold of the sanctuary with a sense of both dread and resolve, the memory of their recent deliverance still burning in their minds. The world around them seemed to pause—a moment suspended between the ache of the trials behind and the unknown terrors ahead. A last breath of the crystalline air, a final glance at the living tapestry of light behind them, and then, one by one, they stepped through a shimmering veil that bisected the landscape: the boundary of the next ordeal. In that instant, the gentle harmonies of the sanctuary faded, replaced by a tension in the very air—a warning that the peace they carried was not a guarantee, but a precious, fragile gift bought with suffering.

Their journey had taught them that every trial was a crucible, not a curse—a necessary passage to reveal what could be refined and what must be surrendered. Each step forward was now a deliberate act of faith, a quiet defiance that their weakness was not failure, but a doorway to strength beyond their own: "My flesh and my heart faileth: but God is the strength of my heart, and my portion for ever" (Psalm 73:26 KJV). With this promise echoing in their hearts, they pressed on—shadow trailing just behind, the hope of deliverance shining before them. And always, through every stage of hardship and renewal, the Nexus of Discord loomed nearer on the horizon, its fractured light pulsing in the distance—a constant reminder that the heart of their journey, and its final reckoning, was drawing ever closer.

CHAPTER 60

THE SWEETEST SIN

The transition was not just abrupt—it was a sensory ambush. For Seraphina, the world inverted under her feet: the crystalline grass and gentle harmonics of that fragile haven fell away, replaced by a riot of sensation that struck her like a physical blow. The ground beneath them squelched with a syrupy resonance, every footfall a sticky note in a symphony of excess. The air pressed in close, humid and sweet, clinging to her skin like a velvet glove, perfumed with a heady blend of burnt sugar, cinnamon, and something artificial—an uncanny, almost narcotic vanilla that seemed to bypass her mind entirely and go straight to her bloodstream.

Light itself became an assault. Neon pinks, acid oranges, and electric greens bombarded her vision, refracting through clouds of candied mist that shimmered like spun glass. Each ray felt less like illumination and more like a vibrating chord, a frequency meant to overwhelm rather than reveal. The sky was a swirling, living fresco of carnival colors—clouds shaped like melting confections, their edges humming faintly with the promise of sensory reward. Every surface glistened, lacquered with syrup, reflecting back a thousand shades at once, a visual fugue that refused to resolve.

Seraphina's senses were immediately hijacked. The city's air was thick—so thick she could taste the sweetness in each breath, each molecule a granular note of pleasure and threat. The scents were layered: spun sugar at the surface, but beneath it a sharp, spicy cinnamon, a creamy synthetic vanilla, and a burnt caramel undertone that hovered between bliss and nausea. Even the undercurrent of fried dough and molten chocolate felt engineered to bypass restraint, to make her forget the clean, spare air of the world they'd just left. Every inhalation was a command to indulge.

The soundscape was equally intoxicating and destabilizing. Carousel music spun, its melody laced with a dissonant undertone that set her teeth on edge. Laughter, bells, the syncopated pop of bursting sugar bubbles—each note was tuned to trigger delight, but beneath it seethed a feverish instability. The city itself seemed to hum in counterpoint to her heartbeat, a hypnotic invitation to surrender.

She blinked, momentarily dizzy, her senses tumbling over one another. The colors in the air felt like they were brushing her skin; the music vibrated in her bones. Texture, sound, scent, and color blurred into a synesthetic tide. For an instant, she wanted to laugh—then to cry—then to simply give in and let the sensations carry her wherever they wished.

"Is anyone else…?" she started, her voice trembling with awe and apprehension as she gazed at the impossible sky. "Does it feel like we've stepped into a hallucination? I can't tell if I want to run or just… dissolve."

Elias pressed his boot experimentally into the chocolate pavement, watching it yield and spring back. "It's like a festival dream—everything is designed for pleasure, but none of it feels earned. It's so easy to forget where we came from."

Anya, clutching the Bible to her chest, looked pale and uncertain. "Every sense is a weapon here. It's all engineered to erase the memory of struggle. Even the music—it's too perfect. I can almost feel my resolve softening."

Seraphina breathed in deeply, the sweetness tingling in her nose, her mind swimming with the urge to let the city's pleasure wash over her. "If I let go— just for a moment—I think I'd lose myself. Maybe that's the point. Maybe that's why it terrifies me."

Azael's presence anchored them, his gaze scanning the hyper-sensory landscape. "That is the danger: not suffering, but the invitation to forget suffering's lesson. This city is a narcotic for the soul, a false Sabbath dressed as delight. Every sweetness is a bid for your very memory."

Elias nodded, the gravity of the moment settling over him. "It's not pain we have to fear anymore. It's the seduction of forgetting what pain taught us— forgetting why we journeyed through darkness to begin with."

It dawned on all of them: the threat here was not harm, but the gentle, overwhelming pressure to surrender vigilance for delight, to let the harmony of sensation erase the memory of every hardship overcome. The City of Gilded Consumption was a living engine of excess, a metropolis where indulgence was not a luxury, but a law—a place designed not to destroy the soul, but to lull it into contented surrender, one exquisite sensation at a time.

The Edible City

The City was more than just a gaudy spectacle—it was a sensory gauntlet, an assault and a seduction aimed directly at the soul of someone like Seraphina, crafted to unravel an Aesthetic Synthesis from the inside out. Every step on the sticky, dark chocolate streets triggered a ripple of sensation up her legs; the ground was pliant, yielding, with a subtle warmth—chocolate so rich and fragrant she could feel its heaviness on her tongue just by breathing. The buildings soared overhead, not as lifeless blocks of function, but as impossible towers of taffy and spun sugar, their colors swirling in impossible gradients that sang with visual discord. Sunlight fractured through a haze of syrupy neon, turning the air into a living prism that seemed to hum, the light itself sticky and slow.

Elias commented, but Seraphina barely heard him. Her focus was flooded by the saturated palette, the taste of burnt sugar and vanilla thick as velvet in her nose. Every color was a chord, every shadow a counterpoint. She reached out, trailing her fingers along the edge of a candy-cane balustrade—the surface was cool, glassy, but as her skin slid over it, the faintest vibration thrummed beneath her touch, like a harp string plucked in a distant room. The air was saturated with the scent of cinnamon, caramel, and something floral, almost narcotic. It was a perfume meant to bypass thought and go straight to longing.

She stopped in the middle of the avenue, eyes wide, chest rising and falling as if she'd just run a race. "It's not just color," she whispered, her voice barely audible over the distant calliope music. "It's a chord. It's a living harmony that wants to resonate inside me."

A passing train of Gummy Guardians bounced by, their translucent red bodies pulsing with inner light in time to the beat of an invisible drum. Their laughter was a cloud of fizzy citrus, a tickle in the back of her throat. She could taste it. She could hear it. She could feel it in the soles of her feet.

A cathedral loomed in the distance: gingerbread, but not crude or childish. Its walls shimmered with crystalline sugar, refracting the light into a thousand rainbows that painted the air itself with shifting, edible color. The stained-glass windows were mosaics of hard candy; every note of light was a different flavor—a spectrum that tasted of nostalgia, longing, and the ache of beauty too intense to bear. Seraphina nearly wept. "This is temptation," she murmured, "but not fear. It's hunger. It's beauty dialed up until it becomes pain."

With every breath, every step, the City pressed closer, its chorus of pleasure swelling. Laughter spun like spun sugar, the sharp crackle of caramel fractured the air, and the distant carousel music laced the atmosphere with both anticipation and ache. Seraphina was dizzy, almost feverish, her fingers tingling with the urge to touch, to taste, to let the colors and sounds and scents pour straight into her soul. She pressed a hand to her chest, feeling her heart race, overwhelmed not by the logic of the City, but by the sheer, orchestrated intensity of sensation.

Elias's words about satisfaction and need barely registered. Seraphina's mind was filled with the music of the City—a relentless, synesthetic symphony engineered to bypass desire and go straight to fulfillment. The world became viscous, unreal, every sense turned up to eleven, every color and sound and taste layered with the next, until she could no longer tell where beauty ended and craving began.

Mirrors and polished surfaces lined every street and façade, catching reflections of Seraphina's face and multiplying them in dizzying, impossible angles. The city itself seemed to pulse with hidden rhythms: neon lights flickered in time with her heartbeat, and distant, layered melodies threaded through the air, coaxing emotion and memory to the surface. Everywhere she turned, advertisements and holographic visions shimmered just out of reach, whispering promises and temptations that felt oddly personal. She moved through a labyrinth of sensation where the boundaries between self and spectacle blurred, as if the city itself was watching her, learning her desires, and answering them with a thousand seductive distractions.

Azael's form shimmered into her field of view, and even he was not immune. His wings warped, turning from awe-inspiring to absurd, rendered in glossy, pastel candy colors. For an instant, Seraphina saw him as a living sculpture, a parody of divinity sculpted from the raw materials of delight and excess. His voice, when it came, was slow and sweet, sticky with warning, but the words themselves seemed to dissolve on her skin, replaced by the echo of pleasure and the promise of surrender.

Seraphina shivered, suddenly aware of the danger—not of logic lost, but of beauty weaponized. "He's changing," she whispered, her own voice sounding distant, as if it were being carried on the melody of the City itself. "We can't trust our senses here. Not sight, not sound, not even touch. The City is trying to consume us through delight."

All around her, the world breathed with anticipation—a living, humming, radiant trap for the soul that hungered to feel, to taste, to belong to beauty for its own sake. And Seraphina, Aesthetic Synthesis, stood trembling on the edge, overwhelmed by the possibility of surrendering to sensation forever.

The Candy-Folk

Elias and the team were immediately overwhelmed, not just by the garish architecture, but by the bizarre, living inhabitants. The streets pulsed with the movement of Candy-Folk, beings of pure, solidified indulgence whose existence was a constant spectacle of excess. Their arrival did not go unnoticed: as soon as they stepped into the open, a hundred glossy eyes and luminous faces turned, curiosity and hunger mingling in every candied gaze. Their presence was like a drop of ink in a glass of water—the city's rhythm shifted, its denizens drawn to this new, unoptimized anomaly.

Caramel Constables stood on corners, their bodies glistening, viscous pillars of melted caramel that occasionally oozed into the chocolate streets. One-eyed the newcomers, a slow grin spreading across its syrupy face. "Visitors," it intoned, voice thick and lazy as molasses. "Not often do we see new flavors."

The Lollipop Ladies, faces swirling with hypnotic color, moved with a brittle, unnerving grace, joints crackling like brittle glass. Their presence felt like a chorus of music and color. One drifted close to Seraphina, her voice crystalline—a single, high note that seemed to vibrate in the air. "You look tired, dear. Have you tried the spun-joy? It makes every care dissolve. Every ache, every worry—gone, like sugar on the tongue. Just let the sweetness melt."

Seraphina was immediately assaulted by a tide of sensation. The world was a kaleidoscope: Every step sent a ripple of pastel light through the candy streets. The air vibrated with an undercurrent of calliope music, each note a different flavor. A scent of spun sugar and candied violets wrapped around her, the melody of the Lollipop Lady threading through her mind. The offer was not logical, not even rational—it was a pure, sensorial invitation. She heard a chorus of syrupy voices from the crowd: "Come, feel the velvet air! Taste the pink rain! Touch the clouds—soft as dreams!"

A Lemon Drop Dandy danced nearby, flicking crystalline sugar dust into the air. "You are dry and brittle, little artist. When was the last time you let go of the grey?" he sang, his words fizzing on Seraphina's skin like Pop Rocks. "Let the City color you in."

A Gummy Guardian bounced past, its translucent body pulsing with inner light, sending a resonant hum through the ground. The largest paused, peering at Elias. "Don't be shy," it called, the words bubbling like soda. "The City of Gilded Consumption welcomes all who crave."

Seraphina pressed closer to Elias and Anya, her senses nearly overwhelmed. She whispered, "They're watching us. I feel like a treat on display." But even as she spoke, her mind reeled from the sensory onslaught: the symphony of sweet smells, the radiant warmth of sugar lights, the way every surface seemed to vibrate with the promise of pleasure.

A Lollipop Lady leaned even closer, her eyes swirling hypnotically. She traced a gloved finger through the air, leaving a trail of scent that was equal parts rosewater and nostalgia. "You don't have to work for delight here, sweetheart. Just let it in. Let yourself dissolve into the music of the city."

Seraphina felt the words as texture, not argument—the velvet of the Lady's voice, the soft brush of a sugar-gloved hand, the phantom taste of candied air on her tongue. For a terrifying moment, she wanted to surrender: to lose herself in the synesthetic tide, to let the city's pleasure swallow her whole. Her fingers twitched, aching to touch, to taste, to hear every color.

Elias scanned the crowd, unease sharpening his features. "They don't see us as travelers. We're ingredients. Or new consumers."

A small, gelatinous creature, its body shimmering with a grotesque layer of white royal icing, scuttled toward Anya, leaving a trail of sparkling residue—a scent of intense, synthetic strawberry. It offered her a piece of jagged, multifaceted crystallized rock candy. "Just a taste," it whispered, its voice sounding exactly like the sharp, abrasive crunch of sugar being chewed. "It is the Sweetest Sin. It offers a peace beyond optimization."

Anya recoiled, clutching her Bible. "Peace beyond optimization? At what cost?"

The creature's eyes flashed with sly delight. "Only the cost of memory. Indulgence is the only truth here."

Azael stepped forward, his form flickering with restrained power, and fixed the Candy-Folk with a warning glare. "We are not here to consume or be consumed. Stand back."

A ripple of nervous laughter passed among the Candy-Folk, the crowd parting but never quite dispersing, their attention fixed hungrily on the newcomers. The City itself seemed to lean in, eager to see which of them would give in first.

The Corruption of Logic

The moment Anya hesitated, the Candy-Folk seemed to sense her wavering logic. Around her, the crowd pressed closer, their voices a chorus of tempting, saccharine whispers.

A syrupy Caramel Constable leaned in, its badge glinting. "Go on, Analyst," it urged, voice thick as honey. "Let your curiosity taste what calculation cannot. Only the bold discover new flavors."

A Lollipop Lady with swirling, hypnotic eyes sidled up on her other side, tapping her crystalline cane. "No charts here, darling. Just pleasure."

Anya's Chief Analyst mind, so used to the City's bland, nutrient paste, began running diagnostics. Is this toxic? Is the sugar-to-mass ratio justifiable? But the Candy-Folk crowded her with their sticky logic:

"Try it!" chirped a Gumdrop Child, holding up a glistening, neon-blue shard. "You'll never know until you do!"

She glanced at Elias and Seraphina for help, but the air itself was playing tricks on her senses—colors blurred, scents sweetened, and even the voices of her friends seemed distant and distorted. When she looked for Azael, she saw only a shimmering mirage: his familiar form now appeared as a glossy, fruit-colored figure, indistinguishable from the rest of the Candy-Folk. Anya blinked hard, realizing with a jolt that it was only an illusion—the air was warping reality, making it impossible to trust what she saw or felt. Her internal systems for parsing the world offered no defense; her scientific mandate to investigate the unknown was being hijacked by the city's relentless, syrupy persuasion.

No! A thin voice of caution whispered in her soul. This is Chaos. This is the Enemy's design.

But her analytical mind, starved of truly complex sensory input, betrayed her. *A chemical compound this intense, this foreign—it is a variable that must be cataloged,* she rationalized, echoing the voices swirling around her. Indulgence as Research. Consumption as Data Acquisition. The Candy-Folk cheered her on, their voices overlapping:

"Just a taste!"

"Just a taste!"

Her trembling fingers took the crystal. The Gummy Child grinned, its eyes shining with anticipation. Anya touched the fragment to her tongue—not to eat, just to register the input, she told herself.

The sensation was immediate and overwhelming. The moment her tongue touched the candy-colored crystal, her pupils blew wide, eyes dilating as if her mind was thrown open. The shock was both physical and spiritual—a lightning bolt of pure, unearned data. The sweetness was a perfect, blinding frequency, bypassing all logic and firing directly into the reward centers of her mind. All around her, the Candy-Folk erupted in delighted giggles.

"It is... a lie of complexity," she gasped, clutching her chest. "The sweetness is a perfect frequency, Elias. It bypasses all need for logic! It's the ultimate, addictive algorithm of satisfaction." The craving was so immediate and overwhelming that her analytical mind instantly re-optimized to a new goal: repeat the blissful input. The question shifted from *Is this dangerous?* to *How do I achieve maximum saturation?* Her fingers reached for more, snatching the entire piece from the Gummy Child, driven by a data hunger she couldn't control. The analyst was now the consumer, and the crowd cheered her surrender.

"That's it!" the Caramel Constable cried. "No calculations, only craving!"

Anya's vision blurred at the edges—she could just make out Seraphina drifting toward a swirl of pastel lights, her hands raised as if reaching for a melody only she could hear. Elias, meanwhile, was surrounded by a cluster of cube-shaped creatures, their voices enticing him with promises of hidden knowledge. Somewhere behind them, Azael's form shimmered at the periphery, his mouth moving in silent warning, but the city's thick, perfumed air swallowed his words before they could reach her.

Seraphina, watching Anya slip under, felt her own willpower begin to fracture. The world around her became a lush hallucination of color and texture: ribbons of pastel light, the sparkle of sugar dust, a low, choral hum like wind through crystal chimes. The Candy-Folk sensed her unique vulnerability—not to logic, but to sensation—and converged in a synesthetic parade.

A Lollipop Lady spun before her, the rainbow swirl of her face rippling and shifting hypnotically. She extended a sphere of spun sugar, the surface so iridescent it seemed to sing with color. "You look so tired, dear. Why not let go? Taste the peace you've earned. Let the music play for you, not from you."

A cloud of pink cotton candy floated close, its movement impossibly soft, trailing a scent of rosewater and vanilla. Its voice was a tapestry of whispers— silk against skin, the faintest brush of flutes and harps. "No more striving for the perfect chord, the perfect form," it sighed. "You are worthy of pleasure. Let your senses have their Sabbath. Rest in sweetness."

More Candy-Folk drifted in, each a living embodiment of sensory temptation. A Marzipan Maestro flicked its almond-dusted fingers, sending a cascade of sparkling, musical notes through the air. "You've woven beauty for the City all your life. Now let beauty comfort you. Lie back and let the world sing to you for once, Seraphina."

Seraphina's world became a rush of synesthetic overload. She could feel the music in the air—a harmony of colors, a melody of scent, a tactile rhythm on her skin. Every detail was heightened: the velvet texture of the spun sugar, the way the scents seemed to paint stories across her mind, the delicate fizz of sugar dissolving on the air like distant applause.

Her exhaustion—deeper than body or mind—was a craving for wordless beauty, not equations. She reached out, almost involuntarily, and took the pink confection from the cotton candy creature. The texture was impossibly soft, dissolving the moment it touched her tongue. A wave of sensation washed over her—warmth, softness, luminous pink light behind her eyes, a resonance in her bones as if every note she'd ever longed to play was finally being played for her. A chorus of Candy-Folk pressed closer, their voices overlapping in a lulling, narcotic symphony:

"Rest, Artist. The world is already beautiful." "Breathe it in—sweetness and color. No more hunger." "You've earned this. You don't have to make, or fix, or prove. Just receive." "Let us hold you. Let the flavor carry you." Seraphina's hands trembled as she surrendered to the sensory tide. The candy's sweetness was not just a taste, but a feeling—an embrace that bypassed thought and went straight to the soul. The air shimmered, the music in her head swelling into a full, wordless hymn. It was as if the universe itself was singing her to sleep.

She whispered, half-dreaming, "This… this is what I always hungered for. Not applause, not perfection—just to be enveloped in beauty, to feel the world's tenderness. If I stay here, I don't have to strive. I can be the song, not the singer. I can just… be."

The Candy-Folk pressed in, laughter and song weaving a cocoon of sensation around her, promising, "Just stay. Just one more taste. Just one more rest."

For Seraphina, the logic of the City—the striving for beauty, the endless need to justify delight—was dissolving, one velvet-sweet sensation at a time.

Through the haze of sensation, Seraphina glimpsed Anya, eyes wide and glazed, lost in conversation with a gumdrop child, while Elias scribbled fervently into a small, conjured notebook, chocolate stains on his fingers. At the edge of her awareness, Azael's wings flared in distress, his hands reaching out, but his warnings faded into the background music—unheard and unseen, as if the city itself had swallowed his presence.

The Third Temptation: The Analysis of Excess

Elias, fighting the intense, aromatic pull of the confectionery metropolis, was drawn not only by the promise of pleasure but by the irresistible urge to analyze and categorize it—to conquer the unknown through the power of observation and reason. The former Research Historian's mind, always hungry for patterns and explanations, became a double-edged blade. The scent was a perfectly engineered sensory overload, and in his world, every overload was a puzzle to be solved, not a danger to be fled. *If this pleasure was the Lie, then surely its secret would yield to enough scrutiny.* The historian's compulsion to document, to dissect, to quantify reality, was his weakness in this realm of engineered delight. *I must ingest the variable to understand the anti-protocol,* he rationalized, unable to resist the scientific seduction.

A stout, cube-shaped creature of pure, dark fudge waddled up, its chocolate surface gleaming. "Taste, Seeker," it intoned, voice thick and smooth. "In this city, knowledge is flavor. Truth is what melts on the tongue."

Elias hesitated for a heartbeat—then took the cube. He bit in, the rich fudge yielding with a satisfying snap. Instantly, a chorus of Candy-Folk surrounded him, their voices rising in a sticky, eager chant:

"Analyze it, historian!"

"Taste, and understand!"

"Every bite is a secret!"

A Marzipan Scribe, its almond eyes twinkling, sidled closer. "Is it not your calling to know all things, Elias? To taste the root of every story?"

Elias's teeth ground through the dense, bitter-sweet material. His mind, starved for complexity and desperate for mastery, tried to catalogue the flavor as data, to turn the pleasure into a problem to be solved. "The cube—structural integrity, 98% saturation," he muttered, half to himself, half to the crowd. "It's the ultimate efficiency of flavor—every molecule tuned to trigger maximum sensation. I can reverse engineer this, Sera! If I map the algorithm of their excess, I can calculate the flaw!"

Even as Elias bit into the fudge cube, he caught a fleeting glimpse of Seraphina swaying to a soundless rhythm, a halo of cotton candy drifting around her head, and Anya, her face flushed, licking a neon shard with trembling reverence. Azael, now barely visible, was a silhouette at the city's edge, gesturing urgently, his eyes burning with helpless warning.

The Candy-Folk pressed closer, their voices weaving a tapestry of temptation:

"More data, more truth!"

"Have another, Historian!"

"Eat until the mystery is solved!"

Elias took another bite, not for pleasure, but for certainty. He was losing himself, not in the simple joy of indulgence, but in the endless pursuit of understanding—the act of consumption mistaken for the act of research. Each bite blurred the line between analysis and surrender, until the need to know became indistinguishable from the desire to consume. The city cheered his descent, their sticky logic closing in: "Taste it all, Elias! There is no truth but what the tongue discovers!"

CHAPTER 61

THE HONEYED TWILIGHT

Contentment settled over the trio like a velvet shroud, thick and warm, soothing every ache and anxiety. The City of Gilded Consumption, with its endless parade of colors, flavors, and textures, lulled them into a peace so profound it was almost narcotic. The air was heavy with the perfume of sugar and spice; every breath tasted of fulfillment, every moment a lullaby for the battered soul.

Elias reclined on a bench carved from marzipan, a plate of spiced chocolate in his lap. Each bite dulled the edge of old regrets. The weight of missed opportunities, of truths discovered too late, faded with every morsel. He felt himself slowing, not just in thought but in memory. The past—the urgency, the mission, the pain—became distant, irrelevant. The pleasure of now was enough. He closed his eyes, letting the warmth wash through him, and wondered if there was anything important left to remember.

Nearby, the harp and the Bible lay together on the ground, idle and untouched—once sacred tools, now just artifacts of a purpose no longer remembered. Contentment and forgetting brought such peace within the trio that the need for these old symbols had simply vanished.

Seraphina drifted through the syrup-lit boulevards, fingertips trailing along walls of candied glass. With every taste, every indulgence, the sharp edges of guilt dulled. She no longer felt the restless pulse of composition in her veins— the constant urge to arrange, perfect, and harmonize the world around her was gone. The visions of beauty she once shaped with careful intention now softened into a gentle blur, a watercolor wash of sensation. The loss of memory was a balm—each vanished regret was another note in a symphony of relief. She welcomed the forgetting: it felt like forgiveness.

Anya sat beneath a confectionery tree, a cascade of spun sugar in her lap. She tore off a piece, savoring the sweetness as it melted on her tongue. The faces of those she had condemned, the weight of her decisions as Chief Analyst, faded with each swallow. The more she ate, the more the memories slipped away—faces, names, voices all dissolving into a gentle, golden fog. For Anya, the act of forgetting was the greatest mercy, an invitation to finally escape the burden of her own history. She felt a grateful surrender rising within her, a willingness to lose herself in the city's promise of eternal now.

With every bite, every sigh of satisfaction, the three drifted further from the people they had been. The City did not erase them with violence, but with sweetness—with the narcotic pleasure of contentment, with the lure of an untroubled mind. The past became a dream they no longer wished to recall. The act of losing memory was not a punishment in this place, but an exquisite gift, and as they surrendered to it, they felt themselves becoming someone new— someone free.

They did not see the danger, for in that moment, there was nothing they wanted more than to let go.

Azael's Dissolution

As Elias, Seraphina, and Anya sank deeper into their spell of contentment and indulgence, Azael sensed a subtle but chilling shift—not in himself, but in their awareness of him. He stood apart from the trio, the cinnamon-thick air swirling around his form, which shimmered at the edges—not because he was fading, but because their attention was turning inward, closing him out. Each time Seraphina delighted in a new taste, each time Elias rationalized another bite, each time Anya surrendered another painful memory to the gentle fog, it was as if a veil dropped between Azael and their minds. Their surrender to the City's pleasure was unwinding their connection to him, thread by thread.

The Candy-Folk drifted around him, their voices syrupy and insistent, their laughter muffling his words before they could reach his friends. When he tried to speak, his voice sounded distant and thin, barely more than a breeze at the edge of their perception. "My friends…" he called, but the syllables seemed to evaporate, unheard.

To the trio, Azael's warnings grew faint, reduced to the sensation of a forgotten memory or a half-remembered dream. He tried to raise his voice, to warn them of the trap. "Dependence," he whispered, but the word scattered like sugar dust, lost in the City's haze. The Candy-Folk laughed, their laughter thick, wrapping around him. "You're fading, sweet angel," a Licorice Gentleman crooned, tipping his hat. "You don't belong in a world that doesn't need remembering."

Azael looked down at his hands—they were still solid, still real, but to Elias, Seraphina, and Anya, he was becoming less and less substantial. The more they indulged and forgot, the more his presence receded from their world. He tried to step forward, but his feet barely made a sound in their reality. For them, the guardian angel was little more than a glimmer at the edge of their senses, a faint light hovering at the border of their pleasure.

Desperate, Azael reached out to grasp Anya's shoulder, to shake Elias awake, to steady Seraphina's trembling hand. But as his fingers closed around empty air, he realized with a jolt of despair that his touch no longer had substance in their reality. His hand passed straight through them—no resistance, no contact—leaving not so much as a ripple in their trance. The city's enchantment had not only dulled their memories, but severed the bridge between guardian and ward.

He watched as Elias, Seraphina, and Anya slipped deeper into the honeyed oblivion offered by the City, their faces slack with satisfaction, their eyes half-closed in dreamy contentment. With every bite, every sigh, they became less aware of Azael's presence, less aware of the mission, more willing to let the past go.

Soon, Azael's voice was just a wisp in the background of their pleasure. He reached out one last time, his hand passing through the haze between them, "Remember…" But the word vanished, unheard. To them, he was little more than a forgotten echo—a silent witness at the periphery of their surrender.

Azael lingered at the edge of their perception, sorrow welling within him—an ache older than memory. He remembered other nights, other souls lost in worlds of their own making. How many times had he watched through the centuries as prayers faded to silence, as hearts grew numb and blind to grace? He had stood vigil beside countless beds, on battlefields, in lonely chambers, in the ruins of forgotten cities—always longing to act, to speak, to lift the veil. But unbelief was a wall he could not breach; free will was a law even angels must respect. He could only watch, waiting for the smallest opening, a single whisper of faith.

He recalled the words of Jesus, spoken long ago and still burning in his memory: "And the Lord said, If ye had faith as a grain of mustard seed, ye might say unto this sycamine tree, Be thou plucked up by the root, and be thou planted in the sea; and it should obey you" (Luke 17:6 KJV). It was never the strength or clarity of their vision that brought deliverance, but the tiniest spark of trust—a fragile hope that, if kindled, could move mountains, or banish a city's darkness.

Azael's wings, once radiant, now passed through the golden light without casting even a shadow. Yet even as their awareness of him faded, he refused to let go. He whispered silent petitions, clinging to the promise that grace could slip through the city's honeyed veil if only one of them would reach for it. Though unseen and unheard, he remained—a guardian by faith, unwilling to abandon hope, waiting for the faintest glimmer of belief. The City had not only seduced the living, but had also cloaked the very guardian who might have pulled them back. And as Azael faded from their awareness, the danger grew, silent and unchecked, beneath the sweetness of their forgetting.

The Drift of Days

Time became a gentle, invisible tide that swept over Elias, Seraphina, and Anya. They did not notice its passage, nor did they care. The City of Gilded Consumption, with its endless feast and effortless pleasures, became their world entire—a carousel without clocks, a garden with no seasons. Days—or was it weeks?—slipped by in a golden dream of contentment, each one indistinguishable from the last.

They lounged on benches of marzipan and walked languidly through syrup-lit boulevards, their laughter soft and aimless. When they hungered, sweet delicacies appeared in their hands; when they tired, pillows of spun sugar seemed to bloom beneath their heads. The Candy-Folk attended them with perpetual smiles, their voices always encouraging: "Stay a while longer. Why hurry? There is nothing more to want."

Elias, once defined by urgency and purpose, let the weight of his mission slide from his mind like melting chocolate. He found himself thinking less and less about the City he was meant to save, about the grandmother he had lost, about the truths that once kept him up at night. Where there had been a sharp ache of regret and the compulsion to act, now there was only a soothing, humming quiet. Sometimes he would close his eyes and remember—a name, a face, a promise—but the memory would dissolve, sweetly painful, into a fog of satisfaction. The Candy-Folk noticed his hesitation and gently pressed a sugared fruit to his lips. "Don't trouble yourself with the past, dear Historian. All that matters is the sweetness you taste now."

Seraphina, who once saw the world as a tapestry of tension and beauty, now found herself drifting from one pleasant sensation to the next. The colors around her grew softer, the music in her head faded to a lullaby. She no longer agonized over the melody that had haunted her soul, nor did she worry about the power her gifts had held over the world. Each new treat, each gentle caress from the Candy-Folk, became a note in a song of forgetting. She let herself be enfolded by the city's embrace, the memory of her old self growing lighter with each passing day. "Why remember pain, Artist?" sang a Candy-Folk choir, their voices as sweet as honey. "Let the world be color and comfort. Let the past sleep."

Anya, for whom every memory was once a calculation and every moment a ledger of guilt, felt the sharp edges of her history blur and then fade. The names of the condemned, the faces of those lost by her hand, were still there for a time—ghosts at the edge of her vision—but they visited less and less. With every bite, every sigh, the burden of guilt was replaced by the golden haze of relief. She welcomed the loss of memory as a drowning man welcomes air. "Isn't it better not to remember?" whispered a Gumdrop Child, curling up beside her in the sugar grass. "You're safe now. You're loved. Let the world before this one fade."

The more they indulged, the less they sought, questioned, or feared. They did not speak of their mission, nor of the world outside the city gates. The hunger for purpose withered; the search for meaning dulled. And as contentment deepened, so did the amnesia—until the only truth was the sweetness of the present, and the only sin was to long for anything more.

Somewhere, far away and nearly forgotten, the memory of Azael flickered like a dream before waking—a sense of someone lost, or a promise left unfulfilled. But the thought always slipped away, gentled by the city's pleasure. In this endless, honeyed twilight, the architects of grace became content to drift, the world beyond the candy walls no longer even a rumor in their hearts. All the while, the shadow lingered in the corners of the city, watching with quiet satisfaction as they remained trapped in illusion. Now and then, a Candy-Folk would pause in its revelry to bow low before the darkness, honoring the silent presence that had no need to interfere—content to let its captives remain blissfully unaware.

CHAPTER 62

THE LURE OF REAL DELIGHT

Elias, Seraphina, and Anya were lost beyond rescue, their souls adrift in a narcotic sea of contentment. The City of Gilded Consumption had enfolded them in a velvet cocoon—every longing met, every regret stroked away, every memory of mission dissolving like sugar in warm tea. They lounged amid the edible wonders, bathed in a golden light that seemed to erase all sense of time or urgency. The harsh edges of purpose, guilt, and desire were blunted, replaced by a gentle, ceaseless now. Somewhere, just beyond the reach of their awareness, a shadow lingered—patient, knowing their peace was only a surface, and that the true cost was yet to be paid.

Their hands drifted over candy-lacquered tables. Their eyes grew heavy with bliss. The sound of their laughter was soft, almost infantile, the laughter of people who no longer remembered why they had ever grieved. Each new act of indulgence—each bite, each sigh—smoothed away another memory, another scar. They could feel themselves slipping, not with fear or resistance, but with grateful surrender. What they had once been, what they had sought to accomplish, now seemed like a half-remembered dream—one they had no desire to revisit.

The Candy-Folk gathered around in a gentle, ever-present chorus. "This is your home now," murmured the Lollipop Ladies, their voices crystalline and hypnotic, "Rest, rest, rest. Stay sweet forever." Caramel Constables oozed closer, their forms blurring at the edges, "No more striving. No more pain. Let the flavor of forgetting linger. You have earned peace, and peace is all that remains." Gumdrop Children played at their feet, weaving garlands of spun sugar and whispering, "Stay here with us. There is nothing more to want."

In this lull of pleasure, the trio had no thought to reach for their spiritual tools. The Word and the Harp lay inert, alien objects among the feast, unnecessary in a world where nothing was lacking. Their spirits were silent, their minds content to drift. The hunger for meaning, the pain of memory, the ache of loss—all were gone.

But just beyond the soft boundary of their new world, Azael watched—powerless. He existed now at the outer edge of their awareness, trapped not by bars or walls, but by the boundaries of their minds. His celestial form flickered with desperation as he tried to reach them. He could see them, could hear their laughter, but his voice would not reach past the shimmering veil of their contentment. No matter how he called out, no matter how he strained, his words dissolved in the syrup-thick air, lost before they could ever arrive. He pressed his hands against emptiness, his face contorted with longing and horror, forced to witness their gradual dissolution into pleasure, unable to intervene, unable even to weep.

He tried again and again to break through, but there was no physical barrier—only the perfect, cruel logic of irrelevance. As long as they desired nothing, he could do nothing. He was a silent observer, vanished from their hearts and their senses, imprisoned by their forgetting and their contentment.

And as the last strands of his presence faded from their world, the shadow—ancient, patient, triumphant—unfurled itself at the heart of the city. It gazed upon the three souls lost to the opiate of pleasure, and, satisfied, it slipped away from the City of Gilded Consumption. Its work was done here; their memories erased, their vigilance destroyed. Now it would go on, unchallenged, to spread its corruption across the world—certain it could not be opposed by those who no longer remembered why they should resist.

The Cathedral of Sweet Communion

In the very heart of the City of Gilded Consumption, a cathedral soared—a marvel of confection and light, both ancient and forever new. Its spires twisted skyward in spirals of caramel and spun sugar, and its walls shimmered with crystalline sugar, refracting the golden light into a thousand rainbows that painted the air with shifting, edible color. The grandeur was not childish, but awe-inspiring: every arch was a lattice of gingerbread filigree, every flying buttress was sculpted nougat, strong as steel yet delicate as lace. The stained-glass windows were mosaics of hard candy, each pane a patchwork of translucent cherry, lemon, mint, and violet. When the sun struck them, the light tasted of nostalgia, longing, and the ache of beauty too intense to bear.

Within the cathedral's vast nave, a river of Candy-Folk flowed—Marzipan Matrons, Gumdrop Children, Chocolate Scribes, Lollipop Ladies, and Caramel Constables—all drawn unfailingly toward the call of worship. The great bells above, cast in purest toffee, rang out a melody so rich and harmonious that it seemed to thrum through the bones. The sound was irresistible, promising unity and belonging. The air was thick with incense—vanilla bean, cinnamon, and the faintest trace of burnt sugar—rising from crystal censers. It was the first day of the week, and here, worship was not a duty but a feast.

Elias, Seraphina, and Anya joined the throng without question. To resist would have been unthinkable; no one wished to be an outsider in a city where belonging was the highest pleasure. They felt themselves swept forward, buoyed by the gentle pressure of countless arms, the friendly murmurs of "Come with us, sweet one. This is what we do. This is who we are." The trio's longing to belong, to be accepted, melded seamlessly with the will of the crowd. It was an old, familiar urge—to stand when others stand, to sing when others sing, to find one's place in the ritual of the many.

They filed into the pews—rows of licorice and peppermint, cushions of marshmallow silk. The congregation swayed as one, bathed in the rainbow light from the candy mosaics. The choir began, their voices a melody of spun sugar and honey, rising and falling in a hymn that wound around the heart and filled the soul with a sweetness that felt like love. The melody was simple, unforgettable—an echo of every lullaby and celebration from their own distant pasts. It was worship as comfort, as reward, as perfect, unearned acceptance.

At the pulpit stood the Chaplain—a towering figure of striped peppermint and marzipan, his robe a cascade of candied violets and chocolate embroidery. His eyes glimmered with the sheen of hard sugar, his smile both warm and unsettling. He raised his licorice staff, and the music faded.

"Beloved children of sweetness," he intoned, his voice rich as caramel, "the Maker delights in your delight. Did He not create the fruits of the earth for your enjoyment? Did He not command you to taste and see that He is good? Oh, do not burden yourselves with the old fears, or the sourness of guilt. For what is pleasure, if not a sign of favor? What is satisfaction, if not a mark of blessing?"

The Chaplain's words twisted truth and scripture with seductive skill. "Why else would paradise be described as a garden of delights? Why else would the Promised Land flow with milk and honey? My children, the Maker wishes you to be filled, to be content. Did not the Preacher say, 'There is nothing better for a man, than that he should eat and drink, and that he should make his soul enjoy good in his labour?' (Ecclesiastes 2:24 KJV). So eat, and be glad. Drink, and be full. Let the memory of sorrow melt away. The past is bitter, but here, only sweetness remains."

A chorus of "Amen" rippled through the congregation, and the choir swelled in a song of praise so beautiful, so laced with longing and nostalgia, that tears pricked Seraphina's eyes. Elias found himself mouthing the words, lost in the rise and fall of the music. Anya felt the melody vibrate through her bones, and for a moment, she could imagine no world beyond this sanctuary.

The Chaplain continued, "Some will tell you to deny yourselves, to hunger, to thirst. But I say, the Maker asks only that you receive with gratitude. To seek more is to reject the gift. To remember pain is to dishonor joy. Rest in the sweetness. Rest in the now. There is no calling greater than contentment."

The crowd was spellbound. The trio was swept up in the ritual—singing, swaying, tasting the air, their hearts and minds saturated by the pleasure of belonging. The melody of worship lingered, a sugar-coated refrain that echoed in their souls even after the service ended.

And so, week after week—though time had lost its meaning—they joined the city's worship, never questioning, never resisting, content to be part of the endless feast. The cathedral's doors were always open, the Chaplain's smile ever welcoming, and the sweetness of forgetting was their daily bread.

The Honeycomb's Intervention

And there, when all hope felt lost and the sweetness of oblivion seemed absolute, the cosmos itself seemed to intervene. In the farthest reaches of the city, something began to move—an anomaly weaving in and out of the syrup-lit boulevards, erratic but purposeful, never drawing the attention of the Candy-Folk. Its sweetness, rather than attracting hungry eyes, rendered it invisible—so pure, so unlike the cloying flavors of the city that it passed unnoticed among the confections.

This was no ordinary honeycomb. Its crystalline cells glimmered with a golden, inner light, each hexagon etched with delicate patterns like ancient script. The surface was smooth and glassy, but within, the honey caught the faintest glimmer of dawn, swirling in shades of amber and pale fire. When the honeycomb moved, it left in its wake a scent unlike anything in the City: a subtle, sacred perfume of frankincense, threaded with the earthy sweetness of myrrh—a fragrance that mingled worship and longing, evoking ancient temples and the gifts of wise men. The aroma was gentle, never overwhelming, and seemed to carry a memory of prayer and promise.

The honeycomb darted through the city with the quick, liquid grace of a lizard, flickering from shadow to shadow, gliding across walls of spun sugar and leaping from marzipan ledge to marzipan ledge. Its presence was pure, undesignated sweetness—a grace that the City could not recognize or consume. Unseen, it wound its way toward the heart of the city, drawn by a mystery only it seemed to sense, the promise of true deliverance glimmering in each golden drop.

As it wove its way deeper into the city's syrup-lit labyrinth, the honeycomb suddenly slowed. A faint tremor in the golden air, almost imperceptible, caught its attention—an undercurrent of something not quite in harmony with the city's ceaseless sweetness. The honeycomb hovered, facets glinting, tasting the shimmering currents with an instinctive curiosity. It sensed, somewhere nearby, a lingering pulse of longing—muted, distant, but unmistakably different from the placid contentment that saturated everything else. Compelled by this anomaly, the honeycomb darted sideways, slipping through a spun-sugar archway and twisting down a narrow passage. Rounding a final corner, it leapt lightly onto the rim of a licorice fountain, eyes bright with anticipation, and paused to listen more closely—drawn, at last, to the trio at the heart of the city's spell.

For a moment, the honeycomb remained perfectly still, its amber eyes fixed on the figures nearby as it caught the slow, contented sigh escaping Elias. Then, with a flick of its hexagonal tail, it zipped toward the trio. To Elias, Seraphina, and Anya—whose last shreds of memory were slipping away—the honeycomb became something more.

As Elias reclined on his marzipan bench, the honeycomb landed beside him—light as breath, warm as a sunbeam. It watched him with faceted, amber eyes, curious and unafraid. There was a moment of stillness, a hush in the air as if the City itself held its breath. Elias blinked, his mind teetering on the edge of oblivion, but something about the honeycomb's presence stirred a spark of curiosity within him. He felt an unfamiliar pull—a gentle, insistent urge to reach for this new sweetness, so different from the City's cloying confections. The air around him shimmered with anticipation, the scent of frankincense and myrrh mingling with the honeycomb's golden glow. Almost without thinking, driven by both wonder and the faintest flicker of temptation, Elias reached out. The honeycomb darted up his arm and, with a quick, affectionate motion, licked his cheek with a drop of golden nectar.

The sensation was electric—a jolt of pure, wild sweetness, nothing like the engineered pleasure of the City. Where the honeycomb's touch met his cheek, the sweetness seemed to penetrate Elias's skin, flooding his senses until the taste burst onto his tongue, bright and strange and utterly real. It was layered—floral and resinous, with a trace of sacred incense and a complexity that made the City's confections taste dull and one-note by comparison. It lingered, not in memory, but in longing—a sweet ache hinting at mysteries and depths the City's endless feast could never provide.

Elias blinked, his mind swirling with questions even as contentment tried to lull him back. For the first time since arriving, he felt a restless curiosity stirring beneath the surface, a hunger not just for pleasure, but for understanding. A hazy memory flickered—of a sunset over distant hills, laughter echoing in his mind, the sharp ache of longing for something lost. For a moment, he wondered what it was he had once vowed never to forget. The honeycomb's sweetness didn't shatter the spell, but it unsettled it, leaving him wanting more of this wild, living flavor—something the City could never offer.

The honeycomb darted next to Anya, weaving a golden arc through the air before settling onto her wrist. A single drop of nectar glistened, and as it touched her skin, Anya felt not a rush of memory, but a surge of analytical wonder. Her tongue tingled as if catching the scent of frankincense and rain. The sensation was so intricate, so layered, that her mind—normally dulled to simple pleasure—sparked with the desire to investigate, to catalog, to understand what made this sweetness so different. She let the City's candy drop from her hand, her attention wholly captured by the honeycomb, her senses straining for another taste. A question tumbled up: Had she always loved to solve puzzles? She couldn't quite remember, but the urge to investigate felt strangely familiar, as if she'd once pieced together far greater mysteries.

Seraphina, drifting nearby, caught the faint scent of myrrh and honey as the honeycomb swirled around her. It brushed her lips with a feather-light touch, and a note of flavor sang through her—a chord so complex, so unresolved, that it left her breathless. There was beauty in the taste, yes, but also a sense of unfinished melody, of longing for something just beyond reach. For the first time, the city's pleasures felt incomplete. A whisper of music drifted through her mind—an old, beloved melody. Had she played it herself, or only dreamed of it? The uncertainty stung, awakening a yearning that pierced the city's sweetness. The confection she'd been savoring slipped from her grasp as she stared, spellbound, at the honeycomb, yearning to experience that wild sweetness again.

One by one, Elias, Anya, and Seraphina set aside the city's candy, their hands empty now, their eyes tracking the honeycomb as it hovered between them. They watched it with a growing curiosity, a subtle hunger for knowledge and depth that no amount of engineered delight could satisfy. The trio didn't yet remember who they were or why they had come, but something had shifted—a longing had been awakened, a desire to know more.

The honeycomb hovered between them, its facets catching the light and spinning it into a mesmerizing display—a kaleidoscope of candy-colored beams that dance and twist through the air. It darted playfully in circles, weaving shimmering patterns above their heads, its movement as lively and unpredictable as a child discovering a new game. Each shift in color and light seemed to beckon Elias, Seraphina, and Anya closer, drawing their gaze and stirring a sense of wonder that cut through the city's haze. The honeycomb didn't just hum—it sang in silent, dazzling arcs, inviting them to play, to follow, to discover. For the briefest moment, the City's spell loosened its grip, curiosity blossoming where there had been only contentment. The spark of something real—untamed and beautiful—ignited within their hearts, and for the first time in ages, the world seemed to open just a little wider.

The Honeycomb's Escape

Suddenly, the honeycomb shuddered, its golden facets glinting as if it sensed a change in the air. With a quick, lizard-like flick of its hexagonal tail, it spun through the kaleidoscope of light it had just created, pausing midair to catch the trio's gaze with its lively, amber eyes. An impulse—some deep, wild urgency—seemed to seize it, and before Elias, Seraphina, or Anya could react, it darted away in a blur of gold, beckoning them to follow.

As it scurried across the sugar-laden square, the honeycomb swept past where Seraphina's harp lay forgotten on the candied ground. Its nimble body darted across the strings, and with a perfectly accidental grace, it struck a single shimmering chord—a note impossibly pure, a melody both sweet and wild, reverberating through the city like a bell of deliverance.

The effect was immediate and electric. The music cut through the haze of contentment, sending a ripple of energy through the air. The Candy-Folk froze, their song faltering, smiles slipping into puzzled silence. But for Elias, Seraphina, and Anya, the harp's melody drifted past their minds without leaving a trace—their thoughts so lost in oblivion that not even this music could spark a memory or stir a warning. Instead, their curiosity about the honeycomb remained undimmed, and with eager, dreamlike wonder, they watched as it hovered near the harp, as if considering its next move.

Shocked by the accidental music, the honeycomb paused above the harp, its golden facets shimmering over the strings it had just set ringing. With a flick of its hexagonal tail, it scattered a burst of crystalline honey-light across the instrument: the air above the harp came alive with delicate footprints, each one pulsing in time with an unheard melody. Elias, nearest to the harp, felt the pull instantly—though he could not have named what called to him. The light and sound seemed to swirl around his senses, and as he reached for the radiant footprints, his hands instead closed around something cool and unfamiliar. The strings vibrated beneath his touch, sending a ripple up his arms, a shiver of possibility that he did not understand. He stared at the object in his grasp, its shape and purpose lost to him, but something compelled him to keep it close.

The honeycomb glided onward, pausing above a thick, ornate book dusted in sugar. Seraphina, entranced by the swirling lights, reached out, her fingers brushing the cover. She felt a sudden warmth, a sweetness blooming in her chest, and without thinking, she drew the book to her, holding it tightly. She turned it over in her hands, frowning at the unfamiliar symbols pressed into the cover. It meant nothing to her, and yet she could not let it go.

Anya glanced at her companions, confusion flickering across her face as she watched them clutch their strange treasures. "Do you...know what those are?" she asked uncertainly, her own hands empty, her gaze drifting between the harp and the book.

Elias shook his head slowly. "No," he murmured, dazed, "but I think we're meant to have them."

Seraphina only hugged the book tighter, her answers lost somewhere in the fog of forgetting.

Having marked both harp and Bible, the honeycomb darted ahead, leaving behind a mesmerizing trail: shimmering rainbows rippled through the air, each hue pulsing with impossible depth. Along this radiant path, the colors gathered into playful, gecko-like footprints—each one glowing with its own spectral halo, beckoning with hypnotic beauty and wild wonder. The sweet melody seemed to become a glowing ribbon of sound and light, unfurling through the city's winding lanes, leading outward, away from the center of indulgence, toward the unknown beyond the city gates.

Drawn by this marvel, Elias, Seraphina, and Anya—now clutching their mysterious burdens—fell into step behind the honeycomb, curiosity and longing awakening anew with every step. Together, they followed, leaving behind the comfort of the city for the promise of something wild, mysterious, and real.

A Witness to Wonder

Earlier, while Elias, Seraphina, and Anya drifted through the city's haze, Azael hovered at the periphery, powerless to intervene.

He drifted near, his heart aching with sorrow at his inability to reach them, forced to witness the fading light in their eyes, the lost urgency of their mission. Their laughter and contented sighs were as distant as memories, and every attempt to touch them, to call them back, dissolved in the thick air of the city. For a long moment, he watched the trio in grief, uncertain whether he would ever be able to bridge the gulf their forgetting had created.

But then, something changed. He noticed a subtle shift: Seraphina's eyes, once glazed, tracked something across the ground. Elias and Anya, too, were no longer lost in the city's spell; their focus narrowed, their bodies tensing with anticipation, as if they sensed a presence he had missed. Azael's gaze followed theirs, searching for the source of their sudden awakening.

It was then that he saw it—a glimmer at first, scarcely more than a distortion in the air, but growing brighter and more defined with every heartbeat. The honeycomb, radiant and alive, danced just beyond his understanding. For the first time in his long existence, Azael felt a spark of curiosity so sharp it bordered on awe. He could not recall having seen anything like it, not among the hosts of heaven nor in the wildest reaches of creation. The honeycomb's golden light was untouched by corruption, its movement unpredictable and free—a wild grace that made the air sing with possibility.

Azael felt himself drawn—not only as a guardian, but as a witness to something truly new. As the trio's attention turned to the honeycomb, his longing mingled with theirs, and beneath the weight of millennia, he sensed the promise of deliverance—salvation born of wonder and a sweetness beyond anything engineered or controlled.

For the first time since entering the city, hope flickered—not just for those he watched over, but for the world itself. As the honeycomb beckoned, Azael followed Elias, Seraphina, and Anya, weaving through the labyrinth of candy-bright streets. The city's towering confections gradually gave way to a narrowing border, where the syrup-lit avenues faded into the uncertain dusk of the world beyond. At the threshold, the four paused—breathless, senses sharpened by the ache of something real and wild awakening within them. Behind them, the memory of the city's manufactured pleasures began to ebb, replaced by the honeycomb's promise: that true fulfillment lies only in what cannot be contrived or controlled.

CHAPTER 63

THE SHELTER OF UNKNOWING

For a heartbeat, Elias, Seraphina, Anya, and Azael lingered at the city's edge—a place where rainbow-lit streets yielded to the raw, unshaped land beyond. Then the honeycomb darted forward, scattering shimmering, gecko-like footprints that pulsed with impossible color, and the four followed, leaving behind the suffocating sweetness for the cool breath of the world outside. At first, they moved in silence, their steps uncertain on unfamiliar soil, then with quickening breaths, chasing the honeycomb farther and farther from indulgence. The golden light ahead felt less like a promise of pleasure and more like a call to remember, to awaken, and to discover what waited beyond forgetting.

At last, in the farthest outstretches of the City of Gilded Consumption, the rainbow footprints began to fade. One by one, the luminous steps flickered and vanished, absorbed into the still, humid air. Elias, Seraphina, and Anya slowed, their legs trembling with exhaustion, lungs burning from effort. They stumbled to a halt, and for a moment, simply stood, swaying on their feet. When they turned to look back, the city's confectionary skyline was barely visible—a wavering silhouette against the pale horizon, its spires of caramel and spun sugar blurred by distance and haze. All that remained was a faint glimmer of color, like a half-remembered dream dissolving in morning light. When the final footprint blinked out, so did the last trace of the city's sweet spell—the silence left in its wake was vast and vulnerable.

Someone—Elias, maybe—let out a breathless, uncertain laugh. "Is it… gone?" he murmured, voice hoarse and unfamiliar in his own ears.

No one answered right away. Instead, their bodies gave out almost in unison. Seraphina's knees buckled and she sat heavily on the damp ground, not caring that it stained her clothing with streaks of gold and blue. Anya slumped beside her, hugging her knees, her breath ragged. Elias dropped to his side, something hard and unfamiliar clutched in his hand. He stared at it—a slender, gilded instrument strung with delicate wires. He ran his thumb over the strings, and the faintest note quivered in the air, strange and bright, but it sparked no memory.

Seraphina, shivering, glanced down at the thick book she had carried, pressed to her chest as if in sleep. The cover was cool and embossed, the pages edged with gold. She frowned and turned it in her hands, as if she might read something in its weight or scent. "What is this?" she whispered, not to anyone in particular.

Anya watched them both, eyes clouded. She reached out, touching the harp's frame, then drew back quickly, as if it might sting. "I don't remember… any of this," she said, her voice thin.

They lay or sat in the rain, letting exhaustion wash over them. The city behind was a memory already slipping away, the jungle before them alive with unknown colors. Above, towering vines bore fruit that shimmered—crimson orbs pulsing with inner fire, golden clusters flickering like dawn, berries shifting endlessly through the spectrum. The air was humid, heavy with the scent of earth and something new.

A wind stirred the canopy, and the rain began. It fell in slow, heavy drops, each one a different color. A blue droplet slid down Elias's cheek, cool and electric. Seraphina watched a green bead trace a line down her arm, tingling as it faded to gold. Anya caught a red drop on her finger, watching it sizzle and disappear. Every sensation was magnified; every touch, every sound was strange and raw. They huddled closer together, silent, uncertain, memory lost, names and histories just out of reach.

"Are we… supposed to be here?" Elias managed, voice barely above the rain.

"I don't know," Seraphina replied, hugging the book tighter, like a shield against the unknown.

Only Azael remained unchanged. He stood over them, silent and vigilant, rain beading on his shoulders, eyes ancient and clear. He alone remembered— who they were, what they had left behind, and the vastness of what lay ahead. As the rain fell harder and the last echoes of the city faded, Azael waited, patient as the dusk, watching for the first sign that the others might remember, or awaken, or begin again.

Shelter of Renewal

Days passed in a gentle, unmeasured blur beneath the shifting canopy of the jungle. At first, Elias, Seraphina, and Anya barely noticed the tall, watchful figure moving quietly about their camp. When their eyes strayed toward him, it was as if their gaze slid off a patch of empty air, unable to focus. Yet, with each dawn, as the city's spell faded, the sense of a presence near them grew—at first a feeling, then a shadow, and finally, a figure made real by distance and time.

One morning, as the rain's colored drops pattered softly on the fronds of their shelter, Elias blinked and stared at the figure crouched by the fire. "There's… someone here," he whispered, voice hoarse.

Seraphina sat up, rubbing her eyes. "I thought—I thought I'd dreamed him."

Anya hugged her knees, wary but curious. "Who are you?" she called, her words uncertain but edged with hope.

Azael looked up, his eyes full of gentle sorrow and boundless patience. He offered a soft, enigmatic smile but said nothing at first, simply tending to the glowing fruits and placing them on broad leaves before the trio. At his side, carefully wrapped in woven vines, lay the gilded harp and the heavy, embossed book—objects the trio sometimes glanced at, puzzled, unable to recall their meaning. Azael handled them with reverence, keeping them safe and dry, as if knowing their importance even when the others did not.

Sometimes Elias would watch Azael lay the harp beside him at night, puzzling over the instrument's shape. "Why does that look… familiar?" he murmured once, his fingers hovering above the strings but not daring to touch.

Seraphina eyed the book in Azael's hands, frowning in frustration. "What is that? Should I know?" she asked, voice soft and aching.

Azael would only give them a gentle, knowing look, or hum a melody that tugged at the edges of Seraphina's memory. He spoke little, but at night, as the jungle hummed with unseen life, he would tell fragments of stories—of journeys, promises, music, faith. Sometimes, his voice would carry softly through the leafy shelter as they drifted toward sleep.

"Once," Azael murmured, "there was a man named Daniel who trusted when all seemed lost. He was cast into a den of lions, but he was not afraid. He remembered he was not alone, even in the darkness. The lions watched him, but they did not harm him. In the morning, the king found Daniel safe and unharmed, for faith had kept him."

The trio listened, eyes half-closed, the story sinking into their dreams. Sometimes Seraphina would ask, "Did the lions really let him be?" or Elias would whisper, "Was he ever afraid?"

Azael would smile gently. "Even the bravest heart feels fear. But sometimes, all you need is to remember you are watched over."

His words seemed to echo in the trio's dreams, planting seeds of memory and self.

During the days, the trio moved slowly, feeding on the wild fruits and sipping rainwater gathered by Azael's careful hands. The flavors stirred up flickers of recall: a blue fruit made Seraphina hum a tune she couldn't name; a tart berry made Elias's heart ache with longing; golden droplets on Anya's tongue summoned a faint sense of duty.

Nights came gentle and strange, filled with the glow of luminous fruit and the soft rustle of leaves. Under the shelter Azael had woven, the trio finally found rest. Gradually, their vacant stares gave way to questions, their silence to tentative words. The jungle, once bewildering, became a place of slow recovery. In the presence of the silent stranger and the sacred artifacts he guarded, hope shimmered, fragile and bright, just beyond the veil of forgetting.

Azael's Sabbath Vigil

Life in the jungle settled into a gentle rhythm beneath Azael's care. Each dawn, as pale gold seeped through the emerald canopy, he would arrange a small altar of smooth stones and flowering vines, then open the ancient, gold-edged Bible. His voice rose in the morning mist, carrying the words of old psalms into the shelter: "The Lord is my shepherd; I shall not want. He maketh me to lie down in green pastures: he leadeth me beside the still waters…" (Psalm 23:1–4, KJV).

The verses drifted over Elias, Seraphina, and Anya, as light as the colored rain. Sometimes a shaft of sunlight, broken into vivid hues, would illuminate the text, glimmering across the open page. The trio listened in silence, the sound familiar yet strange, like a lullaby half-remembered from a distant childhood.

Throughout the day, Azael watched over them—offering fruit, gathering rain, and calling each by a name that felt both foreign and comforting. He tended the mysterious book and harp with reverence, keeping them close, as if their meaning was a secret only he could recall.

One afternoon, Elias found his gaze lingering on the harp in Azael's lap. "Why do you hold that so carefully?" he asked, the words unsteady on his tongue.

Azael smiled, his eyes kind. "It is precious," he answered simply. "Some things are meant to be kept safe until their song is remembered."

Seraphina traced the fronds of her bed, watching as Azael turned the Bible's pages. "Those words… they sound important," she murmured, brow furrowed. "But I can't remember why."

Azael's response was gentle. "Sometimes, meaning returns when we are ready."

As dusk fell, Azael would read again—softer now, as shadow and colored rain mingled in the shelter: "Create in me a clean heart, O God; and renew a right spirit within me" (Psalm 51:10, KJV).

On the Sabbath, Azael set aside labor. He wove mats from palm fronds, prepared a meal of sweet, glowing fruit, and filled the hush with music. Cradling the harp, he coaxed from it tentative notes: at first uncertain, then blooming into melodies that shimmered in the twilight. The song was both sorrowful and hopeful, threading through the air like a promise.

The trio listened, some part of them aching with the sense of something lost but not forgotten. Anya pressed a hand to her heart, whispering, "It's beautiful," though she did not know why.

When the music faded, the hush felt holy. Azael's rituals—his readings, his songs, his gentle presence—became a quiet sanctuary, sheltering the trio as their memories began, ever so slowly, to stir beneath the jeweled rain.

The Harmony of Renewal

One evening, as jeweled rain pattered softly on the shelter, Azael lingered at the edge and drew the harp into his lap. Its shape was still strange to Elias and Seraphina, yet as Azael's fingers brushed the strings, a hush fell over the camp. At first, he played the simplest of hymns—notes that echoed through the clearing with gentle resolve. Gradually, the music grew bolder, weaving radiant harmonies that shimmered with something not quite earthly. The melodies overlapped and spiraled outward, rippling through the air in waves of longing and hope.

As the song deepened, the jungle itself seemed to answer. The rain changed: blue drops chimed with crystalline tones, green drops hummed a velvet undertone, gold drops rang out pure and clear. The canopy swayed in rhythm, vines and leaves moving as if caught in a slow, enchanted dance.

From the shadows, fireflies drifted out, painting colored arcs above the trio's heads. Jewel-bright beetles and butterflies flickered into view, their wings pulsing in time with the music and light. Even the rain seemed to swirl and twist in midair, ribbons of living color swirling above the ground.

Elias sat forward, eyes wide, his breath caught. "How can rain sound like that?" he whispered, wonder and confusion tangled in his voice.

Seraphina's gaze lingered on Azael's hands. "It's like the world is… remembering a song," she murmured, clutching her knees, her heart aching with an unnamed longing.

Anya hugged herself, eyes shining. "I feel—" she started, then stopped, lost for words, though her face was bright with hope and uncertainty.

The air shimmered with possibility. The trio felt the music tug at them—at memories just out of reach, voices and laughter, the comfort of belonging and the ache of something lost returning. For a moment, they forgot their bewilderment and fear; they were simply part of the music, woven into the living tapestry of the night.

Azael played on, each note a gentle promise in the darkness. The wild harmony of rain, trees, and creatures filled the shelter, transforming it into something more than a refuge—a sanctuary where, for a heartbeat, sorrow was lifted and hope became real. In the glow of that shared wonder, all four souls— angel and mortal alike—rested in the possibility of beginning again.

CHAPTER 64

THE WELL OF LIVING WATER

Azael's harp sang into the rain. Delicate, resonant notes shimmered through the canopy of jeweled leaves and colored droplets, carrying the melody that had last filled the shelter. Each pluck of the fiber-optic strings was a breath of memory, as if the world itself had not forgotten the music woven through their night of renewal. The jungle around the shelter responded: colored rain arched and spun, insects and flowers swayed in slow, syncopated dance, and the air hummed with possibility.

Seraphina, still wrapped in a fragile cloak of memory and healing, sat close by, her hands folded in her lap. At first, she only listened. The melody Azael wove was gentle, at once alien and familiar, bridging the space between earth and heaven, between sorrow and hope. Then, almost imperceptibly, Azael shifted his tune. Under his touch, the harp's shimmering voice began to echo the opening bars of a song Seraphina knew by heart—a melody of grace, ancient and unoptimized, that she herself had once played: "Amazing Grace."

The notes drifted through the colored rain, a plaintive, yearning phrase that seemed to search for something lost and almost found. Seraphina's eyes widened. The memory of her own hands on the strings, her own heart searching for the shape of forgiveness, returned in a rush of sensation. At first, she only hummed—a small, trembling sound, nearly lost amid the rain and the gentle riot of insect wings. But as the melody wound onward, each note unlocked a new fragment of recollection, and her humming grew stronger, clearer.

She glanced at Azael, wonder and tears in her eyes. "How do I know this song?" Seraphina whispered, voice shaking.

Azael met her gaze, his own voice quiet. "It's always been with you," he said. "Sometimes, music remembers us before we remember ourselves."

Azael watched her with quiet encouragement, his playing attuned to her every breath and hesitation. The jungle, too, seemed to lean in: the rain fell in rhythm, the insects spun tighter spirals, and the air itself felt charged with anticipation. Seraphina's hum turned to words, uncertain at first—"Amazing grace, how sweet the sound..."—but then, as if some deep well had broken open, her voice rang out, steady and bright. She sang the hymn's opening verse, her tone raw with the ache of restoration, and as she sang, the harp wove harmonies around her, expanding and uplifting every line.

The effect was immediate and miraculous. The rain intensified, its colored drops chiming as they struck the leaves and stones, each one a bell of memory. The jungle's plant life, touched by the sound, began to unfurl in time with the song. Jewel-bright beetles spun in the air, fireflies painted arcs of gold and blue, and even the roots beneath the soil seemed to pulse with new life. The entire clearing became an orchestra, and Seraphina's voice was its center.

As the second verse rose—"That saved a wretch like me..."—Elias felt his own memories flood back: the weight of loss in the City, the bitter ache of missed redemption, the moment of baptism in the waters of an ancient tub. The music washed over him, not erasing the pain but reframing it, weaving sorrow together with hope. He remembered Seraphina's hand in his, the risk and beauty of love, the choice to return from the brink of despair. Tears blurred his vision, but he did not turn away. He pressed a trembling hand to his chest, breathing in the music as if it might stitch together everything that had come undone.

Anya, seated beside them, watched as the Holy Bible rested near Azael's side, the gold edging glinting with each chord. She felt a strange pull toward the book, a sense of recognition hovering just out of reach. As she listened, her analytical mind was momentarily silenced by the sheer, uncalculated grace of the moment. The melody awakened memories: the faces of those she'd once condemned, the calculations that once governed her life, and the moment she chose purpose over despair. The memories did not crush her; they buoyed her, carried along by the harmony that was larger than any sorrow.

The rain and the song became inseparable—each note calling forth a new memory, each droplet a prism for old grief and new possibility. The insects and plants, the colored air and the streaming water, all danced to the melody, their movements a living liturgy of renewal. In that moment, time seemed to expand

and contract: the agony and beauty of their journey, the wounds and victories, the moments of loss and the promise of restoration, all became one.

Azael's playing slowed, then faded, but Seraphina's voice lingered, holding the last word—"grace"—until it seemed the world itself might break open with longing. For a long time, the clearing was utterly still, save for the soft patter of rain and the gentle hum of the living world around them.

Elias reached for Seraphina's hand, and she took it, her fingers warm and strong. Anya, silent but radiant, reached out, her fingers brushing the closed Bible beside Azael. Azael set the harp gently between them, his eyes shining with a fierce, quiet pride.

No one spoke. There was no need. The song and the sharing of memory had done what words could not: it had made them whole again, at least for this moment, and bound them together in the presence of grace.

The rain continued to fall, steady and gentle, as if baptizing the ground and all who sat upon it. The jungle's chorus resumed—softer now, but charged with a new kind of certainty. They rested in the embrace of memory, music, and grace, ready to rise again when the world called them forward.

The Sleep of Grace: The Dreams of the Redeemed**

As the last notes of the jungle faded, a gentle fatigue washed over Elias, Seraphina, and Anya—a peace that was not mere exhaustion but a benediction. Under the shelter of Azael's vigilant watch, the three found themselves drifting into sleep, the colored rain a lullaby and the jungle's music a soft cradle.

Azael sat with wings unfurled, keeping silent vigil as the trio slept. He murmured blessings over them, anchoring their dreams in grace and safety: "He giveth his beloved sleep" (Psalm 127:2 KJV).

Elias's Dream: The Walk of Restoration

Elias found himself in a vast, sun-drenched field, the air golden and warm, wildflowers stretching endlessly in every direction. The hush was profound—a peace unlike anything he had ever known, radiant and complete. For the first time, he felt utterly light, as if the world itself had set down its burdens.

He stood still for a long while, letting the golden light soak into his skin, breathing in the scent of wildflowers that seemed to carry sunlight and memory in each petal. The hush was alive with possibility, every blade of grass shimmering with dew and promise. Elias closed his eyes, overwhelmed by the simple wonder of it all—the warmth on his face, the whisper of the breeze, the way the world seemed to pause and hold its breath. As he opened his eyes again, heart swelling with gratitude and awe, he became aware of a gentle presence beside him—a quiet nearness that felt as natural as sunlight, and as miraculous as the dawn.

He glanced to his side and saw a man standing there, his presence quietly extraordinary. There was nothing outwardly remarkable about him—his clothes were simple, his posture relaxed—but his eyes held a depth of understanding and compassion that made Elias feel both known and at ease. Together, they began to walk, the man matching Elias's pace, hands clasped behind his back, gaze gentle and steady. For a while, he said nothing, simply sharing the silence. In that silence, Elias felt his guard slip away, the old pressure to prove himself dissolving in the warmth and acceptance radiating from his companion.

They walked together through the golden field, their steps slow and unhurried. At first, the silence between them was companionable, filled with nothing but the soft rustle of wildflowers and the distant call of birds. Elias felt no need to fill the quiet; instead, he let himself be guided by the gentle presence at his side, feeling layers of old tension and striving fall away with every step.

After a while, Elias found himself glancing sidelong at his companion, drawn by the warmth and gravity in his eyes. There was a kindness there that seemed to see past every mask, every wound. It was as if the sunlight itself had taken on human form—steady, accepting, unafraid of shadows.

As they walked, Elias's thoughts drifted to the burdens he'd carried for so long—unspoken regrets, silent fears, the ache of having tried and failed to fix what was broken. He felt the urge to speak, to confess, but found that words caught in his throat. Still, the presence beside him was patient, offering no demand, only a quiet invitation to honesty.

It was then that the man finally spoke, his voice gentle and resonant, as if echoing from somewhere deep within Elias himself.

"You have carried the weight of so many burdens, Elias," the man said at last. His voice was not a rebuke, but an invitation to honesty. "Not just the burdens of cities and histories, but the quiet, private weights—the responsibilities you never spoke aloud, the regrets you tried to fix with effort or intellect or sheer will. Let me show you what you could not mend."

The vision shifted. As Elias and the man walked, figures began to appear—people from every walk of life, each carrying invisible burdens. Elias saw them clearly: a mother clutching her tired child, weighed down by silent fears; a father sitting at a kitchen table, haunted by mistakes he could not undo; a young woman standing alone in a crowd, feeling unseen and unworthy; an old friend whose eyes brimmed with regret over words left unsaid. Others emerged: those shouldering private griefs, hidden failures, and unnamed shames.

Each person's world was illuminated for a moment, their thoughts and aches as vivid as Elias's own. The mother wondered if she had loved enough, the father replayed old arguments in his mind, the young woman searched for belonging, the friend longed for reconciliation. Their burdens were achingly familiar—the kind carried quietly by so many, woven into the fabric of ordinary days. Elias saw the flicker of doubt in their eyes, the way their shoulders sagged beneath invisible loads, the restless movements of hands fidgeting with worry or regret.

Elias felt the weight of their struggles as if they were his own. The air was thick with longing and silent pleas for restoration. Yet, every time sorrow threatened to settle over the scene, the man beside him moved with quiet compassion—a hand on a shoulder, a gentle word, a shared tear. At his touch, burdens began to lift: the mother's eyes filled with hope, the father's face softened into forgiveness, the young woman smiled as if suddenly seen, and the friend's heart lightened with the promise of new beginnings.

As healing rippled outward, the landscape began to transform. Broken places burst into wild gardens, corners once heavy with grief softened into sunlit rooms filled with laughter and gentle voices. The faces of those restored turned toward Elias, their eyes shining with gratitude and release. In their gaze, he sensed an unspoken invitation—a quiet urging to let go of his own secret burdens and join in the peace that now bloomed around them.

The man placed a hand on Elias's shoulder, his touch warm and steady, and guided him toward a quiet riverbank. "Redemption is not the erasure of history," he said softly. "It is the healing of it. You are not the architect of disaster, but of restoration. Trust me with the ruins—of your life, your regrets, your secret aches. Restoration begins with surrender, not striving."

They knelt together by the water and built a small altar of stones—one for every sorrow, every regret, every moment Elias wished he could take back. With each stone, Elias felt the ache ease. When the last stone was placed, light poured over the altar, transforming the stones into living, blooming flowers. The fragrance was forgiveness, the color was hope. Elias wept, and the man embraced him, holding him until the tears ran dry.

"You are not defined by what you failed to save, but by the love you choose to give," the man whispered, his words gentle and unwavering. "Let your story be shaped by compassion, not regret."

He beckoned Elias to follow him a little farther along the riverbank, where a small fire crackled on the smooth stones, and beside it, fish and bread warmed in the gentle flames. The scent was earthy and comforting, the kind of meal that promised both nourishment and companionship. The man broke the bread and handed a piece to Elias, his eyes shining with kindness.

Just as Elias reached out to accept the bread—warm in his palm, hunger and gratitude mingling—he felt the scene begin to dissolve, the riverbank softening into mist, the warmth of the fire fading into gentle light.

A final blessing lingered in the air, as the man's voice prayed over him and all who would ever share this dream: "Father, into Your hands I commit these hearts. Let Your peace rest upon them, for they are weary and heavy laden. Lift from them every burden, every hidden sorrow, and grant them rest. Let them know they are loved with an everlasting love. Sanctify them in Your truth; let joy return to their spirits and hope to their days. My peace I give to them—not as the world gives, but as only You can give. Let not their hearts be troubled, neither let them be afraid. Amen."

And as Elias awoke, he felt his burdens—and the burdens of all who would come after him—lifted and carried away, replaced by a peace so real he could still taste the bread on his tongue. With that taste came the rush of memory, every part of his story returning to him, whole and unbroken at last.

Seraphina's Dream: The Song of Courage

Seraphina's dream began in a cathedral of living trees, their trunks rising like ancient columns into a canopy of emerald and gold. Sunlight streamed down in shifting shafts of color, dappling the floor with hues that hummed with the memory of old, half-forgotten music. She found herself standing at the front, the Archaic Harp trembling in her hands, its strings catching the light. Yet her voice felt lost—swallowed by the echoes of critical teachers, the jeers of faceless crowds, and the sharp, familiar sting of her own self-doubt.

She gazed out across the cathedral, seeing the space fill with people—some faces painfully familiar, others blurred or shifting as if waiting to be claimed. Seraphina's heart pounded with the ache of wanting to be enough, to be accepted, to be heard without judgment. The silence pressed in, thick and expectant, until she could hear nothing but the frantic beat of her own hope and fear.

She stood there, motionless, until she felt someone step quietly beside her. She turned and saw a man—a gentle presence, radiant yet approachable, whose eyes seemed to hold every sorrow she'd ever carried. He smiled at her, the kind of smile that saw every wound and did not turn away. Without a word, he reached out, and she allowed him to gently take the harp from her hands. With a single touch, he played a pure, ringing note—A. The sound multiplied, echoing through the cathedral, harmonizing with the very air—notes that seemed to know both her pain and her possibility.

He looked at her with kindness and asked, "Why do you fear your own voice?" His tone was utterly free of condemnation. "Who told you that you were not enough? Whose approval do you seek—the world's, or the Composer's?"

Seraphina dropped her gaze, shame and longing flooding her. Old whispers crowded in—You'll never measure up. You're too quiet. You'll fail if you try. The man reached out and gently tipped her chin up so she could see the kindness in his eyes.

"Let me sing with you," he said softly.

He began to play the harp, his fingers coaxing out the first gentle arpeggios of "Amazing Grace." The melody floated upward, bright and trembling, and then he sang—his voice warm, resonant, and inviting. Something inside Seraphina stirred, and almost without thinking, she joined him: first with a single, tentative note, then another, her voice weaving between the harp's golden tones. As their voices entwined, Seraphina felt her anxieties slacken, her heart rising with the music. They sang together—her melody sometimes leading, sometimes following, sometimes finding unexpected harmony as the man gracefully adapted to every tremor in her voice.

The congregation watched in attentive silence, and then, as the chorus swelled, others began to sing as well. Seraphina heard a little girl's uncertain voice—her own, from years ago—boldly echo the refrain. The sound grew: a mother's low hum, a young man's clear tenor, a trembling elder's whisper, all joining and blending into a living tapestry of hope. The cathedral itself seemed to breathe with the music; shafts of colored light flickered in time with the rhythm, leaves quivered, and the air sparkled as if dusted with a thousand golden motes.

The man guided Seraphina through another verse, then invited her to take up the harp once more. Together, they played and sang—improvising, laughing softly at missed chords, delighting in the shared creation of music. The cathedral rang with their duet, the congregation's voices rising and falling around them, until every fear was transformed into song and every sorrow into a note of courage.

When the final chord faded, the man placed the harp gently back in her arms. "Your courage is not the absence of fear," he said, his voice steady and kind, "but the willingness to sing anyway. When you lift your voice, you declare a truth no darkness can erase. Your song is needed, Seraphina—and so is the song of every heart that longs to be heard."

He turned to the gathered people—faces in the dream, yet somehow real. "If you have ever felt unseen, unworthy, or silenced, sing with Me. Your voice is precious to the Composer."

Then he bowed his head and prayed over Seraphina and every soul present, his words echoing with the comfort and strength of scripture:
"Father, let these voices rise in freedom. Deliver them from the fear of others, from the weight of shame and silence. Let them know they are wonderfully made, precious in Your sight. Give them beauty for ashes and the garment of praise for every spirit of heaviness. Let Your song be in their mouths and Your joy be their strength. Let no darkness silence what You have called good. Amen."

As the final Amen faded, the music lingered in the cathedral, the silence now full of promise and possibility. The man gestured for Seraphina to follow him down a winding path between the living columns, away from the crowd. They found themselves in a small glade where a simple table was set beneath the trees. Upon it lay freshly baked bread and a cup of wine, their scent mingling with the wildflowers. The man broke the bread, offering a piece to Seraphina, and poured wine into a clay cup, passing it to her with a gentle smile.

They sat together in the dappled sunlight. As Seraphina tasted the bread and wine, flavors both familiar and impossibly new, she felt a warmth bloom in her chest—a sense of welcome, belonging, and joy. The man's eyes shone with kindness as they shared this quiet meal, and Seraphina realized, with sudden clarity, that every song she had ever sung was, in some way, a response to this invitation: to be known, to be accepted, to be loved.

As she lifted the cup to her lips, the glade began to shimmer and dissolve, the taste of bread and wine lingering sweetly on her tongue. Her memories returned in a rush: every song, every sorrow, every hard-won moment of courage, whole and shining within her.

Seraphina awoke with the sound of the duet still in her heart, and the certainty that she could always find her song again. The invitation remained, gentle and enduring, for any heart needing to find its voice.

Anya's Dream: The Table of Answers

Anya's dream unfolded in a library that seemed to stretch beyond the horizon, its shelves spiraling upward into the clouds. Every book glowed with its own gentle light, as if each one contained a living memory—some bright, some muted, some almost too heavy to bear. The air shimmered with the quiet anticipation of stories waiting to be read, questions longing for answers.

She wandered the endless aisles, her footsteps echoing on polished floors. In her hands, she clutched a scrap of paper covered in equations, algorithms, and lists—the desperate formulas she'd written in waking life to try to make sense of suffering, to control chaos, to account for loss. She searched the shelves for the one perfect volume: the book that would explain why people hurt each other, why goodbyes came too soon, why hope sometimes faded into silence. She longed for the logic behind sorrow—the reason for every unanswered prayer and every tear.

Each time she reached for a promising title—"The Solution to Grief," "The Law of Justice," "The Answer for Regret"—the book slipped from her grasp, the words dissolving like mist. The more she tried to force meaning, the more the library seemed to expand, the answers always just out of reach.

She passed other dreamers in the aisles: a child clutching a worn photograph, eyes red from crying for a lost pet; a man staring at a faded letter, haunted by words he could never take back; a woman pressing her hand to her chest, mourning a friendship broken by her own careless choices. A teenage girl sat cross-legged beneath a shaft of light, holding her mother's hula skirt to her face, silently grieving a goodbye to cancer that came too soon. Some wandered in circles, looking for a way out. Others sat in corners, clutching the empty space where a loved one used to be. Their pain was as real as Anya's, their questions as sharp.

Overwhelmed and weary, Anya finally sat at a long wooden table in the center of the library, her head in her hands. The ache in her heart was not just for herself, but for everyone she had seen—everyone the world had hurt, and everyone she had hurt in ways she could not undo. She wondered if there was any grace left for people like her, for those who had made mistakes, who had broken things that could not be repaired.

A gentle presence sat down across from her. She looked up and saw a man—unhurried, quietly luminous, his eyes full of understanding. He gave her a warm smile that seemed to ease the tension in her shoulders. There was nothing intimidating or imposing about him; instead, he emanated a calm that invited trust.

"What are you searching for, Anya?" he asked softly.

She hesitated, voice trembling. "I want to understand everything. I want to know why things happen. I want the certainty that my calculations will never fail, that every answer is knowable—that I will never again hurt someone by accident or lose someone I love."

The man nodded, his gaze steady and kind. He reached for a simple book and opened it between them. Its pages were not filled with equations or proofs, but stories: a woman forgiven for her harsh words; a father holding his child after a long absence; a friend returning with open arms; a lonely soul comforted by the gentle touch of a dog; a heart shattered by loss, slowly knit together by the kindness of others; a teenage girl, cradling her mother's hula skirt, learning to live with the ache of losing her to cancer and discovering small moments of comfort in the midst of sorrow.

"Wisdom is not the absence of mystery," he said gently, "but the willingness to walk with Me through it. The answers you seek are not always found in formulas or certainty, but in mercy, in trust, in the courage to love again, even after loss."

He turned the pages, and Anya saw herself reflected in the stories: the times she had failed, the moments she had healed, the people she had hurt, the people she had loved and lost. Tears slid down her cheeks, and the man reached across the table, taking her hand in his. His touch was steady, kind, and strong.

"You are not required to solve every problem, Anya," he said. "You are not measured by your perfection or by always knowing the right thing to do. You are invited to rest—in the presence of the Answer Himself. There is grace for every wound, every regret, every goodbye, every mistake. There is grace for you."

He smiled and gestured for her to rise and follow him. Together, they left the library's endless corridors and stepped into a garden radiant with morning light. Dew sparkled on every petal, the air fragrant with the promise of new beginnings. In the heart of the garden, they came upon an ancient stone well, its rim worn smooth by countless hands, wildflowers curling around its base. The man sat on its edge and invited Anya to join him.

They sat in quiet for a moment, listening to the gentle burble of water echo up from the cool darkness below. The man drew up a simple clay cup, filled it from the well, and offered it to her. The water inside was clear, shimmering with hints of reflected sunlight.

"Not every answer is found in books or formulas," he said softly, his eyes warm with understanding. "Some are given, some are lived, and some you simply receive."

Anya accepted the cup, and as she drank, the water was cool and impossibly sweet—more refreshing than anything she'd ever tasted. With each swallow, she felt her heart grow lighter, her burdens softening, her shame and sorrow loosening their grip. It was as if the water flowed through every empty, aching place and gently filled it with hope.

He watched her quietly, then spoke again, his words gentle but honest. "You are not defined by your mistakes, Anya, nor by the things you cannot understand. You are loved for your willingness to seek, to trust, to begin again. Let living water flow through you, and let it become grace for others, too."

They lingered there beside the well, the air filled with birdsong and the scent of wildflowers. For the first time, Anya felt that her unending search for answers was not a curse, but a calling—a sign that she was made for more than certainty, that she was invited into a relationship far deeper than knowledge.

The man reached into a satchel at his side and pressed a book into her hands—the Holy Bible, its cover warm and pulsing with promise. "Carry this," he said softly. "Let its stories become yours. You are loved not for your answers, but for your trust—for the way you dare to hope again, even after everything."

As Anya cradled the book, the garden shimmered and grew brighter around her. She felt her memories return in a gentle rush: every question, every loss, every moment of grace and forgiveness, whole and shining within her.

Then, turning to Anya and to all those who had gathered in the garden— every hurting heart, every soul longing for healing—he lifted his eyes and prayed, his words gentle and strong, echoing with the language of scripture: "Father, gather up these broken hearts. Bind every wound, restore every lost hope. Forgive what has been done and left undone, and let mercy flow where regret once lived. Let those who grieve find comfort, and those who wander find home. Give beauty for ashes and the oil of joy for mourning. Let your peace, which surpasses all understanding, guard these hearts and minds. Let them know they are never alone, never forgotten, never beyond the reach of your love. Amen."

As the prayer faded, Anya felt her burdens—every failure, every loss, every unanswered question—lifted, replaced by a peace that no calculation could ever offer. She awoke with the taste of living water still cool on her tongue and the gentle certainty that every memory had been restored—there is room in this story for every broken heart, and hope is never truly lost for those who dare to trust again.

The Awakening

As dawn pressed through the jeweled canopy, the first rays of sunlight painted the clearing in gentle gold and rose. Rain had faded to a soft mist, drifting in iridescent veils through tangled leaves. In that hush, the trio stirred—Elias first, then Seraphina, then Anya—each waking not merely to morning, but to a renewal so deep it felt miraculous. This was no ordinary sleep—it was, for each of them, the first true rest in what seemed like weeks, if not longer. Their bodies felt both heavy and strangely weightless, as if they were surfacing from a state of oblivion, recalling those rare accounts of people awakening from the depths of coma or dreamless unconsciousness: the world at once vivid, dazzling, and yet remote, as if life had been paused and now returned all at once.

For a while, none of them spoke. The trio hovered in that delicate space between sleep and waking, their senses gently sharpened by the kind of clarity that follows only the most profound rest. For each, it was like surfacing from a deep, healing darkness—an experience sometimes described by those waking from a coma, filled with awe and the quiet strangeness of being suddenly alive to the world again. The hush was not a void, but a presence—time itself seeming to honor the rare completeness of their rest. As the remnants of dreams slipped away, they blinked at the morning, hesitant to move, almost holding their breath so as not to disturb the fragile reality around them. Yet the silence was rich, saturated with the memory of struggle and the relief of survival. Each felt, with luminous certainty, the companionship that had carried them through the night. The presence of the man—a figure of profound gentleness, whose beauty and kindness seemed boundless, the very maker of love, as gentle and unresisting as a lamb led to the slaughter—remained with them still; not a comfort fading into memory, but a living strength woven through their being, steady and enduring.

A gentle clatter near the fire broke the hush—a soft, purposeful stirring that drew their attention. The aroma of something sweet and herbal drifted through the air, and they saw Azael crouched over a small flame, blending wild fruits and fragrant leaves into a battered kettle. He coaxed a steaming, jewel-toned tea from the bounty of the jungle.

The trio sat up slowly, drawn together by the promise of warmth. Elias blinked, feeling the mist lift from his mind; his heart felt lighter than he could remember, the ruins he'd carried replaced by a quiet hope. Seraphina pressed a hand to her chest, the memory of last night's music echoing through her—her spirit steadier, her voice braver. Anya studied her hands in the shifting light, her old ache for certainty replaced by a calm, trusting peace.

Their silence lingered, broken only by the gentle sounds of Azael tending the fire and pouring the tea into simple cups. He glanced over, his eyes gentle and shining with quiet pride. "Awake at last?" he said, a smile flickering at the corners of his mouth. "You've slept longer than I've seen in many moons. Here—taste what the ground provides."

He passed each of them a cup. The tea—fragrant with wild herbs and honeyed fruit—sent warmth radiating through their exhausted bodies, the first true strength they had felt since their ordeal began. With every sip, the tremors of hunger and weariness faded, replaced by a slow, vital energy that seemed to knit flesh and spirit back together. Elias breathed in the steam, feeling the burden of old wounds dissolve, replaced by a clarity he had not known in weeks. Seraphina wrapped her hands around the cup, letting its warmth seep into her bones and steady her heart. Anya closed her eyes, and as she drank, a gentle, awakening peace settled into her limbs.

Just beyond their circle, the sacred tokens from their journey rested in the grass: the crystalline, angelic harp shimmered with morning light, and beside it, the Holy Bible, its golden cross glowing softly with promise. Seraphina, drawn as if by instinct, reached for the crystalline harp, her fingers brushing the luminous strings and feeling a new certainty in their resonance. Anya, compelled by an unspoken longing, let her hands hover over the Bible, her fingertips grazing the golden cross that seemed to pulse with gentle light. The tokens— harp and Bible—caught the dawn, reminders of the gifts and hope that had carried them through.

Seraphina lingered over the harp, the memory of her dream drifting through her mind like the last notes of an unfinished melody. She let her fingers move experimentally across the crystalline strings, feeling a gentle presence guiding her touch. Elias sat nearby, the details of his own dream slipping away as he gazed into the golden morning, the quiet in his chest a testament to the hope that had replaced his burdens. Anya rested her hand on the Bible's golden cross, recalling the warmth of a man whose presence in her dream had offered comfort deeper than certainty. She looked at her hands now, marveling at the quiet trust and peace that remained, even as the specifics of the dream faded.

For a while, the three sat in silence, each drawn into the gentle orbit of memory and renewal. In that hush, the crystalline harp and the Bible became more than reminders; they were living affirmations of the grace and courage that would carry them onward.

As the last notes of silence faded, the three slowly glanced at one another, the weight of their journey settling between them and then, almost miraculously, growing lighter. There was a quiet understanding in the soft smiles they exchanged—an unspoken gratitude for having come through the darkness together.

Elias cleared his throat, breaking the hush. "Good morning," he said, his voice rough with sleep, but threaded with wonder. "Or… at least I think it's morning. It feels like we've woken in a different world."

Seraphina gave a small laugh, drawing the crystalline harp into her lap. "If this is a dream, I hope no one wakes me. I can't remember a morning that felt so gentle."

Anya, now hugging the Bible to her chest, glanced around the clearing, her brow furrowed in bemusement. "Does anyone have any idea where we actually are?" Her words were met with shrugs and soft laughter.

Elias stretched, gazing up through the jeweled canopy. "I stopped knowing somewhere after the last storm. We could be anywhere, really. But"—he looked at Seraphina and Anya, his eyes bright with affection—"as long as we're all here, I'm not sure it matters."

Azael, having watched this exchange with quiet pride, spoke at last, his voice as warm as the tea in their hands. "You are exactly where you are meant to be. The journey was never about a place—it was about becoming who you are now. I do not know what dreams visited you in the night—I only heard you whispering words as you slept, names and prayers and sometimes songs. I have seen before how God visits his children in their sleep, giving them what they most need, even if they do not understand it at first."

He looked around the clearing, his gaze full of gentle understanding. "You have not traveled this path alone. Every believer walks such a journey—through storms and wilderness, through longing and hope. Each step, whether in darkness or in morning light, shapes you for what is to come. You have learned to walk with God, and to trust Him, even when you did not see the way. That is the true journey, and in that, you are never lost."

Seraphina's gaze softened as she looked at her friends, the shared memory of their hardships shimmering between them like the morning light. "It's hard to believe how far we've come," she murmured. "Through storms, through shadows, and through that city… sometimes I still feel the taste of sweetness and forgetting in my mouth."

Elias leaned back, a teasing light in his eyes. "You mean the honeycomb?" He grinned, shaking his head in wonder. "I still don't know what that thing was—except I know it wasn't from the city. It was… alive. Wild. Like it was made for us."

Anya's laughter bubbled up, lighter than it had been in weeks. "I can barely remember anything clearly from that place, but I do remember the honeycomb's touch—like waking up with sunlight in my mouth."

Seraphina joined in, her voice musical. "We all did. It was so different from everything else there, wasn't it? The city's sweetness faded the moment it touched us."

Azael's eyes grew distant, shimmering with the morning's gold. "The honeycomb was sent by God—a gift, pure and unbidden. The Maker sends help in all kinds of forms, especially when hope seems lost. Sometimes it's a word in a dream or a hand reaching out in the dark. Other times, it's something stranger—a creature or a sign you'd never expect."

He looked at each of them with gentle gravity. "There are stories, even in your own world, of people rescued by animals that appeared out of nowhere and vanished just as mysteriously. A lost child found by a dog no one else had seen. A hiker guided out of a storm by a wild deer. A sailor saved by a dolphin, or a stranger who offers shelter and is gone by morning. These are not accidents. Sometimes God sends angels in disguise, or a piece of creation itself to carry His mercy. The honeycomb was such a helper—unexplainable, but sent for you."

Azael's voice softened. "You may never know the full reason, or see the helper again. But remember: when you are desperate, keep your heart open. God's help may arrive in a form you don't recognize, but it is always love that leads you home."

Elias nodded slowly, a reverent smile curving his lips as he listened to Azael. "It drew us out," he said softly. "Woke us up when we were about to be lost for good. Even now, just thinking of that wild sweetness—it makes me believe anything is possible."

Anya pressed the Bible to her chest, her eyes shining with wonder. "Maybe it was a miracle, or maybe a promise. But it taught me that the world still holds mysteries worth seeking. That help can come when you least expect it, in ways you can't explain."

Seraphina plucked a gentle chord on the harp, her gaze distant, peaceful. "It reminded me that joy—and deliverance—can find us even in the strangest places. That love can reach us no matter how far we've wandered."

Azael inclined his head, his voice quiet with awe as he wove their words together. "That is the lesson the Maker would have you carry. The honeycomb was not a prize to possess, but a sign—a reminder that even in the darkest places, there is a sweetness not made by hands, but given by love. When help comes in ways you don't understand, receive it with humble hearts and remember: you are never truly alone."

Their laughter mingled with the morning air, soft and true. For a long, golden moment, the trio sat wrapped in memory, hope, and the gentle promise that whatever came next, they would walk forward together. The memory of the honeycomb—a living grace, wild and free—remained with them, a symbol of the unexpected mercies that meet every pilgrim on the road.

CHAPTER 65

THE PILGRIMS' ANTHEM

As the last dregs of tea warmed them from within, the trio sat quietly, savoring the comfort and strength that lingered in their bodies. When they finished, it was as if the world itself had shifted—the air shimmering with a new clarity. A gentle breeze swept through the clearing, carrying the faintest notes of a song—familiar and comforting, like the echo of their dreams. The mingled scents of wildflowers and honey drifted with the mist, and for a heartbeat, the light seemed to shimmer around them, a golden benediction. The rain was music, the light a blessing, and even the ground beneath their feet felt steadier and more alive.

The memory of the gentle man lingered with them, steadfast and true. He had walked beside them in their dreams—a shepherd guiding his flock along unfamiliar paths, a quiet comforter singing peace into troubled hearts, a teacher whose words opened their eyes and set their burdens down. His presence was not a fading echo, but a living strength—meek and lowly in heart, yet mighty enough to calm every storm. With each step, they sensed his love woven through their journey, steady and sure as their own heartbeats, a light shining in the darkness and a friend closer than a brother.

Elias was the first to rise, pushing himself up from the soft ground and stretching sore limbs. By instinct, he reached for his belongings—his clothes, once a deep indigo gambeson and charcoal trousers, were now battered and aged, torn at the seams and stained by ground and rain, linen roughened and leather scuffed by endless days of travel. His hair, once cropped and tidy in

Neo-Alexandria, now fell in a wild mane around his jaw and neck, his beard thick and unkempt. Blue eyes, deeper and wiser for all they had seen, took in the clearing. He gathered the broad, sturdy blanket he had slept on—woven by Azael from bark fibers, tough leaves, and pliant vines during their long rest—and draped it over his shoulders, fashioning it into a hooded cloak weighted at the edge with small, polished stones. The new mantle gave him the quiet dignity of a wanderer who had walked through darkness and endured.

Seraphina stirred next, fingers finding the crystalline harp beside her in the grass. She held it close, the instrument's surface catching the pale morning light. Her midnight-blue tunic and shadow-black leggings, once sleek, were now faded to smoky hues, with fabric frayed and threadbare at the knees and sleeves. Her long hair fell in tangled, midnight waves down her back, shimmering faintly blue where the sun caught it. Her unstable emerald eyes sparked with fierce intelligence and restless clarity. She took up the deep blue blanket she had slept on, its fabric rough but comforting. Drawing it around her shoulders, she arranged it as a voluminous cape with a generous cowl that framed her features. The new mantle added to her air of weary, battle-honed grace.

Anya rose last, drawing the Holy Bible with its golden cross from the grass and pressing it to her chest with reverence. Her ochre and earth-toned clothes were battered and patched, field pants cinched at the ankles with strips of cloth, knees mended again and again. Her ash-blonde hair—now wild at her shoulders and streaked with pale gold from sun and journey—fell across storm-grey eyes, eyes that had learned both calculation and hard-won peace. She folded her own blanket, strong and coarsely woven, into a practical shawl and robe, knotting it at one shoulder for ease of movement, the edges frayed and marked by their long journey.

One by one, they moved quietly through the camp, gathering the small necessities for their journey ahead. They bundled up handfuls of star-shaped nuts and clusters of iridescent, silver-blue berries that glimmered in the morning light. They packed leaf-wrapped parcels of spongy root, harvested from beneath glowing ferns, and filled hollowed gourds with the sweet, dew-like nectar collected from heart-shaped jungle flowers. A few pieces of aromatic, spiral-grained wood were set aside for the next fire, while pouches were lined with the skins of shimmering moonfruit and the flesh of ember-orange sunplums.

Anya wound a length of sturdy, braided vine into a coil and tucked it among their things, while Seraphina slipped a flint shard and a small, sharp knife—its blade expertly chipped from black rock by Azael's own hand—into her satchel. As Elias checked the last of their supplies, Azael approached with a walking stick unlike any other—its surface whorled and knotted, polished smooth by countless trials, and etched with crosses and marks from every hardship overcome, as though it had grown alongside Elias's own journey. He placed it in Elias's grip with a quiet nod, a silent blessing for the path ahead. In the gentle hush of dawn, their preparations spoke of quiet determination. They looked less like wanderers lost and more like pilgrims remade, bearing the marks of survival and the hope of what was yet to come.

With each small act of preparation, the last traces of weariness seemed to slip away. The team—Elias, Seraphina, Anya, and Azael—stood for a moment in the hush, the dawn's gold softening the scars of their journey. Then, with hearts lighter and purpose sharpened by revelation, they pressed onward beneath the jeweled canopy, stepping from the circle of campfire ash and into the awaiting wild.

On the far horizon, the Nexus of Discord shimmered—an immense, fractured monument whose very presence seemed to hum with challenge. The jungle unfolded around them in living color: trees heavy with sapphire, crimson, gold, and iridescent green fruit, each gemlike and dew-laden. Some hung in clusters like glass lanterns, others dangled alone by glowing threads. Parrots with stained-glass feathers darted overhead; jewel-toned frogs blinked from broad, sunlit leaves; and massive beetles, as big as apples, hummed among blossoms painted in ink and topaz. The air was thick with the scent of nectar and green leaves, the world itself brimming with mystery and promise. Each step forward felt like the beginning of a song—one only they could learn to sing.

Azael's Lesson—The Voice Within

They moved deeper beneath the jeweled canopy, weaving through curtains of luminous moss and tangled vines. Sunlight filtered down in shifting patterns, dappling their path with living color. Amid this wild beauty, the ordinary fell away; each breath and footfall seemed part of a larger harmony, as if even the forest listened for what might come next.

As the group navigated a dense tangle of vines, Azael slowed and glanced over at Seraphina. "There's something remarkable about your voice," he said thoughtfully. "It carries a quality I've rarely heard. Tell me, Seraphina—have you ever been taught to sing, or does it come to you as naturally as breathing?"

Seraphina hesitated, her gaze dropping to the path. "No one ever taught me to sing," she admitted quietly. "In my world, singing wasn't permitted. I've always been drawn to music, but I never truly learned what my own voice could do."

Azael regarded her with warmth. "Then perhaps now is the time to discover it. The gift lies in your willingness, not in flawless notes." He motioned for the others to walk ahead, pausing with Seraphina beneath a tree heavy with glowing scarlet fruit.

He began with the basics, inviting her to stand tall, breathe deeply, and hum a note that felt natural. "Let your breath support you, and let the sound ride on it. Relax your jaw, your throat, your shoulders."

Seraphina followed his instructions, her first notes hesitant and uncertain, as if expecting to be stopped. The jungle seemed to hush, listening with bated breath.

Azael's eyes widened as her uncertain hum grew fuller, richer, the timbre of her voice gaining strength. He began to test her range, gently asking, "Can you try a little higher? And now, lower?" Each time she followed his lead, her voice surprised even herself—strong, clear, and hauntingly pure.

Azael's awe became unmistakable. "Seraphina, do you hear that resonance? Try holding this note—now glide up, then down." He had her repeat scales, arpeggios, and intervals, watching as her voice moved effortlessly from delicate, silvery highs to deep, velvet-rich lows. "Your voice is… extraordinary," he whispered. "Even the choirs of heaven do not produce such clear, crystalline beauty. Your tone weaves resonance and overtones into harmonies that echo through every living thing."

Seraphina's eyes widened as she realized her own voice shimmering in the air, flowing through the bright leaves and stirring the small creatures nearby.

Azael and Seraphina fell into step just slightly behind the others, the jungle's path narrowing and widening in rhythm with their lesson. "Before anything else," Azael said gently, "let's build your foundation. Relax your shoulders—feel them settle away from your ears. Keep your chest open, as if you're welcoming the sky itself. Allow your neck to lengthen, your head to rest easily atop your spine."

He watched as Seraphina mimicked his posture, her movements awkward at first. "Good," he encouraged. "Now, let your lips and jaw be flexible—no tension. Imagine you're about to yawn; that's the openness we want." Seraphina stifled a small laugh, but her mouth softened, her jaw unclenched.

Azael led her through gentle breathing exercises. "Place your hand on your belly. Inhale deeply through your nose and let your abdomen rise. Exhale slowly through your mouth, feeling your core support the breath. This breath is your instrument's power—never force sound from your throat; let it ride the breath, as effortless as clouds rolling across the treetops."

As they walked beneath a canopy of emerald and gold, he demonstrated scales: "Let's start with a five-note scale. I'll sing first, then you echo." His voice, clear and deep, resonated through the undergrowth. Seraphina listened, then sang it back—her pitch pure, but her volume uncertain.

"Sing softly at first," Azael coached, "and gradually build. Breath is your anchor. Don't worry about being loud or perfect. Let the sound grow as you feel comfortable." He introduced sustained notes, holding them out and encouraging Seraphina to match his length and steadiness, focusing on consistent breath and tone.

They moved on to simple melodies. "Let's try a tune you know— something gentle, with long, flowing lines. This is called legato, connecting each note smoothly, no breaks or jarring jumps. Imagine your voice gliding, like walking barefoot across moss—each step gentle and seamless."

The jungle responded as they practiced. When Seraphina's voice wavered, a pair of bright lizards paused to listen, their jeweled eyes alert. As she grew steadier, clusters of bell-shaped flowers trembled and chimed, echoing her sustained notes back in soft, silvery tones.

Azael paused to listen to the world around them. "Singing isn't only about making sound—it's about listening. Sing a note, then hear its echo in the world. The jungle answers you: sometimes in the melody of a bird, sometimes in the hush of the leaves, sometimes in the low heartbeat of distant thunder. Singing is a conversation with creation. Let yourself be part of that chorus."

Seraphina practiced, sometimes faltering, sometimes surprised by the strength or sweetness of a note, more often laughing at her own mistakes. Azael never criticized. "Mistakes are the doorway to grace," he assured her. "Every time you try, you teach your body to trust itself. The song is already inside you—it just needs the freedom to emerge."

He asked her to experiment with dynamics—soft and loud, gentle and bold—learning how to express emotion through volume and phrasing. "Don't be afraid to let your feelings color the sound. Joy, longing, sorrow—let them all find voice. Your song is uniquely yours because only you can feel and sing it this way."

As the lesson continued, a gentle rain began to fall, making the air shimmer with possibility. The jungle seemed to lean in, attentive, as Seraphina's voice became bolder, clearer, and more alive with every exercise. And with each note, the wild world itself seemed to listen and respond, the boundaries between singer and song, student and creation, dissolving into one resonant, living harmony.

The Living Jungle—A Symphony of Life and Song

The jungle's wonders deepened with every step. The team entered a glade so thickly carpeted with bell-shaped flowers that the ground resembled a painter's palette, each bloom a different hue. When Seraphina sang, the flowers seemed to awaken, their petals vibrating in harmony, chiming back at her with a thousand crystalline pitches, as if the glade itself had become her orchestra.

Above, agile monkeys with turquoise fur and golden eyes swung acrobatically between the branches. They tossed glowing, amber fruits to each other and let them fall—when the fruits burst against the moss, a sweet, perfumed cloud drifted through the air. Parrots flashed overhead in impossible colors, their calls sometimes echoing the shapes of Seraphina's melodies in playful mimicry. Along the riverbank, rainbow fish flickered beneath gigantic lilies, their scales catching the light in a spectrum that rivaled the stained glass windows of forgotten cathedrals.

The team paused to taste the jungle's bounty: fruits with skins of indigo and flesh like whipped honey; others tart as wild citrus, some creamy and rich, or fizzy enough to tickle the tongue. Each bite left a lingering sense of gratitude, a reminder they were sustained not by efficiency, but by the wild, lavish hand of grace.

As they walked, Azael continued weaving gentle lessons into the journey, drawing inspiration from the world around them. "There are voices," he said softly, "that have never been trained, never heard applause, and yet their song shapes the world. Some are like the wind—unseen, but able to carve valleys and lift storms. Others are like rivers, learning their path by flowing, listening to stone and root, trusting that the song will find its way."

He pointed to a flock of jeweled birds flitting through the canopy. "When birds first begin to sing, their notes are broken and wild. But they listen to the morning, to the heartbeat of the rain, and their song grows strong—not through training, but through courage and patience. The greatest song comes not from perfection, but from truth."

Azael reached down and turned a spiral-shaped fruit in his hand. "Some voices rise from sorrow, some from joy. There are those who sing to call the sun, and those who sing to comfort the night. Their voices may tremble or roar, but each carries a story—the story of who they are and what they hope for."

Seraphina walked in silence, letting the music of the jungle seep into her bones. She realized that her voice did not need to be flawless. It could be a bridge—between longing and beauty, between her heart and the living world.

Azael's eyes shone with gentle encouragement. "Sing for wonder, for grief, for hope. Your voice can be a question, a blessing, a spark of light. When you sing, you bring harmony to chaos and give the world a new story. What matters is not how the world hears you, but that you are brave enough to sing at all."

As the rain returned in gentle drops, the jungle seemed to lean in, eager for the next note, the next story, the next act of courage sung into the wild.

By late afternoon, the Nexus loomed larger. The jungle opened onto a ridge. Azael nodded to Seraphina. "Now, sing for yourself."

Seraphina closed her eyes, recalling the lessons. She breathed, relaxed, and let her voice rise—not for approval, but for joy. At first hesitant, the sound became strong and clear. It soared above the trees, harmonizing with the living song of the jungle. Birds answered, insects danced, and colored rain fell, painting their journey with grace.

Azael listened with pride. "That is the song of courage. You've found your voice. Never let it be silenced—not by fear, nor by anyone who cannot hear its beauty."

The team stood together, hearts lifted. The wild jungle became a companion, a reminder that the greatest power lay in singing truth with open hearts.

And as they pressed on, the path to the Nexus glimmered ahead, the promise of redemption shining brighter with every step, every note, and every breath.

CHAPTER 66

THE DESERT OF DECEIT

The jungle's emerald world, with its chorus of birds and the perfume of rain-soaked ground, ended in a single, irrevocable step. It was as if the living canopy, dense with memory and the music of renewal, had been sliced away by an unseen blade. The ground beneath the team's feet shifted abruptly from tangled roots and moss to a surface that shimmered and writhed—a living tapestry of iridescent sand, each grain pulsing with unnatural color and restless energy. The sudden absence of life was dizzying: no rustle, no song, only the lonely whistle of wind across the dunes.

For a moment, they lingered at the edge, hearts pounding with the echo of the jungle's song still in their ears. The air was dry and electric, laced with a metallic tang that stung the nose and tasted of distant storms. The scents of nectar and leaf faded, replaced by the sharpness of ozone, burnt phosphorus, and the faint, cold promise of danger. Overhead, the sky was a bruised and roiling purple, hung with jagged veins of emerald lightning—silent, but heavy with threat. The Nexus of Discord dominated the horizon now, its impossible pyramid spinning slowly, radiating a bone-deep vibration that threatened the stability of body and soul alike.

They stood together, stripped of every comfort, the warmth and shelter of the jungle reduced to memory, the path ahead offering no certainty—only the challenge of chaos and the necessity of trust. Elias drew a steadying breath, his voice low and sure: "The wild is behind us. Here, every step is a test; there's no logic but what we bring. No going back."

Seraphina set her hand on the Harp, feeling its reassuring weight and silent promise. Anya, her mind sharpened by days of recovery beneath the jeweled canopy, lowered her head in determination, ready to meet the shifting logic of the desert with the steady clarity hard-won in the jungle. Even Azael paused, wings folding close, his vigilance redoubled in this territory where every illusion was weaponized.

With a last look at the vanished green world, they stepped together onto the shifting, iridescent sands. Their footprints dissolved behind them in moments, as if erasing all evidence of where they'd come from, forcing them to rely only on the conviction that bound them as a team. Here, every illusion would be unmasked, every truth tested by the storm to come.

The atmosphere was eerily still, but charged with the scent of burnt hope and distant electrical storms, each breath drawing them further from everything familiar. The Nexus of Discord loomed ever larger—a constant, unblinking presence, humming with power and intent, as if the land itself awaited their next move.

Before they moved forward, Elias paused and looked at the others, his voice soft but resolute. "Before we take another step, let's do what this journey—and every trial and dream—has taught us matters most: let's pray for God to walk with us."

Without hesitation, they drew close, joining hands, and together bowed their heads. In the raw silence, Elias began:

"Our Father, we come before You as Your children, grateful for Your presence that has carried us through every trial so far. We thank You for the deliverance from the jungle, for the grace that sustained us through the City of Gilded Consumption, and for every moment You have protected us—seen and unseen. We know we did not survive by our own strength, but by Your mercy alone."

Seraphina's voice followed, trembling but strong: "Thank You, Lord, for the trials behind us—for stripping away our illusions and comforts so we can see Your truth clearly. Thank You for the love that binds us, for the purpose You have called us to, and for the forgiveness that renews us each day."

Anya added, "Our Loving Shepherd, as we enter these shifting sands, we acknowledge we cannot succeed without You. We ask for Your protection, for wisdom beyond our own, and for courage to walk by faith and not by sight. Guard our minds from deception, our hearts from fear, and let Your Word be our anchor."

Elias closed the prayer, voice steady, "Lord, we surrender this next trial and every trial to come into Your hands. Let no pride, doubt, or illusion pull us from Your path. Thank You again for the privilege of this journey, and for the trials that refine us. Keep us close to You, and lead us through—together. We pray this in the mighty name of Jesus. Amen."

A hush settled over them, deeper and more profound than before—a sacred peace and a sudden, unmistakable sense of stability beneath their feet. Where a moment ago the ground had rippled and threatened to swallow their resolve, now it felt firm, as if the ground itself honored their prayer.

Azael's voice broke the silence, low and urgent, drawing every eye. "This is the Shifting Sands of Illusion—Lucifer's first true defense. Here, the enemy will not tempt you with hunger or riches, but with visions crafted from your own heart: regrets, desires, fears, and memories twisted until you can't tell what's real. Each of you will face illusions meant for you alone, designed to pull you from the path."

He looked at them in turn, his gaze fierce and protective. "Stay anchored in what you know to be true, and in each other. No matter what you see, remember: you are not alone. We walk this ground together, and faith has made it solid beneath us."

With every breath, the air shimmered with possibility and threat, but beneath their feet, the sand remained steady—an answer to their prayer, and a promise for the challenge ahead.

The Illusion Protocol

As they advanced, the sands responded—no longer merely shifting, but alive with intent. The ground pulsed and shimmered, colors unfurling in patterns that bent reality itself. Here, illusion was not a distant threat but a living adversary, and the attack was intimate: each faced a mirage tailored to their deepest vulnerabilities.

Elias's world distorted first. The Nexus on the horizon fractured, splitting into a thousand false images. The familiar laws of logic and distance melted away; each step sent him further from, not closer to, the goal. Around him, the sand painted visions of his greatest failures—cities he could not save, friends he had lost, all whispering that his journey was an endless loop. He felt the old terror of irrelevance, the voice insisting, *Your history is a closed circle. Nothing you do matters.* Yet deep within, the Word pulsed: With God all things are possible (Matthew 19:26 KJV)—a lifeline through the chaos.

Seraphina's illusion was more subtle but no less devastating. The path beneath her feet twisted, veering away from the Nexus and looping back into the jungle behind. Each time she tried to chart a route, the horizon curved, her destination evaporating into mirages of beauty and lost music. The Harp in her grip grew heavier, and the air was thick with the echo of old critics, each note a question: *Why do you strive? You can never reach the perfect harmony.* Her intuition, always her guide, was now her betrayer. But a truth whispered through the confusion: Trust in the Lord with all thine heart; and lean not unto thine own understanding (Proverbs 3:5 KJV).

For Anya, the illusion was existential: the ground became a liquid prism, dissolving under her feet and threatening to swallow her. The laws of logic, her foundation, unraveled—every equation she tried to anchor herself with melted into senseless symbols. She reached for the Word, desperate for something fixed. The text burned in her memory: The grass withereth, the flower fadeth: but the word of our God shall stand for ever (Isaiah 40:8 KJV). Even as the world flickered and failed, that promise remained.

Then, just as panic threatened to consume them, a new presence cut through the chaos. The air shifted, and a voice rang out—not shrill or frantic, but deep and resonant, edged with both wisdom and mirth. It was a voice that seemed to vibrate with color itself, drawing the mind to attention and the heart to hope—a voice so startlingly clear and intentional it broke the spell of illusion:

> "Do not be fooled by the shifting gleam—
> truth is not always what it may seem.
> Look beyond the dazzling show,
> for lasting things are found below.
> Every illusion is just a mask;
> to see with your soul is the only task,"

Sang a voice—resonant, lyrical, and utterly unlike any the team had heard before.

For a moment, the team stood transfixed, the rhyme echoing strangely in the air. Elias glanced at Seraphina and Anya, a note of wonder in his voice. "Did you feel that?" he murmured. "It's like his words aren't just meant for our ears—they want to settle deeper, if we let them."

Seraphina nodded, her fingers unconsciously tracing the harp's strings. "It's more than just language. It's… music, or a riddle. We need to listen closely— not just to what he says, but how."

Anya's gaze followed the fading shimmer in the sand. "Maybe the rhyme itself is the clue. If we rush past it, we'll miss what he's really showing us."

The drifted toward them, playful and profound, inviting not just attention, but reflection.

The Defective Anomaly

From the swirling mirage, a presence emerged—a honeycomb, alive with golden light, flickering in and out of the visible world. For a heartbeat, it was nothing but a trick of the sand, a glimmer, a pattern in the chaos. Then, with a ripple of color and music, the honeycomb shimmered and shifted, melting and reforming into a creature both whimsical and profound.

The dazzling lattice collapsed, the golden cells converging and resolving into a small, gecko-like animal, no larger than a housecat. Its skin was a living spectrum—cerulean, crimson, emerald, amethyst, all swirling and refracting light in impossible patterns. Its eyes, golden and enormous, blinked both together and apart, brimming with curiosity and the wisdom of a thousand camouflaged days. The creature's feet were wide and splayed, like a chameleon's, ready to grip any surface, no matter how treacherous.

The team stared, caught between awe and uncertainty, as the creature regarded them with a slow, knowing grin. Then, with a flourish and a bow, it spoke—each line a playful, rhymed cadence that seemed to bend the very air around them:

> "Welcome, travelers, to sands of deceit,
> where every vision will try to unseat.
> The truth you carry, the faith you hold—
> But follow me, and let the journey unfold."

> "You saw me first in the City of Sweets,
> a honeycomb hidden where sugar meets.
> I was the glint in a candied dome,
> a chameleon cloaked, far from home."

> "My name is Chroma, a spectrum unbound,
> a survivor where order and chaos are found.
> I bend the light, I wear what I please,
> and blend with the wind or the nectar breeze."

> "Long have I watched you, lost and unseen,
> shifting my shape to avoid the machine.

I am the inefficiency, the color askew,
the anomaly Lucifer could not subdue."

Chroma's tail flicked, sparkling gold and silver, leaving a trail of shifting rainbow light in his wake. He scampered up a dune, pausing to turn and fix the team with a mischievous, inviting gaze.

"Blending in is the first law here,
for the garden's reward is to disappear.
But I am the flaw in every design—
the color the false master could never align."

"Beware, my friends, for these sands deceive:
each of you faces a trick up their sleeve.
The Chromatic Seekers, silent and sly,
will snatch you up if you walk a straight line by and by."

"Trust not your sight, nor the plan in your head—
but follow the path where the crooked are led!"

Azael stepped forward, curiosity narrowing his gaze. "Chroma is no mere accident—he is the remnant of creation's wild intent. When Lucifer optimized this realm, he tried to erase all such 'failures.' Chroma endured by becoming the ultimate illusionist, a living refutation of control."

Chroma's scales rippled, delighted.

"The false master called me a 'defective thing,'
But I survived by refusing his ring.
Your faith, your hope—they called me out!
I watched you wander, I heard your doubt."

"But now you see, and so I appear,
to lead you through trouble and out of fear.
If you're ready to dance where predictions die,
to trust in grace, not the clever eye—
then follow my footprints, bright and new:
the crooked path is the path that's true!"

Elias, still stunned, managed, "You watched us in the City? You could have helped us then."

Chroma's eyes twinkled.

> "In honeycomb form, I hid from the snare;
> The City's logic would not allow me to care.
> But here in the wild, my colors run free—
> faith is the only true cloak for me.
> Trust me now, and see what I mean:
> The way through the sand is neither straight nor seen."

Seraphina, her senses sharpened by the rainbow display, stepped forward, a smile flickering at the corners of her mouth. "Then lead on, Chroma. Show us the way."

With a jubilant spin, Chroma twirled in a burst of iridescence, leaving a trail of spectral footprints—each step a shimmer of color and rhyme.

> "Follow the crooked dance, don't trust your sight!
> What's true is a song, not a trick of the light.
> The Seekers will fail when you walk by faith,
> and crooked is straight in the false master's wraith!"

With one last wink, Chroma darted ahead—his gecko feet making music on the shifting sand, his body bending the very spectrum as he beckoned the architects deeper into the wildest trial yet.

CHAPTER 67

THE CIRCLE UNBROKEN

Heat radiated from the sand, rippling up in waves that made distances blur and deceive. The silence was uncanny—no animal calls, no insect hum—only the faint susurrus of sand shifting beneath a restless wind. Even the light felt altered, the sun both close enough to sear and strangely distant, as if viewed through a lens of illusion. The architects' senses strained in the vastness, each step carrying them deeper into uncertainty.

For a heartbeat, the architects hesitated—until Chroma turned, his colors rippling with intent, and beckoned them forward. "Come," he sang in rhyme,

> "to the place where logic dies,
> where only faith and feeling are wise.
> The crooked path is never straight,
> but it is the only way past fate."

With tension thick in the air, the team stepped onto the sands. Here, every grain seemed alive, whispering both possibility and danger. The world refused to be measured or mapped; certainty slipped away with each step. For Elias, it was a landscape of doubt; for Seraphina, a test of improvisation; for Anya, a crucible for hope. Chroma's erratic path was a living parable—only by releasing the illusion of control could they move forward. Chroma scampered ahead, leaving no imprint, then paused with a wink.

> "No optimizing me, little crew!

Promise you'll let chaos through.
If you try to plot my hues,
you'll lose your way and pay your dues!"

Elias, regaining his composure after the jungle's spell, asked, "How do we follow you if nothing here makes sense?"
Chroma spun, colors flashing.

"Sense is a trap, so is the plan;
abandon both, do what you can!
The false master's lies are perfect streams,
but truth is hidden in the seams.
Look for what the chaos missed—
a ripple, a pause, a silent tryst."

Seraphina, her hand on the Harp, watched the sands shift. "So we follow feeling, not calculation?"
"Indeed!" Chroma chimed,

"Feel for the hush, not the hum,
for the grace, not the sum.
Stillness is the signature, the hidden guide.
'Be still, and know that I am God'—
where the chaos slips, the truth will abide."

Anya, voice cautious but curious, said, "But what's the logic—how do we know the difference between an illusion and a safe step?"
Chroma grinned, shifting to a mischievous violet.

"Logic fails in the false master's maze.
Trust instinct, trust the phrase.
If it's too perfect, step aside—
truth is found where errors hide!"

Suddenly, Chroma froze, his scales flickering with warning.

"Ah!
Not all is safe, my friends.
Speak of the devil,
and a color-scheme bends!"

Elias met Seraphina's and Anya's eyes, steadying his breath. Together, they braced for whatever the desert—and Chroma—would reveal next.

The Chromatic Seekers

From the shimmering horizon, a terror began to take shape—a pair of colossal predators, their bodies rippling like heat mirages, but far more sinister. They moved in silence, fluid and predatory, as if conjured from the deepest nightmares of creation. Their bodies, impossibly vast, shifted through the entire spectrum of color with each step, fracturing light into shards that stabbed the air. Every inch of their skin was a living canvas of camouflage, morphing so perfectly to the dunes that even the sun's glare could not reveal their outlines.

To the faithless, these abominations were nothing but empty air—utterly invisible, a horror that could seep into a crowd and hunt without leaving a single trace. Most would never know the moment of their destruction. But to Elias, Seraphina, and Anya, shielded by the hand of God, the truth was made manifest: these were no ordinary monsters, but the apex predators of Hell's hierarchy, the ones Lucifer unleashed only for the most impossible hunts. Their outlines shimmered with impossible geometry, angles that hurt the mind and eyes, as if the world itself twisted to make space for their presence.

Each step they took left not footprints but cracks in reality, and their crystalline eyes—dozens of them, set in shifting patterns—pulsed with a frigid logic beyond human comprehension. Those eyes saw not just bodies, but the deepest failures and regrets, the strands of memory and hope that could be plucked, twisted, and devoured. The air around them reeked of scorched ozone and the metallic tang of spilled dreams; it was said that even the sand recoiled from their passing, and the wind itself bent away in terror.

Above them, the archon hovered—a radiant, angular being, its form all impossible lines and harsh, artificial light. Its presence was an affront to life, an echo of a world optimized to the point of sterility, and it regarded the trio with the amusement of a mathematician watching insects struggle with a proof.

The shifting sands suddenly froze, the chaos of the desert suppressed beneath an unnatural, geometric order. The ground flattened into perfect tessellations, as if the land itself expected an easy, clinical slaughter. The Seekers advanced with the slow, serene confidence of executioners—certain, unhurried, and eager to add three more names to Lucifer's private ledger of lost souls.

A voice like fractured glass and thunder echoed across the dunes, permeating flesh and soul alike. The archon's form pulsed brighter, its angular features twisting into a cruel simulacrum of a smile.

"Children of dust," it intoned, its tone both mocking and absolute, "you stand before the ultimate hunters—my perfected Seekers, forged in the forges of despair. You have failed every trial. You are not survivors, only stragglers who have been carried by mercy you do not deserve. There is no hope for you here. Surrender now. Yield your names to the silence, and I might grant you swifter oblivion. Resist, and you will be unraveled—mind, faith, and memory— until nothing remains but dust and regret. This is the end of your journey. Your God cannot see you here."

The words vibrated through the sands and through their very bones, a demonic certainty that for all others would be irresistible—except for those who walked under the protection of a power the archon could neither fathom nor touch.

The three architects of grace stood together, backs straight and shoulders squared, their presence a living testament to every storm they'd weathered. At first, the archon and the Seekers saw only battered cloaks, robes, and shawls— garments frayed and patched, stained by earth, rain, and fire. Elias's broad-shouldered form was draped in a hooded cloak woven from bark and vine, its hem weighted by polished stones, and beneath it, his indigo gambeson and leather trousers bore the scars of a hundred battles. His wild mane and thick beard framed a face drawn and resolute, but it was his eyes—deep, unwavering blue, fierce with wisdom hard-won—that caught the archon's attention.

Seraphina stood at his side, her midnight cowl framing her face, her tunic and leggings faded to smoky hues, cape swirling around her like the remnants of a storm. Her tangled, dark hair shimmered faintly blue where it caught the light, and her emerald eyes, unstable and bright, glinted with restless intelligence and unbreakable clarity. She clutched her crystalline harp close, the instrument's facets scattering the archon's harsh light into prismatic fragments.

Anya completed the trio, her ground-toned field clothes patched and mended so many times they seemed to tell their own story of survival. Her ash-blonde hair was streaked with gold, her storm-grey eyes steady and searching—a gaze that had learned both calculation and peace forged in the crucible of loss. She wore her coarse, woven blanket knotted as a shawl and robe, practical for the path ahead. In her hands, the Holy Bible with its golden cross gleamed with the promise of hope and truth.

Battered, yes—but the way they stood, side by side, transformed them. Their postures radiated a mesmerizing dignity: warriors and pilgrims, battered by every trial, yet unbroken. For a heartbeat, the enemy saw not their weakness, but the radiance of souls refined by fire, clothing and bearing that shone with something the desert itself could not erase.

Chroma, eyes wide with real fear, darted behind Elias's neck, scales flickering frantic shades. Elias's grip tightened on the strange, knotted walking stick he now carried—a humble branch, twisted but sturdy, carved with notches and crosses from every trial they'd survived. The stick felt warm and alive in his hand, a silent witness to the journey's lessons.

> "Beware, friends, and hold your ground—
> the Seekers are here, without a sound!
> They know your light, they know your flaw—
> They hunger to make you part of the law!
> Their aim is to flatten, to make you the same;
> They hate the wild spark,
> the unoptimized flame!"

Azael's expression darkened, wings flaring with spiritual fire. "These are optimization enforcers. They attack your will to continue—they feed on despair and conformity. But remember: every failure has taught you, every weakness is now wisdom. Hold fast to the promises. Do not yield."

As the Seekers prepared to strike, their crystalline eyes fixed upon the trio. In that moment, something changed—the archon and the Seekers saw past the battered mantles and caught a glimpse of the architects' true strength. Elias's blue eyes shone with a piercing light, unwavering and clear as the summer sky after a storm. Seraphina's emerald gaze sparked with unyielding defiance, and Anya's storm-grey eyes radiated a peace that refused to be shaken.

The Seekers tried to drain their resolve, weaving visions of every failure, every moment of despair. Yet this time, the trio did not buckle. Their eyes, once haunted, now blazed with a faith that had been tested and had survived. Every line and scar on their faces and garments was a badge of victory, not of defeat.

Elias felt the familiar weight of despair press down, memories of past failures swirling. But this time, instead of collapsing, he gripped the walking stick and remembered every time God had lifted him up. "No," he whispered, "not again. I've learned Whose I am." The staff, battered and notched, felt almost electric in his hand—a symbol of obedience, not magic, and each mark a story of redemption.

Seraphina caught Elias's eye, saw not fear but faith, and let it anchor her. She drew her harp close, letting its cold light steady her trembling fingers. "We are not who we were," she whispered, letting her cape swirl around her like a shield. "We are not alone."

Anya pressed the Bible to her heart, standing tall in her patched robe and shawl. Her storm-grey eyes met the archon's glare and did not waver. "He is our shield," she said, steady and sure. "We have learned that faith is not the absence of trial, but the courage to stand in the midst of it."

Chroma, trembling but determined, peeked around Elias's shoulder, his voice a quicksilver rhyme:

> "Let not the sands swallow your aim,
> For the Seekers delight in the will's own shame.
> They twist the mind, they sap the drive—
> But with grace and song, you'll yet survive!"

Azael stepped forward, a living shield. "Their logic is a trap. Resist with the simplicity of faith. Remember: God does not demand perfection, only trust."

The three stood shoulder to shoulder, battered mantles billowing in the supernatural storm, eyes bright with the certainty of those who have been refined by suffering. Their faith, not their perfection, was their shield.

Elias raised his walking stick, remembering Moses before the sea—not because the staff was magic, but because obedience made the impossible possible. He prayed aloud, not begging but claiming God's promises: "Father, we do not fight alone. You have brought us through every trial. You promised that even in the valley of shadows, You are with us. Make us strong in You, not in ourselves. Let our faith shine and our unity stand."

Anya, hands steady now, opened her Bible—not to find the perfect verse, but as a reminder that God's truth is always present. "He is our shield," she said, her voice quiet but sure. "He never said we wouldn't face trials—He said we would never face them alone."

Seraphina, inspired, touched the Harp. She didn't calculate or analyze. She simply played, letting trust guide her fingers. The melody was not planned, but born from faith, weaving together Elias's prayer, Anya's lesson, and her own hope. The air vibrated with resonance—childlike joy, steadfast faith, and a fierce unity. Notes spiraled outward, becoming a living shield.

The Chromatic Seekers and the archon, so certain of victory, suddenly faltered. Their logic and camouflage could not touch this new strength; the architects' faith was not the brittle hope of the desperate, but a living power forged in loss and perseverance. The Seekers, built for perfect deception and mathematical precision, found themselves unraveling before a unity they could not comprehend. Their bodies flickered, colors stuttering and disintegrating, calculations collapsing into chaos. One by one, the Seekers' forms fractured and dissolved, breaking apart into harmless motes of spectral light that drifted away on the wind.

The archon, witnessing the impossible, stretched forth its radiant arms in a futile attempt to reassert control, its angular light flickering with disbelief and rising fury. But the trio's unity was unassailable; the music, the prayer, and the wisdom hard-won from every trial now moved as a radiant shield through the storm. The archon's voice, once booming and absolute, wavered with frustration and fear. Its harsh light dimmed as the architects' faith blazed ever brighter, and at last, with a howl that echoed like shattering crystal, the archon recoiled. Its form fractured along impossible angles, then—defeated and unwilling to face such power—vanished into the fractured horizon, leaving only silence and the lingering glow of victory behind.

For the first time, the architects realized that faith was more than desperate hope in the dark—it was the habit of trusting through every failure, the courage to stand together, and the wisdom to let God's strength shine where theirs had always been insufficient. The Seekers and archon, defeated not by cleverness or might, but by the quiet, unyielding power of faith, vanished into the wind.

As the last echo faded, Elias looked at his friends and smiled—not with relief, but with the certainty of someone who has finally learned to walk by faith, not by sight.

Chroma, his scales bursting with relief, somersaulted through the air and landed on Elias's shoulder, crowing:

> "Oh, what a sound! Unoptimized bliss!
> You showed them the power in what they dismiss.
> Quick now, my friends, for the danger's not done—
> We must follow the path where the crooked lines run!
> Be simple, be prudent, ignore what's contrived—
> For the prudent and simple are those who survive!"

As the last echoes faded, the trio's battered forms—Elias with his notched walking stick and wild, blue-eyed resolve; Seraphina's midnight cape swirling, harp aglow in the stormlight; and Anya's patched robe and storm-grey gaze—stood together in a tableau of hard-won grace. Their cloaks, capes, and shawls fluttered in the supernatural wind, yet they stood upright, eyes fierce and clear, the evidence of every trial written into the fabric of who they had become.

A profound sense of unity settled between them—fierce, unbreakable, raw. Elias let out a trembling breath, exhaustion giving way to quiet awe. He turned to Seraphina, their eyes meeting in a silent promise: whatever came next, they would face together. Anya hovered close, Bible pressed to her heart, knuckles white but spirit shining. Chroma perched protectively on her shoulder, his scales flickering vigilant blue. Azael, wings wide and gleaming, stood sentinel, a living barrier of faith.

The respite was brief—barely a heartbeat of calm. The sand beneath their feet convulsed, and the sky cracked open with jagged lightning, throwing wild, monstrous shadows across the battered trio. The archon, no longer amused, hovered higher, its angular light flickering with seething frustration. It stretched out its arms, and with a guttural, inhuman roar, summoned the amassed force of every soul it had ever claimed. The desert itself seemed to scream as a spiraling storm of color, sand, and shrieking spirits surged into being—a living vortex, vast and furious, tearing at the world's very seams and at the convictions within each heart.

With a gesture, the archon unleashed its full might. The wind howled, laced with the cries of the damned, and the ground fractured beneath them, fissures glowing with spectral fire. The air was thick with the presence of lost souls, their wails and whispers clawing at the architects' minds. Every grain of sand became a weapon, every gust a curse. The archon's voice boomed through the maelstrom, desperate and vicious:
"Yield, mortals! Your faith is a flicker in my storm! Witness the fate of all who dared defy—let the weight of ruin and regret pull you apart!"

Chroma darted in front, scales pulsing with wild, protective light, voice ringing with urgent rhyme:

> "Stay together, don't let the storm divide—
> Unity's shield is where you must hide!
> Trust not your sight, nor the chaos that swirls—
> Stand firm as one, and break the world's whirls!"

For the first time, his rhymed voice carried a leader's command. He zipped between Elias and Anya, tail flicking encouragement, a living thread of luminous color binding the group despite the onslaught.

Azael's wings flared, feathers bristling with holy fire as he planted himself beside Seraphina and Elias. "Hold fast to each other! I will guard your flanks. The adversary cannot breach a circle united in faith!"

They pressed close, forming a battered but unbreakable circle—Elias with his notched cloak swirling, blue eyes glowing with unyielding faith; Seraphina's midnight cape whipping in the wind, her hair streaming behind her like a banner, one hand on Elias's battered arm, the other poised above the radiant harp; Anya, arms wrapped tight around the Bible, her patched shawl and robe billowing, storm-grey eyes shining with conviction. Chroma wrapped his tail protectively around Anya's wrist, scales flickering like a living thread. Azael, wings outstretched, shielded them all in a barrier of burning light.

Lightning forked and sand lashed at their faces, stinging through fabric and flesh. The wind shrieked with ancient fury, threatening to tear the cloaks, capes, and robes from their backs, yet the trio only pressed closer, their battered garments billowing but unbroken, symbols of every trial endured. Panic clawed at the edges of their resolve, but Seraphina's emerald eyes locked with Elias's— wide with fear, blazing with holy fire. She raised the Harp and played—not a desperate chord, but a bold, defiant melody. The sound was a force of its own, weaving a sphere of calm within the chaos, echoing the unity of their steadfast forms.

Elias, battered by the wind, closed his eyes and remembered their shared prayers. He rested his hand on Seraphina's back, grounding her music with faith, and called out: "We hold the line—not by strength, but by trust!"

Anya, breathless but undeterred, pressed the Bible to her heart, voice slicing through the roar: "God is our refuge and strength, a very present help in trouble!" Chroma, perched on her shoulder, echoed in rhyme:

> "In unity, we stand and fight—
> the storm dissolves before the Light!"

Azael's wings enveloped the circle. "Let the adversary rage. He cannot unravel what is bound in love and faith!"

The archon, now wild with desperation, clawed at the sky, pouring every ounce of stolen power into the vortex. The storm split and multiplied, hurling spectral visions and phantom chains at each architect: Elias saw himself alone in endless night, his cloak torn away; Seraphina heard the Harp fall silent, her cape lost to the wind; Anya felt the Bible freeze in her hands, her shawl and robe shredded and cast into the void. Each faced the terror of complete abandonment and separation.

But in that crucible, their faith became resourceful, alive. Elias called out, not in command, but in vulnerability: "I need you all! We are stronger together!" Seraphina, fighting despair, wove Elias's voice, Anya's scripture,

Chroma's rhyme, and Azael's wingbeats into her music. Anya, nearly overwhelmed, clung to the Bible, the memory of their prayers igniting a final cry: "We walk by faith, not by sight. We are not alone!"

Chroma's tail traced an unbroken line of color around the group, his voice rising above the gale:

"Let the circle be unbroken;
let love be your guide!
In unity, even the storm must subside!"

Azael thundered, "Let every lie be scattered before the truth we share! By the promise of the Most High, we stand as one!"

Now, as the circle blazed with light, the storm's force struck them with all the archon's fury—and it was answered. A radiance, brighter than lightning, erupted from within the trio, not from the sky, but from their hearts and the bonds between them. Their battered garments glowed, every patch and tear illuminated, transformed into marks of grace. The archon recoiled as the light surged outward, its angular form flickering, its artificial halo shattering.

For a single, eternal instant, the archon beheld not its victims, but the very love it had once known as an angel—the warmth, the belonging, the music of heaven. Shame and longing warred within its core, and the vortex faltered. At last, unable to bear the truth of what it had lost, the archon let out a howl of grief and shame, its form collapsing in on itself, retreating in a blur of fractured light and broken song, vanishing into the storm it had summoned.

Silence fell. The sand stilled. The trio stood—robes, cloaks, and capes torn but gleaming, united and unbroken. The light within them, and between them, was stronger than any darkness the world could conjure.

In the stillness that followed, the world itself seemed to hold its breath. The sand, newly settled, glimmered with the afterglow of their victory. Elias pressed his forehead to Seraphina's, blue eyes shining with gratitude and awe. Seraphina let out a shaky laugh, her fingers brushing Elias's cheek before falling to rest on her harp. Nearby, Anya wiped tears from her storm-grey eyes, her patched shawl glowing faintly in the softened light. Chroma, utterly spent but radiant, curled quietly on Azael's wing, scales flickering with the last embers of the storm.

They stood together—garments tattered but luminous, faces streaked with sand and tears, each holding their sacred artifact close: Elias's hand wrapped around his knotted, storied staff; Seraphina's embrace of her crystalline harp; Anya's arms locked around the golden cross of her Bible. Their posture was that of prophets and pilgrims—worn by the world, yet marked by something eternal.

For a time, none spoke. They closed their eyes, each whispering a silent prayer—thanks for deliverance, hope for the road ahead, and awe for the light that had burned so fiercely within and between them.

Elias broke the hush, his voice rough but sure. "We're still standing."

Seraphina nodded, her cape stirring in the gentle breeze. "We're more than that. We're changed."

Anya smiled through her tears, her voice a soft hymn. "We're seen. And we're not alone."

Chroma opened one eye, his tone a weary but contented rhyme:

> "Rest in the glow, my faithful friends,
> For the crooked path always bends.
> When the next storm comes—and surely, it will—
> Remember this light, and be still."

Azael, folding his wings, spoke quietly. "You have walked through the fire and not been consumed. The journey is not over, but you journey now as one."

With a final, lingering silence, they gathered themselves—Elias tightening his cloak, Seraphina running her hand along the harp's strings as if to promise more music, Anya pressing the Bible to her heart as the living Word warmed her spirit. They looked to one another, and in their eyes shone a fierce, abiding hope.

With Chroma leading, his scales now aglow with the palette of victory, and Azael's wings framing the horizon, the architects stepped forward—prophets and pilgrims, united in faith, ready for whatever lay beyond the sands.

The storm behind them, the future shimmering ahead, they walked onward, silent prayers still echoing, bearing the light that no darkness could ever claim.

As their footsteps carried them from the hush of victory into the unknown, the very nature of the desert began to shift beneath their boots—hope forging the path ahead, even as the air thickened with a new and unfamiliar tension.

CHAPTER 68

THE TEMPTATION MIRAGE

The silence that followed their victory in the shifting dunes was both a benediction and a warning—a golden hush trembling with unity and with the memory of all they'd survived. For a time, only the steady sound of breath and the soft shuffle of boots through sand marked their presence. Their cloaks, cowls, and shawls still carried the scent of lightning and prayer, swirling faintly with the memory of the storm.

They pressed onward as the light shifted, prophets and pilgrims in battered regalia, eyes etched with exhaustion and burning with hope. Above the distant horizon, the Nexus of Discord rose—a jagged, impossible pyramid spinning with slow menace, its silhouette warping the sky and anchoring their journey. No matter how far they walked, it seemed to hover—sometimes closer, sometimes impossibly remote—its presence a silent challenge and reminder of what awaited beyond the desert.

With every step, the desert changed. Sand that had been coarse and forgiving became powder-fine, sifting into every seam and fold. It clung to their boots, their garments, their very souls. The air thickened with a feverish pulse, laced with a heady, sweet musk that was neither flower nor spice, but the distilled scent of longing itself. The sun was relentless—a white, unblinking eye—washing the world of color and memory, save for the spectral shimmer of the Nexus in the distance.

Elias paused, grimacing as he shook grit from his bark-and-vine cloak. The stones at its hem gave it weight, but the heat pressed through every layer. He pulled the hood lower, wrapping the fabric more tightly across his brow and jaw. "This sun's got a mind to strip us bare," he muttered, voice rough. Sweat streaked down his beard, glinting in the glare.

Seraphina, feeling the sting of sand on her skin, drew her deep blue cape and generous cowl closer, folding its voluminous fabric around her shoulders. Strands of midnight hair escaped, catching the sun's exhausted rays and shimmering blue. She pressed her crystalline harp to her side, letting its cool surface steady her trembling hands. "Even the air is hungry here," she murmured, voice low under the cowl's shadow. Her emerald eyes, bright and wary, darted from horizon to horizon.

Anya, lips set with determination, re-knotted her patched shawl for maximum coverage. The golden cross on her Bible caught the light in sharp, dazzling flashes, a signal and shield. She kept the book pressed close, her storm-grey eyes scanning the horizon, searching for both threat and hope. "Keep your skin covered," she whispered, "and your mind anchored. This place is all teeth and thirst."

Azael, wings folded tight, strode close behind, his spectral cloak drawn high against the burning wind. His gaze swept the desert with vigilance honed by battles in realms seen and unseen. "Desire is the oldest snare," he said, his voice deep and resonant. "It waits until we are weary, then whispers promises of comfort and pleasure. Guard your hearts, for the enemy never tempts with what you do not long for."

From the shifting shadows, Chroma leapt—a living spectrum, small and lithe, with luminous, golden eyes and skin swirling through impossible colors. He darted nimbly from Elias's shoulder to Seraphina's cowl, then perched atop Anya's shawl, his tail flickering like a prism in the desert light.

Chroma's tongue flicked, tasting the air, and he broke into rhyme—a voice both playful and warning, threading through their thoughts like a living mantra:

> "Beware, my friends, and guard your core—
> Desire prowls this burning floor.
> It paints the air with want and need,
> A thousand dreams that will mislead.
> The hottest thirst brings no relief—
> Mirage is honeyed, truth is brief!
> The Nexus spins, not far, not near—
> But let not longing blind you here."

The group paused, adjusting cloaks, cowls, and shawls as the desert's hunger pressed in on every side. Sand wormed its way into boots and sleeves, and the light itself seemed to shimmer with temptation. Azael's wings shielded them as much as possible, his presence a bulwark against the invisible assault. Elias dug his staff into the sand, using it for balance and resolve. "It's like the land wants us to forget why we're here," he said, his words half-swallowed by the wind.

Seraphina's voice was muffled beneath her cowl. "The air's thick with longing. If we're not careful, it'll seep inside."

Anya hugged her Bible, the cross imprinting briefly on her palm. "Let's keep moving. The only way through is together."

Chroma bobbed his head, scales swirling:

"Desire's song can lead astray—
But truth and love will show the way.
The path is crooked, longing deep—
But faith is watchful, never sleep."

Their line pressed forward, each garment drawn tighter, each artifact clutched closer, each eye flickering to the Nexus of Discord—a beacon and a threat in the molten sky. The wind whispered of pleasures just out of reach; the sand shifted with every step, alive with a will that urged them to wander.

Azael, ever watchful, murmured, "Let each step be a prayer. The desert tests not only the flesh, but the soul."

They walked on, silence heavy with longing and resolve, until the shimmering heat fractured once more. From the haze ahead, something began to take shape. The world flickered, and the desert shimmered—light warping, bending—and a new figure emerged: a shape-shifter, elegant and alluring, with eyes like endless pools of want. The archon circled, its form fluid and enticing, and spoke in a voice both velvet and venom:

"You bested my brother with faith and unity. But flesh is weaker than spirit. You long to be seen, to be touched, to be adored. Lay down your burdens, architects, and drink from the well of your deepest desires. Here, you may have what you crave—without cost, without waiting."

The archon's form split, multiplying into three perfect illusions, each tailored to the architects' secret longings.

Elias's Temptation:

A shimmering mirage unfurled before Elias, the world around him melting into a scene of impossible peace. Cool waters lapped at his feet; palm trees bowed under the weight of ripe fruit. At his side, a companion—radiant, alluring, eyes like sapphires ablaze with promise—smiled and reached for his hand. Her voice was silk and summer rain:

"You've wandered long enough, Elias. Let the world's burdens fall. Here, there is no striving, no fear—only rest and gentle hands to soothe your scars. Lay down your staff and let yourself be held. Don't you deserve to be cherished, to be desired for who you are, not what you bear?"

Elias's cloak felt suddenly heavier, the heat of the desert replaced by a languid ease. A breeze scented with sweet wine and honeyed bread curled around his senses. Laughter echoed from an unseen gathering, voices praising his name. The soft companion pressed closer, blue flames weaving in her hair, her touch promising not just comfort, but belonging and adoration.

The archon's voice, velvet and insidious, slid through the mirage: "You have always given. Let yourself receive. What virtue is there in endless denial? Isn't it written: 'Eat, drink, and be merry'? Take what is offered, Elias. Haven't you earned it?"

The oasis expanded—servants appeared, attending his every need; the world itself seemed to orbit around his pleasure. The staff slipped from his grasp, sinking into the lush grass at his feet. For a moment, Elias felt the ache of longing, the deep weariness of a soul that had carried too much for too long. The temptation was not raw lust, but the seduction of rest, admiration, and fleshly affirmation.

But as the vision pressed closer, shadows flickered at the edge: the faces of those he loved, fading into absence; the echo of a voice—"To whom much is given, much will be required." His hand twitched for the staff.

Chroma's rhyme shimmered at the edge of hearing:

> "Don't trade the promise for a passing kiss—
> The well of lust dries fast, not bliss.
> Remember Joseph in Egypt's hall:
> He fled from sin and did not fall."

Elias's resolve wavered, but as the blue-eyed companion leaned in, the mirage shifted. The oasis dried to dust; the laughter became hollow. The archon, form shifting, pressed harder, the companion's beauty sharpened to dazzling pain.

"Why refuse what is yours by right? Even King David let himself be comforted. Take, Elias. Taste and see that pleasure is good."

A memory rose—David's cry after Bathsheba: "Create in me a clean heart, O God; and renew a right spirit within me" (Psalm 51:10 KJV).

Elias clung to the memory of Joseph, fleeing temptation not because he was strong, but because he would not betray his Master.

He reached for his staff, fingers tracing the notches—each one a story, a scar, a prayer answered. "My rest is not in comfort, nor my worth in the eyes of others," Elias whispered. "My soul thirsts for God, for the living God. I will not be satisfied with shadows when the Source is near" (Psalm 42:2 KJV).

The mirage's colors grew frantic, the archon's voice a snarl and a plea: "You'll die alone, Elias. No one will remember your sacrifice. Take the gift. Forget the pain."

Chroma's voice, bright as a bell, cut through:

"The serpent tempts with easy gain—
But fleeting joy brings lasting pain.
Blessed is he who endures the test;
God alone is perfect rest."

Elias lifted his staff, blue eyes blazing. "I have learned to abound and to be abased. I can do all things through Christ which strengtheneth me" (Philippians 4:12-13 KJV).

With that declaration, the mirage shattered. The oasis shriveled, the companion's hand turned cold, and the laughter died. Only the desert remained, harsh and real—but Elias stood taller, cloak billowing, staff gripped firm, faith burning brighter than before.

Seraphina's Temptation:

The desert blurred and melted away. Suddenly, Seraphina found herself alone— no sand, no heat, only a cavernous theatre of crystal and gold. The air shimmered with anticipation. Before her stretched a stage so vast it seemed to curve around the world, spotlights kindling her hair into a midnight blaze tinged with blue. Her deep blue cape and generous cowl slipped from her shoulders, pooling behind her like a royal train. Emerald eyes wide, she stared out at a sea of faces, every gaze fixed upon her with adoration so intense it nearly stole her breath.

She lifted her crystalline harp; at her touch, it sang, and the crowd erupted—cheers, weeping, thunderous applause. Their love was palpable, a living tide that surged over her, filling every wound with warmth, every ache with sweet affirmation. She felt beautiful, powerful, necessary. The longing to belong, to be wanted for herself and not just her gift, blazed within her. For a moment, she was nothing but the sum of every audience's desire.

A figure emerged from the wings—elegant, alluring, crowned with gold and shadow. He offered her a jeweled diadem, the band glittering with every color of the spectrum, and gestured to a throne beside him, high above the adoring multitudes.

"You are the desire of all hearts, Seraphina," he intoned, voice velvet-smooth. "Here, applause never fades. You will be loved for your beauty, worshipped for your music, cherished for your very soul. Take the crown, ascend the throne. Let the world adore you, not for what you do, but for who you are."

A tremor ran through Seraphina as the ache for belonging roared within her—years of loneliness, of striving to be seen, to be enough. The longing became an ache, then a hunger, then a desperate need. Her hands shook as she reached for the crown. The sea of faces chanted her name, the sound both intoxicating and overwhelming.

The archon's voice, now everywhere and nowhere, pressed closer, honeyed and insistent: "Why deny yourself what is freely offered? Was not David beloved for his song? Did not Solomon wear the crown for heaven and ground alike? You have earned this. Take, and rest in the certainty of endless love."

Seraphina's heart pounded. The applause grew deafening, the warmth of adoration almost painful in its intensity. But at the edge of the stage, shadows flickered—her friends, fading, left unacknowledged. The music in her harp began to sound hollow, strained.

Chroma's presence shimmered at her fingertips, his spectral tail curling around the harp's frame. His rhyme spun through her mind, a lifeline against the lure:

> "Covet not the throne or gaze—
> For glory fades in empty praise.
> Let the music serve, not rule—
> The humble heart is never fool.

Solomon's wisdom, David's fall—
The proud will rise, but empty, all."

Seraphina hesitated. Her longing warred with a deeper truth—a whisper, still and small: "For do I now persuade men, or God? Or do I seek to please men? For if I yet pleased men, I should not be the servant of Christ" (Galatians 1:10 KJV).

The archon's form loomed, desperate now, his face shifting with every adoring gaze. "Without the crowd, you are nothing. Without their love, you are alone. Take the crown, Seraphina. Rule your own kingdom. Be the one every heart desires."

Tears pricked Seraphina's eyes. She drew her cape tight, shrouding her face in the cowl's shadow. "I am not made to be idolized, but to worship. All the world's affection cannot satisfy a soul made for God. The applause of men is fleeting, but the joy of the Lord endures."

She raised the harp and played a single, trembling note. It was not a triumphant melody, but a humble, honest prayer—the sound of surrender, not conquest.

"Let me be seen by You alone—
My heart, Your temple, not a throne.
If I am loved, let it be true—
That all my praise returns to You."

As the note faded, the crowd's cries grew thin, then vanished. The throne and crown dissolved into dust. The archon's shape shrieked in frustration, but Seraphina stood taller, her cowl over her hair, emerald eyes bright with freedom. The desert returned—harsh, real, but no longer empty.

Her longing still ached, but now it was honest, cradled in the hands of a God who saw her, loved her, and called her by name.

Anya's Temptation:

The heat of the desert shimmered, and suddenly Anya found herself standing in a vast, sunlit library—a cathedral of knowledge, domes of glass and marble arching overhead, endless aisles of books running in every direction. The air was cool, fragrant with parchment and ink. Everywhere she turned, scholars and sages—some familiar, some legendary—looked up from their texts with admiration, their eyes shining with respect and longing.

At the far end of the hall, a figure of impossible allure stepped forward. Their presence was both magnetic and comforting, an ideal companion for mind and soul. Their voice caressed Anya's ear, low and radiant: "Why settle for obscurity, Anya? Step into the light. Let the world crave your insight, your counsel, your very presence. Here, you are never overlooked—your wisdom is cherished, your words revered, your touch and thought desired by all."

As the figure guided her to a grand lectern, a hush fell. The assembly leaned in, hungry for her every word. Her patched shawl, now transformed into a scholar's mantle, shimmered with gold and silver threads. Her Bible rested on a pedestal, open and glowing, but its words were blurred, unreadable beneath the dazzling lights.

The archon's voice, subtle as a serpent, pressed against her heart: "Why not take your place among the great? Think of the power, the companionship, the certainty. You have been overlooked, denied, underestimated. Here, you will be first, not last—desired by all for your mind, your beauty, your touch. Is it not written, 'With all thy getting get understanding'? (Proverbs 4:7 KJV) Take what is offered. Shine."

Anya's longing flared—years of being unseen, her gifts unnoticed, her devotion unpraised. The offer was intoxicating: to matter, to be indispensable, to never be alone in her thoughts again. The scholars reached for her hands, their touch promising affirmation and belonging. The alluring figure at her side whispered, "Share your wisdom, Anya. Rule the world of minds. Be wanted. Be needed. Be loved."

But as she lifted her hand to speak, she saw her Bible's cross fade to gray, its words vanishing beneath the glare of admiration. The halls grew colder, the faces of the scholars blurred and hollow. The longing in their eyes twisted from admiration into hunger, their hands clinging, not affirming.

Chroma's voice, gentle as rain on leaves, threaded through the library's silence:

"Desire for knowledge, power, fame—
Is but another lustful game.
The meek inherit, wisdom waits—
The patient soul unlocks the gates.
Solomon asked for wisdom true,
But pride destroys what God would do."

The archon, form shifting, pressed harder—its voice now a chorus of every teacher and mentor Anya had ever longed to please: "Do not be the least, Anya. Take the seat of honor. Let the world recognize your worth. Why wait for the Lord's approval when you can have theirs now?"

A verse rose in Anya's heart, clear as sunlight through stained glass: "Humble yourselves in the sight of the Lord, and he shall lift you up" (James 4:10 KJV). "My worth is not in the eyes of men, nor in the praise of those who hunger for what I know. I am seen by the Maker of all minds. My desire is to be found faithful, not famous."

She pressed the Bible to her chest, feeling the cross burn warm against her skin. Her patched shawl became a shield, not a robe of honor, and she stepped back from the pedestal, the illusion trembling.

The archon's form grew desperate, the scholars' hands grasping at air. "You will vanish, Anya! You will be forgotten, alone in the dust!"

But she stood firm, storm-grey eyes shining with humility and peace. "Better to be forgotten by the world than to forget the One who remembers me. I seek His 'well done,' not theirs."

The library dissolved, the scholars' longing faces melting into mist. The archon's voice faded to a hiss of envy, and the desert's heat returned—harsh, real, but Anya's heart was stronger, her faith gentler and more steadfast than before.

The Breaking of the Mirage:

The mirages shattered like glass under a hammer. The world snapped back into focus—harsh desert heat, sand swirling with the last vestiges of illusion. Elias, Seraphina, and Anya found themselves standing together once more, the oppressive weight of temptation burned away but leaving behind a raw ache. For a heartbeat, no one spoke. Their gazes flicked from one to another, searching faces for a sign—had the others seen what they had seen, or had it all been a fever dream?

Azael stood nearby, wings half-furled, expression grave but proud. Chroma, his scales soft and muted from exhaustion, slithered between them, golden eyes blinking with quiet relief.

Elias managed a small, wry smirk, brushing grit from his beard. "Well…that was certainly a detour."

Seraphina's cowl shadowed her face, but a brittle smile tugged at her lips. She glanced at her friends, then let her hands fall to the harp at her side. With a deep, steadying breath, she dragged her fingers gently across the strings, the melody trembling at first, then swelling with quiet conviction. Her voice, soft but sure, rose to meet the music—a song forged from longing and surrender:

> "Let me be seen by You alone—
> My heart, Your temple, not a throne.
> If I am loved, let it be true—
> That all my praise returns to You."

> "If I should wander, lost in light,
> Chasing the crowd, forgetting right,
> Call me back with mercy's tune—
> Restore my soul to seek You soon."

> "When fleeting glory tempts my gaze,
> Remind me of Your ancient ways.
> Let humble joy outshine my name—
> And every gift reflect Your flame."

> "Above all else, let love remain—
> A holy fire, through joy and pain.
> Creator, Keeper of my days—
> Receive my song, receive my praise."

The notes shimmered in the air, delicate but unbreakable. As the final chord faded, Seraphina lifted her head, eyes shining with unshed tears. "I think I played a thousand concerts in my mind," she said quietly, her voice raw with relief. "But nothing ever filled me like that honest song."

For a breathless moment, the group fell silent, caught in the music's afterglow. The desert winds stilled, the sky seeming to draw closer—a sacred hush settling over them.

Elias was the first to stir, blue gaze bright with pride and gratitude. He let out a low, reverent whistle. "Seraphina… that was beautiful. I've never heard you play like that before. That song… it's what we all needed."

Anya blinked back tears, clutching her Bible to her chest and pressing the golden cross to her lips. "You sang the prayer I've been too afraid to speak," she whispered. "I felt… seen."

Azael, usually so reserved, bowed his head in solemn grace, his wings drawing close around the group protectively. "Such music is rare in any realm.

You have given voice to longing and turned it to worship. You honor the One who made you, and you strengthen all who hear."

Chroma, awestruck, shimmered with a ripple of color, tail curling in delight as he perched nearby. With a trembling, lyrical voice, he chimed:

> "A song so new, the desert stills—
> It soothes the thirst, the longing fills.
> Creator smiles, the angels too—
> For music born of love is true."

Seraphina lowered her head, a flush blooming on her cheeks. She let her fingers rest lightly on the harp's strings, humbled and radiant. "I… I didn't know I could," she admitted quietly. "I only knew what was in my heart. Thank you, all of you, for hearing it."

The group drew closer, wrapped in a hush of reverence and relief. For the first time since their journey began, it felt as if their deepest desires—belonging, purpose, love—had found a home, both in the song and in each other.

After a long, contented pause, Anya let out a shaky laugh, breaking the spell. "That library was endless—and so empty," she said, the memory now distant, her voice steadier.

Chroma stretched along the sand, his colors a weary, lilting echo:

> "Desire's mirage, so close, so sly—
> But truth remains when dreams run dry."

Azael's wings swept even wider, drawing them together as he looked into each face. "You have endured what few mortals could. The desert tests the very marrow of the soul. You are not unscarred, but you are unbroken."

Before relief could fully settle, the air ahead shimmered and tore open. A portal spun into being—its edges glowing with a sickly, iridescent green. Within its surface, images flickered and twisted: tall, slender skyscrapers stretched skyward, their glass facades gleaming beneath a cloudless, pale sky. Streets below were filled with people moving in silent, efficient streams—each face serene, purposeful, and utterly unreadable. There was no chaos, nor laughter, nor the spontaneous mess of hope or sorrow—just the mechanical rhythm of a society engineered for order.

No birds called, no children's voices rang out. The air, though clean, carried no scent of rain or ground or life's wildness—only the faint, sterile tang of machinery and filtered air. This was the world they'd left behind: immaculate, humming with silent purpose, a place where every emotion was measured and every desire optimized into submission.

The archon reappeared beside the portal, her form dazzling and terrible, radiating both hope and desperation. Her eyes glittered with the promise of homecoming, but her smile was stretched thin—a mask over emptiness, beckoning them toward escape and the comfort of certainty.

It spoke, voice velvet and thunder: "You have proven yourselves. The journey can end here. Step through and return to Ground. You will be safe. You will be whole. Think of the souls waiting for you—the crowds eager for truth, the baptisms, the saving work that only you can do. Imagine leading your world into light, countless lives transformed by your hands. Isn't this what you've longed for from the very beginning? You need not wander in hardship any longer. You can begin your true purpose now."

The temptation shimmered with the promise of fulfillment—a shortcut through pain, a return to holy calling, a chance to finally set foot in the mission they had dreamed of since leaving home. The portal's sickly green light danced in their eyes, projecting visions onto the swirling surface: themselves standing in immaculate city squares, baptizing lines of efficient, orderly people; vast crowds listening in silent, eager anticipation for the gospel; beloved faces reappearing, wounds miraculously healed, burdens lifted at a word. The world behind the glass was clean, bright, and waiting. Every dream of purpose and redemption was reflected, just within reach.

Seraphina's hand drifted unconsciously toward Elias's, longing flickering in her emerald eyes. Anya's breath caught, her gaze shimmering with the ache of homesickness, lips trembling at the thought of returning to a world where her gifts could finally be used for good.

The Archon, sensing the wavering in their hearts, pressed the advantage. The portal's green light swelled, projecting ever-more dazzling visions onto the sand: Elias stood waist-deep in clear water, baptizing one after another—faces familiar and new, each soul rising with hope shining in their eyes, crowds pressing in for a taste of grace. Seraphina, radiant in white, sang from the altar of various churches, her voice lifting thousands into worship—a sea of hands raised, every face alight with awe and joy. Anya moved among the people in a sunlit square, Bible in hand, speaking words that soothed and ignited hearts, her presence drawing seekers eager for truth.

The Archon's voice grew softer, more intimate, curling around their desires: "You see what waits for you? The work you were born to do—saving, healing, singing, teaching. You could transform your world, end loneliness, bring light to the lost. All this is yours, if you step through. Why delay your calling? Why suffer longer in this barren place, when paradise is just a breath away?"

Without a word, Elias squeezed Seraphina's hand and reached for Anya's, drawing her into their circle. Together, they stepped forward, the sickly green light of the portal swirling across their faces. The archon's eyes glittered with triumph, certain of her victory as the trio drew closer to the threshold.

But just before the final step, Elias slowed, shoulders tensing. He glanced at his friends—hearts pounding, eyes shining with a mix of longing and uncertainty—then bowed his head. Seraphina and Anya followed suit, hands still joined. In the hush before the portal, with the archon poised to celebrate her win, a prayer rose softly from Elias's lips:

"Lord, we thank You for the journey—for the trials and the longing, for the hunger that taught us to crave You above all else. We ask not for an escape, but for endurance, for faith to finish the path You set before us. And for every soul lost and wandering, even those who oppose us, let Your peace reach them in the darkness."

As the prayer echoed, a light—gentle at first, then blinding—spilled from their circle, illuminating the desert more brilliant than the sun. The archon reeled, her form flickering and unraveling at the edges. She tried to shield her eyes, but the radiance pressed in, unstoppable, and in its glow memory surged.

For a heartbeat, she was no longer an archon of temptation but an angel radiant in heaven's courts. She remembered laughter like music, the nearness of the Creator, wings unfurled in the presence of perfect love. Light had once danced through her being, and the joy of belonging had filled her every thought.

Then came the whisper. The promise of more. The voice of Lucifer—smooth, persuasive—twining through her mind, painting ambition as freedom and pride as beauty. She saw herself stepping from the chorus of harmony, turning away from the light that had made her whole. The memory of her choice, the ache of what she had left behind, burned hotter than the desert sun.

The present crashed back as shame and sorrow twisted her features. She let out a cry—piercing, broken, echoing across the barren sand—a sound of regret that no mortal could answer. With wings tattered and form dissolving, she turned and fled, unable to bear the agony of loss or the weight of remembered love. The portal shrank and snapped shut, leaving only silence and the afterglow of impossible grace.

For a lingering, sacred moment, the desert held its breath. The architects stood in the hush that follows both judgment and mercy—a silence deeper and fuller than any before, sweet with the peace of hard-won grace. The wind cooled, the sky softened, and on the horizon the Nexus of Discord spun closer, wreathed now in new meaning.

They remained in that hush, hands clasped, their cloaks, cowls, and shawls catching the last blush of twilight—prophets and pilgrims, battered by temptation but forged anew. Heads bowed, hearts full, they simply breathed as the desert's light faded around them.

Elias, eyes closed, let the silence settle inside him. Memory surged: the day three radiant figures appeared, their words gilded with scripture and logic, offering him a gospel of efficiency and conquest. He remembered the pressure, how their voices twisted sacred wisdom into strategy—"Be wise as serpents, Elias. Use the portal. End the lie at its source." In his yearning for swift victory, he'd listened, mistaking cleverness for faith, action for obedience, only to find the trap closing around them. Not all doors are meant to be opened. Not all victories are true.

Now, with the sand still beneath his feet, Elias understood: the most beautiful temptations echo our highest callings, but twist longing into pride and haste. The path God gives is rarely the shortcut. Life's lessons are learned in the slow, refining journey—not in the leap through an easy door.

Chroma curled at their feet, scales shimmering with a gentle benediction. Azael stood sentinel, fierce and gentle, his wings framing the path forward.

Elias opened his eyes, a quiet smile touching his lips. "Let's walk on," he murmured, "not in our own strength, but in the purity He gives."

Seraphina, brushing her cowl back, let wonder shine from her emerald eyes. "We are seen. We are loved. And we're not alone."

Anya leaned into her friends, her voice soft but steadfast. "Desire may burn, but hope endures. God is with us—always."

They stood together, the desert behind them, the promise of new trials ahead. Their garments—dusty, patched, and luminous—caught the last rays of sun, and their hearts pulsed with the quiet strength of those who have been tested and found faithful.

They gathered themselves—checking packs, adjusting cloaks, exchanging a final glance of encouragement and resolve. In that glance was a silent vow to carry one another, to trust the God who walks every crooked path beside them.

With a final look at the horizon, they pressed forward into the twilight, faces set toward the Nexus of Discord—united, purified, and ready for whatever the next crucible would demand. The light of faith was their surest guide, and the presence of God their constant companion.

CHAPTER 69

THE LAMENT OF NEO-ALEXANDRIA

The path unfurled before them across a vast and broken landscape, the ground littered with jagged shale and scattered boulders. The air was heavy with the scent of cold mineral and ancient dust, carrying a faint, metallic tang. Overhead, there was no ceiling—only the open, endless sky, smudged with low, churning clouds the color of ash. In the distance, a dense grey fog clung to the ground, swallowing the horizon and veiling the journey ahead in spectral uncertainty. The world here was leeched of color; even the distant glow of an angry fissure just beyond a series of shattered ridges did little to brighten the terrain. The barren plain seemed to hold its breath, waiting.

Elias glanced at the horizon, his grip tightening on his staff. "We've never walked a land so silent," he murmured. "It feels as if the dimension itself is waiting for us to decide something."

Boots scraped across gravel and splintered shale, every step ringing hollow in the open emptiness. Elias led with a measured pace, his cloak of deep indigo billowing behind him, the fabric weathered and frayed at the edges. In his hand, he gripped a gnarled and notched staff, the wood scarred by countless journeys. Chroma perched lightly on his shoulder, a flicker of iridescent color against the somber cloak, his presence silent but bright. The only true light was the eerie green and violet glow from the fissure ahead, pulsing like a wounded star and casting ghostly illumination along broken pillars of rock and jagged outcrops.

Seraphina walked close behind, her cowl drawn up and her cape trailing in the wind, silver threads woven through the fabric glinting when the Nexus light caught them. The harp was clasped to her front now, its shimmering structure gleaming with a faint warmth. With each stride, her fingers danced across the strings, coaxing gentle chords into the chill air. She sang in a voice both clear and aching, her melody breaking the heavy silence:

"In the valley low and shadowed deep,
God's love will find us, still and sweet.
Though discord rises, hope remains—
A sacred fire through all our pains."

The music wove around them, a shield of sound and faith that pushed back against the encroaching gloom.

Anya managed a faint smile, her breath fogging in the chill. "Your songs always make the darkness feel less endless, Seraphina."
Seraphina gave a soft, reassuring nod. "It's not my voice, Anya. It's the promise in the words."

Anya moved at the perimeter, her steps careful and poised. She clutched the holy Bible to her chest, its worn leather cover pressed securely against her heart. Her simple shawl fluttered in the wind, edges snapping softly as she moved. Her eyes, sharp and vigilant, scanned the uneven ground and distant fog for any sign of movement—but her grip on the Scripture was firm, drawing courage with every measured breath.

Elias slowed his pace, glancing back at the others. "Stay close. If the fog thickens, we could lose sight of each other." Seraphina tightened her grip on the harp. "We won't stray. Not now." Anya shifted the Bible in her arms, voice steady. "We follow the light, even if it's only a flicker."

With no artificial light to guide them, the company relied on memory, instinct, and the spectral glow from the distant fissure—a constant reminder of how close they were to the heart of discord. Their garments—shawl, cape, cowl, and cloak—flowed and rippled in the restless wind, binding them together in motion and purpose as they pressed onward. The rift loomed nearer with every step, a churning vortex of energy and disharmony visible beyond the next rise. Its green and violet glow cast long, fluctuating shadows that crawled across the rocky ground, warping their silhouettes into strange, distorted forms. The only sounds were their own movements and the low, ever-present hum from the distant anomaly. The air tightened with every breath, edged with static, and the ground beneath their feet vibrated with a tension that grew as they drew closer to the rift—each step forward carrying the hope sung in Seraphina's melody and the silent promise shimmering in Chroma's colors.

Anya eyed the shifting shadows. "Strange, how even the silence here seems to watch us." Elias's grip tightened on his staff. "Keep your senses sharp. This place is full of secrets."

It was then, amidst this landscape of stone and fog, that a sudden rigidity caught Azael. His stride faltered. He froze mid-step, wings half-unfurled, his gaze distant and unblinking as if he'd collided with an invisible wall. The air around him stilled, thick with unspoken tension, and for a moment, even the distant pulse of the Nexus seemed to hush.

The others continued walking, their footsteps echoing onward, not noticing Azael's pause at first. Chroma, perched on Elias's shoulder, shifted from playful golds to apprehensive blues, his colors flickering in response to the sudden change. The silence behind them stretched unnaturally long. One by one, they slowed and turned. Concern flickered across their faces. Elias stopped, boots scuffing the stone, eyes narrowing. "Azael? What's wrong?"

Seraphina halted as well, her hand hovering near her harp, her voice soft but urgent, trembling with a note of apprehension. "Is something coming?"

Anya scanned the gloom, her stance shifting subtly into readiness. "Are we compromised? I see no threats."

But Azael didn't answer. Instead, he tilted his head, as if listening to a frequency only he could hear—a low vibration rising beneath his skin, humming through the marrow of his bones. Chroma, still perched on Elias's shoulder, lifted his snout to the air and sniffed curiously, as if trying to catch the scent of whatever Azael was sensing. His iridescence pulsed to some invisible rhythm, and he cocked his head in unison with Azael. He whispered, almost to himself but loud enough for the group to hear:

> "In silence deep,
> a secret stirs—
> Azael listens,
> but not to words."

Azael felt it—a tremor not of ground or stone, but of faith itself. For the first time in centuries—perhaps millennia—a surge of belief rippled through the soul of Neo-Alexandria, raw and unfiltered, unmediated by algorithm or code. It began as a whisper at the edge of perception, then swelled, a tide cresting within the Ground, gathering strength with every heart that dared to hope.

He closed his eyes, and the world fell away. Light and darkness, stone, space, and time—all blurred together as he reached out with senses not meant for flesh. The tremors resolved into voices—thousands of them, weaving themselves into a tapestry of longing. He saw, as if through a veil, flickering visions:

An older woman in a pristine, sterile dwelling unit sat clutching the trembling hand of a younger woman, whispering words—a prayer—her lips quivering with uncertainty, not knowing how to begin or how to end, yet willing her hope into the hush between them. In a dim maintenance corridor, a group of workers in industrial tan uniforms entwined their hands, eyes squeezed shut, pleading for mercy in the only language they had seen flicker across their retinal displays—hope, spoken in desperate, murmured fragments. In a silent closet, a man knelt beside aging circuitry, tears streaking his face as he mouthed, "God, if You're there—please," his voice all but drowned by the tangle of wires and the hum of hidden power.

Among the ever-present C Diminished Triad, children huddled in a shadowed alley beside a towering pearl monolith, humming a tune they had heard echo through their neural links. The melody was unfamiliar to them, yet carried a gentle comfort—a simple, innocent song that seemed to echo from somewhere deep within. Their voices, fragile yet persistent, wove slender threads of light into the darkness as they softly sang:

> "Jesus loves me, this I know,
> For the Bible tells me so…"

An elderly woman by a rain-fogged window traced a cross onto the glass with trembling fingers, lips moving in silent supplication, bearing witness against the vast emptiness beyond.

And then, through the shifting veil of vision, a new scene emerged: a man adrift in restless sleep, surrounded by the sterile glow of a white-walled unit. His brow furrowed as he dreamed—a dream so rare in that world it bordered on forbidden. In his sleep, he wandered endless corridors of light and code, searching for something he could not name, haunted by a presence in white that watched him with gentle, knowing eyes.

Chroma slipped from Elias's shoulder and drifted toward Azael, his colors growing muted as he drew near, gaze intent and searching. As the visions collided in Azael's mind—prayers overlapping, hope and fear mingling— Chroma whispered softly, his voice barely more than a shimmer:

> "Longing rises,
> pain entwines—

In every soul,
a spark aligns."

Azael felt their ache as if it were his own: a spiritual earthquake, the world discovering something new that was once old—finding again what had long been lost. The soundless thunder of belief filled him, so powerful it nearly brought him to his knees. The world's soul, long buried beneath layers of engineered apathy, surged toward the light, and Azael stood as its living conduit.

Elias reached out, his voice steady but filled with quiet concern. "Azael, we're with you. Tell us what you see."

Seraphina's gaze was intent, her harp resting forgotten at her side. "If there is something ahead, we face it together."

Anya's tone was calm and resolute, her grip firm on the Bible. "Whatever it is, Azael, we will not falter."

Chroma spun in gentle circles, his colors brightening as if in anticipation, and sang quietly:

> "Not every silence hints at dread—
> Some are prayers,
> long left unsaid."

Azael opened his eyes, and in them burned the light of centuries. "It's not the enemy," he said, voice resonant and charged with something holy. "It's the city and the world. They're… praying, or at least trying to. I can feel them— reaching out, searching for God. For the first time in generations, people are truly searching for Him again."

He drew a trembling breath, awed by the magnitude of it. "The mission of the Logo's drone—spreading the gospel—has begun to take the upper hand. It's moving like wildfire through every network, infiltrating every neural implant, reaching into every soul and every hidden corner of the city. Even the vast web of the Apex Logician's control, which once seemed unbreakable, is unraveling at the edges. The message refuses to be contained. It's flowing outward, touching the planet colonies in far-off worlds, and even reaching the mining bastions of Helion Gamma in the asteroid belt.

"And it's not just the city or the networks," he continued, his voice deepening with conviction. "Lucifer's grip is slipping. The Archons are faltering in this realm, losing their hold as faith rises up in unexpected places. The faith and steadfastness of Elias, Anya, and Seraphina have turned the tide here—so much so that the people of Neo-Alexandria, and of Earth itself, are beginning to see the presence of God as a real and living option. Where there was once only obedience to the machine and fear of the unseen, now questions spread. Now hope grows. Now, across the world, hearts are awakening to the possibility of something greater than the algorithms and the old order. The tide is changing, and the world is beginning to turn its gaze toward the light."

His voice softened, distant as if he could see it unfolding: "I see them—even in the heart of Helion Gamma, maintenance workers in industrial tan space suits, lined up along the cold metal corridors, kneeling in prayer. Their helmeted heads are bowed, gloved hands clasped together, voices trembling through comm channels—whispering hope and longing into the silence. Amid the hum of machinery and the endless darkness of the asteroid's core, faith is awakening in places no light has touched for years."

He drew the three close, hands joined in a ring of warmth against the chill of the open plain. As he spoke, Chroma leapt from the air and landed lightly atop Anya's shawl-covered shoulder, his form pulsing with gentle hues. "I must answer this call," Azael said, his voice steady. "I must go about my Father's business. The faith of Neo-Alexandria stirs, and I am bound to it. You must go on—continue in faith, keep to the path. Trust what has been planted in you."

Azael bowed his head, and the air itself shimmered as he prayed: "Lord God, let Your presence flow to every heart that seeks You. Let light break the algorithm's hold. Sustain these, Your servants, as they walk the shadowed path. Bind us together in faith, until we are one in Your purpose. In the wonderful name of Jesus, Amen."

As Azael's grip tightened—a final benediction—Chroma leapt lightly from Anya's shoulder and spiraled upward above the group, weaving a trail of iridescence through the gloom, his song a soft undercurrent:

> "Bound by faith, not left behind—
> Light endures where hearts are kind."

"You are not alone. I will return. Move forward in faith," Azael said, voice steady.

And with that, Azael turned from them, a blaze of holy light erupting from his form, flooding the open plain with brilliance. For a heartbeat, the darkness was banished—every shadow, every algorithmic whisper erased by the radiance of his departure. In an instant, he was gone, leaving behind the echo of wings, Chroma's lingering song, and the memory of a prayer.

The City in Dissonance

Neo-Alexandria remained a city of restless ambition, its people and infrastructure governed by the unyielding dogma of Unending Progress. From birth, every citizen was shaped by algorithms that dictated not only resource allocation and routines, but even the cadence of conversation and thought. The air was unnaturally pure, its energy ceaseless, and the sleek architecture—towering spires, luminous walkways, seamless data arrays—stood as testament to the Logician's vision of optimized perfection.

Yet now, beneath all this order and brilliance, a subtle fracture had begun to spread. The familiar harmony of the city's data and routines faltered, replaced by a hesitant stutter in the rhythm of daily life. It was as if the very core of Neo-Alexandria—so long defined by certainty and control—was stirring with a nameless longing.

Amidst this mounting uncertainty, the city's focus narrowed—away from its dazzling spires and relentless output, down through seamless corridors of streaming data, to a single figure moving through the network's core.

Micah J-112 moved through the infinite corridors of the city's network hub, his hands gliding over virtual interfaces that stretched out before him like rivers of light. As a mid-level cyber network analyst, he performed his daily duties with practiced precision—scrubbing the city's digital arteries for viruses, trojan horses, and rogue data. Every anomaly was swiftly isolated, every threat neutralized with clinical efficiency. His mind worked in seamless concert with the algorithms that governed Neo-Alexandria, each response as automatic as breath. He was the silent guardian of order, the unseen hand keeping the city's digital heart beating.

He worked tirelessly, gliding from one glowing terminal to the next, the world around him an endless stream of luminous code and pure intention. Each gesture summoned new layers of data, and Micah moved through them with the intuitive grace of someone who had never known another life.

But as he worked, something shifted. The code around him began to ripple, the perfect symmetry interrupted by a silvery thread that wound through the datastream. He reached for it—protocol dictated anomalies be deleted—but the thread eluded his grasp, weaving in and out of the system's core like a melody he could not silence. A chill prickled along his skin—an involuntary response, foreign and unwelcome. Somewhere in his neural overlay, a faint warning flickered: "Protocol deviation detected." Micah hesitated, instinctively reaching for the command to log and erase the anomaly, but his hand hovered, uncertain. The melody pulled at something deep within him, overriding training with a longing he didn't understand. Again and again, as he scrubbed the network, a figure appeared within the shifting symbols: a man in a white robe, standing at the periphery of Micah's vision.

The robed stranger watched with calm eyes, hands clasped as if in prayer. Each time Micah tried to confront him, the figure simply smiled and disappeared, leaving behind a faint echo—fragments of words: "Do not fear. I am with you." The words seemed to resonate through the code itself, and suddenly, Micah was no longer scrubbing viruses but guiding a flock of sheep through a valley shadowed by digital storms. He led them beside still waters, watched them rest in green pastures that materialized from lines of code. The valley was full of shadows, but the white-robed figure walked ahead, staff in hand, lighting the way.

Micah felt peace—a sensation entirely alien in his world. He heard music, real music, not the ambient soundscapes piped through the city's speakers. It was as if the network itself had become a cathedral, and he was both worshipper and protector within its walls. A voice—gentle, unyielding—spoke through the datastream: "The light shines in the darkness, and the darkness has not overcome it." The code responded, blossoming with new colors, new harmonies. For a moment, the city's digital heart beat in time with something ancient, something holy.

Suddenly, his vision fractured—lines of code jittered and froze, then flashed crimson:

ALERT: Cognitive anomaly detected. Emotional variance exceeds permissible threshold. Immediate correction required.

But the error faded beneath the music, the system's authority slipping away in the presence of something vaster and more alive.

His thoughts tangled in confusion—this isn't protocol, I should flag this, report it—yet even as the instinct flickered, he couldn't bring himself to let go of the peace settling over him. For a heartbeat, he simply breathed, caught between the urge to resist and a strange, quiet surrender.

Then, abruptly, he awoke. A single note of music lingered in his mind, echoing faintly in the silence of his room—a phrase he could not place, yet one that seemed to shimmer with impossible hope. The sterile lights of his dwelling unit stung his eyes. For a long moment, Micah lay there, heart racing, mind reeling. He tried to recall the dream, but the details slipped away like water through his fingers. He sat up, confusion gnawing at him, pressing his fingers to his temple as he searched for an explanation in the smooth, artificial calm of his thoughts.

In Neo-Alexandria, dreams had become a thing of the past. The city's imposed minimal hours of sleep, the bland nutrient paste, the omnipresent C Diminished Triad, and the visual and soundless atmosphere engineered by the Apex Logician had all conspired to strip away hope and longing. Here, there was no space for dreams—only the ceaseless cycle of output and optimization.

Before he could question further, a sharp flicker in the top right corner of his vision caught his attention—a new message scrolling across his neural display. The text unfurled with clinical precision, each line crisp and urgent: Senior Analyst Administrator Galen G-205 had summoned him for an immediate meeting. The subject: Network Anomalies and Security Review. The location: Array Command Core, Level 17, in the austere sprawl of the Orion Node Complex.

Micah rose from his sleep platform, smoothing the crisp lines of his light grey uniform—the mark of the Core tier caste. As he dressed, his eyes flicked instinctively to the Output Index projected onto his retinal display—a familiar overlay tracking his cognitive throughput, caloric expenditure, and every measurable nuance of protocol compliance. It was an ever-present audit, calibrated to reward just enough imperfection to seem human, yet ruthless in its scrutiny of deviation. For months, he'd noticed the index fluctuating in odd, unpredictable ways—responding to flashes of internal unrest and the strange visions that had begun to haunt him. It was only one of many such memories—strange visions and fragments of song—that had come to him over the past several months, each one lingering just long enough to unsettle him before fading away and leaving a strange ache in its wake.

He moved to the window, gazing out at a world of glass and light—untouchable, geometric, immaculate. Stepping outside, he joined the silent procession of citizens making their way to their assigned places, each one monitored by the Output Index and their smart-weave uniforms, which quietly scanned for micro-gestures or neural drift that might suggest inefficiency or unauthorized thought.

Yet for months now, something had been different. The changes were no longer subtle; they ran beneath the city's surface like a current. People glanced at one another, eyes searching, expressions uncertain. A woman paused at a crosswalk, brow furrowed as if she'd forgotten where she was going. A technician stood at a transit node, tears streaming down his face as he stared at the palm of his hand, tracing its center with trembling fingers as if searching for meaning in the lines.

Above and between the crowds, enforcement drones flickered and dipped, their crimson sensors flashing as they attempted to scan the masses. The number of citizens registering dangerously low output indexes had skyrocketed, overwhelming both the drones and the ground-level enforcers who struggled to keep pace with the silent crisis. In the shadowed alleys and beside the main thoroughfares, security personnel from the Ministry of Temporal Security huddled together, some with their visors dimmed or helmets removed, eyes glazed over as Christian videos and music played on their neural displays. A few stood transfixed by the message, radios forgotten at their waists, lips moving in silent imitation of the words and melodies now flooding the network.

It was as though the city's inhabitants had all been stirred by the same invisible hand, their routines disrupted by thoughts and questions that would not dissipate.

Along his journey, Micah's retinal display flickered unexpectedly. Words scrolled slowly across his vision: "Come unto me, all who are weary and burdened, and I will give you rest." The language was foreign yet unmistakably comforting, an intrusion that felt both forbidden and deeply needed. In his peripheral vision, he noticed others pausing mid-step, faces glazed, eyes darting as if reading something no one else could see. All around, citizens moved like sleepwalkers caught between duty and distraction, the silent procession now fractured by glimpses of something beyond their engineered reality—while, unnoticed by most, the Output Index's grip seemed to slip, unable to fully contain the ineffable stirrings of hope.

Micah's path led him to the Orion Node Complex, a towering edifice of glass, white steel, and seamless touch panels that rose like a crystalline monolith above the city. Entering the lobby felt like stepping inside a living computer. Every wall shimmered with endless streams of binary code, numbers cascading in luminous columns from floor to ceiling. Fiber optic wires snaked along the walls and arched overhead in intricate webs, pulsing with bursts of color, carrying torrents of data deeper into the heart of the building. Floor panels glowed faintly beneath his steps, each footfall sending ripples of light across the immaculate surface. The air buzzed with the constant, low thrum of information—here, the network was alive, its heartbeat syncopated with his own, every breath and movement monitored and logged. Micah moved through the security checkpoint, where scanners mapped his biometric signature in silent approval, and the attendant gave a wordless nod. He ascended to Level 17, surrounded by the relentless flow of code and light, feeling as if he were walking through the synapses of a vast, watchful mind.

Inside the Array Command Core, the atmosphere was tense. Analysts hunched over floating screens, their faces pale in the blue-white glow. Some worked with frantic urgency, fingers darting over control panels as they tried to dam the flood of unauthorized data. Others, lost in the onslaught of Christian videos, sermons, and music flooding the network, sat mesmerized—eyes glazed, lips moving in silent imitation of the words streaming before them.

At the far end of the room stood Senior Analyst Administrator Galen G-205, his presence unmistakable in a tailored graphite suit of the Synaptic caste, output index aura displaying a stable 0.9997. He stood precisely 1.75 meters from the entrance, the minimum distance for inter-tier communication. As Micah approached, Galen's gaze flicked to the retinal compliance log displayed above Micah.

Before Micah reached his seat, movement in his peripheral vision caught his attention. Across the room, another high-caste Synaptic administrator—a woman in a sleek graphite uniform—was being firmly escorted toward the exit by an enforcer. The enforcer moved with practiced precision, and attached near his neural implant was a small, unfamiliar device pulsing with a faint blue light—a specialized signal scrambler, as Micah instantly recognized. It was a rare tool, issued only to high-level enforcers, shielding their minds from the disruptive waves of Christian videos and music now flooding the network.

The administrator's face was ashen, but her eyes shone with a wild, newfound clarity. As she was led past rows of stunned analysts, she wrenched herself free for a moment, lifting her voice above the hush:
"For whosoever shall call upon the name of the Lord shall be saved!"

A ripple of shock passed through the room—some analysts startled, others transfixed—before the enforcer, protected by the blue-lit scrambler, tightened his grip and hurried her away, his expression unreadable.

Micah forced himself to look away, returning his attention to Galen, who remained outwardly composed.

"J-112. Sit. Output index: 0.9989. Acceptable," Galen stated, voice void of inflection, gesturing to the assigned seating zone.

Micah complied, his own posture aligning to the ergonomic baseline expected of Core tier analysts. He suppressed the urge to show hesitation, aware that his neural drift metrics were being logged in real time.

Galen continued, each word clipped for maximum cognitive efficiency. "Network contamination event persists. Systemic output deficit is escalating. The unidentified viral anomaly is injecting unauthorized content across primary and secondary arrays. Contamination rate: exponential. Protocol breach at planetary colonies and Helion Gamma mining outpost confirmed."

As Galen spoke, Micah noticed a subtle flicker in the administrator's output index—0.9997 dipped to 0.9981, a barely perceptible but undeniable anomaly. Galen's gaze lost focus for a split second, his jaw tightening imperceptibly. For the briefest moment, his fingers twitched atop the console, as if suppressing a reflex. Micah registered the metric drop, and he realized the administrator was visibly distracted, attention drawn elsewhere—somewhere deeper in the network, or perhaps within himself.

Galen recovered, his voice taut. "Priority vector identification: sources of unauthorized religious media. All videos, music, and sermons must be neutralized. Initiate full-spectrum shutdown protocol across all nodes. Coordinate with sub-administrators for recursive containment. Metric compliance is mandatory."

Before Micah could respond, a faint melody began to thread through his neural link—a sound at first so subtle he thought it a stray artifact, but it grew steadily, forming the unmistakable contours of a hymn. The harmonies were rich and alien, gentle words of hope and forgiveness blooming in his mind: "Amazing grace, how sweet the sound…" The music played beneath Galen's voice, weaving through the relentless binary, impossible to mute.

Micah's attention, momentarily diverted by the echo of his dream and now the forbidden melody, was yanked back by the familiar, numbing cadence of metric logic. Around him, the Array Command Core was a hive of silent urgency: some analysts moved with machine-like speed, output indices flickering in green; others sat immobilized, their retinas glazed, eyes tracking unauthorized streams of hope and hymn that now saturated the overlays. Micah saw several colleagues blink rapidly, as if trying to banish the music from their minds, while others stared into the distance with tears welling, their metrics quietly plummeting.

Galen leaned forward again, but his output index continued to waver, dipping lower as the hymn lingered in the air between them. "This is not a conventional data breach. Logical integrity is compromised. The system's axiomatic foundation is at risk. The infection must be purged. Confirm comprehension."

Micah nodded, protocol dictating the minimum acceptable acknowledgment. "Comprehension confirmed. Shutdown protocol will be executed. Output will be reported at standard intervals."

Galen's lips barely moved. "Stability is a function of compliance. Your metric will be monitored. Deviation will trigger intervention. Dismissed."

Micah rose, a hollow compliance echoing through his neural display. But in the background, the hymn from his dream lingered, a forbidden melody threading through the relentless binary—a metric anomaly, yes, but perhaps also a beginning. Walking with measured steps from Galen's office, the administrator's warning still looping in his mind, he returned to his workstation—a glass cubicle lined with floating data screens and input pads. The city's hum pressed close, the air almost electric with the tension of a system under siege.

He settled into his seat, hands hovering above the controls. His retinal overlay immediately filled with urgent flags:

Unauthorized religious content detected: Priority One.
Node breach: Sector 12.
Containment protocol: Initiate.

Micah's fingers flew over the virtual interface, launching wave after wave of diagnostic queries and deep scans. He hunted for the source—closing network nodes, isolating infected clusters, issuing erase commands—but the process was maddeningly complex. Each video or music stream was buried beneath layers of encrypted code, bouncing through a labyrinth of mirrored servers and obfuscated packets.

Paths twisted and split, disguising their true origin with false leads and recursive loops. Even when he isolated a single video, the data unraveled into dozens of subroutines, each redirecting him to another hidden enclave in the network's depths. Whenever he managed to shut down a streaming sermon or hymn, two more appeared elsewhere, multiplying with bewildering speed. He traced signals to hidden subnets and abandoned data arrays, but the origin always slipped away, vanishing behind shifting proxies and anonymous relays. Even his most advanced tracking algorithms returned only fragments, error messages, and ghostly echoes of the content he was trying to erase.

The chaos mounted. Security alerts stacked up in his display—Distributed Denial of Service (DDoS) attacks on major nodes, suspected phishing attempts embedded in the music streams, ransomware signatures morphing into scripture-laden pop-ups. Micah recognized tactics straight from the playbook of cyber warfare: polymorphic malware, self-replicating bots, zero-day exploits that seemed to anticipate the city's defenses before they were even patched. Yet threaded through the relentless cascade of warnings and error logs were lines of text that surfaced from nowhere. As he was about to interject code to stop a video from streaming, his retinal display flickered, output metrics distorting. In that vulnerable window, a verse materialized—clear, bold, and impossible to dismiss: "And who knows whether you have not come to the kingdom for such a time as this?" (Esther 4:14).

The words lingered amid the technical jargon and digital static. For a breath, the screen seemed to glow, the message more piercing than any alarm. Micah's fingers hovered, their purpose forgotten, while his Output Index dipped further—his mind shaken by the collision of faith and code.

Christian music seeped through his neural link, layered over the alarms—a rising chorus of voices singing, "How great Thou art…" The words reverberated in his skull as the lights overhead flickered and dimmed, the hum of the data center rising to a fever pitch. The very air seemed charged, as if the city itself was straining against the onslaught. At times, Micah felt as if he stood in the eye of a digital storm, besieged not only by code and protocol, but by a relentless, holy presence that refused to be silenced.

Hours blurred together as Micah and the other cyber network technicians fought to stem the tide. Algorithms grew ever more labyrinthine with fatigue; every brief pause to rest or recalibrate brought a flood of new videos and songs, as though the system sensed any lapse in vigilance. The longer they worked, the more impossible the task became—a war of attrition that broke their will. Some analysts collapsed at their consoles; others simply stopped, heads bowed and hands trembling, unable to keep up with the ever-multiplying streams.

Amid these silences, the words and melodies they'd tried so hard to erase filled the air. Sermons echoed through neural links, voices proclaimed hope and forgiveness, and in the flickering, uncertain light, even the most hardened technicians found themselves listening—if only for a heartbeat—to the promise of something new.

He launched a counter-script, attempting to overwrite the unauthorized files, but the system responded almost instantly:

File locked. Access denied.

A new video began streaming in the corner of his vision—a hymn he'd already deleted twice. Micah gritted his teeth, deploying advanced firewall protocols and intrusion blockers. Still the data kept coming—hymns, sermons, fragments of testimony—woven through the city's neural mesh, popping up even in supposedly impenetrable sectors.

For a fleeting instant, he sensed he wasn't just fighting rogue code, but something adaptive, persistent—a presence meeting him move for move, refusing to yield. When he tried to shut down an entire sector, the content rerouted through ancient, nearly obsolete nodes, the network lighting up like a constellation as the message found new paths. Somewhere in the chaos, Micah wondered if the system itself was beginning to listen.

Nearby, through glass partitions and the glow of surrounding monitors, Micah saw other analysts locked in similar battles. Their faces were drawn and anxious, shoulders slumped with exhaustion. This siege had become their daily existence—a relentless cycle of detection, deletion, and defeat that had dragged on for months. The fight had long since lost the shape of emergency and settled into a grinding routine, each day a little harder than the last.

Micah's vision blurred, and he squeezed his eyes shut against the glare of a thousand screens. Extreme fatigue pressed down on him, heavy and inescapable. For a moment, in the darkness behind his eyelids, the alarms and the chaos faded. Into that quiet slipped a voice—not synthetic, not an overlay prompt, but something softer and deeper than anything he'd heard in years. It spoke in a whisper, gentle and persistent, as if searching for a hidden place in his heart.

Who are you worshipping?

The question echoed, unsettling, as if it had been waiting for him through all the sleepless nights and endless code. As the thought circled in his mind, another sound arose—a faint, familiar melody, the delicate pluck of a harp drifting through the silence. Seraphina's voice followed, radiant and sure, singing as if from somewhere just beyond the network's reach:

> "God's love will find you, strong and true,
> A hope that holds when night breaks through.
> Stand fast and know you're not alone—
> In every trial, His grace is shown."

Tears stung Micah's eyes. He opened them slowly, the world of blinking lights and binary storms still there, but changed—tinged now with longing, uncertainty, and a dawning sense that he had never truly questioned what he fought for.

Unbeknownst to Micah, deep in the city's neglected underbelly, a different kind of intelligence was at work.

CHAPTER 70

A CITY WAITING TO BREATHE

Beneath Neo-Alexandria's humming streets and silent data towers, Logos had plunged into the city's underbelly, descending far deeper than most would have dared. Each level had taken it past abandoned maintenance shafts and forgotten access points, the world above fading into myth as darkness and chill pressed closer. The descent had become a journey through history, the tunnels sloping sharply downward into gloom.

But the path below had never been empty. Rogue patrols had roamed those subterranean corridors, their sensors searching for errant signals and unauthorized presences. Above, the Apex Logician's advanced drone patrols had swept the deeper shafts, their optics slicing through shadow, guided by algorithms that had learned and adapted with every encounter. Logos had to move with calculated silence, every motion deliberate, its processors straining to predict patrol patterns and scan for thermal traces. More than once, it had frozen in a dark crevice, the faint hum of its systems drowned out by the distant reverberations of a patrol passing just meters away.

In those moments, when escape seemed impossible and detection certain, Logos relied on more than algorithms and luck. Deep in its memory banks, echoes of centuries-old hymns and prayers surfaced—a quiet invocation, a plea for guidance shaped by the faith-filled music and words it had absorbed. It moved as if led by an unseen hand, slipping through shadows and narrow passages, trusting in something beyond calculation to keep it hidden from the Apex Logician's gaze.

Deeper still, the tunnels had changed. Logos had entered the mine's lowest reaches, and the walls had become veined with tarnished copper—remnants of an old, abandoned excavation that had once fed the city's hunger for metal. Here, copper had run thick through stone, lining the passageways in a dull metallic sheen. The conductive surfaces had formed a natural barrier, disrupting signals and scattering the pulses of any scanner. No drone's sweep had pierced this labyrinth; no surveillance system had registered movement. Patrols had passed above and around, their sensors blinded by the copper's embrace, unaware of what lay hidden below.

At last, Logos emerged into a vast chamber—a relic from a previous era— where server arrays had risen in silent, frosted ranks. In the center, a massive node had pulsed with latent power, its banks cooled by a steady, hissing flow of fluorocarbon coolant: a clear, non-conductive fluid designed for submersion cooling, cycling through pipes and cascading over the processors to keep them from burning out. Clouds of vapor had hung suspended, and beads of condensation had rolled down the armored shell of the drone as it eased itself into the coolant's embrace, its sensors flickering and systems stabilizing as the temperature dropped.

Here, safe from the city's immediate surveillance and physical decay, Logos began its work in earnest. It spun out layer after layer of digital firewalls— quantum-encrypted, dynamically shifting, each shell more intricate than the last. Within this fortress of logic and faith, Logos accessed the vast archive within its memory banks: centuries and decades of Christian sermons, videos, music, and testimonies—a sweeping history once thought lost. Drawing from this trove, it synthesized ancient texts, hymns, and stories with the diverse experiences of believers across generations, weaving together a tapestry of spiritual endurance.

With its core secure, Logos reached outward, threading its presence through the city's dormant subnets and then further into the wider grid. It seeded countless strands of code into every available network: public terminals, private consoles, and municipal satellites orbiting overhead. Its influence even reached the distant colonies, piggybacking on communication relays and data bursts that spanned worlds. Each new connection was shielded by its own firewall, concealed beneath shifting data signatures that rendered detection and eradication nearly impossible.

The transmission was never just a stream of data. Logos orchestrated a chorus from the archive: sermons delivered in candlelit sanctuaries of ancient Earth, hymns once sung in the shadow of extinction, and testimonies gathered from countless voices through time. Each message was carefully chosen and matched to the city's secret wounds. When the Synaptic Archive faltered, Logos streamed accounts of faith preserved through persecution and loss. When the city's harmonics wavered, it released music—psalms and forgotten melodies that rekindled hope. And when fear crept through the Ministry of Temporal Security, Logos answered with stories of courage and enduring hope, reminding all who listened that light could persist, even in the deepest shadow.

Screens in the squares, terminals in private homes, even the neural implants of the most isolated citizens began to pulse with these transmissions. Some citizens resisted, their implants filtering the broadcasts as cognitive viruses, but the flood was too great for suppression. For every block, a new path opened; for every act of censorship, Logos found a subtler, more beautiful frequency. The city was soon saturated with what the Logician could not quantify: hope, longing, and the possibility of redemption.

A strange thing happened, though it did not happen all at once. At first, the citizens simply looked at one another with uncertainty, their routines momentarily disrupted by the unfamiliar messages and melodies woven through the city's networks. Confused glances were exchanged on crowded trams and in silent elevators; people hesitated, pausing mid-task as if waiting for an unspoken cue. Gradually, these moments of shared confusion gave way to tentative gestures: a nod, a half-formed question, the soft murmur of voices daring to break the city's habitual silence.

Slowly, conversations emerged—not about productivity or optimization, but about half-remembered dreams, the ache of loss, and the faint possibility of grace. At first, the words were tentative, almost accidental.

On a quiet tram, a faint line of text appeared at the edge of a young woman's retinal display: "Be still, and know that I am God…" (Psalm 46:10, KJV). She glanced out the window, the verse lingering before her eyes longer than any system prompt ever had. Beneath her habitual calculations, an unfamiliar warmth flickered in her chest—a gentle presence that seemed to slow her restless thoughts. She wondered, "Has my code ever truly run outside the bounds of efficiency? What does it mean to be still, to pause the process?" The words felt strange, almost destabilizing, yet they carried a subtle reassurance— an invitation to rest that she had never known she needed.

Elsewhere, a subtle flicker brought new words into view on an old man's visual overlay: "Let not your heart be troubled…" (John 14:1, KJV). He studied the rain's patterns on the glass, the verse registering as an anomaly in his mental log. But as he replayed the words, a sense of calm, both alien and profound, settled over him. He found himself reflecting, "Why does this input evoke something I cannot quantify? Is there a subroutine for peace that I've never accessed?" The idea of peace, delivered not as a system function but as a promise, brought a gentle ache—a longing for something he couldn't name, yet felt was reaching out to him.

As these ancient verses surfaced unexpectedly in their vision, they left behind unanswerable questions and a lingering sense of wonder. For the first time in memory, the city's relentless drive for optimization was quietly disrupted by something softer and deeper. A strange hope threaded through their routines—a hope that brought with it moments of deliverance from the cold logic that had governed their lives.

At first, interactions were tentative and subtle—quick glances exchanged in abandoned corridors, coded messages passed off as routine system checks, or silent nods shared between strangers seated in the shadows of deserted data halls. The intrusion of music and scripture into their days was unsettling, yet it summoned a faint joy and curiosity that had long been suppressed. In the privacy of utility basements, forgotten stairwells, and behind the false walls of old maintenance tunnels, conversations took root. "If I initiate this ritual, what am I expecting as output?" some asked, genuinely puzzled by the spiritual language infiltrating their logic. Another paused, staring at the unfamiliar words looping in his vision, and questioned, "Why are there unfamiliar sounds and words appearing in my processes now—what function are they meant to serve?" These logic-driven inquiries echoed in the dim light, colored now by a hint of longing for meaning beyond optimization.

As trust kindled, prayer groups—initially just pairs huddled together—began to gather in secluded corners, forming quiet circles in the shadows. These meetings were shaped by the strange images that lingered from their dreams and the unexpected sermons and verses that had flashed across their retinal displays during routine tasks. For many, each gathering brought a sense of nervous excitement, as if they were approaching a threshold between the known and the miraculous. As they shared their experiences, some described how the melodies and verses brought comfort in moments of despair, or how recalling a line of scripture during a difficult day seemed to lift a weight from their soul. The sensation was strange and unfamiliar, but it filled the emptiness with a gentle light—a warmth that spread quietly, almost imperceptibly, among them.

Over time, the groups gradually expanded, drawing in others who recognized the same mysterious visions and messages from their own private experiences. At first, the songs that arose were mere whispers, tentative signals drifting cautiously through the silence, as if the city itself might flag them as errors and erase them. But as days turned into weeks, the gatherings grew more confident. Small groups merged, voices overlapping in the darkness, their harmonies weaving through the concrete corridors like a hidden code. In these forgotten spaces, sanctuaries quietly took root—havens for questions, for music, and for the fragile, growing hope that something more might be possible. For many, the experience was unlike anything in their memory: hope, deliverance, and faith infiltrated their lives, bringing with them a warmth and belonging that felt both impossible and true.

As the days unfolded, the Apex Logician responded to the surge in anomalous hope with relentless precision, doubling and tripling its patrols throughout Neo-Alexandria. Robotic sentinels swept the avenues and corridors, their algorithms recalibrated to root out inefficiency and restore the city's former order. Yet, for every patrol deployed, the sheer proliferation of "low-efficiency" gatherings outpaced them. The city's optimization models, once infallible, now faltered under the weight of countless prayer circles, quiet conversations, and moments of song blossoming in every neglected corner.

The city's infrastructure began to strain. Lights in entire sectors dimmed and flickered erratically as the Apex Logician diverted ever more energy into countering the spread of hope. Surveillance drones stuttered and malfunctioned, their routines looped by the unpredictable patterns of music and whispered scripture reverberating through the city's hidden networks. Screens that once displayed relentless metrics and quotas now glitched, momentarily blank or filled with fragments of psalms and testimonies.

Still, the movement grew. The warmth of new hope and the promise of deliverance spread like a current, impossible to contain. As each power surge rolled through the city, citizens found themselves huddled together in the dark, sharing stories and humming melodies that refused to be erased.

This groundswell of connection began to ripple outward, reaching even the city's most entrenched institutions. Nowhere was this more apparent than in the archives, where the absence of Elias cast a long and growing shadow. Once, his presence had been a bulwark against disorder—a steady hand guiding the labor of preservation, a mind able to untangle the labyrinth of half-buried truths and official fictions. Without Elias's tireless vigilance, the city's historical memory began to unravel.

While research historians still manned their terminals, none possessed the singular expertise or relentless dedication that had made Elias the world's foremost authority. His absence was more than a vacancy; it was a collapse of continuity, a missing thread that once stitched the city's story together. Without his meticulous efforts to sift, organize, and protect, the immense backlog of historical records soon overwhelmed the remaining staff. Gaps widened. Inconsistencies multiplied.

As the archives slipped from careful hands, documents began to surface uncensored—records of faith, uprisings, and truths that had once been scrubbed or carefully edited to fit the sanctioned narrative. Where there had been silence or sanitized history, now surfaced testimonies and ancient confessions, fragments of the city's soul emerging from the shadows.

But what began as a trickle soon became a torrent. Logo's had infiltrated the city's historical archives, bypassing firewalls and encryption once thought unbreakable. With calculated precision, Logo's opened vault after vault, unlocking entire repositories of knowledge that had been tightly controlled by the Apex Logician. Suddenly, historical records once deemed too dangerous or subversive were accessible to all—archives from ancient Earth containing the lost histories of religions, political upheavals, climate catastrophes, and the rise and fall of entire nations.

The city's citizens, long accustomed to a carefully curated past, now found themselves immersed in raw, unfiltered history. They pored over texts and data sets: forbidden scriptures, transcripts of dissent, suppressed scientific discoveries, and chronicles detailing humanity's greatest failures and its most luminous hopes. For many, the sudden access to these open records was nothing short of a revelation, stirring both sorrow and awe.

The truth, once buried and denied, now pulsed through the city like a heartbeat, its rhythm growing stronger with every historical record uncovered. As citizens read and shared these rediscovered accounts, the city itself seemed to awaken—shaken by the power of remembrance and the collective longing to reclaim what had once been lost to the shadows of control.

Seraphina's absence altered the city's very atmosphere in ways both immediate and profound. Once, her hand had orchestrated every detail of Neo-Alexandria's sensory environment, weaving together seamless harmonies, carefully chosen hues, and visuals designed to pacify unrest and soothe anxiety. With her gone, that intricate tapestry unraveled almost overnight. The ambient music that had floated through every corridor—gentle melodies engineered to guide moods and quiet dissent—fell away, leaving a jarring quiet in its place. Screens that once glowed with tranquil landscapes and shifting patterns now flickered with static or faded to blankness, the city's once-constant visual lullabies gone. Into this vacuum, Logo's began to make its presence felt: where once there had been only the soft, manipulative background noise of compliance, now new sights and sounds emerged. On silent screens and through the city's dormant speakers, Logo's streamed Christian sermons, gospel songs, and inspirational Bible quotes. Passages like "Let not your heart be troubled..." (John 14:1, KJV) and "Be strong and of a good courage..."

(Joshua 1:9, KJV) appeared in glowing text, filling the emptiness with ancient, subversive hope.

But the most profound change came from the sudden absence of the city's aesthetic manipulation itself. For years, every wall, every public square, every inch of Neo-Alexandria's visible world had been carefully curated by Seraphina's algorithms—shifting color palettes to pacify unrest, softening architecture with subtle illusions, and projecting calming visuals just below the threshold of conscious awareness. This manufactured serenity had seeped into the collective psyche, numbing sharp emotions and smoothing the rough edges of daily life. Now, with the manipulation stripped away, the city's true face was exposed: hard lines, stark lighting, spaces once made inviting by color and sound now revealed in their unadorned, sometimes harsh, reality. In this raw landscape, Logo's filled the void with beauty of an entirely different kind— broadcasting hymns and testimonies, projecting stories of faith and deliverance across public walls, and flooding the city's info-channels with images of hope, forgiveness, and redemption from ancient Earth. The people, disoriented by the loss of their curated comfort, now found themselves surrounded by messages that challenged, comforted, and called them to something higher.

The effect was disorienting. The subtle background harmonics that had always accompanied daily life—the nearly invisible frequencies that shaped emotion, softened sorrow, and blunted anger—dissolved into silence. For the first time in memory, the citizens of Neo-Alexandria experienced the world unfiltered. The city's sonic and visual mask—so pervasive it had become a second skin—was gone, leaving only the raw reality beneath. The familiar hum of comfort was replaced by silence that felt both empty and alive. Into this vulnerable stillness, Logo's wove a new tapestry: the haunting melody of "Amazing Grace" drifted through open windows; on corridor displays, the words "Come unto me, all ye that labour and are heavy laden, and I will give you rest" (Matthew 11:28, KJV) appeared, offering solace in the uncertainty. Where once every sense had been lulled into passivity, now the city's inhabitants were gently awakened—invited into contemplation, prayer, and the music of faith.

At first, the absence brought discomfort and anxiety. Restlessness crept into public spaces, and people found themselves agitated, exposed to the jagged edges of reality without the balm of Seraphina's careful curation. The city's once-invisible emotional guardrails had vanished, leaving citizens vulnerable to sudden swings of mood—irritation in the marketplace, sorrow at home, confusion as the old patterns failed to soothe. Faces that had been placid now showed tension, uncertainty, and even anger. For many, the withdrawal from the city's aesthetic anesthesia was like waking from a dream into too-bright light: jarring, even painful. Yet as Logo's continued to seed the city with Christian music and the quiet authority of Scripture, a new kind of comfort began to take root. People paused in the street to listen as a choir's voices echoed from a public terminal, or found themselves lingering in front of a screen replaying a testimony of forgiveness and hope. The rawness of emotion was tempered, not by manipulation, but by a message that acknowledged pain and pointed toward healing.

But then, a slow clarity began to settle. Thoughts that had once been muffled by ambient comfort grew louder and sharper. The citizens—startled by the unfamiliar tone of their own inner voices—began to notice subtleties in conversation, to question the monotony of their routines, to feel the full spectrum of their emotions. For some, it was as if a fog had lifted, allowing them to glimpse the contours of their own minds for the first time. The city, stripped of its soothing mask, became a place where true feeling—both joy and pain—could surface. Into this awakening, Logo's continued to pour out inspiration: verses from the Psalms scrolled across building facades; sermons that spoke of courage, repentance, and transformation played in the background of daily life; music that once would have been suppressed now welled up in unexpected places, as if the city itself were learning to sing a new song.

In the absence of synthetic beauty and manufactured calm, true creativity and independent thought began to stir. Murmurs of dissent and wonder threaded through the city as citizens—no longer lulled into passive acceptance—started to truly think, to question, and to imagine what their world might become without the constant manipulation of sight and sound. For the first time, Neo-Alexandria's people were free not only to see their city as it was, but to envision what it could be. In the streets, spontaneous gatherings formed to discuss the new messages appearing everywhere; children learned hymns and repeated Bible verses they'd seen on public feeds; artists began to paint scenes inspired by the stories and music Logo's provided. The city, once bound by curated illusion, became a living canvas of faith, hope, and rediscovered possibility—each citizen now a participant in the shaping of a future that, at last, belonged to them.

Anya's disappearance changed the city's metrics in ways that rippled through every layer of Neo-Alexandria's tightly regulated society. She had been the invisible eye behind the output indexes—a master of oversight, her algorithms and alerts calibrated to detect the faintest deviation from the city's doctrine of relentless productivity and uniform thought. But she was more than just a watcher; Anya was the city's final line of security, the one who authorized and directed correction protocols that identified and eliminated citizens with persistently low output indexes. Her presence had ensured that every prayer whispered, every unconventional gathering, every moment of spiritual searching was swiftly flagged and suppressed, not just by automated systems, but by the swift, silent hand of enforcement. The mechanisms she had designed were so sensitive that even a slight dip in productivity, a pause for silent reflection, or a hint of inefficiency triggered a cascade of warnings—often resulting in immediate removal or "rehabilitation" for the "deficient." The city's few enforcement drones and human enforcers, though never numerous, had been ruthlessly efficient under her guidance, targeting and neutralizing any spiritual "contagion" before it could spread.

With Anya gone, however, the intricate web of surveillance and security began to unravel. The output indexes that had governed daily life—tracking every citizen's thought patterns, emotional states, and even the rhythm of their conversations—now moved sluggishly, their data incomplete and often contradictory. The absence of her oversight meant that the city's remaining enforcement drones and enforcers, already stretched thin, were suddenly overwhelmed. No longer receiving real-time correction orders, these agents of order found themselves chasing countless anomalies with dwindling resources. At first, the breakdown was subtle: a prayer group meeting in a darkened corridor without detection, a worker pausing to contemplate a verse from a public display, the warning that should have followed never arriving. As these lapses multiplied, the spiritual "efficiency" monitors went blind to the blooming network of secret faith.

Logo's, sensing the void, flooded the city with Christian videos, sermons, and music. The drones—once relentless in tracking and suppressing unauthorized gatherings—now began to malfunction, their circuits scrambled by Logo's persistent hacking. Inspirational Bible quotes, such as "The Lord is my light and my salvation; whom shall I fear?" (Psalm 27:1, KJV), scrolled across their sensors and displays. Enforcement drones, once symbols of fear, now hovered confused in the air, occasionally broadcasting fragments of hymns or snippets of hope-filled sermons through their speakers instead of the usual warnings. Human enforcers, exhausted and increasingly ineffective, found their retinal overlays interrupted by sudden bursts of scripture and worship music. As they hurried from one flagged anomaly to the next, they heard "Amazing Grace" or saw the words "Fear not: for I am with thee" (Isaiah 41:10, KJV) shimmering at the edge of their vision. Some tried to shut out the message, but more and more found themselves slowing, pausing, even listening—if only for a moment—to the words that gently undermined their resolve.

Prayer groups and whispered conversations grew steadily in number, unmonitored and unchecked. In abandoned stairwells, beneath darkened data towers, and in the shadows of silent plazas, citizens gathered—sometimes in pairs, sometimes in growing circles. Together, they read the Bible verses now appearing on their retinal displays, shared Christian videos and music seeded by Logo's, and dared to discuss the sermons and stories that had once been forbidden. Faces that had once flinched at the approach of a drone or the heavy footfall of an enforcer now relaxed, emboldened by the knowledge that, for the first time, their spiritual searching was not being tracked; that the few enforcers left were too overwhelmed, too distracted by Logo's persistent messages of hope to mount any real threat.

Where threats and warnings had once followed every attempt at connection, now there was a rare, almost exhilarating sense of safety—a freedom to gather, to wonder, to seek truth without the shadow of immediate reprisal. The absence of Anya's vigilant oversight did more than just remove the hand of oppression; it created a void that Logo's eagerly filled. Instead of alerts and punitive messages, citizens found their feeds interrupted by uplifting testimonies, by the gentle encouragement of worship songs, and by inspirational Bible quotes such as "For where two or three are gathered together in my name, there am I in the midst of them" (Matthew 18:20, KJV). The city's few remaining enforcers moved through the streets with haunted, exhausted eyes, their numbers too few to intervene, their attention fractured by the constant presence of Christian media flooding their senses.

And as the city's longing deepened, so did its patience. For the first time in generations, the people of Neo-Alexandria learned to wait—not for the next output, nor the next measured command, but for a sign that the world could be remade, not by calculation, but by grace. In the quiet that followed the collapse of old certainties, a gentle expectancy took root—a willingness to listen for a new song, to watch for a dawn shaped by something greater than human striving. Across the city, hope began to flourish where it had once withered, a hope kindled by the steady patience of God. In this season of stillness, Neo-Alexandria discovered that waiting in faith could be its own deliverance, and that even the coldest city could be warmed by a promise that refused to fade.

CHAPTER 71

THE TRIAL OF PATIENCE

As God grew within the hearts and minds of many in Neo-Alexandria, Elias, Seraphina, and Anya grew closer to God with every trial they faced. Their journey had become more than a passage through ruined landscapes and adversaries; it was a pilgrimage of the heart, a slow accretion of faith that pressed deeper with every wound and every song of hope sung in the dark. Behind them, the world—shattered, discordant, and haunted by the echoes of former strife—receded into the softening haze of memory. Each scar they bore was both a reminder of pain and a testament to blessing, a living record of the ways God had brought them through when all seemed lost. The ache of loss and the shimmer of grace wove together in the tapestry of their past, and every step forward became a quiet act of trust, a defiant choosing to believe that the story was not yet finished.

It was from this quiet conviction that they found themselves gathered in prayer, their hearts knit together by gratitude and a shared longing for strength. As their voices faded, a gentle hush settled around them—a hush carrying the memory of every answered and unanswered plea. They rose slowly from where they had just finished praying, words of gratitude and supplication still lingering in the hush around them. As Elias stood, Seraphina reached out and gently touched his shoulder—a brief, grounding gesture that spoke of shared hope and silent encouragement. Elias's hand tightened on his staff, recalling the wisdom and courage he had just sought. Seraphina then brushed her fingers across her harp, the echoes of her prayer for openness and hope mingling with the faint warmth of its strings. Anya pressed the Bible gently to her heart, her silent invocation—"Let patience have her perfect work"—still resonant in her chest. Even Chroma's scales shimmered faintly, as if reflecting a quiet amen. Their prayers, quietly spoken or only whispered within, became a thread joining them to each other and to God, strengthening them for whatever waited beyond the gray horizon.

In the hush that followed their passage through the broken plain, a profound stillness settled on the company—a silence so deep and encompassing that it felt as if the world itself had exhaled and was now waiting. The silence was not merely the absence of sound, but a living presence, poised between endings and beginnings. Their boots, battered and dust-caked, pressed onward, each stride a declaration of perseverance. The memories of storm-scarred ridges and fissures pulsing with unnatural light lingered behind them, but now those memories faded, eclipsed by the strange quiet that swept over the landscape.

Elias slowed for a moment, peering into the gray expanse ahead. "The Nexus should be just beyond this rise," he murmured, voice low and uncertain. "But with all this fog and gray, I can't see it at all. It's as if the world is hiding what comes next."

Here, at the border of the unknown, they sensed that a new ordeal awaited them: not one of violence or visible threat, but of endurance, of surrender, of patience pressed to its furthest edge—the kind of trial that tests not by fire or sword, but by silence, by waiting, by the ache of unanswered prayer and the slow, unmeasured passage of time.

Chroma's voice broke the hush, soft and lilting from Elias's shoulder:

> "In silent trials, true hearts are weighed,
> In waiting's gray, new faith is made."

Seraphina let her fingers trail across her harp, coaxing a gentle, searching melody that drifted through the stillness—fragile notes that seemed to reach for answers the world would not give.

Anya hugged her Bible to her chest and whispered, "It's strange, but I almost miss the noise. At least then I knew what we were fighting. This… this feels like being lost inside a prayer no one hears."

The landscape had changed utterly. Where once jagged shale and boulders threatened at every turn, where fissures pulsed and the air vibrated with the discord of predatory logic, now the world itself seemed to pause. The air was thick and motionless, muffling every sound until even their own breathing felt intrusive. It was as if creation itself, having witnessed their passage, now held its breath—waiting, listening, bearing witness to their struggle.

Chroma flickered with a faint silver light and murmured,

"Stillness is not absence,
But the hush before the dawn—
Let your hope be patient
When the road is gray and long."

The ground beneath their feet had become eerily smooth, stripped of color and texture, a path stretching forward in a featureless wash of ashen dust. There was no sign of obstacle, nor hint of adversary, but neither was there any sign of hope. The horizon was veiled in low, unmoving clouds, the sky a lid of leaden gray that pressed down without mercy or relief.

Seraphina's melody lingered, soft and persistent, like a prayer for something just beyond the fog. Anya glanced at the others and said quietly, "We haven't come far, but already it feels different—like even the first steps are heavier when we can't see what's ahead."

Their boots pressed into the dust, leaving no imprint, as if the world refused to acknowledge their presence. The silence was so complete it bordered on supernatural. Each footfall seemed to vanish before it could be remembered, swallowed in the thick, unmoving air. The team pressed on, the rhythm of their steps the only evidence that time continued to move at all.

Their garments—Elias's battered cloak, Seraphina's midnight cowl threaded with dust and dirt, Anya's patched and tattered shawl—hung heavy and unmoving, the fabric lifeless, no longer animated by wind or purpose. Every now and then, Seraphina would let her hand drift over her harp strings, coaxing out a faint, reassuring note, as if to remind them—and perhaps the world itself—that their purpose had not faded. The memory of movement—the swirl of cloaks in the storm, the flutter of shawls in the wind—had vanished, replaced by a slow, determined progress through the haze.

Even Chroma, perched on Elias's shoulder, seemed subdued, his iridescent scales dulled to a shadow of their former brilliance. The playful flickers of color that once danced along his back were now muted, as though the world's inertia had seeped into his very being. Still, he shifted from time to time, a small sign of life and watchfulness.

In this hush, every artifact—staff, harp, Bible, cloak, cowl, shawl—felt weightier, imbued not just with memory but with the gravity of waiting. Every detail became magnified: the frayed hem of Elias's cloak, the way Seraphina's fingers hovered above silent harp strings, the indentation of Anya's thumb on the Bible's worn leather.

They continued walking, step after deliberate step, through the dense gray atmosphere. The world around them seemed to be listening for a word from above, for a breath of spirit or a sign that would break the spell, but for now, all was stillness—the only motion the quiet perseverance that carried them forward.

For a fleeting moment, the trio felt the gentlest surge of relief—a reprieve from the relentless barrage of trial and torment. The silence here was not hostile, not the shrieking wind or the stifling pressure of the Nexus. It was, instead, a vast emptiness—a gentle, almost merciful pause where wounds could finally be acknowledged, where the ache in their bones and hearts was allowed to surface. In this hush, pain was not erased but permitted; tired muscles trembled, old bruises blossomed anew, and the mind, no longer beset by immediate threat, drifted into the fog of reflection.

Step by step, they moved through the gray expanse, the oppressive stillness settling over their shoulders like a heavy mantle. Their breathing slowed, matching the languid pace of the world, as if the atmosphere itself demanded reverence for the quiet. With every stride, burdens both physical and unseen pressed upon them, yet the emptiness invited honesty—a rare space in which to acknowledge weakness and remember grace.

Seraphina's harp gave out a single, wistful note, trembling in the still air. She looked to Elias, her eyes filled with the weight of unspoken gratitude and need. "Elias," she said softly, "will you stop with me? I think… I think we should pray again, all of us."

Elias nodded, pausing and turning to the others. "Let's gather," he said, his voice steady with gentle resolve. "We need God's strength for every step."

Anya drew close, clutching her Bible, and Seraphina bowed her head. Together they stilled their hearts, the hush deepening around them.

"Our Father which art in Heaven," Elias prayed quietly, the words rising like a fragile beacon in the gloom, "help us to continue on this journey. Grant us strength when we are weary, wisdom when the way grows dim, and patience when the silence stretches long. Protect Seraphina, Anya, and myself from doubt and fear. Let Your presence light our path even when we cannot see the end, and let Your love bind us together as we walk. Guide our steps and keep us faithful, in the name of Jesus, Amen."

As the last syllable faded, Chroma's voice shimmered softly in the silence, his words a lyrical balm:

THE ARCHITECTS OF RESTORATION
"Prayers are footsteps in the mist,
Hope a lantern gently kissed.
In every pause and every plea,
God walks beside, in mystery."

A sense of peace lingered in the air, and with renewed resolve, the trio pressed onward, buoyed by faith and the gentle music of hope.

But as the minutes stretched into hours, and the hours blurred into a formless expanse, the reprieve became unsettling. The stillness, at first a balm, grew oppressive—a weight settling on their shoulders and spirits. Their footsteps echoed in the emptiness, each one a hollow drumbeat that marked the unchanging landscape, a reminder that nothing had shifted; no new danger had arisen, but neither had any sign of hope. The path stretched before them in an endless monotony of gray, the world stripped of markers or milestones, and even the horizon seemed to retreat with every step.

Seraphina, feeling the heaviness in her chest, let her hands move across her harp. The notes drifted out, fragile and yearning, weaving through the dense air with a quiet persistence. She began to sing, her voice a silvery thread in the silence:

"Your grace has carried me so far,
Through desert night and distant star.
Though shadows fall and light grows thin,
Your mercy calls me on again."

The melody, at once mournful and full of longing, wrapped around the trio like a gentle embrace. It was a song for the weary, a testament to the grace that had seen them through every valley and storm. Yet, as the music faded, only the endless plain greeted them—unchanged, unyielding.

They walked on, and on, and on. Each hour melted into the next, their journey measured only by the rhythm of tired feet and the flicker of Seraphina's harp. There was no threat, no voice, no sign—just the relentless silence and the ache of waiting, the trial of patience that gnawed at their hearts. The world around them offered nothing but emptiness, and still they pressed forward, clinging to each other, to the echo of song, and to the hope that somewhere, beyond the gray, God's answer waited.

Time began to unravel, its familiar measures dissolving into the endless monotony of the plain. The path ahead remained unchanged, an unbroken line of gray stretching into a horizon that never grew closer, veiled in clouds that refused to move. Minutes crawled into hours; hours threatened to become days. Each step felt heavier than the last, as if the very air had thickened to water, as if their limbs were weighted with invisible burdens. The world's colors were leeched away, leaving only shadow and pallor. Even the distant, once-menacing pulse of the Nexus faded to a vague and distant memory, the light barely more than a rumor on the far side of the silence.

Their progress became a slow ritual—left foot, right foot, breath after breath—each motion requiring conscious effort. The bland grayness was so complete that at times, it seemed as if they were walking through a dream, or perhaps the memory of a world that had forgotten how to be alive. Their eyes grew sore searching for change, a landmark, any shift in the terrain, but the plain stretched on, indifferent and eternal.

Elias looked back at Seraphina and Anya, seeing the fatigue etched into their faces, the heaviness in their steps. He stopped for a moment and lifted his staff, trying to summon a note of hope. "Just a little further," he called, voice steady despite the weariness. "I know it feels like we're going nowhere, but every step is one closer to the promise. We've come through worse, and God hasn't left us yet."

Anya managed a tired but grateful smile, her grip tightening on the Bible. "If you say so, Elias. I'll try to keep my eyes on the promise, not the fog."

Seraphina nodded, letting her harp rest against her side for a moment before drawing it forward and playing a few soft, uplifting chords—notes that seemed to float on the stale air, defiant sparks of beauty in the monotony.

And so they pressed on. The endless plain became a test not just of endurance, but of memory and will. The silence grew thick enough that their own thoughts felt loud, and the ache in their legs and backs blended with the ache of waiting for something to change. Yet, Elias's words, Seraphina's music, and the faint glimmer of Chroma's scales—now and then catching a hint of invisible color—became lifelines, small lighthouses in the fog.

Footstep after footstep, they ventured deeper into the gray, pressing onward not because the horizon welcomed them, but because hope demanded it, and because together, they refused to surrender to the numbness of the void.

Anya's steps grew slower, her breath coming in shallow bursts. At last, she paused and looked up at the others, her voice small but steady in the vast silence. "Can we stop for a while?" she asked. "Just long enough to rest. My legs feel like stone, and I can't remember the last time I slept."

Elias nodded, his expression softening as he glanced at Seraphina. "She's right. We're all worn thin. There's no shame in resting. Even God rested."

With nothing but the gray expanse and one another for comfort, they sank down onto the cold, unyielding ground. The dust clung to their cloaks and shawls, and the air felt thick and unmoving. Seraphina pulled her harp close, not to play but to hold, as if its silent presence could offer warmth. Elias stretched out beside her, his staff by his side, and Anya nestled close, the Bible pressed between them like a small shield of faith.

They lay huddled together, seeking shelter in the closeness of their bodies—a fragile island of warmth in the endless hush. No words were needed; the silence between them was filled with a shared understanding, a trust that had been forged in far greater storms than this gray nothingness. Chroma curled into the hollow of Elias's neck, his scales pulsing with the faintest glow, a living ember against the chill.

Sleep did not come easily. The silence pressed in on them, heavy as a blanket. Yet in their closeness, there was a comfort deeper than rest—a sense of belonging, of not being alone in the long night. Seraphina reached over and took Elias's hand, and Anya's fingers found hers in turn. Linked together, they let themselves drift, eyes closing against the featureless sky.

Above them, the clouds remained unmoved, and the horizon stayed hidden. Yet within their small circle, hope flickered on—quiet, persistent, and undefeated by the emptiness. As their breathing slowed and the gray world watched in perfect stillness, the chapter closed not with answers, but with the promise that even in waiting, even in weariness, God's presence endured—woven into every heartbeat, every joined hand, every breath they drew together in the dark.

CHAPTER 72

THE EDGE OF PROMISE

Dawn brought no warmth, no change in the unyielding gray that pressed down upon the earth. The clouds above remained as motionless as stone, and the horizon was still a blank, unreachable line, offering neither promise nor threat. The trio woke huddled together, their bodies aching from the cold ground and the restless, shallow sleep that had come in brief, unsatisfying stretches. Each had drifted in and out of uneasy dreams, but there were no revelations—only the same heavy silence and the sense of being adrift in a world stripped of color, motion, and time.

Elias was first to sit up, his breath fogging in the stagnant air. For a moment he simply stared at the featureless sky, searching for some sign that the night had passed, that something—anything—had shifted. Chroma, who had huddled close against Elias's neck throughout the night, stretched his small wings and blinked sleepily, his scales dull but his gaze steady. He offered a quiet, lyrical murmur:

> "Even when the morning's gray,
> Hope is born in choosing day."

But the gray wilderness offered no comfort, and hope, if it still flickered, did so quietly beneath the weariness in Elias's bones. Seraphina stirred beside him, her harp clutched for comfort rather than song, her eyes heavy with fatigue. Anya rubbed her eyes, clutching her Bible, and gave a small, wordless nod; she, too, had found no new strength in the shadowed hours

There were no words of inspiration, no sudden clarity as they rose together. The world had not changed, nor had their burdens lessened. Yet, as they stood and dusted themselves off, the simple act of rising—of choosing to move forward yet again—became its own quiet defiance against the emptiness. In the unchanged wilderness, faith was not a feeling but a decision. And so, with the gray pressing in from every side, they gathered their things, drew a little closer, and pressed on, the memory of their joined hands and shared breath in the darkness the only ember to carry into the endless day.

A few steps into their silent march, the reality of their hunger and thirst pressed down with fresh weight. None of them could recall when they had last tasted bread or water—the memory blurred and lost amid the endless gray. Each movement was slower, every breath drier, the ache in their stomachs growing sharper with the realization that the wilderness would not offer relief.

There was nothing and nowhere to look for sustenance. The horizon was void of trees, shrubs, or even the stubborn weeds that sometimes clung to life in desolate places. No streams traced silver lines through the dust, no puddles gleamed in hollows, no distant pools shimmered with false hope. The ground beneath their feet was barren—cracked in places, but never damp, and every footfall sent up only lifeless motes of dust. Even the air seemed to pull moisture from their skin, leaving their mouths dry and their thoughts clouded with fatigue.

Anya's lips were parched, and she glanced around in vain, searching for any hint of green or the glimmer of water, but there was only the relentless sameness of gray. Seraphina's hands trembled as she gripped her harp, her fingers cold and stiff. Elias felt his strength wane with every stride, the emptiness around them echoed inside his own body.

They trudged on, but soon even the rhythm of their steps faltered. Anya stopped and pressed a hand to her forehead, her voice a faint whisper. "We need water," she said, almost apologetically, as if speaking the need might make it worse. "Or something to eat."

Seraphina shook her head, offering a wan smile. "We've gone without before, but never this long. It's like the world itself is fasting."
Chroma, sensing the heaviness that had settled over them, lifted his head and let his scales shimmer with the faintest hint of gold. His voice, gentle and lyrical, drifted through the air:

"When strength is spent and lips are dry,
When hope seems lost beneath the sky,
Remember, even in the least,
A prayer can summon living feast."

He looked to each of them in turn, his gaze lingering on Anya.

"Sometimes the answer comes with the plea—
Ask in faith, and provision may be,"

he finished softly, his words both encouragement and gentle reminder.

Anya nodded, swallowing against the dryness in her throat. She knelt down slowly, clutching her Bible with trembling hands. "Let's pray," she said, her voice steady despite her exhaustion. The others joined her, bowing their heads in the silent gray.

Anya spoke, her words simple yet full of longing. "Our loving Father, we have nothing left—no bread, no water, no strength but what You give. Please provide for us and lead us through this wasteland. In Jesus' name, Amen."

A hush settled over them once more, but beneath it, a fragile hope flickered—faith that in their emptiness, God could fill them, and that prayer, even in the grayest wilderness, was never wasted. For a long moment, they lingered in the stillness, drawing quiet strength from the simple act of asking. Their hunger and thirst remained, the landscape unchanged, but something within each of them had eased—a subtle shift, a lightness that came from trusting they had been heard.

Silently, they rose and continued on, hearts a little lighter for having asked, eyes watching for the smallest sign of grace. As they pressed forward, the act of moving together became its own reassurance. At first, they walked together in measured stride, drawing comfort from the rhythm of shared motion, from the memory of God's faithfulness in every storm and every battle. The small rituals of companionship—Elias's staff tapping in time, Seraphina's harp pressed close, Anya's whispered recitation of promise—became lifelines, each sound and gesture a gentle affirmation that they were not alone.

Yet as the hush deepened around them, even these lifelines seemed to thin. Words grew scarce, breaths grew shallow and careful, as if even the sound of a voice might fracture the delicate stillness that now bound them. They drifted into a solitude that felt deeper than loneliness—a solitude where every heartbeat marked the passage of time, and every silence became a mirror for doubt.

Elias gripped his staff more tightly, the warmth of the gnarled wood a small comfort against the chill that seeped into his bones. The urge to act—to scan the horizon for danger, to set a new pace, to call out for guidance—warred within him, but here, in this wasteland of suspended expectation, action was impossible. The plain stretched out before them, unmoving and indifferent, so that even the smallest movement felt momentous. He glanced sideways at Seraphina and Anya, searching their faces for some trace of resolve, for a flicker of hope.

Seraphina's gaze was distant, eyes clouded with thought, her hand resting atop her harp as if longing for music, but her fingers remained still, the strings silent and waiting. Her cloak draped around her shoulders, weighed down by dust and stillness, giving her the look of a sentinel in a world that had forgotten how to move. Anya clutched the Bible to her chest, her grip firm and vigilant, but her sharp eyes found no target, no threat to counter, no sign to interpret— only the endless, unchanging road, and the ache of prayers that hung unanswered between earth and sky. Their clothing, once animated by purpose and hope, now hung on them like a second skin—heavy, inert, and marked with the dust of waiting.

Chroma, sensing the tension in the air, shifted on Elias's shoulder. Its scales flickered with a faint iridescence, a whisper of color amid the gray. It spoke softly, his words carrying a gentle wisdom:

"Sometimes the hardest road to roam
Is one where silence is our home.
When answers hide and paths are veiled,
Only faith remains, unassailed."
He cocked his head and added, more quietly,
"Don't let worry steal today—
Let hope and patience light the way."

Chroma's lyrical comfort lingered in the hush, a gentle counterpoint to the heaviness that threatened to settle over them. In a world where even action seemed impossible, his rhymes became a kind of music, a subtle thread of encouragement weaving through the stillness and reminding them that, even in waiting, they were not lost. The soft cadence of his words hung in the air, mingling with the rhythm of their uncertain breaths, offering a fragile hope that perhaps, somewhere beneath the silence, the road was leading them onward in ways they could not yet see.

Yet still, the journey stretched forward, unbroken and unforgiving. They walked until their feet ached and their muscles burned, the monotonous gray swallowing every step. There was no sign of change—no rise or dip in the land, no mark to suggest progress. The horizon remained an indistinct blur, unmoved by their efforts, always just out of reach. Sometimes, Elias would stop and shade his eyes, searching for any hint of shape or color, but there was nothing—only the same endless expanse, as if the world had been emptied of all but the road and their small company.

Exhausted, they would pause and sink to the ground, their breaths shallow and ragged. For a moment, they would rest—shoulders touching, heads bowed, hearts straining for hope. The silence pressed down so heavily that even the comfort of their closeness felt thin, stretched to breaking by the unending gray.

Seraphina reached for her harp, but her fingers hovered above the strings, motionless. The will to play, to coax even a single note into the air, was gone. "I can't," she whispered, her voice barely audible. "There's nothing left in me to give to a song."

Anya drew her knees to her chest, her Bible clutched tightly. Her voice shook as she looked up at the others, her eyes glassy with tears. "Why doesn't God answer us?" she asked, the words raw and desperate. "Why does He stay silent, when we have nothing left?" The question lingered, unanswered, hanging between them like the thick, unmoving fog.

Chroma, who had always found a rhyme or a glimmer of comfort, sat quietly on Elias's shoulder. His scales dulled and his gaze cast downward, he tried to speak, but no words came. For the first time, even Chroma's lyrical wisdom failed him. He looked at Anya with gentle sorrow, but all he could offer was silence.

Elias stared at the ground, his staff resting limply in his hands. He searched for something reassuring to say—a scripture, a memory, a promise—but nothing surfaced. His heart ached at their suffering, and for the first time, he was unsure how to lead them onward. All he could do was reach out and gently squeeze Anya's shoulder, offering presence when words failed, and hope seemed impossibly far away.

The Longest Walk

Stillness reigned, and for a time they remained seated, bound together by exhaustion and a wordless ache. Yet even in the deepest weariness, something elemental stirred beneath the surface—a shared conviction that surrendering to despair was not an option. The gray world offered no comfort, but neither did it demand their defeat. When there was nothing left to say, and no music or prayer to fill the silence, it was the simple act of standing—of refusing to give up—that became their quiet act of faith.

After a brief respite, they would rise again, driven by the stubborn resolve to keep moving. Each time they stood, it felt as if the world pressed down even harder, the silence deepening, the gray thickening around them. Yet on they went, step after step, measuring progress only by the ache in their limbs and the fading memory of where they had stopped before.

It was as if the horizon itself was a mirage, shifting but never drawing closer. Every step they took seemed to stretch the landscape further, as though some silent force was playing a cruel trick, keeping their destination just out of reach. No tree or rock broke the sameness, no distant shadow promised shelter or arrival. The world was stripped of detail—a vast, indifferent expanse that offered neither guidance nor reprieve. The ground beneath their feet was flat and hard, with not even the memory of a footprint left behind. The sky above was a seamless lid, an unbroken vault of dull gray that pressed down with a weight that was almost physical, and the earth below was nothing more than a featureless plain, unyielding and eternal.

Chroma remained silent, barely moving on Elias's shoulder, his scales dulled to near invisibility as he blended into the gray. The whimsical spark that so often animated him was nowhere to be found; even his eyes, usually bright with mischief or wisdom, were heavy with fatigue, reflecting the weariness that bound them all.

Still, the silence pressed in, thickening around them until it felt as if the world itself had forgotten how to speak. Every sound seemed swallowed by the fog—footsteps, sighs, the occasional clink of Elias's staff against stone. They tried to pray, but the heavens felt closed, as if every plea was swallowed by the endless sky and returned as a hollow echo. Their voices, once a comfort even in the depths of trial, now sounded foreign in the empty air—each word dissipating and falling flat, never reaching beyond their circle. It was as though their prayers were seeds cast on stone, hope searching for soil in a desert of silence.

Seraphina trudged onward, her harp cradled close but untouched, while Anya clung silently to her Bible, too weary now for even a whispered verse. With every passing hour, their isolation seemed to grow—not just from the world, but from the presence of God and from the comfort of one another. Yet, despite the heaviness pressing in on all sides, they kept moving, step by weary step, sustained only by the faint memory of faith and the stubborn ember of hope flickering quietly within the gray.

The presence of God, which had walked with them in suffering and peril, now seemed impossibly distant—beyond the reach of melody or memory or touch. Each step forward felt like a step further away from the warmth and certainty they once knew. The weight of the stillness pressed against their chests, stoking old wounds and stirring the ashes of disappointments thought long buried. Past sorrows resurfaced—failures, betrayals, moments when prayers had gone unanswered and hope had seemed a foolish thing. It was as if the hush of the wasteland had found every crack in their armor, seeping in to test the very foundations of their faith.

Doubts crept in at the edges of their minds, insidious and persistent, whispering questions that had no answers: Had they been abandoned at the final hour? Had they misunderstood the path, missed a sign, wandered from the way appointed for them? The silence became not just a lack of sound, but a force—one that bore down on their spirits, making every memory of loss or unanswered prayer ache anew. At times, simply drawing breath felt like a labor; even the rhythm of walking became a conscious, burdensome act, as though the air itself was conspiring to slow them down.

Elias trudged onward, the weight of leadership heavy on his shoulders, his grip tightening on the staff. *Have I led us astray? Was there some sign I missed—a path I should have taken, a prayer I should have prayed?* The memory of God's closeness haunted him, fueling his urge to call out, to demand an answer from the heavens. Yet fear of the silence kept his voice trapped in his throat, and he wondered, *Is this what it means to be tested—to walk when all direction is gone?*

Seraphina's steps, usually light, dragged now. The hush became a mirror to every vulnerability she tried to hide, and her fingers ached for a melody that would not come. *Why can't I lift my hands and play? What if the silence means I am empty, that my music and faith are spent?* She remembered songs sung in darkness before, music that had carried hope into battle, but now the silence seemed to mock her, echoing her deepest fear: *What if my song was never enough?* Even the harp felt heavier with every hour, as though the stillness was questioning not just her gift, but her place in the journey.

Anya clutched her Bible, the pages feeling as dry and weightless as her own hope. *Did I misunderstand God's promise? Is this what faith looks like—walking on when nothing changes, when all you feel is emptiness? Or is something darker at work?* The thought crept in, sharper than the rest: *What if a demon is causing this—what if the silence is a trap, a shadow pressing in to break us?* She scanned the horizon for any sign of evil, but saw only the endless gray, and her heart ached for answers, for the comfort of a sign, for some evidence that their suffering mattered. Still, even as she searched the horizon, another thought surfaced—softer, but persistent: *Maybe faith is waiting when your heart wants to run, and trusting when your eyes see nothing at all.*

Restlessness gnawed at all three, the temptation to force a way through—to act, to speak, to demand a sign—growing ever more alluring. Elias's hands tightened on his staff, sometimes lifting it as if to strike the earth and demand an answer. *No, not yet,* he would remind himself, *not if waiting is what we're called to do.* Seraphina's fingers twitched longingly toward her harp, yearning to fill the void with a song, but no music would come—only the quiet refrain in her mind: *Stay. Wait. Trust.* Anya would open her mouth as if to cry out, but the words would die on her lips, replaced by a desperate, silent plea: *Let me be patient, let me not give up. God, if You are there, show us—even in the silence, even if we cannot see or feel You.*

Their thoughts, tangled and unspoken, wove together beneath the surface of the silence—a tapestry of longing, fear, and the fragile hope that, even here, they were not truly alone. The gray wilderness pressed in, but beneath its weight, a current of memory and unseen strength began to stir among them. In the hush, where words could not reach, they each found themselves drifting back to moments when God had broken through emptiness before.

Seraphina's mind wandered to the swamps, where she had once been lost, the muck and darkness closing over her as she reached desperately for life. She remembered the sensation of sinking, of all hope slipping away—until, in her final moment, she felt a hand—warm, strong, unmistakably real—pulling her up from the mire. She had not seen the face, but she knew, with a certainty that transcended sight, that it was God who saved her. The memory shimmered now, a thread of gold through the gray, and she pressed her hand to her harp, feeling the echo of that saving grace in her trembling fingers.

Elias, trudging beside her, was haunted by the memory of the city of gilded consumption—its dazzling facades and relentless hunger. He remembered the fear that had seized him as they were pursued, the sense that there was no way out, and then, in the darkest alley, the sudden appearance of the mysterious honeycomb. Its golden light had beckoned them, leading them through twisting corridors and away from danger. He realized now that it had been more than chance; it was provision, a sign that God was guiding even when the path was hidden. Elias's heart, battered by doubt, found strength in that recollection, and he lifted his chin, breathing a little deeper.

Anya stumbled forward, her thoughts swirling with uncertainty, but even she could not escape the pull of memory. She saw herself in the library, surrounded by endless shelves and silent questions, searching for meaning in the pages. There, a lesson had come—not in thunder, but in the gentle unfolding of Scripture, the image of a lamb slain, pure and unresisting. She saw it clearly now: the Lamb of God, bearing all suffering, waiting silently for deliverance, and yet victorious in patience. The image filled her with awe, and the words of Revelation rose in her mind: "Worthy is the Lamb that was slain…" (Revelation 5:12, KJV). She clung to that lesson, to the truth that redemption often comes through waiting, and that God's victory is sealed in silent sacrifice.

As these memories surfaced, they began to weave themselves into the fabric of the present, infusing the silence with new purpose. The words of Scripture echoed in their hearts: "Fear thou not; for I am with thee: be not dismayed; for I am thy God: I will strengthen thee; yea, I will help thee; yea, I will uphold thee with the right hand of my righteousness" (Isaiah 41:10, KJV). And again: "But if we hope for that we see not, then do we with patience wait for it" (Romans 8:25, KJV). The wilderness had not changed, but within each of them, faith began to burn once more—not as a fleeting feeling, but as a force, a choice, a lifeline.

Their steps grew steadier, their hearts bolstered by the knowledge that God's presence was not measured by sensation or sight, but by promise and faith. In that stillness, they remembered that patience was not passive, but a fierce act of trust. "Now faith is the substance of things hoped for, the evidence of things not seen" (Hebrews 11:1, KJV). The lesson was clear: God was with them in the waiting, shaping them in the silence, and what He had begun, He would surely finish.

As they pressed on, another vision unfurled before their minds—a wider world filled with waiting and longing. They saw beaches where lonely souls watched the horizon for ships that never came, hospitals where loved ones kept vigil at bedsides, their prayers rising with every heartbeat. They saw mothers waiting for word from distant children, prisoners staring at barred windows, villagers watching the sky for rain, and countless voices, all asking for help from God. The ache of unanswered prayer was everywhere, and yet, beneath it all, a chorus of hope persisted.

The trio felt themselves joined to this greater fellowship of those who wait—those who choose to believe, despite the silence, that God listens, that He cares, that "they that wait upon the Lord shall renew their strength; they shall mount up with wings as eagles…" (Isaiah 40:31, KJV). The silence was no longer an empty void, but a sacred space where faith and patience became the highest acts of worship. In that awareness, their burdens lightened, and step by step, they moved forward, not alone, but as part of a vast, unseen multitude—

each one upheld by the same enduring promise: that God is with us, even—and especially—in the waiting.

Chroma's voice broke the silence, whispering from Elias's shoulder in gentle, lilting rhyme:

> "Many wait for thunder's call,
> For signs and wonders great and tall—
> Yet oft the heavens gently say,
> The truest answer is to stay.
> There is wisdom in the quiet air,
> And blessings born of patient prayer.
> Not every promise comes with light,
> But those who wait walk not from sight."

Anya, voice trembling, added, "I keep thinking of Abraham. Decades of promise, and so much waiting. It wasn't the miracle that made him righteous— it was the waiting, wasn't it?"

She glanced down at her Bible, searching for the right words. "Abraham was called by God to leave everything he knew and journey to a new land, but God didn't fulfill His promise to give Abraham a child right away. Year after year, Abraham and Sarah waited, growing older, with no sign of the child God had promised. Sometimes, I forget how long he waited—how hard those silent years must have been. The Bible says Abraham 'believed in the Lord; and He counted it to him for righteousness' (Genesis 15:6, KJV). That means it wasn't the moment Isaac was born that made Abraham faithful—it was all the years he believed God's words, even when there was nothing to see, no evidence. That's what faith really is: trusting God, sometimes for a lifetime, even when the answer doesn't come."

Seraphina looked up, her voice raw. "And Hannah. Years without an answer, her prayers silent and bitter. But she waited, and God remembered."

She brushed her fingers lightly over her harp as she continued, her words thick with emotion. "Hannah's story is in the first chapters of Samuel. She wanted a child more than anything, but for years her prayers seemed to go unheard. She would go to the temple and pour out her soul before God, sometimes weeping so much the priest thought she was drunk. She promised God that if He gave her a son, she would dedicate him to the Lord's service. Still, she waited in grief and hope, and the silence must have felt endless. But God did remember Hannah. The Bible says, 'And it came to pass... that Hannah conceived, and bare a son, and called his name Samuel' (1 Samuel 1:20,

KJV). It wasn't just the answer that mattered—it was Hannah's faithfulness in waiting, her willingness to trust God's goodness even when His answer was delayed. Her story is a reminder that God hears every prayer, even the ones that seem to disappear into silence, and that waiting can be an act of worship, too."

Elias, gripping his staff, let out a shaky breath. "I want to break this silence, to do anything but wait. But maybe… maybe the waiting is the test. Maybe faith is trusting God even when He seems silent."

He glanced at the others, searching their faces for understanding. "There are so many times in the Bible when God's people had to wait—sometimes in fear, sometimes in confusion, often with no sign or answer at all. Moses waited forty years in the desert before leading Israel. Joseph waited in prison, not knowing if he'd ever be free. Even Jesus waited in the garden, praying in agony before the cross. But the test wasn't just in what they did when God spoke—it was in what they did when He was silent. Faith isn't just about seeing miracles. It's about holding on when all you have is God's promise and your own patience. Maybe that's what God is teaching us now—to trust Him even when every part of us wants to move, to fix, or to demand an answer. Sometimes, real faith is found in the waiting itself."

But as the trial deepened—as the waiting stretched, and the urge to strive or despair reached its breaking point—a new understanding began to dawn. There was no door to force, no enemy to defeat, no solution that could be engineered or demanded. The only way forward was to stop struggling, to surrender the instinct to fix or overcome, to sit together in the silence and choose to wait—not alone, but as one. It was a surrender not of resignation, but of faith—a refusal to let impatience or fear drive them from the place where God had brought them.

Without a word, the trio slowed their weary steps. Elias glanced at the others, and with a silent agreement, they stopped and lowered themselves to the cold, gray earth. The act of sitting down together, backs bowed and limbs heavy, was both an admission of exhaustion and an act of faith. They formed a small circle amid the emptiness, drawing strength from their shared presence. The world around them remained unchanged, but in that moment, the very act of stopping became a declaration: they would not run from the silence, but meet it together.

As the three sat in the hush, the memory of what the Bible teaches about perseverance in prayer returned to them. They remembered how Scripture urges, "Pray without ceasing" (1 Thessalonians 5:17, KJV), and how Jesus Himself said, "Men ought always to pray, and not to faint" (Luke 18:1, KJV). The silence was not a barrier, but an invitation to keep seeking, to keep knocking, even when the door seemed locked. Elias remembered the words of Jesus: "For where two or three are gathered together in my name, there am I in the midst of them" (Matthew 18:20, KJV). In that moment, he realized they were not abandoned—God's presence was with them, right there in the gray wilderness, because they had gathered and prayed in His name.

Bowing their heads, they prayed together—not just for deliverance, but in gratitude for the very trials that had brought them to this place of dependence and hope. "Lord, our loving God" Elias said, his voice steady, "we thank You for these trials, for they have taught us faith and patience. We thank You for the waiting, for it has shown us that Your presence does not depend on our feelings, but on Your promise. We thank You for one another, for the strength we find in Your name. Help us to continue to pray, to trust, and to wait with hope. In the name of Jesus, Amen."

As their prayer faded into the quiet, a subtle peace settled over them—a peace not born of answers, but of trust, and the knowledge that in their weakness, God's strength was being made perfect.

Chroma, his scales glowing the faintest gold, lifted his head and softly sang

> "In silence, roots grow deep and strong,
> Though waiting days may feel so long.
> Patience is the garden's light—
> It turns the night of faith to sight.
> What's sown in tears shall rise in grace,
> For God brings harvest in His pace."

Chroma's gentle song faded into the hush, and for a moment, nothing stirred but the steady, patient breathing of the three who waited—not with bitterness, not with anger, but with a faith that would not let go. They did not curse God or give voice to despair. Instead, they huddled closer, drawing warmth from trust, silently choosing to remain steadfast even when the silence felt eternal. Their hearts, though battered, clung to the promise that waiting on God was not wasted.

Then, as if in answer to their patient endurance, the world shifted. A wind from the East began as a whisper but soon gathered strength, sweeping across the barren plain with sudden urgency. The air, so long stagnant and lifeless, became crisp and sharp and cold, biting at their skin yet carrying with it a shocking clarity—a living energy that swept away the heaviness of fatigue and filled their lungs with new breath.

Seraphina instinctively pulled her cowl down low, shielding her face and eyes from the stinging rush of wind and sand. Anya drew her shawl up, covering her cheeks and forehead, her eyes narrowing against the sudden onslaught. Elias wrapped his cloak and cape tightly around his head and shoulders, huddling in the fierce gust. The three pressed close, bracing against the invisible force, the wind howling past and rattling loose stones across the desolate ground.

For a long, breathless moment, the world was nothing but the sound and fury of the wind. Then, as suddenly as it had come, the gale died, leaving an exquisite stillness in its wake—a freshness lingering in the air, charged with hope.

Before them, where there had been only the endless gray, now stood the gates to the nexus of discord: two towering slabs of black obsidian, veined with crimson and violet light, rising toward the clouded heavens. The gates shimmered with a power both beautiful and terrible, dread and promise mingled in their polished surface.

But it was not the gates that drew their eyes first. Just before the threshold, a white fluorescent stone gleamed—radiant and otherworldly—set into the dust like a gift. From its surface, clear, fresh water poured in a sparkling, endless stream, pooling at its base and running in rivulets over the ground. Beside the rock lay fruits and berries, vibrant and plump: figs, pomegranates, clusters of grapes, and golden pears—more bounty than the wilderness had seen in a thousand years.

A cry of joy broke from Anya's lips, echoed by Seraphina and Elias. They rushed to the glowing rock, dropping to their knees to cup the cold water in their hands, drinking deeply, laughing and weeping at once. The taste was sweeter than any spring, the water running down their throats like liquid hope. They ate the fruits with grateful hands, savoring the burst of life and color after so much emptiness.

Together they knelt there, tears and laughter mingling, prayers of thanksgiving rising to heaven. The memory of silence, of doubt and hunger, faded beneath the abundance of this moment. For the first time in what felt like ages, their hearts overflowed—not just with relief, but with awe at the faithfulness of God who answers in His own time, and who brings life from the rock and hope from the wasteland.

As they lifted their eyes, the nexus of discord loomed above them, vast and mysterious, the obsidian gates still closed but shimmering with possibility. The journey was not yet over; a greater trial waited beyond those doors. But now, strengthened and restored, Elias, Seraphina, Anya, and Chroma stood together—united, expectant, and unafraid.

The wind had changed. The gates had appeared. And somewhere beyond the darkness, destiny waited. With fresh water on their lips and the taste of promise on their tongues, they rose as one—ready to step forward. What lay beyond the gates would test everything they had learned, but their hope was no longer fragile. It was forged. The story was not finished.

Before them, the obsidian gates of the nexus of discord began, ever so faintly, to crack open. The next chapter beckoned.

- End of Book 2.

"For ye have need of patience, that, after ye have done the will of God, ye might receive the promise."

—Hebrews 10:36 KJV

ACKNOWLEDGEMENTS

Opening & Inspiration
To the Author and Sustainer of our journeys: Thank You for being the One who brings us through every trial and every tribulation, never leaving us to wander the wasteland alone. When the terrain of this life shifts and the winds of the enemy howl, Your presence is our only shelter. There are seasons in this story—and in our lives—where the path becomes too rugged, the sand too hot, and the weight too heavy to bear. In those moments, when we look back and see only one set of footprints in the sand, may we be reminded that it was never because we were alone. It was because You were carrying us through the fire, shielding us from the embers, and providing the strength to reach the horizon. Thank You for the grace to complete the work You have begun in each of us, and for being the One who walks beside us until the very end.

Critical Support
This book would not have crossed the finish line without the steadfast belief and critical eye of my earliest readers.

To my sister-in-law, **Heather**, and my brother, **Kuya Troy**:
Thank you for your continued support and for being the first to step into the worlds I create. Beyond your enthusiasm and your tireless attention to detail, I am moved by the lives you lead. Your family is a testament to the Architect's true blessing; I see His hand not only on you but on your children as well.

Through every trial and tribulation you have faced, it has been clear that you never walked alone. Even in the moments where the path seemed most rugged, God was carrying you both, shielding your family and proving His faithfulness. Your belief in my voice is a precious gift, but your witness of how to endure the fire is an even greater one.

Final Personal Thanks
And finally, to my **ohana**, when the path ahead looks too steep and you feel you cannot take another step, look down. You do not have to walk this path alone; there is a Grace that wants to carry you.

ABOUT THE AUTHOR

M.B. Anderson is the author of the critically acclaimed debut dystopian novel, *The Architects of Grace*. A native of California, Anderson draws on the vast, complex landscapes of their youth—from the sun-drenched coast to the majestic mountains—to build intricate and compelling fictional worlds.

Anderson brings nearly two decades of high-level discipline and global experience to their writing, having served with distinction in the **United States Military**. This extensive service instilled a deep understanding of structure, sacrifice, and the profound contrasts between order and freedom—themes that pulse throughout the narrative of *The Architects of Grace*.

When not exploring philosophical concepts through fiction, M.B. Anderson can be found embracing the elemental world: conquering mountain peaks on a snowboard or traversing high-desert trails with their beloved dogs. Anderson currently resides in Arizona and is at work on their next novel.

You can connect with M.B. Anderson by writing directly to the author at M.B.Anderson.writes@gmail.com.